REVENGE

OF THE

PHANTOM PRESS

A BOLINGBROOK BABBLER STORY

BOOK 3

WILLIAM BRINKMAN

For the latest news about William Brinkman and the Bolingbrook Babbler stories, subscribe at https://bolingbrookbabbler.com/mailing-list

Praise for the Bolingbrook Babbler Stories

Pathways to Bolingbrook:

"Two smart women trying to survive in difficult times. *Pathways to Bolingbrook* captures your imagination and leaves you wanting to know what happens next. Can't wait for the publication of the novel. Well worth reading." — Amazon reviewer.

"This is a very short introduction to what is sure to be an entertaining series, if just for ONE THING: Iowa is not boring." — Amazon reviewer.

"Keep reading. Keep writing, Mr. Brinkman, and all the best with your Anti-Psychic Kitty Press. Breathlessly waiting for your next publication. Six stars!" — Amazon reviewer.

A Fire in the Shadows:

"A thrilling 'vampire' fantasy packed full of twists, turns – and danger!" — Wishing Shelf.

"This was a fast-paced and exhilarating supernatural and sci-fi YA fantasy! The world-building and mythos that the author built into this series were evident immediately." — Author This was a fast-paced and exhilarating supernatural and sci-fi YA fantasy! The world-building and mythos that the author built into this series were evident immediately." — Anthony Avina, author

"I have never read a book so fast before! It sucks you in from the very first sentence. I can't wait to read more books from this author." — Goodreads reviewer.

The Rift:

"A richly written novel filled with memorable characters. Highly recommended!" — The Wishing Shelf.

"A quick, easy and interesting read that had good writing, a good storyline and well developed characters." — Goodreads reviewer.

"Every new development in the story surprised me and -- there are weredeer!I don't usually read fantasy or sci-fi, but this book made me want to take another look at the genre. I highly recommend it!" — Amazon reviewer.

"*The Rift* is a wild adventure, sprinkled with humor, duplicitous characters, and extraterrestrials. You never know who is working for the good of mankind or creating a rift in the world." — Amazon reviewer.

To my wife, for her love and support.
In memory of Edward Rosenthal, zekher tsadik livrakha.

1

Tom Larsen aimed his smartphone camera at the three float-ing ducks in front of him. "Which one of you is the Hidden Lakes Monster?" he asked.

The ducks watched Tom watching them. *One of them has to be a decoy,* he thought. He knew the Hidden Lakes Monster had a retractable plume of feathers that resembled an ordinary duck. That plume might deceive visitors and the other ducks, but it wouldn't fool Tom. This time, he would take a picture of the half-duck, half-sea serpent creature that called the former trout farm home.

"I just need one picture," Tom said to the ducks. "You want to be in the fiftieth anniversary issue of the *Bolingbrook Babbler*, right?"

The ducks replied by spreading their wings and taking flight. Tom ducked to avoid a collision.

All three of them are real ducks!

Tom started to curse but stopped when he noticed a family watching him from a picnic blanket. Two preschoolers waited for Tom to say something. The parents frowned at him as if they knew what he was holding back.

"Gosh darn it!" he said.

Both preschoolers giggled.

The dad asked, "Did you say you work for the *Babbler*?"

Tom straightened his stance and smiled. "Yes, I do."

"Do you really think your stories are funny?"

Tom gritted his teeth to stop himself from swearing. "No. We're a serious tabloid that's been covering Bolingbrook since it was incorporated."

"So, the stuff about UFO bases, weredeer, tree people?"

"All real," Tom replied. "Bolingbrook is home to the largest urban UFO base in the world, and we have the highest concentration of cyprids in Chicagoland." He forced himself to smile.

"I told you they were crazy," the mother said.

Tom shrugged. "It wouldn't be the Brook without the *Bolingbrook Babbler*." Tom glanced at his phone. "I've got to get back to work."

One preschooler said, "Bye, crazy guy!"

Tom hurried away from the family. He sighed as he wiped some sweat off his forehead. *August heat is the worst,* he thought. At least he was at one of the prettiest nature spots in Bolingbrook. The park's commercial past would be unknown to most visitors if it weren't for the name Hidden Lakes Trout Farm. Now it was a park and a popular fishing spot. Some visitors fished along the shores of the four ponds. Others passed through the park as they walked along the DuPage River Greenway Trail. A few visitors walked across the wooden bridge and followed the elevated path towards Whalon Lake. Some, like the family Tom walked away from, sat under the weeping willow trees, appreciating the scenery.

In the parking lot, staff from the Parks District and Bolingbrook Public Works Department attached a banner to the streetlight. It read, "Village of Bolingbrook 50th. Bridging the past, the present, and the future. 1965–2015." Several summer events celebrated this milestone anniversary. The highlight was going to a summer festival and concert headlined by Trip Monkey, a popular band from the 1990s and a step up from the cover bands that usually performed at village events.

To mark the *Babbler's* fiftieth anniversary, the staff was working on a special edition marking the anniversary of the village and of the *Babbler* itself. *Babbler's* motto was "The Truth is unbelievable" as most residents didn't believe its articles.

Tom's phone vibrated. He pulled out his phone and saw the call was from Shavana, a fellow reporter. Both joined the *Babbler* around the same time last year, yet Tom felt like their careers were moving in different directions. She had contacts within Bolingbrook's three covert departments — the Department of Paranormal Affairs, the Department of Interstellar Affairs, and the Restoration Department, also known as the Clean-Up Crew. Tom had some contacts in the DIA and the Clean-Up crew, but none within the DPA. Shavana had several solo cover stories, while Tom had only one.

"What's up, Shavana?"

"Is this a bad time?" Shavana asked. Her soft voice hinted at her anxiety.

Tom lowered his phone so Shavana couldn't hear his frustrated sigh.

"Tom?"

"As good as any time," he replied.

"Are you still at Hidden Lakes?"

Tom nodded. "Yes."

"Is Robert there?"

Tom spotted Mayor Robert Clark's white sports car pulling into a parking spot. "He just arrived."

"Do you think you could ask him some questions for me?"

"Sure," he replied, trying to sound upbeat. "I could use a break from trying to find the Hidden Lakes Monster."

"Still haven't taken a picture of her?"

"Not yet," said Tom. He forced himself to smile to lighten his voice and added, "But I'm not giving up."

"I'm sorry," she said. "Maybe try just before Hidden Lake closes."

And get arrested by the DPA?

"I'll think about it," he replied. "So, what do you want me to ask?"

"Thanks!" Her previous anxiousness turned to excitement. "Ask him to confirm whether the DPA is investigating a possible occult ritual."

Tom furrowed his brow. "Occult ritual?"

"Yeah," she said. Tom imagined her face brightening like it always did when she told him about a story she was working on. Shavana continued, "Last night, there was a bonfire next to Bolingbrook High School. Someone was burning White Sox apparel. It was all over the police scanner."

Tom was too embarrassed to admit he'd skipped listening to his police scanner today, though he was impressed Shavana could listen to the scanner and pick out the calls regarding paranormal activity.

"And how is this an occult ritual?" Tom asked, hoping to steer away from the police scanner. "It could have been Roaming Roul camping out for the night?" Roaming Roul was Bolingbrook's most visible homeless resident.

"It wasn't a campfire," Shavana replied. "And he doesn't burn sports apparel, just branches or garbage. Plus, whoever started this fire also trampled the grass to make a spiral pattern. Almost like a crop circle."

"But what's different?" Tom asked.

"Pieces of White Sox apparel were placed at specific points on the spiral. Each piece had a runestone on top. I took some pictures before the police and DPA secured the area."

"They didn't let you stay?" asked Tom. "I thought the DPA liked you."

"They're just willing to answer my questions. Big difference."

Tom nodded though he wished he had Shavana's problem with the DPA. "What did they tell you?"

"Nothing."

"Nothing?" Tom raised his eyebrows. "Seriously?"

"Seriously. It's so strange. Normally, I can at least get a statement from the DPA. So, do you think you could ask Robert about this? He's not returning my calls, and you always get at least one quote out of him."

Tom noticed Robert walking out of the parking lot. He was wearing a black polo with Bolingbrook 50th Anniversary embroidered on the pocket, standing out against the bright sunlight. He was a white male in his late 60s with gray hair combed and parted on the right. His khaki slacks appeared tailored for him, and his polished black shoes reflected the summer sun.

"Did you try contacting Steve?" Tom asked, referring to Steve Peterseim, the head of the Bolingbrook's Department of Paranormal Affairs.

"I did," she replied. "He's not returning my calls."

Tom looked back and noticed Robert entering the park. To Tom's surprise, he also saw Steve who, along with a photographer, appeared to have been waiting for Robert.

Steve was a white male in his late 60s. Despite the summer heat, he was wearing a Village of Bolingbrook polo shirt and black slacks. Though Tom was standing several yards away, he could still make out the old scar on the right side of Steve's face.

"I see Steve now. I guess he's doing a photoshoot with Robert."

"Oh! Can you ask them about the ritual?"

Tom tensed. "I might get something out of Robert, but I don't know about Steve. Every time I ask him a question, he either ignores me or looks at me like he's about to order my disappearance. If he's not answering your calls, I doubt he's going to talk to me."

"Could you try?" she asked. "I really need your help. Please?"

Tom raised an eyebrow. Shavana had never begged for his help.

Shavana continued, "I promised my mother I'd run an errand for her, and I'm the only one available. Steve will be gone by the time I arrive. Could you at least ask them if they believe the ritualists were targeting the White Sox? Maybe they were trying to help the Cubs by cursing the White Sox?"

Tom shook his head and laughed. "It's a bit late for that."

Shavana was silent for a moment. "What do you mean?" she asked with a hint of embarrassment in her voice.

Tom felt pride for surpassing Shavana's knowledge on a subject. *This is a rare opportunity to impress her,* Tom thought.

Tom cleared his throat. "The Royals are running away with the AL Central. Honestly, a Cubs/Indians World Series is more likely than the Sox making the playoffs."

The thought of the MLB's worst franchises facing each other in the World Series amused Tom. He wondered if that series would trigger an apocalypse.

"I see," Shavana replied, still hiding her embarrassment. "Tom, if you can get anything from Robert or Steve, that would help me so much!"

Tom looked back at Hidden Lakes. "Well, I can, but I need a clear photo of the Hidden Lakes Monster if I want to get back on Sara's good side."

It was true, thought Tom. Sara Langston, the editor of the Babbler, took a chance hiring him over a year ago. He was internet famous for debunking paranormal claims back then, but after discovering that monsters and aliens were real, he quit the skeptical movement that had once embraced him as a future leader. Tom valued uncovering the truth more than the rewards of participating in the greatest cover-up in human history. A year later, Tom couldn't help but think that Sara was disappointed in him despite her encouragement.

"Please?" Shavana pleaded. "We can share the byline. Helping me write a cover story will impress her, too."

Tom's spirits rose. Helping Shavana write a major cover story would improve his standing with Sara. At the very least, it wouldn't hurt his reputation within the *Babbler*.

He replied, "Since you put it that way, I'll ask them to comment on the ritual." Tom shrugged. "Maybe Robert can coax Steve into saying something?"

"Thank you!" said Shavana, sounding eager. "You're the best."

Tom chuckled. He didn't feel like the best, but co-writing a cover story with the *Babbler's* rising star reporter was a step in the right direction.

"Send me the pictures, and I'll get to work."

Shavana ended the call. Moments later, her messages streamed onto his phone. Tom walked under a tree and sat down to review them. From her photos, Tom recognized the area as the field north of the Bolingbrook High School football stadium. The fire was near the banks of Lily Cache Creek. The photos matched Shavana's description of the scene. While he wasn't a rune expert, he recognized that the runes the occultists used were from different rune alphabets. Most rituals involving runes used a single alphabet, like Anglo-Saxon or Elder Futhark. Each set of runes had its own unique power. Tom wondered if the occultists had figured out how to combine the power of different rune sets. *Then again,* he thought, *maybe they were amateurs copying runes without understanding their significance.*

The two people who might have the answer were yards away from Tom. One had an explosive temper but tolerated him occasionally. The other was even-tempered but ignored him. But if he was going to share a byline with Shavana, he needed to pry something out of them.

Tom forced himself to smile as he approached Robert and Steve. Robert was talking to the photographer, gesturing towards the trees and the 'lakes.' Steve stood beside Robert, nodding as Robert spoke. Steve noticed Tom, locking eyes on him like a hunter about to pull the trigger. Robert glanced at Steve, then noticed Tom coming to a stop. He sighed and gave Tom a harsh glare.

"Tom," said Robert, shaking his head. "Why am I not surprised to see you?"

Tom chuckled but braced for one of Robert's rants. "Because you make the news, and I cover the news," he replied, hoping humor would defuse Robert's temper.

Steve shook his head as Tom smiled. "He does more than make the news," he said, looking away from both men.

Robert snickered and then approached Tom. "Make it quick. We're busy."

Tom pulled out his phone and started recording. "What can you tell me about the bonfire that was next to Bolingbrook High School?"

Robert scowled for a moment. Tom braced for the rant. Instead, Robert took a breath, then folded his arms. "Let me guess." He almost sounded bored. "It was no ordinary bonfire."

Feeling like he had avoided a verbal attack, Tom pressed on. "Can Steve or you confirm if it was used in an occult ritual?"

Steve turned and locked his eyes on Tom. Tom felt a chill from Steve's staring.

The photographer gave Tom a confused look, then turned to Robert.

Robert unfolded his arms. "Fifty years," Robert said to the photographer. "The *Babbler* has been at it for fifty long years. Do you know how many years I've been the mayor?"

The photographer shook his head.

"Twenty-nine years. Twenty-nine years of questions like that. Steve, how long have you worked for the village?"

"Since 1971," he replied, showing little emotion.

"Forty-four years," Robert said. "That's how long he's had to put up with their questions." Robert walked up to Steve. "It also shows his dedication and commitment to the village." Robert patted Steve's back. "And he's been with me ever since I became the mayor. That kind of loyalty and commitment is so rare nowadays. You're not an employee. You're like the brother I always wanted."

Steve shrugged. "Because I'm always cleaning up after you."

"And I appreciate it." Robert walked over to the photographer. "Steve runs the Public Works Department."

The photographer chuckled.

Robert looked around Hidden Lakes. "When I was elected, Bolingbrook had more cornstalks than people. If you wanted to buy something, you had to go to Naperville. Today, we're the second-largest village in the state. We have twenty-four corporate headquarters in the village, including WeatherTech." Robert looked up. "Clow Airport started out as a small private airport. Now it's a certified international airport." He looked back at the photographer. "We have so many stores now that people from Naperville come here to shop." Robert smiled. "There's so much more to Bolingbrook than *Babbler*. The Golf

Club. The Promenade. Our fine parks. Maybe we wouldn't be the Brook without the *Bolingbrook Babbler*. But look around you."

The cameraman glanced around Hidden Lakes.

"This is the Bolingbrook I built. With Steve's help."

"Of course," Steve replied. "History didn't start until Robert was elected."

"Damn right," Robert replied.

Tom cleared his throat. "Getting back to the occult ritual?"

Robert narrowed his eyes as he focused on Tom. "I don't care if they were Satanists, pagans, or rabid Cubs fans, no one gets away with vandalizing my village. Especially on its fiftieth anniversary. I will give them what they deserve."

"If—"

Robert smirked. "That's my quote for today, Tom."

"But—"

Robert shook his head. "We're done. Now, if you don't mind, I have a photoshoot with the new deputy mayor." He looked past Tom. "Speaking of which."

Deputy Mayor Simon Williams slowed as he approached Robert. Simon was an African American man in his thirties. He was wearing a Bolingbrook S.T.E.A.M. Association polo shirt and black pants that contrasted with his white walking shoes.

"Just got off work," Simon said, catching his breath.

"Perfect timing," said Robert. He motioned to the photographer. "We can start taking pictures by the bait stand."

"I'll catch up," Steve said.

"Don't take too long. You deserve to be in these shots, too."

"But you deserve so much more," Steve dryly replied.

Robert chuckled. "Flattery isn't your strong suit." Robert looked at Simon. "You'll learn a lot from Steve."

Tom and Steve watched as Robert and Simon left with the photographer.

"So," Tom said as he pointed his phone at Steve. "Can you confirm the bonfire was part of an occult ritual?"

"No comment," Steve replied, looking down at Tom.

"If it was a ritual, were the White Sox the target?"

Steve shook his head. "I don't do interviews with the *Babbler*."

"Come on," Tom protested. "You've talked to Shavana."

"I give her statements," Steve said, sounding bored. "Statements are not the same as interviews. Again, I don't do interviews with the *Babbler*." Steve turned his back towards Tom.

"I've read the archives," Tom said. He felt himself tense up. "You used to grant interviews to Don."

Steve turned his head towards Tom. "You're not Don."

As Steve walked away, Tom still felt the sting of his words. Don was a legendary reporter who retired last year. Tom had taken Don's position at the *Babbler*. Steve was right. He wasn't Don. Tom's shoulders slumped as he felt the weight of Don's reputation on his back.

"Tom?" asked a young girl.

Tom turned and knew the girl with warm brown skin and blue eyes. "Meggy." His mood brightened. "You've grown."

"You haven't," Meggy replied.

Tom snickered. "I think I stopped growing a while ago. So, how have you been?"

"Great!" Meggy said as her eyes lit up with excitement. "I won first place for the best space drawing!"

"You did? Congratulations!"

A year ago, Meggy was an introvert bullied by her half-brother. Tom was pleased to see her happy and outgoing.

Tom continued, "I loved the picture you made of us on the moon."

"Thanks, but I've gotten better since then."

"I would hope so."

"So, what about you?"

"Me?"

"What are you up to? Are girls being nice to you now?"

Tom wondered how he could answer her question in a way the ten-year-old would understand. "Let's just say, the ones that don't like me leave me alone, and I leave them alone. I talk only to the ones who like me. Make sense?"

Meggy nodded. "Yes."

"Speaking of girls," Tom looked towards the ponds. "I'm looking for a very special girl." He looked around and then whispered, "I'm looking for the Hidden Lakes Monster."

Meggy gasped and then whispered, "Any luck?"

"No. I've been waiting for her to raise her head out of the water, but no luck." Tom realized Meggy was the only person outside of the *Babbler* who wouldn't laugh at him searching for the Hidden Lakes Monster.

Meggy looked towards Robert and the gathering. They were holding a long, horizontal fiftieth-anniversary banner while smiling for the camera. She looked back at Tom. "I've got an idea. Follow me." She walked towards the wooden fishing deck over the largest pond. Tom followed.

Nothing else has worked.

They reached the far end of the deck. Two men were fishing. One watched his line, while the other slowly reeled his in.

Meggy walked up to the railing, which was almost as tall as her. She looked back at Tom and said, "Come on."

Tom glanced at the two men as he approached Meggy. They continued to ignore Tom and Meggy. He stopped beside Meggy and looked down into the cloudy green water.

"Call her," said Meggy.

Tom blinked. "Call her?"

"Yeah," said Meggy. "When my mom wants me to come inside, she'll call for me. Maybe she'll come if you call her."

Tom couldn't see the bottom of the pond, let alone the Hidden Lakes Monster.

"Try it," Meggy said. "It might work."

To Tom, the mere thought of calling the Hidden Lakes Monsters embarrassed him. However, he knew that if he helped Shavana, Sara might not be disappointed in him for not getting a photo.

"Here, Hidden Lakes Monster," Tom heard himself say. "Come here, Hidden Lakes Monster! Come on!"

One fisherman finished reeling in his line. He gave Tom a strange look before he walked away. The other fisherman looked away from Tom, trying to ignore him.

Meggy shook her head. "You're doing it wrong."

Tom's face felt warmer. "How?" Tom asked, wondering if he should take advice from a ten-year-old.

"You're using its full name," Meggy explained. "You don't call someone by their full name unless they're in trouble. Just ask my parents."

"And mine," Tom sighed.

"Try calling her by her nickname."

Tom furrowed his brow. "Nickname?"

"Yeah. Just like Meggy is my nickname."

Tom pondered Meggy's answer for a few moments. "Okay... what is her nickname?"

Meggy looked around, then whispered into Tom's ear. "HLM."

Tom's eyes widened for a moment.

"Really," Meggy replied. "My friend Rachel said that's her nickname. She's almost never wrong."

Tom looked back at the water and pondered calling out for HLM. Could it get any worse?

Before he could try, he heard Simon's distant yell.

"Meggy!" he yelled. His voice hinted at a Southern accent. "Come here right now."

"I've got to go," said Meggy. "That's my dad calling me."

Tom nodded. "Good to see you again."

"Good to see you, too." Meggy ran towards her father.

Tom once again faced the murky water. He took a deep breath. "Hi HLM! Want to come out?" He waited for a few moments. The Hidden Lakes Monster didn't surface. People around the pond stared at Tom. He blushed and sighed.

2

Tom clasped his hands in his lap as he sat while Sara, sitting at her desk, read the article. She was an African-American woman in her late thirties. Sara wore a blue blouse and wire-framed reading glasses. Next to her laptop docking port was a framed photo of her husband and two children. Beside the photo was a worn copy of the book, Night Whispers: The Chicago Reaper Case of 1928.

"I have a question," said Sara, as she put her reading glasses in their case.

Tom nodded but worried this would not end well.

"Shavana explained her contributions to the article." She closed the case, and the sound startled Tom. Sara pushed the case aside. "What did you contribute to this article?"

Tom tensed.

Uh oh.

He cleared his throat. "I got the quote from Robert, and the no-comment from Steve." Tom paused for a moment. "Oh, I asked Wendy to confirm that the runes were off."

"Meaning?"

Tom froze. "Meaning?"

"Why is it important to note that the stones were marked with seemingly random runes?"

"Because you can't mix and match runes for a ritual. It's like trying to plug a US electrical cord into a European outlet. They're not compatible. I checked with Wendy, and she said I was right. And I let Shavana know." Tom fidgeted as Sara waited. "It was a last-minute ask. I was trying to get a picture of the Hidden Lakes Monster when she called. She was the one who offered a joint byline."

"She told me that."

"I can add more," Tom said. "If you need me to reach out to confirm—"

Sara shook her head. "You were right about the mixing of runes. It was up to Shavana if she wanted you to do more research. Tom, the point I'm trying to make is she took the lead, and you just followed. That seems to happen with every cover story you're involved with. Except for your first one, of course."

Tom nodded in defeat. "And that was under exceptional circumstances. Normally, we don't encounter our future selves threatening to unleash a weredeer army on the Bolingbrook Golf Club."

"No," Sara replied. "And I understand it's a big shift from being an internet influencer for the skeptical movement."

"That's one way to put it." Tom shifted in his chair and tried to smile.

Sara didn't return it. "You've done great work on your interior stories. I like how your Hidden Lakes Monster is coming together."

Tom nodded and said, "I just wish I could add a photo of the Hidden Lakes Monster."

"It would have been nice. But that's not the problem. The problem is you should be further along in your development as a reporter."

Tom's eyes watered.

REVENGE OF THE PHANTOM PRESS

"Tom?" Sara asked, tilting her head.

"I'm sorry." Tom sighed as he wiped his eyes. "It's just that Shavana is such a natural fit. She came here right after graduation and made an impact. I wasted three years of my life attacking Jamie Kyle when I should have apologized for making her feel uncomfortable on that elevator ride." Tom looked down at the desk. "Hell, I almost slipped down the secular rabbit hole. I thought I was a rising star in the secular movement, destined to be one of the great rationalists. Until I found out monsters were real, and Bolingbrook really has the world's largest urban UFO base."

Sara pushed her box of tissues closer to Tom. "But you discovered the truth."

Tom pulled out a tissue and wiped his eyes. "True. But it took the death of Reese Habenstein and seeing that future version to make me see what the skeptical movement was doing to me. And sometimes I wonder if I'm still destined to become someone like him."

Sara waited for Tom to finish wiping his eyes. "Tom," she said with sympathy in her voice. "You went through a very traumatic experience. I understand that. I'm happy to recommend a therapist who might help you."

"As long as they don't consider working here a sign of mental illness."

Sara smirked. "No. Now, let me ask you some more questions. Are you training Megan Simon to be a high-tech assassin?"

Tom blinked in surprise. "No."

"Are you writing about the evils of radical feminism?"

Tom shook his head. "No. My friend Pamela is a Humanist Heart Board member. She took the time to point out the flaws in my argument. Now I can enjoy Jamie's songs again. I even bought her new album."

Sara nodded. "Do you still believe Matthew Bennett is a great man?"

"Fuck no!" Tom blushed. "Sorry. No. Not since I learned what he's done to women and what he almost did to my mother."

Sara leaned back in her chair. "Seems like you're a long way away from being that future version of you."

Tom nodded.

"When you joined us last year, I didn't expect you to be a superstar reporter."

"That was Don," Tom replied. "He had all those solo cover stories. I can't do that yet."

"But there have been many successful reporters here who have never written a solo cover story. That was one thing that made Don an exceptional reporter. I don't expect you to be Don. But at this point in your career, I expect you to contribute more to a team than you have been. Maybe take the lead on a story."

Tom grabbed another tissue. "I'll try to lead a team. I just need to find the right story. It would help if I had more sources in the Department of Interstellar Affairs and any sources in the DPA."

"That comes with time." Sara leaned back in her chair. "Let me tell you something about Shavana."

Tom nodded.

"When she started, she had one of the worst cases of imposter syndrome I'd ever seen. Don even told her off when she tried to investigate the girls in green. Now, look how far she's come. There's no reason you can't be in her position someday."

"I hope so." Tom wiped his eyes again. "Thank you for taking a chance on me last year."

"Now you have to take a chance on yourself." She looked at her phone. "I have a meeting with Chris. Take as much time as you need to clean up."

"Thanks," Tom said. "I'll think about what you said."

Sara left her cubicle. Tom cleaned up his discarded tissues and took a few moments to compose himself. The meeting wasn't a total disaster. He struggled to envision himself taking the lead on a cover story.

Tom tossed the tissues and stepped out of Sara's cubicle and into the newsroom. The room was alive with sounds — people talking on the phone and the clicking of keyboards. Deadline day always brought the newsroom to life.

Tom knew he would leave at a decent hour because he was almost finished with his Hidden Lakes Monster article. All he needed to do was check the *Babbler*'s archives to see if there was an article explaining why HLM was so camera shy.

A familiar voice asked, "You okay, Tom?"

Tom turned and saw Wendy sitting at her open desk. She was a white woman in her fifties, wearing a white blouse and black slacks. Tom was surprised that her normal pale skin had tanned. Like Tom, she'd quit the skeptical movement to work for the *Babbler*. She was Tom's role-model and friend.

Standing next to Wendy was Jenna Olson. She was in her early thirties and had medium-length blonde hair and was wearing a gray pantsuit. Jenna was a sales representative and Chris's granddaughter. She was also a psychic with precognition. Though her visions of the future were symbolic, they were helpful.

Tom approached. "Rough meeting."

Wendy gave Tom a sympathetic look. "Sorry about that."

He shrugged. "Sara says I need to take the lead on a cover story."

"And you will," Jenna replied. "Maybe sooner than you think."

"You saw that?" Tom asked as he perked up.

Jenna nodded. "I can't tell you any more than that. There's still a big event that's clouding my visions."

"Are you still hearing screams?" he asked, suddenly feeling like his problems were small compared to Jenna's.

She nodded. "Yes, but they stopped giving me migraines. I was just telling Wendy that it looks like a storm, but there are countless people in the clouds. All of them are screaming. Some are terrified. Some sound enraged. But they're all contributing to the storm. Sometimes, I can see a red glow. Like a fireball obscured by clouds." Jenna sighed. "If you're worried, I'm positive it's not a vision of the end of the world. But something big is going to happen."

"We're just glad you're feeling better," Wendy replied.

Tom smirked. "Maybe it's the rage from Trump supporters reacting to Hillary Clinton's victory."

Jenna smiled. "We can only hope."

"I'm not too worried," Wendy replied. "I think the NWO will stop Trump before the primaries. He'd wreck all their long-term plans if he won."

"I'm kind of worried," said Tom. "Motivate enough voters, and you can overwhelm any covert group's agenda."

Wendy started to reply when Jenna said, "I think Shavana has a big announcement to make."

"About what?" Tom asked.

"Not sure. Something involving a light. A light that's pulling her away from a dark place. We'll find out right about... now."

Shavana, wearing dark jeans and a red blouse, rushed through the front door, holding her smartphone. She was an African-American woman in her early twenties with black curly hair.

"I got it!" she called out, her voice bursting with excitement. She lifted the flip-up counter that separated the 'lobby' from the newsroom and ran towards Wendy. "I got a picture of a girl in green!"

Tom dropped his jaw. "A girl in green clothing or *the* girls in green?"

The girls in green were a mystery that baffled every *Babbler* reporter since they were spotted in the 1970s. Eyewitnesses could never remember their faces or other features. They would only remember them wearing green. Tom always wondered if they were clones designed to spy for the village, or some kind of Fae that watched over the residents.

"Both!" She held the phone up. Tom recognized the Bolingbrook Historical Museum in the background. A green motion blur on the right side of the image caught his attention. It kind of looked like someone wearing a green dress. If it was a woman, most of her body was off camera. On top of the green blur was a streak of black. Tom wondered if it was her hair. The rest of the photo was in focus, and he knew Shavana wasn't the type of person who would submit a fake photo, especially of something as major as a girl in green sighting.

"Send it to me," said Wendy, rushing to grab her phone.

Shavana started sharing the photo. "I was in Rotary Park when I glimpsed her. You know they always disappear if you look in their direction. She didn't, but she was moving fast. So pulled out my camera, and I got the shot just before she vanished."

Wendy plugged her phone into her computer. Others gathered around Wendy as she downloaded the historic photo.

Shavana had pulled off the greatest feat in the *Babbler's* history. Tom felt inadequate.

3

Tom savored the smell of meat sauce as he poured it onto his steaming hot spaghetti noodles. His mother, Michelle, dumped the remaining noodles onto her plate. His father, Jason, finished serving the tossed salad.

"Smells great," said Tom. His mother's meals were the best part of his visits. He hoped that this would be the dinner that didn't end in an argument.

"Thank you," said Michelle as she sat back down. "This time I used your grandmother's recipe."

"She spent over thirty minutes making it," Jason added.

"You didn't have to," said Tom before he took a bite. The taste took him back to his childhood visits to his grandmother.

"Nonsense," she replied.

Tom wiped his mouth. "So, I hope things are going well with the library board."

"They're fine." Michelle set down her fork. "I got to tour the vault a couple of days ago. The staff showed me the items they were going to put in the fiftieth anniversary display, like the minutes of the very first board meeting and the first two issues of the *Phantom Press*."

"Cool," said Tom. He lowered his fork filled with spaghetti. "Are they finally going to display the Broken Scepter letter as well?" Tom then realized he shouldn't have mentioned it. He resumed eating dinner, hoping his parents wouldn't press him for details.

"Broken Scepter letter?" asked Jason. He had a slight sauce stain on the front of his white polo shirt that displayed the name and logo of his electronic repair shop.

Tom considered how to escape the minefield he'd just wandered into. He swallowed. "Yeah." He took a sip of water. "You know. It's the letter Robert sent out with a picture of a broken scepter on it. I've heard there's a copy in the vault. I always wondered what he wrote." Tom knew better than to mention that it was rumored to be the letter Robert sent to the Illuminati announcing his defection to the New World Order.

Michelle and Jason gave each other a long look.

Oh shit.

"Tom," Jason finally said. "Simon says he saw you talking to his daughter."

"Yeah," Tom replied, as if nothing was wrong. "I met her last year, along with her brother. He was a sexist pig and bully. When he said he liked my blog, that's when I started thinking about shutting it down. Because if people like him—" His parents looked at each other again. "Anyway, Meggy said hi to me, and I said hi back. She's so much happier now. Apparently she won a contest for one of her drawings. It's like Marty's departure set her free." Tom knew better than to mention that her brother was a prisoner of the Plutonian Matriarchy. He hoped to change the subject. "You know, since I've met Pamela, I've learned so much about intersectionality and—"

"About that," said Jason. He fidgeted for a few moments. "Tom... we listened to the Skeptical World podcast yesterday."

Tom pretended to cough. Jamie co-hosted the podcast with hosts from around the world. He knew which episode his parents were about to ask him about. Tom looked down at his plate and wondered how much he could eat before the argument started.

"They," Michelle said, then paused. "They mentioned one of your articles."

"I heard that episode, too," Tom replied, still trying to sound upbeat. "It's so rude and unprofessional to diagnose a person you've never met. Don't you think?" He looked at the salad bowl. "Could someone pass the salad, please?"

His parents didn't reach for the bowl.

So close to a peaceful dinner.

"Tom." Jason sighed. "Your mother and I had a talk." He hesitated and then looked at his wife.

"We think you should check into Alexian Brothers," Michelle quickly added.

Tom dropped his fork. He knew they were referring to their mental health inpatient unit.

Jason cleared his throat. "You're still on my health insurance."

"And we can get you a private room. It wouldn't be like your apartment, but I think you would still like it."

Tom stared at his parents in disbelief. "You want to commit me to a mental ward because of a podcast?"

"We're worried about you, Tom," said Michelle.

"We heard you were trying to summon the Hidden Lakes Monster," Jason added.

"Summon?" Tom asked and tried to laugh. "I'm not a magic user. I was just trying to take a focused photo of it."

Michelle looked at Jason, who nodded. "I did some research, Tom," she said. "The deepest pond in Hidden Lakes is only eight feet deep. It's too shallow to house a sea serpent."

"And there's no such thing as a sea serpent." Jason added.

Tom raised his index finger. "Normally, it is eight feet deep. But the Hidden Lakes Monster can burrow down to its original cavern, which is over a mile—"

"Listen to yourself!" Jason yelled, standing.

"Jason!" Michelle touched Jason. "We talked about this." She faced Tom. "Tom, I know it seems very real to you. But do you remember all the things Reese and the other skeptics taught you? Isn't it more likely that you have some kind of mental illness?"

Tom leaned back in his chair. "Considered and rejected."

Jason leaned forward. "I'm wondering if your issues with Jamie and the skeptical movement go back to when you found out Juanita Vega found a boyfriend in college."

Tom remembered Juanita from the Chicago Anti-Superstition Society's Lunch and Learn sessions. Though she was a high school senior and he was younger, it didn't matter. She was beautiful, smart, and an atheist. The perfect woman, he had thought.

Michelle said, "Your father and I are worried that we didn't recognize how traumatic that was for you. We thought it was a harmless teenage crush. We should have recognized it was something that needed professional attention."

Tom's jaw dropped. "Oh, my God!" He shook his head. "That was years ago. We moved on. She's now the president of the Chicago Anti-Superstition Society. You're saying I'm still upset because she brought her boyfriend to a Lunch and Learn?"

Jason replied, "Tom, until you saw him, you used to love going to Lunch and Learns. That obviously wounded you. If you don't treat a wound, it only gets worse."

Michelle added, "And now it's gotten to where you're suffering from delusions. Those *Babbler* people are making them worse."

Tom scowled at his parents. "I'm not delusional! I know what I've seen!"

Jason threw his hands up in frustration. "You should know better than that. After all the books, CASS meetings, podcasts, and everything else I did to teach you about skepticism. I even persuaded Reese Habenstein to send you his first DVD. How do you think he would feel if he knew you were working for the *Babbler*?"

Tom shrugged. "He'd appreciate my commitment to the truth?"

Jason slapped the table. "*The Babbler*, Tom! We sacrificed so much so you could grow up free of woo and promote science. To carry on my work." He stood up, knocking his chair over, and pointed to Michelle. "Your mother thinks you're sick, and I hope she's right. Because I don't know what I would do if I thought you were deliberately trashing Reese's legacy, turning your back on the movement I helped build, and embarrassing your mother every week."

Tom trembled. He hadn't seen his father this angry in years. But he wasn't going to back down. "Did Robert put you two up to this?" Jason and Michelle exchanged knowing glances. "Is that it? Robert wants Mom to run for Village Trustee, but it would look bad if her son still worked for the *Babbler*?"

"Tom," Michelle replied with a shaky voice, "we just want you to get better. If that means not running for trustee, I won't run. I'll even resign as library trustee if that's what you need. You're not well, Tom. You need help." She stood up and held Jason's hand. "Your father and I are trying to help you. You must understand that."

Tom gritted his teeth and then said, "Oh, they'll help me, alright. They'll help me deal with Juanita, Jamie—anyone they think messed me up." He raised his voice as he stood. "The problem is, I won't lie to them. I won't lie about seeing the men in blue. I won't lie about being inside Clow UFO Base, and I'm not going to lie about surviving a weredeer attack. I'll even tell them Robert thinks he's the most important mayor in the galaxy. You think they would let me out after saying that? Huh?"

Michelle put a hand up to her mouth. Jason put his other hand on her shoulder.

Tom continued, "The only way I'd be let out is if Robert sent his men in blue to scramble my mind. Then they would let me out, but I wouldn't be your son anymore. I'd just be an empty shell, wasting my life away as one of the village's menial employees. Is that what both of you want? Because I sure as hell don't want that.

"I'm going to keep telling the truth, even if it costs my mother a seat on the board, or makes my dad feel uncomfortable listening to the Skeptical World. Because Robert's campaign fund isn't big enough to make me lie. Hell, I may suck at my job, but at least I'm writing the truth. For the first time in my life, I'm writing about the truth, and not being a cog in the skeptical movement's schemes." Tom stepped away from the table. "It's my turn to address the village board on Wednesday. You should skip that meeting so you won't be embarrassed."

He stormed out of the house.

4

As THE FOUR YOUNGER members of the Bolingbrook S.T.E.
A.M Association., including Meggy, posed with their winning
works of art, Tom and the children's parents snapped pictures.
Robert smiled as he posed behind them. The light of the setting
sun shone through the village boardroom's bay windows. On
the elevated platform behind Robert, the village trustees and
other high-ranking officials waited for the meeting to resume.
Simon focused on Tom, with a hint of suspicion on his face.

"Okay," Robert said as he looked at one of the automated
cameras streaming the board meeting over the internet and onto
Bolingbrook Community Television. "The Bolingbrook S.T.E
.A.M. Association is one of many things that make Bolingbrook
great." He looked down at the children. "I don't think you want
to stick around for the boring part."

"No," replied a boy.

"I'm getting a banana split!" said Meggy.

"Wow," Robert replied. "Just don't spend all the money on
your gift card tonight."

"We won't," Meggy's mother replied.

The parents and the children filtered out of the boardroom
while Tom returned to the movie theater-style seats from the
audience. As he sat down, a man wearing a Suburban Star Pub-
lications polo shirt walked by.

"You're leaving?" asked Tom.

"Yeah," he replied.

"Now? They haven't voted on anything yet."

The man shrugged. "I took my pictures. The team in the Philippines is writing the article."

Tom's jaw dropped. "Are you serious?"

The man shrugged. "Like anything important is going to happen."

The man walked away, and Meggy approached Tom. "Did you meet HLM?" she asked.

Tom shook his head. "Nope."

Meggy thought for a moment. "Maybe I can meet her first? Then I can introduce you to her."

Before Tom could answer, Meggy's mother rushed up to her and grabbed her hand. "We have to go." She looked at Tom with suspicion. "Don't make her an alien or monster in your story."

Tom shrugged. "She's not."

Meggy said goodbye as her mother escorted her out of the boardroom.

After most of the audience left, Robert called the meeting to order. The trustees snapped to attention.

Tom started reviewing his list of questions. Robert allowed only one *Babbler* reporter to address the board during public comments, so Sara rotated the responsibility among all the reporters. Depending on Robert's mood, he'd either lash out at the reporter or dismiss them without comment. When he lashed out, he sometimes said something noteworthy. Whether it was deliberate or an accident, Tom wasn't sure. He just hated being on the receiving end of Robert's rants.

A text message from Pamela popped up.

> Hi. I just heard the podcast. Doing okay?

> Yes. My parents didn't take it well.

> Sorry. Don't worry about the HH board.
> You're not on the agenda.

Tom wasn't sure if he should feel relieved or insulted that he wasn't worth the Humanist Heart's time. A year ago, he thought Humanist Heart was part of a feminist conspiracy to take over the skeptical movement. Pamela helped him realize that wasn't true.

Considering the impact she'd had on his life, Tom found it hard to believe they'd only seen each other twice—once at a Habencon, and once at the Humanist Heart Congress in Bolingbrook. After the congress, they stayed in touch over the Internet. Though she listened to him, she was still a skeptic who didn't know the skeptical movement's involvement in covering up paranormal activity. Even Humanist Heart took part in the cover-up on behalf of the Interstellar Commonwealth, the governing body of the Milky Way. Unlike his parents, Pamala never said he needed to be committed to a mental institution.

> What have you been up to?

As Pamela typed her answer, Tom noticed the board had already voted on half the items on the agenda. One advantage of one-party rule is short meetings, thought Tom.

> I'm going on a date this Friday.

Tom set his phone down and closed his eyes. For over a year, he'd debated telling her how he felt. He hesitated because she lived in Washington state, and there was no way he could move there. Nor could he ask her to move to Illinois and give up her teaching position. Now, even a long-distance relationship was out of the question. Had he blown it again? Just like he blew it with Juanita.

"Any questions or comments?" said Robert. He stared at Tom. Tom noticed there were now five residents, a police officer, and two men in blue in the audience. Typical of these meetings. The men in blue were the village's covert enforcers, like the NWO's men in black.

Tom looked down and sent his reply to Pamela.

Great!

As Tom approached the podium, Robert picked up a stack of folders. "The clock starts now, Tom." He opened a folder and started sorting the papers. "Make it quick."

"Sure," Tom replied, and prepared to speed-read his note-cards. "We have the following questions. Will the DPA confirm that an occult ritual was performed near Bolingbrook High School? Will the village allow the surviving members of the Bolingbrook Yacht Club to be part of the 50th anniversary celebrations? If so, will they be allowed to fly one of their hover yachts? What role will the Hidden Lakes Monster have in the celebrations? Finally, do you have an update about the weredeer abducted by the Interstellar Commonwealth last year?"

Tom prepared to take notes and braced himself for Robert's rant.

Robert quietly shuffled through a few more papers. Then he cleared his throat. "Done?"

"Yes."

Brace for impact.

Robert took a deep breath as he set the papers aside. "You know, there are people who say that Bolingbrook wouldn't be Bolingbrook without the *Babbler*." Robert paused for a few beats. "I understand why. Your first issue appeared just moments after the first board signed the incorporation papers. Nobody knows how they pulled that off." Robert looked at one of the remote-controlled cameras. "Anyway, for the first few years, the *Babbler* was Bolingbrook's first tourist attraction. People traveled from as far away as Crystal Lake to buy a copy. Or so I've heard. That angered some residents enough to establish the park district." Robert chuckled. "Now, sometimes the *Babbler* runs good stories. Like the ones where I save Bolingbrook."

Everyone, including Tom, laughed.

"But seriously. When I became mayor, Bolingbrook was a very different community. It was surrounded by cornfields. The Old Chicago Mall was in ruins. There were roads to nowhere, and one of the previous mayors wasted taxpayer money on expensive wallpaper for the private bathroom." Robert locked his eyes on Tom. "While *Babbler* kept running its silly articles, I started improving the village. I brought in the right people. I brought new business to the village. I secured its boundaries, and I ordered the implosion of the Old Chicago mall. Under my leadership, the cornfields were replaced with stores and factories."

Robert looked at his trustees, like a teacher looking at their students. "Today, Bolingbrook is a great place to grow because I planned it that way. Yet, some people still say that we wouldn't be the Brook without the *Babbler*." He glared at Tom. "Well, excuse my language, but that's bullshit. Residents should say it wouldn't be the Brook without me." He pointed at Tom. "Not you and your friends, The *Babbler*—"

The sound of shattering glass interrupted Robert. Tom turned just in time to see Robert's car flying through the bay window like a toy car tossed by a child. The front of the car impacted the floor, totaling the bumper and hood. After the impact, the car toppled over. Tom froze in horror as the falling car cast a shadow over him. The roof of the car crumpled as it crashed into the floor, shattering the car's windows. It came to rest a few yards from Tom's position.

For a moment, everyone stared at the car in stunned silence, struggling to process what had happened. The car's alarm activated. The room filled with the blaring.

"Spilled milk!" a police officer shouted.

"Spilled milk!" yelled a police officer, who was crouched behind a row of chairs. He kept repeating the phrase "spilled milk" into his radio.

Two men in blue rushed past Tom towards Robert's chair. Robert lifted his head above the table and looked around. In all the years Tom lived in Bolingbrook, he'd never seen Robert as pale and stunned as he was now. When the men in blue offered their hands, Robert's face turned red, and the familiar scowl returned to his face.

"I'm fine," he protested. He grunted as he stood up. The men in blue positioned themselves between the shattered bay window and the mayor. Robert pulled out his keys and deactivated the alarm. "Simon," he yelled. "Get the trustees to Shelter One. Everyone else, follow the officers outside. Evacuation Route Blue."

The trustees jumped out of their seats and rushed towards the side door. Simon stopped next to Robert.

"What about you?" asked Simon. "You can't stay here. It might be rigged to blow."

Robert's face turned a brighter shade of red. "Then what are you doing standing here? Get them to the shelter."

"But—"

"I'm still the mayor," Robert snapped. "Don't argue with me."

Simon looked at Robert in disbelief, and the mayor glared back. A moment later, Simon yelled, "You heard Robert! Clear out!"

Tom realized he was still holding his phone. He switched to the photo app and got a few shots of the trustees and the department heads rushing out the side exit. Hearing footsteps behind him, he turned and took pictures of the attendees leaving through the back exit. Like him, they seemed to be in shock as they walked away from the unexpected crash scene.

Tom then started taking pictures of the wrecked sports car. *How could it have gotten here,* he wondered. The bay window was elevated off the ground outside. It would have needed a ramp and a running start to make the jump through the bay windows. Yet the engines were off, and the wheels weren't spinning. The other possibilities were too frightening to consider. A psychic with telekinesis? A shifter? Aliens?

"Alpha Red!" Robert yelled into his earpiece. "Yes. Alpha Red. Get the emergency command center online."

Robert walked off the platform, accompanied by the two men in blue. As he approached his wrecked car, he lowered his hand from his earpiece. Tom started taking pictures of Robert. To Tom's surprise, Robert didn't seem to notice. He locked his eyes on his ruined sports car. The men in blue walked ahead of Robert, then abruptly stopped. Tom suspected Robert used his implant to give them a telepathic order to stay behind him.

Tom started to ask a question when he noticed movement by the bay window. He turned. Countless sheets of paper drifted down from the sky like giant snowflakes. Robert noticed and watched them fall from the sky.

"All clear," came Steve's voice.

Tom turned and saw Steve wearing a black suit and walking towards Robert. He held an eight and a half by eleven-inch sheet of paper, the same color of white as the ones raining from the sky. At this distance, Tom could see there was text printed on the papers. Three columns of body text and headlines, like a newsletter.

Robert tensed. "Who did this?" he yelled.

Steve handed the sheet to Robert. As Robert read it, his hands shook, and his body tensed.

"They're telling everyone in Bolingbrook," Steve calmly added.

Robert crumpled up the sheet and tossed it onto the floor. "I'm placing you in charge of this. You have emergency authority. All the resources of the village are at your disposal."

Steve nodded. "We've already started."

"Good, and now you can use the resources of the DIA to assist." Robert looked up at the night sky through the shattered bay window. "You had your chance to rest in peace! Now you're about to experience hell on Earth." Robert noticed Tom. "That's your quote for today." He looked back at Steve. "We'll take an APC to the emergency command center."

"It's warming up now," Steve replied. "I'll meet you there."

The Bolingbrook Golf Club was a luxury golf course owned by the village. Many residents nicknamed it the Robert Mahal because it was his dream project. Unknown to most residents, it was also the home of the secret emergency command center.

Robert left the boardroom, accompanied by the men in blue.

"What's going on?" Tom asked.

"This is a perfect example," Steve replied, still calm despite the flurry of activity around him.

"Of what?" Tom asked.

"Of why you need us." Steve turned and walked away at a normal pace.

Tom picked up the sheet of paper and uncrumpled it. The masthead read *The Phantom Press,* and it had today's date.

"We're back" read the headline.

5

Tom's hands trembled as he emptied a sugar packet over his Portillo's chocolate shake. A gust of humid wind rushed through Portillo's patio area. A couple sitting two tables down stared at Tom in shocked silence. He glared back at them.

"It's not sweet enough," Tom said in response to their silent question. In truth, he needed a stronger than normal sugar rush after what he'd just seen at the Town Center.

The couple shook their heads, then resumed reading their copies of the *Phantom Press*. The back page's headline enraged Tom as he read it again: "The Unbelievable Truth about the *Babbler*."

It wasn't enough for the *Phantom Press* to toss Robert's car into the boardroom. They didn't stop with a front-page article attacking Robert. Nor was it enough to rain thousands of copies on Bolingbrook. They had to attack the staff of the *Babbler*, too, including him.

They wrote, "Tom Larsen made a name for himself after propositioning secular podcaster Jamie Kyle in an elevator at 2 AM. Using his blog and social media outlets, he fanned the flames of male entitlement within the secular movement. His efforts led to the Bolingbrook Golf Club riot as his fans tried to disrupt a gathering of secular feminists. After the riot, he snapped and started believing in the same paranormal phenomena that he used to ridicule others for believing in. Now his family wants him committed, and the *Babbler* is on the verge of firing him. To all those atheist influencers out there, look upon Tom's works and despair."

Tom grumbled and looked away from the issue. Normally, Tom liked Portillo's Americana décor and found their 1950s background music comforting. Now they reminded him of ghosts that were haunting him—the ones in his head, and now the real ones exposing his past to the residents.

"Tom!" Wendy called out. She rushed up the ramp onto the patio. "Are you okay?"

Tom shrugged as Wendy took a seat. "As okay as someone who nearly got crushed by a car can be." He made himself smile. "Thanks for coming out on short notice."

"Of course," Wendy replied in a sympathetic tone. "Do you want me to unlock the office?"

Tom shook his head and took a deep breath to calm himself. "Not yet." He opened another sugar packet. "I just need some time to decompress."

Wendy's eyes widened as Tom poured the packet onto his shake. "You're gonna get diabetes if you keep adding sugar to that shake."

"It beats drinking and making an ass of myself."

"Tom," said Wendy. "The not drinking part is good. Overdosing on sugar isn't."

Tom took another sip of his shake. "I think it's just right." He set the cup aside and handed Wendy the issue. "Did you see this?"

"How could I not?" Wendy replied. "It's everywhere. It's so bad, Robert called in the sanitation company to help clean up the mess."

"Did you see the part...?" Tom hesitated, unsure if he should say the next part out loud.

Wendy sighed and glanced around the patio. "Yes," she whispered. "We'll deal with it later."

The new issue outed Wendy as a trans woman. Tom thought the *Phantom Press* just humiliated him. But outing Wendy — that was far beyond embarrassing someone, thought Tom. They had crossed the line into endangerment.

The sound of a bicycle bell startled Tom. It sounded familiar.

"I asked Roaming Roul to join us," Wendy said. She looked out at the large parking lot of the strip mall. "I hope you don't mind."

Tom, like many Bolingbrook residents, knew Roaming Roul as the homeless man who rode his beat-up bike around the village. He always attached handwritten signs to his bike, many of them critical of Robert. If asked, he would insist he wasn't homeless but protesting about Robert. Though Robert could have ordered the police to arrest Roul, he had tolerated Roul's "protest" for several years.

Unknown to most residents, Roul also provided Wendy with tips about paranormal activities in Bolingbrook. Not all his tips were correct, but some of his tips resulted in cover stories. Somehow, Roul always stayed one step ahead of the men in blue, and maybe the girls in green.

Tom replied, "If you think he can help."

Roul pedaled into Tom's view. He was a Latino man with long gray hair that matched his untamed beard. What he could see of Roul's skin looked rough and weathered. Three baskets on his bicycle held bundles of clothes and camping gear. Tied to the front basket was a sign that read, "Resist Robert!"

Wendy waved at Roul and motioned for him to join them. Tom braced himself, expecting to be overwhelmed by Roul's body odor.

"Hola!" Roul called out as he stepped off his bike. "Wendy, you still look great."

Wendy blushed. "You don't have to."

"But it's true," he replied and smiled, revealing his yellow teeth.

The other customers on the patio glanced at Roul as he locked his bike to a railing. They averted their eyes, seeming to hope he wouldn't notice them.

Tom whispered, "Do we owe him?"

Wendy shook her head. "Already taken care of," she whispered back.

Wendy stood up as Roul approached. Tom followed. When Roul reached the table, Wendy opened her arms to offer him a friendly hug.

Roul said, "I wish this were under better circumstances."

Wendy released the hug and nodded. She gestured towards Tom. "This is Tom Larsen. He witnessed the attack."

Tom made himself smile as he braced for Roul's stench. "Thank you for joining us. I hope we didn't make you ride too far."

Roul chuckled. "Nonsense. I'd just finished showering at the Annerino Center. Great place, and it's right by my favorite library."

He offered his hand to Tom. Tom shook his hand. To his surprise, Roul didn't stink. He thought that Roul must be telling the truth, though he wasn't sure how he got access to the locker rooms.

"I wouldn't say it's next to the library." He shook Roul's hand.

Roul flashed a sly smile. "You're thinking of the big library. I meant the small library. It is close to Annerino. They make a great team."

"I'll have to check out that library, then." Tom knew that all the neighboring libraries were nowhere near the Annerino Center.

Roul's expression turned serious. "I hope you never have to." After a beat, he smiled. "Let's get down to business."

The three of them sat down. Roul gave Tom a concerned look. "How are you doing, Tom?"

Tom felt himself relax. "Better. It's not every day that a ghost throws a car at you."

"Really?" Roul asked, sounding puzzled. "Tell us what happened."

Tom recounted the events leading up to Robert declaring a state of emergency and placing Steve in charge. In recounting the tale, Tom felt the shock of the event fade away. Talking, he thought, was better than a super-sweet shake. But it didn't taste as good.

When he finished, Wendy looked at Roul. "What do you think?" she asked.

Roul scratched his beard as he scanned Tom. "Are you leaving anything out?"

"Excuse me?" Tom asked.

Roul leaned closer to Tom. "Anything. Disembodied voices? Hallucinations? Unexpected emotions?"

Tom immediately shook his head. "No. Nothing like that."

"Did it look like anyone else was experiencing those things?" Roul asked.

"No," Tom replied. "The only manifestations were throwing the car into the boardroom and the new issue."

Roul nodded. "Speaking of the issue." He picked up one copy on the table. "What do you two think of the design?"

Tom and Wendy each took a copy and examined it. Tom forced himself to look past the attacks and focus on the design itself. It took more effort than he had expected.

"The fonts look dated," said Tom. "But the layout looks too perfect. I could tell the old issues were literal cut-and-paste jobs. The columns were slightly out of alignment."

Wendy added, "I agree. This looks like it was done on a computer."

Roul nodded. "They wouldn't have access to computers in the Ghost Frequencies."

"Ghost Frequencies?" Tom asked.

"It's where ghosts come from," Wendy replied. Her eyes lit up every time she could explain something. "After death, most of the time a person's mental energy is converted to heat, but sometimes, the energy is powerful enough to shift to a new electromagnetic frequency."

Tom gave Wendy a puzzled look. "The afterlife exists in the electromagnetic spectrum?"

Roul laughed, and Tom felt himself blush.

"Sorry," Roul replied. "Think of it as the edge of a cliff. The afterlife is at the bottom. You can stay near the edge for a long time, but eventually, you're going to fall."

Wendy added, "I have some books you can borrow, Tom."

"Thanks," Tom replied, still feeling embarrassed.

"There's no such thing as a stupid question," Roul said.

"Roul," Wendy said, "Tom's going to write the article about the attack. Do you know anything that might give more insight into what happened?"

Roul cracked his knuckles. "I'll see what I can find out." He extended a hand towards Tom. "May I have your card?"

Tom hesitated, then realized Roul meant his paper card. "I'll get it." He reached for his wallet and started fumbling through it.

Roul looked at Wendy. "This is going to take some extra effort on my part."

Wendy pulled a Portillo's gift card out of her fanny pack. "I think this will make it worth your while."

"Gracias," Roul replied as he accepted the gift card.

Tom then handed his card to Roul. As he accepted Tom's card, Roul scrutinized his face. "Have we met before?"

Tom examined Roul's face. His face seemed familiar, yet the details eluded him. He shrugged. "I'm sure I've driven by you many times."

Roul kept scanning Tom. "Have you ever been to Chicago?"

Tom blinked. "Of course. I used to visit a lot when I was a teenager. Then I went to UIC and got my communication degree there."

Roul nodded as a hint of recognition appeared on his face. "I remember now. *Mi ángel de la razón* blessed you."

"Who?" Tom tried to remember all the invisible urban monsters that could have stalked him in Chicago.

"The Angel of Reason," Roul replied, his voice hushed, a joyous gleam in his eyes that betrayed his calm demeanor. "I saw her bless you many times."

Tom gave Roul a confused look. "I don't... recall ever seeing an angel before."

"But in your heart, you accepted every one of them," Roul replied with a mischievous smile. "Could you do me a favor, Tom?"

Tom blinked. "What kind of favor?"

Roul leaned closer to Tom and whispered, "If *mi ángel de la razón* appears before you again, tell her *el caballero blanco extraña a su pequeño girasol.*"

Tom wished he'd taken Spanish in high school instead of Latin. "El..."

"She'll know what you mean."

Tom didn't know how to reply.

Wendy cleared her throat. "Roul, can we talk in private?"

"But of course."

Wendy and Roul said goodbye to Tom and then walked away. Tom took another sip of his loaded shake.

"Perfect," he said to himself.

6

TOM YAWNED AFTER FINISHING the Fountaindale Library's archive of Phantom Press issues from 1975 to 1985. The morning light passing through the library's glass façade illuminated the second floor reading space. Outside he could see the Town Center and four village employees boarding over the shattered windows. Investigators still examined the parking. Farther away, three TV news crews were doing live remotes, showing the scarred building.

Tom turned his attention back to the binder containing the old *Phantom Press* articles. After reading all the issues, he noticed the contrast between the snarky tone of the original articles and the nastiness of the recent issue. Though the ghost reporters of the *Phantom Press* spied on every major figure in Bolingbrook, most of the articles highlighted embarrassing revelations like a trustee spending hundreds of dollars 'caring' for a pet rock or what a local radio personality really thought about Bolingbrook. They did some investigative reporting, like how a school board trustee was accepting bribes to keep the Valley View School District's year-round school schedule.

Oddly, the *Phantom Press* never covered paranormal activity in Bolingbrook. It was as if they wanted to maintain the illusion that mortals produced the *Phantom Press*. Despite their claims about uncovering the truth, the *Phantom Press* was taking part in the cover-up of paranormal activity. *Just like the leaders of the skeptical movement,* Tom thought.

As part of the coverup, The *Phantom Press* ran articles critical of the *Babbler* and printed gossip about staffers. They described Jenna's great uncle, a reporter in the 1970s, as a drug addict who was always hallucinating.

The only person the Phantom Press didn't attack was Rene McDonald. She served two terms as a village trustee starting in 1973. After a close election in 1981, she won the mayoral race. She was also a techno-shaman and a loyal member of the Illuminati. Her magical powers were the key to defeating invaders from the future during the Bolingbrook Time War in 1984.

During her term, the *Phantom Press* attacked her enemies, especially then-Trustee Robert Clark. The *Phantom Press* depicted Robert as someone who was always arguing with Rene. One of their editorials read that if Rene said the sky was blue, Robert would still argue with her. When Robert accused her of buying expensive wallpaper for the mayor's private bathroom, the *Phantom Press* published accounts of his meetings with local business leaders. They said Robert planned to sell out Bolingbrook and spend taxpayers' money on projects far more expensive than wallpaper. Tom believed that she let the *Phantom Press* operate in the abandoned Old Chicago shopping mall/amusement park in exchange for favorable coverage.

Rene had planned to run for reelection, but in December 1984, a drunk driver killed her husband and her only child, Natalie. Rene ended her reelection campaign and endorsed another trustee to run in her place.

With Rene's endorsement and the *Phantom Press's* relentless attacks against Robert, her chosen candidate won. However, when he was charged with committing a federal crime, he resigned to focus on his criminal defense. The board selected Robert to be the acting mayor.

Once appointed, Robert acted swiftly. According to the *Babbler*, Robert ordered the implosion of the Old Chicago building, using enhanced explosives that also produced electromagnetic pulses. He also imprisoned the *Phantom Press* inside the building. Destroying the Old Chicago Mall would weaken, if not break, the Phantom Press's connection to our world. The EMP-enhanced charges should have obliterated any ghosts that had not passed over.

In the *Phantom Press's* second to last issue, their editorial board accused Robert of breaking the village's promise not to demolish Old Chicago. They warned that if the residents didn't stop Robert's plan, they would hold the residents responsible for the 'atrocity.'

Most residents didn't complain. The implosion happened. The *Phantom Press* stopped publishing.

Until 29 years later.

Though the recent issue was hostile towards his fellow staffers and him, Robert received the brunt of their vitriol. They called him 'a corrupt petty dictator with delusions of being greater than any king.' Tom was aware of most of their accusations against Robert, like pressuring local CEOs to donate to his campaign fund or to an organization of Robert's choice. He hadn't heard about Robert supposedly pressuring bars to donate kegs of beer for his block parties. Maybe it was worth investigating?

Tom checked his smartphone. He'd been at the library since it opened, and it was almost lunchtime. While Robert and Steve weren't answering his follow-up calls, Tom felt like he had enough background material to complete his article before the special staff meeting in a few hours. He was positive this was going to be his second solo cover story, though he wished it were under better circumstances.

Tom checked the binder with the *Phantom Press* issues and noticed that the last issue was missing. The index listed it, so the library had a copy. No one could remove any issues from the library. Where could it be?

Tom left the room housing the Bolingbrook Historical Archives and headed to the reference desk. The librarian behind the desk yawned and then stopped when she noticed Tom. As she stood up, Tom spotted the name 'Sally' on her name tag.

"Did you find what you needed?" Sally asked, sounding friendly.

"I have a couple of questions," Tom whispered. "Can you help me?"

"Of course," she replied. Her drooping eyelids widened.

"I didn't see the last issue of the *Phantom Press* in the binder. Do you know where I can find it?"

She sighed. "It's in the vault."

Tom straightened his back and put on his best fake smile. "Can you escort me to the vault?"

Sally gave Tom a critical look. "Do you have a black card?"

"What's a black card?" Tom asked, though he knew exactly what it was.

Sally's eyes narrowed. "You know what it is, Tom. If you get a black card, I can let you in."

"But I need to read it. It could be the missing link between the issue that fell out of the sky and the original issues."

Sally side-eyed Tom. "That was a hoax," she replied. "They were dropped from an ultralight craft. The police even have suspects. Trust me, you don't need to read the last issue to understand what happened last night."

Tom knew better than to argue the point. "There has to be a way to allow guests into the vault."

"Ask your mother." The librarian turned away from Tom and yawned. She shook her head and then faced Tom. "Next question."

"I was hoping you could find an obituary for Rene McDonald. She was a former mayor of Bolingbrook."

Sally looked at Tom with disbelief. "There was a mayor before Robert?"

"Yeah," Tom replied. "Apparently, Bolingbrook used to play musical chairs with mayors before Robert was elected."

"Wait right there." Sally walked up to another desk with a desktop computer and started typing.

While he waited, Tom sent a text message to his mother.

Hi. Hope you are doing well. Can you get me into the vault? I'm researching the *Phantom Press*. Can you believe that someone dropped a new issue?

Seconds later, Tom received a response.

If I do, will you check yourself in after you're done?

Tom felt his shoulders drop.

The sound of a running printer distracted him. Sally picked up the paper and brought it to Tom.

"No obituary, but I found this article." A smile appeared on Sally's face. "She might still be alive."

Tom accepted the printout. The article originated at the Aurora Times. The headline read, "Former mayor turns trailer park neighborhood into 'Little Bolingbrook.'"

"Thank you," Tom replied.

"I'm always up for a challenge," she replied.

7

WENDY APPROACHED TOM'S CUBICLE, holding a Rolodex in one hand and pulling her chair with the other. "You got a minute?"

Tom hung up the phone. "Yeah. I just sent the article to Sara." He pulled a stack of books closer. "Hey, thanks for these books. I learned a lot."

"Glad I could help," Wendy replied as she sat down on her chair.

Tom glanced at the books. "I didn't realize ghosts need to feed off the emotions and memories of the living. They're almost like psychic leeches." He chuckled.

Wendy didn't react to Tom's comment. "That's one way of looking at it," she replied as she put the Rolodex on Tom's desk. "I think of them as a cloud of mental energy clinging to existence." She pushed the Rolodex towards Tom. "The memories their loved ones have of them eventually fade away. Ghosts can sustain themselves for only so long by siphoning the mental energy of mortals. Entropy always wins in the end."

Tom looked at the Rolodex. "But you're not here to talk about ghosts, are you?"

Wendy shook her head. "I've decided to focus on the production side and step away from fieldwork." She looked into Tom's eyes. "So, I'm going to be introducing you to my contacts. Including the ones in the DPA."

Tom blinked in surprise. "Thank you." He looked at the Rolodex for a few seconds. "I don't know if I'm up for this." He looked in her direction, but not at her face. "Or if I earned this."

"You have," Wendy replied. She smiled. "As far as I'm concerned, you've earned this ever since you started working for us." She rolled her chair closer to Tom's. "You're always welcome to ask for my advice. I'll still be here for a while."

Tom raised his eyebrows. "A while? Are you leaving us?"

Wendy shrugged. "I don't know." She looked around Tom's cubicle, then sighed. "Fieldwork isn't an option since I was just outed to everyone in Bolingbrook. Now I'm more likely to get shot by a resident than mauled by a weredeer."

"But things are changing. They legalized gay marriage only a few months ago. It's getting better."

Wendy shook her head. "Don't underestimate the hate most transphobes have towards us. Some monsters are human."

"Yeah, but—" Tom struggled to find the words he wanted.

"Tom," said Wendy. "Roul already likes you. That's saying something. So don't sell yourself short."

Tom started to talk but stopped when another staffer said, "Don!"

Tom and Wendy looked out of the cubicle. Tom recognized Don, who had just entered the building. He was a white man in his seventies. His khaki shorts and t-shirt had more wrinkles than his face. Jenna accompanied Don. When they reached the countertop, Don lifted it and motioned for Jenna to enter first. She smirked and entered the newsroom first. Don followed, then closed the countertop and made his way into the newsroom.

Sara stepped out of her cubicle and walked up to Don.

"It's been a while," said Don as he looked around the newsroom.

"Welcome back," Sara said as she offered her hand. "And thanks for meeting with us on short notice."

Don smiled as he looked around the newsroom one more time. "I may have retired." He shook Sara's hand. "But part of me never left."

Sara smiled and released Don's hand. "We really could use your help right now."

"Of course."

Don noticed Wendy and nodded in her direction. Wendy nodded back. Don then faced the staffers, who were gathering around him. "If you'll excuse me, we have a meeting with Chris. You know he doesn't like it when people are late."

Sara said, "Don will join us at the staff meeting."

Tom watched as Don, Jenna, and Sara entered the publisher's office. "What's this about?"

Wendy stared at the office's door. "We'll find out in about an hour."

***

Tom and Wendy joined the others in the middle of the newsroom as they gathered around Sara, Jenna, and Don. Sara motioned for everyone to be quiet.

"Thank you," said Sara as she projected her voice. "Thank you for coming here on short notice." She held up the recent issue of the *Phantom Press*. "Last night, the *Phantom Press* attacked the Village Board and literally dropped its first issue in twenty-nine years."

A few staffers chuckled.

"I want to commend Tom for his coverage of the attack." She looked down at Tom, who was sitting in his chair.

Tom smiled as he imagined how his solo article would appear on the cover.

She continued to stare at him. "But this story is too big for one reporter to cover."

Tom's eyes widened, and his jaw dropped.

Sara looked out at the gathered staffers. "The *Phantom Press* isn't just targeting Town Center. They're targeting us as well. Like it or not, we're part of the story." She motioned towards Don. "Don has come out of retirement to help us. He's dealt with the *Phantom Press* before, and that's why I'm assigning the *Phantom Press* story to him."

Tom looked at Sara in stunned disbelief. His solo cover story was now another of his joint articles.

Sara turned towards Don. "I'll let you explain the next step."

She stepped back as Don stepped forward. He flashed a smile and looked at the staff members before him. "Thank you, Sara. I wish this reunion could have been under better circumstances. But it is what it is." Don paced. "I think I'm the only one in this room who remembers dealing with the *Phantom Press*. Honestly, they were just annoying back then. The worst they would do to us is knock over coffee cups. We competed with them, but they weren't our enemy." He looked down at the floor for a few moments, then returned his attention to the staffers. "We need to find out why they've turned to violence and why they're slandering us." He chuckled. "I meant slandering the *Babbler*. Old habits die hard."

Tom nodded, while some staffers chuckled with Don.

"The only way we'll find out is to interview them." The room fell silent. Tom and Wendy looked at each other. Don continued, "I'm the only one they might talk to. With the help of our council of psychics, I should be able to contact them."

Jenna stood up. "The council has agreed to assist Don." She took a breath. "While we have avoided contacting the dead, we will make an exception."

Don nodded. "We'll meet here after sunset and attempt to call them here."

"Excuse me," Wendy said as she raised her hand. "You want to hold a séance. Here?"

Don looked down at Wendy. "That's correct. This is an anchor point for them. And I'm not doing a séance. I just want to talk to them. The council is just going to make it possible to reach out to them."

"Why not meet them where Old Chicago used to be?"

Don shook his head. "Robert destroyed Old Chicago. They wouldn't have a connection with a car auction yard." He gestured around the newsroom. "They do have a connection to our newsroom."

Wendy shook her head. "Nonsense. The psychic resonance in the lot is strong enough to still serve as an anchor point."

Don side-eyed Wendy. "And I suppose you checked it out with your gadgets?"

"Wendy," said Sara. "Chris and I have already approved this attempt."

Wendy stood up. "I'll respect that, but Don? Can you tell us how you're going to protect the council if things get out of hand?"

"I'll be the conduit," Don replied. "The *Phantom Press* won't get past me."

"And if they do?"

"They're not that powerful."

Wendy's eyes widened. "They just threw Robert's car into the boardroom. How can you say they're not powerful?"

"They're not powerful enough to overwhelm my protective measures. And even if they could, it's only a matter of time before they try throwing a car into the newsroom. This way, we can talk to them and work things out before they get out of control."

Wendy stepped closer to Don. "I never knew you were a necromancer."

"I'm not," Don looked into Wendy's eyes. "Neither are you."

Tom cleared his throat. "Excuse me."

The staff stared at Tom. He blushed and then cleared his throat.

"We still have the EMP device," said Tom. He looked at Wendy, who nodded. "Maybe we should arm the EMP device just to be safe? If Don is right, we won't need it. If Don is mistaken, Wendy can trigger the device to protect the council. We installed the device for circumstances like this. Right?"

"You're right," Wendy replied. She faced Sara. "I can get it ready by sunset. If I have your permission."

"You do." She smiled at Tom. "That was a good suggestion."

"Thanks," Tom replied. "I'd also like to watch."

Sara shook her head. "You need to stay at home tonight."

Tom did a double take. "But I've been working on this story since the attack. I think—"

"Later," Sara snapped.

"But—"

"Later, Tom." She looked out at the staff. "Everyone needs to take their laptops home tonight. Once you're home, stay inside until I send an all-clear message. If you have any other electronic devices here, either take them home or lock them inside your desks."

"I'll secure the servers, too." Wendy turned away from Don. "If you hallucinate, try to stay calm. They're trying to evoke a powerful emotion from you. Don't help them by giving in. It will only strengthen them."

Sara stepped next to Wendy. "Good point, Wendy. Everyone, we're running out of time. Please start prepping your area now."

Everyone stood up. Tom approached Wendy.

"Why did you pull me from this story?" Tom asked.

"It's not personal." She looked up at the wall clock. "I'll explain it to you tomorrow. Assuming we don't open the gates of hell tonight."

Sara walked away before Tom could respond. Jenna and Don joined Sara as they left the newsroom. Wendy headed into the backroom, where the device was located.

Tom returned to his desk and started removing his laptop from the docking station. Wendy's Rolodex was still on his desk. It was worn out from heavy use. Still, Tom thought, Wendy's sources could help him uncover important stories.

But if I did the work, wouldn't Sara just give it to someone else?

Tom put the Rolodex and Wendy's books in a drawer and locked it.

8

Tom took one last weary look at the setting sun before closing the shades. The *Phantom Press* could be in the newsroom right now, but he was stuck in his apartment. Worse, Sara had brought Don out of retirement to take the lead on a story that should have been his.

I was about to prove myself, but she took it away from me. What did I do wrong?

Tom looked around his modestly furnished apartment. Back when he was a successful blogger, he went on a shopping spree at the local Ikea. He thought the donations would never stop, but they ceased after he renounced the Men's Rights Movement and told his followers he was incorrect to attack feminism. His mismatched furniture was another reminder of his mistakes. And he couldn't afford to replace it.

Tom returned to the couch and started eating his dinner — a burrito combo meal. If he couldn't interview the *Phantom Press*, he could enjoy a meal from one of his favorite restaurants. It was better than drinking away his disappointment.

Before he could turn on his television, his phone buzzed. It was Pamela.

"Hey," Tom said as he put his phone on speaker mode. "What's up?"

"Taking a break from grading papers," Pamela replied, her voice sounding exhausted. "What have you been up to?"

Tom hesitated. "Promise you won't have me committed?"

"Like I could do that," Pamela replied, her voice now sounding more energetic.

Tom took a deep breath. "I witnessed a ghost attack last night."

Silence consumed the other end.

"Hello?" asked Tom.

"Tell me about it," Pamela replied, sounding sincerely interested.

Tom recounted how Robert's car crashed into the boardroom, mentioning the engine wasn't running. He ended with Robert's declaration of a state of emergency. When he finished, he braced himself for Pamela's reaction. Seconds passed by, but they felt like minutes to Tom.

"You're thinking of a zebra," Pamela finally replied.

Tom's eyes widened in confusion. "A zebra?"

"Yes," Pamela replied. "If you see hoof prints, it's far more likely they were made by a horse than a zebra."

"And?" Tom asked, not sure where she was going.

"I think you're jumping to conclusions," Pamela replied. "You're thinking of a zebra when you should think of a horse."

"What does this have to do with the attack?" Tom asked, his voice reflecting his confusion.

"I don't think you considered all the possibilities before concluding you witnessed a ghost attack."

Tom tilted his head as he stared at his phone. "What else could it have been? Cars don't just fly into the air and crash through windows. The engine wasn't running, so it couldn't have been driven up a ramp."

"Catapult," said Pamela.

Tom blinked. "Catapult?"

"Yes," Pamela replied with excitement in her voice. "It could have been spring-launched into the boardroom. Like one of those human cannonball cylinders, only they shot a car instead of a person."

"Seriously?" asked Tom in disbelief of her suggestion.

"Yes," she replied. "It's far more likely than beings who defy the laws of physics. Try thinking of the horse before thinking of a zebra."

Tom started to reply when he received a text. "Just a second," he said to Pamela. "I just got a message."

> Meet me at Bolingbrook Commons now! RR

Tom guessed RR stood for Roaming Roul. But why was he messaging him instead of Wendy?

> How do I know it's you?

> The Angel of Reason blessed you. Meet in the parking lot. Bring Wendy.

> Wendy is meeting with the Phantom Press. I can't reach her.

> Then meet me on her behalf. This involves the Phantom Press. Last message.

"Tom?" Pamela asked.

Tom reread the messages. He wondered if it was a trap or if Roul had uncovered something major. Something that couldn't be relayed over text or email.

"I've got to go," Tom finally replied. "A source needs to see me right now."

"Oh," Pamela replied, sounding disappointed. "Be careful."

"I will," Tom replied.

"And think of horses first, Tom. Not zebras."

Tom said goodbye and ended the call. If he couldn't attend the interview with the *Phantom Press*, he could at least relay a message from Roaming Roul to Wendy.

***

As Tom prepared to exit I-55 onto Bolingbrook Drive, he saw three armored personnel transports in the Bolingbrook Commons parking lot, which startled him. They parked in a semi-circle in front of the entrance to the former Century Tile store. Parked behind the transports were five Bolingbrook police cars and five Will County Sheriff's patrol cars. At the edge of the parking lot, a mobile command vehicle was parked behind tall plexiglass barriers.

Talk about excessive force to capture one man.

Tom sped down the exit towards the stoplight on Bolingbrook Drive. When the light turned yellow, Tom sped up as he attempted a right turn. For a moment, he remembered when he had attempted a high-speed turn onto Boughton Road to escape an enraged weredeer. He tightened his grip on the steering wheel as he heard his tires screech. This time, his Toyota Echo didn't roll over.

Once he straightened his car, he saw a line of Bolingbrook police cars blocking the northbound lanes. The officer in the front car motioned for Tom to stop. Behind the cars, two officers with shotguns locked their eyes on Tom's car.

Tom slammed on the brakes. The car screeched and skidded, stopping a few feet from the officer. Tom caught his breath. The first officer approached, and Tom rolled down his window.

"Road's closed," said the officer, his voice almost monotone.

Tom leaned his head out the window. "I'm with the *Bolingbrook Babbler*. What's going on?"

"Got a press pass?"

Tom's shoulders dropped. "We've never been granted press passes."

The officer motioned toward the south. "You can wait at the truck stop. This shouldn't take too long."

Overhead, two helicopters approached and pointed their spotlights towards Bolingbrook Commons.

Tom looked at the officer. "Is there someplace I can watch? Put me with the other media outlets."

The officer started shaking his head, then abruptly stopped. He cupped his hand over his right ear. "What's your name?" the officer asked.

"Tom Larsen." Tom wasn't sure if it was a good idea to give his name.

The officer repeated Tom's name and waited. After a few seconds, he removed his hand from his ear. "Park behind the Denny's. Someone will meet you."

One of the police cars backed away, and Tom drove through the gap. He drove past a Department of Public Works truck parked next to a streetlight with a fiftieth anniversary banner attached. Two men waited inside.

They picked the wrong time to work on a streetlight.

Tom turned onto Frontage Road and noticed ambulances parked along Commons Drive. Tom turned onto Commons Drive. Behind the mobile command center was an open-air tent. Uniformed and plainclothes officials huddled around equipment and monitors placed on folding tables. He could see Robert being unusually animated as he talked to the Director of Public Safety and the Will County Sherrif.

Helicopters circled the storefront where the Century Tile store had been, their spotlights trained on the rooftop. This was the first time he'd seen law enforcement helicopters flying over Bolingbrook.

Parked in the area across the street from the command center was a red 2015 Ford Mustang with the dealer's information still taped to the passenger side window. Seeing a spot next to the Mustang, Tom parked next to it, leaving enough room for the driver to open the door.

From the backseat, a little girl's voice said, "Please?"

Tom gasped. He turned around but saw only the junk in his backseat that he still hadn't gotten around to cleaning. As he turned around, he saw someone in the rearview mirror. In the back seat sat a Caucasian girl, her long brown hair cascading down her back, appearing to be about six or seven years old. Her pink dress had blood spatter on it. Tom froze.

A tapping sound startled Tom. After catching his breath, he looked in the mirror. The girl was gone.

Steve stood outside the driver's side window, wearing a black bulletproof vest. The words "Bolingbrook Police" printed on them in bold white letters.

"Come on," Steve said, glancing between Tom and the command center. "We don't have much time."

Tom exited the car. "What's going on?" he asked as he locked the door.

"We found the man responsible for destroying Robert's car," Steve replied as he started walking fast towards the command center. "And the ritual."

"Roaming Roul?" Tom asked.

"I didn't say that," Steve said, not looking back at Tom.

"Then—"

"Tom," Steve interrupted. "If it were up to me, I'd have you taken in for questioning." He paused. "Robert thinks you should see this. So, if you don't want to end up detained or dead, I suggest you shut up and follow my instructions."

Steve resumed walking, and Tom followed. Tom wondered what he'd seen earlier. Was it a ghost? Or did he imagine seeing that girl? Pamela was right. He needed to think of horses before thinking of zebras.

They reached an empty folding chair behind the command center, angled to view the storefront. Steve motioned for Tom to take a seat. "The barriers will protect you. Until the operation is over, stay here."

Tom started to nod, but Steve turned away and walked towards Robert.

"In position," Steve called out.

Robert snatched the microphone from the dispatcher. "Go!" he growled.

Bright flashes appeared inside the storefront, followed by loud bangs. Even at this distance, Tom's ears hurt, and he had spots in his eyes. The doors of the patrol cars behind the APCs opened. A uniformed officer from each car rushed out and ducked behind the APCs.

Another loud bang startled Tom, followed by the sound of shattered glass raining down on the concrete. White smoke and gas billowed out through the broken window. He wondered if it was tear gas.

Steve cupped his hand over his ear. He nodded and then said, "Suspect captured."

"Good!" Robert snarled. "He's got a lot to answer for."

"Though it might take a while to get those answers," Steve casually replied.

"I'll speed things up," Robert replied.

"I won't stop you," said Steve.

Robert stepped out of the tent and walked towards Tom. As Tom stood up, Robert turned his back to him.

Two SWAT officers escorted Roul outside. Roul wore handcuffs, and his eyes were almost too swollen to open. One officer pulled on Roul's arm. The other pulled him by his long hair. Roul struggled to keep up.

Robert walked towards the barriers. Tom followed.

"Tom," said Steve from behind. Tom turned to see Steve stopping inches away. "Why are you here?"

Tom shrugged. "To cover this story."

Steve leaned towards Tom's face. "Did Roul try to contact you?"

"I—" Tom stopped himself. "I cannot divulge that information."

Steve folded his arms. "Yes. You can," he said in a stern tone. "And I suggest you do before I have to pry the answer out of you."

Tom gulped. Was he about to be thrown into a DPA interrogation room? He knew he wouldn't last a minute in there. He tensed. That didn't mean he had to volunteer to answer his questions.

"Why are you asking?" Tom felt his heart racing. "The covert departments monitor all communications in Bolingbrook. You should know who Roul was contacting even if you can't read his encrypted messages."

A voice crackled from Steve's earpiece, making him wince in pain.

"Spheres!" came a man's voice.

The officers escorting Roul broke into a near run, and Roul struggled to keep pace.

"Pull back!" yelled Robert in near panic as he moved his microphone closer to his mouth. "Everyone, pull back now." He repeated the command, his voice mixed with rage and fear, a fear Tom had never seen in Robert. Robert dropped his microphone and signaled the officers to fall back.

The armored vehicles at the entrance backed away. One of them collided with a patrol car that was just starting. The armored vehicle knocked the car to the side and kept going. The damaged car roared to life and backed away. Tom could hear the car's bent frame rubbing against the tires.

Steve regained his composure and then tapped his earpiece. "You know what to do."

Tom took a few steps towards the barrier, hoping to get a better view of what they were running away from.

"You don't want to get any closer," Steve said in a calm voice. "Unless you want to die."

Two SWAT officers sprinted through the door. Before they could step off the sidewalk, an almost blinding flash emanated from inside the building, followed by a thunder-like boom. The shockwave knocked over the officers and rattled the plexiglass barrier. Through the spots in his eyes, Tom saw the officers' violent convulsions against the pavement, as if every nerve in their bodies had just shorted out. Moments later, the officers stopped moving. Too still.

Steve tapped his earpiece. "All clear."

Two ambulances started up and drove towards the store-front.

"Tom," said Steve. "When you write the articles, note that two men died outside, and two died inside. They were the most dedicated men I'd ever worked with, and you can quote me."

"Who were they?" Tom asked.

"Don't take pictures of the bodies," Steve replied as he walked away. "The bodies of sphere victims aren't suitable for publication."

Tom started speaking but stopped when he saw Roul being escorted around the mobile command center. The escorts shoved Roul against the vehicle. He moaned from the pain of the impact. Robert rushed up to him while Tom cautiously approached.

Robert jabbed his finger into Roul's chest. "Those were four good men you just murdered!" the mayor yelled. "I let you stay here for years. I looked away while you stunk up my facilities. I was even willing to ignore the mess you made in front of the high school." Robert trembled as his face turned bright red. "This is your way of thanking me? Wrecking my car? Killing my men? Vandalizing my boardroom? Slandering my family with your fake news? Murdering my men?"

"That wasn't me," Roul said, struggling to hold himself up. "You're being lied to, Robert. Please listen to me. I'm trying to save you. Please!"

Robert struck Roul with a left hook and punched his abdomen with his right hand. The force of the blow made Roul cough up blood and tooth fragments onto Robert's white shirt. Robert smacked Roul. "You have a pretty fucked-up idea of what it means to save someone."

Steve and four men in black suits approached Robert and Roul. Tom froze. It was too dangerous to get closer.

Robert nodded to Steve and looked into Roul's eyes. "You're going to spend some time with the DPA's finest. If you cooperate, I might let you remember your name." Robert looked down at his shirt and shook his head. He then looked up at Steve. "Don't kill him. Yet."

Steve's men took Roul from the officers and started dragging him towards the gas station. Tom wondered if they were taking Roul to the SUV parked by it.

"You can't do this!" said Roul as his face swelled. "I told you the truth! They'll kill every resident to spite you. You can stop them before it's too late."

Robert turned his back to Roul and looked down at his knuckles. He shook his hand and then winced in pain. "Medic," he said.

Roul noticed Tom watching him. "Tom! Listen to me! Tell Wendy it's a legion. They created a legion! The information is in the big and little libraries!" Roul's eyes widened. "Then find *el ángel de la razón*. Tell her *el caballero blanco extraña a su pequeño girasol*. She's the only one who can save us. Find her!"

9

Tom honked his horn as he drove north on Route 53. "Move!"

The driver in the left lane flipped Tom off, and the driver blocking the right lane ignored him. Tom grumbled. He spotted the intersection of Boughton and Route 53 ahead. Almost there, he thought.

Tom called Wendy but got her voicemail. "Wendy, it's Tom. The DPA just arrested Roul. It was bad. Four killed in the raid. Roul said they created a legion. Do you know what he's talking about? Maybe we should hold off on the séance. I'll be at the office in a few minutes."

Seeing an opening in the left lane, Tom swerved over. The car now behind him honked its horn. The stoplight turned green. Tom accelerated towards the turn lane.

Sara told him to stay away from the office during the séance, but this was an emergency, and they weren't taking his phone calls. In this case, it was better to ask for Sara's forgiveness, especially if he saved the council of psychics from the "legion."

As the Barber's Corner strip mall came into view, a bright flash of white light came from behind the auto repair shop where the *Babbler*'s office was located.

That can't be good. Maybe I'm too late?

Tom ran through a stale yellow light. He felt a lump in his throat when the light changed to red. He floored the accelerator and pulled on the steering wheel. The tires scratched as he made a wide turn onto Boughton. Two pedestrians on the sidewalk ran away as Tom neared the curb. He straightened the car's path, avoiding the curb by inches.

"Sorry!" he said.

The pedestrians flipped off Tom. A flash of light startled them, as well as Tom. Both fled.

Tom turned into the parking lot. Four people ran in front of him. He slammed on the brakes, bouncing in his seat. Fear contorted the faces of the two men and two women. They fled away from the direction of the *Babbler's* office.

This really isn't good.

When he saw an opening, Tom shifted to the left-turn lane and sped up. After running through the stale yellow light, he loosened his grip on the steering wheel and prepared to turn into the parking. A few sparks rained down from a fiftieth anniversary banner, puzzling Tom. A bright flash that originated behind the auto repair shop soon followed it where the *Babbler's* office was.

That can't be good.

Three more flashes occurred, and for a moment, Tom thought he heard whispering like members of a large crowd whispering at once. Then it stopped.

Tom parked behind the repair shop. Remembering the EMP device in the office, he left his phone behind and got out of the car. The air felt still, cool. Too cool for a summer evening.

After locking his car, Tom cautiously walked around the shop. He stopped when he could see the *Babbler's* office several yards ahead. The last remaining interior window shade fell to the floor, as it was blown off by a powerful blast of air. The interior window shades swayed as if they were being hit with strong winds. A flash of bright white light through the front door startled Tom. When he finished blinking, a man stood between Tom and the office. He was a white male wearing a battered sports coat and black slacks. On his hat was a piece of paper with the word "Press" printed on it.

Tom straightened his stance and took a moment to focus. "I'm Tom."

The man stared at him.

Tom cleared his throat. "Are you with the *Phantom Press*?"

In an instant, the man's head transformed into a giant decaying human head. Red flames shot out of his eye sockets. Its neck extended and twisted like a snake. Its arms elongated and clinched Tom's head in its impossibly large hands. The ghost screamed at Tom, and a fire ignited in its mouth. The flames danced dangerously close to Tom's face.

Six faceless men, wearing hats with a card marked "Press," grabbed Tom and started pulling at his limbs.

Tom closed his eyes. He recited the motto of the International Ethical Union: "Grounded in reason. Guided by the heart." By focusing on the words, Tom hoped he could control his emotions and stop feeding the ghosts. The ghosts responded by pulling harder, stretching Tom's ligaments to their limits. Despite the pain, he struggled to keep reciting the motto.

A girl screamed, "Stop it!"

The pulling stopped. Tom opened his eyes. He was still between the repair shop and the *Babbler's* office. The ghosts, now translucent and with their bodies distorted beyond recognition, circled Tom like a whirlwind. The girl he'd seen earlier in his car was now sobbing in front of him.

"I'm so sorry!" she bawled. "I don't want to be here. I just want to go home. They won't let me go home!"

"Who?" Tom asked. "Who won't let you go home?"

"I can't make them stop! I'm so sorry!" The girl lost control of her sobbing.

"It's him!" said the ghost circling him. The others joined in. "It's him. It's him!"

Tom faced the circling ghosts. "What do you want?"

Darkness engulfed Tom. He could feel only his feet standing on the ground. He reached out but felt nothing.

"You understand," said someone who sounded like Tom.

Tom looked for any light in the void. "What do I understand?"

"The unfairness of it all. Knowing that nothing you do will appease them. To be cast into oblivion for speaking the truth. But with your help, we will send them into oblivion. Join us and be free."

Tom's heart raced. "You're hurting my friends. Why would I want to join you?"

The time traveler, a future variant of Tom, appeared in front of him. "Because we have so much in common."

"Leave him alone!" said the girl.

The darkness lifted. Tom was once again in the parking lot, along with the time traveler and the girl.

"We need him," said the time traveler.

"No," the girl cried. "We don't belong here." She faded away, repeating, "I just want to go home."

The time traveler screamed in horror. One of his arms stretched out to an inhuman length and grabbed her. The girl's body solidified. Her eyes widened as she cried out in horror. Hundreds of disembodied hands grabbed the girl. She thrashed and struggled to free herself.

"No!" she screamed. "Don't keep me here. I want to go home!"

A flash of light blinded Tom, followed by a shockwave that knocked him to the ground. Something solid rained on him. When the spots faded from his eyes, Tom realized he was lying on the pavement of the parking lot. Broken glass and rubble covered the lot. As he stood up, he saw that the anniversary banners along Bolingbrook Drive and Boughton were on fire. The smell of the smoke reminded him of an electrical fire.

Looking back at the office, he saw that the shockwave had blown out all the windows. Sparks from the ceiling lights rained down inside the office.

Wendy set off the EMP!

Tom rose to his feet, then raced towards the door. He heard Don sobbing.

"Don?" Tom asked.

Tom stepped into the office and froze. The office looked as if a tornado had hit it. Jenna and the other psychics lay unconscious on the floor in a circle. Inside the circle, Don sat curled up in a ball, rocking back and forth.

"You didn't have to do this," he said. "Why?"

Wendy leaned against a wall, holding a black box with a large red button. She dropped the box and slid down the wall to the floor.

"Wendy!" Tom screamed.

Tom ran up to Wendy. She looked in Tom's direction with her glazed eyes. Her face, covered with purple bruises, and her hair, once neatly styled, resembled a bird's nest.

"They've changed." Wendy gasped.

Tom kneeled next to her. "Changed?"

"Into something... far worse." She closed her eyes.

"Wendy?" Tom shook her shoulders. Wendy's eyes partially opened. "Roul said they made a legion. Do you know what that means?"

Wendy's head wobbled. "Not exactly." She grabbed Tom's arm. "Stay on the story. If Roul is right, Don's on the wrong track. Stay on the story."

"I will," Tom replied. He attempted to repeat what Roul said in Spanish. "Do you know what it means?"

"You need to work on your Spanish." Wendy chuckled and then coughed.

"Wendy?" Tom touched her arm. "I'm sorry. But do you know what he was talking about?"

Wendy coughed. "You need to find the Angel of Reason." He glanced over at Don. "Only you."

"But where do I find her? What does she look like?"

Wendy smiled. "You'll know." Her eyes closed, and she fell limp.

"Wendy?" said Tom, catching Wendy's slumping body. He put Wendy in the recovery position by rolling her on her side and extending one of her arms. He learned about the recovery position in one of his first aid classes.

The psychics moaned behind him. He turned around. Don had stopped crying and was looking at a cell phone inside a Faraday cage.

Tom approached Jenna first and kneeled next to her. "Can you hear me? It's over. You're safe now."

Jenna's opened wide with fear. A faint whisper escaped her lips. "Legion."

"What?" asked Tom.

"Legion," said Jenna. Her shivering intensified. "Legion."

The other psychics started saying "legion" too.

"Tom!" Don yelled. "You need to leave. Sara just activated the Scatter Protocols."

A chill ran down Tom's spine. Sara had just ordered every *Babbler* staffer to evacuate Bolingbrook. This was the first time they'd ever been activated.

"I'll take care of them," Don said as he stood up. "I promise."

All the psychics started screaming, "Legion!"

"I can provide first aid. I can help them."

"No!" Don snapped. "If you want to help them, evacuate now. You've only minutes before the DPA arrives. You don't want to be here when they arrive. Trust me."

Tom reluctantly stood up. "Take care of my friends, Don."

"I am," Don replied. "Now go! Before Steve arrests you."

Tom ran out of the office. Behind him, the psychics screamed one word in unison: "Legion!"

10

TOM MADE SURE EVERYONE on the video conference was muted one last time. When he was a blogger, he used to host video chats. After leaving the skeptical movement, he never expected to host a video conference again. But here he was. *Wendy should be hosting this*, he thought. But she was in a coma, while he hadn't slept all night. Outside, the sun was rising, but he couldn't stop thinking about the events of last night.

"Sara," Tom said, fighting off his fatigue. "I just gave you control of the screen. You can unmute yourself when you're ready."

Sara squinted at the screen for a moment, then moved her mouse. "Nod if you can hear me."

Everyone nodded or posted a confirmation on the chat channel.

"Good," Sara replied, sounding exhausted. "Thank you for attending on such short notice. It looks like all of you followed the first step and are inside your homes. I wish this were a drill, but it's not." She took a deep, solemn breath. "I have an update. Jenna, Wendy, and the psychics are alive. They're still in a catatonic state." Sara paused. Tom skimmed the chat screens, seeing the concern reflected in their faces. Sara continued, "The good news is that they're being treated at Alexian Brothers."

The staff's questions flooded the chat channel.

"Chris and I will check on them later today. Which brings me to my next item." Sara paused and looked down at her keyboard. She sighed and looked up. "What I am about to ask has never been asked of any previous *Babbler* staffers. That's because there's never been a threat like this. The *Phantom Press* has attacked us and Town Center. The DPA is unable and/or unwilling to protect us. We don't know whether they can protect the village." Sara paused and took a deep breath. "Chris and I are implementing steps two and three. That means everyone needs to leave Bolingbrook before nightfall."

Staffers unmuted themselves. The cacophony of anger and fear started drowning out everything else.

Sara muted everyone.

"I know this will be a burden. This is a burden for my family, too. However, Don believes the ghosts are spiritually bound to Bolingbrook. In order to protect ourselves and our families, we need to evacuate. Let me be clear." She paused. "Your families are in danger if they stay here." Sara paused again. "Don is the only one allowed to stay in Bolingbrook. He'll cover the *Phantom Press* story for now. No one else."

The staff, including Tom, tried to reply, but Sara kept them on mute. "If any of you return to Bolingbrook, you'll be suspended and possibly fired. No exceptions. If you can't comply with the Scatter Protocols, you can post your resignation in the chat."

No one posted on the chat channel.

"Chris has already arranged your accommodations. We'll send each of you a coded message with the address. Once you're settled in, I will give each of you a new assignment. This isn't a vacation. This is a disaster, but we're going to pull through." She paused for a few moments. Her eyes moved as if she were looking at all the video windows on her screen. She said, "Fifty years ago, the Olson family hired the *Babbler's* first staff. We will not be its last staff."

***

As Tom contemplated how to close his overflowing suitcase on his bed, his phone vibrated. He checked and saw a new email from Pamela.

> Heard about the explosion. Let's chat.

The email included a link to a video chat. Tom looked at the mound of clothes, then sighed. He typed his reply.

> I'll log on right now.

Tom headed over to his desktop computer. The DPA covered up the *Phantom Press's* attack as an explosion. The reports stated the police had already determined it wasn't a terrorist attack. Instead, according to anonymous sources, the police believed a faulty propane tank was the cause.

The DPA's cover story for the raid on Bolingbrook Commons described it as a training exercise, complete with a fake bomb. The *Bolingbrook Star* quoted an anonymous official praising Robert's acting during the drill. Appalled by *The Star's* coverage, Tom appreciated that *The Star* withdrew its job offer. He would have just been editing Robert's propaganda pieces.

About a minute after Tom logged in, Pamela started the video chat. Her strawberry blonde hair was cut into a pixie cut, framing her delicate face. The purple of her shirt matched her eyes, while a concerned look marked her face.

"Were you injured?" Pamela asked. "You look terrible."

Tom looked at himself on the screen. "I'm fine," he replied. He realized he hadn't taken a shower, nor had he shaved. The bags under his eyes reminded Tom he hadn't slept since the attack. "I'm just getting over having ghosts messing with my mind."

Pamela frowned. "Did you think of a horse first?"

Tom scowled at Pamela. "No. Because it's hard to think of a horse when a goddamn zebra is kicking you in the face!"

"Don't shout," Pamela replied, keeping her voice level.

Tom sighed and collected thoughts. "I'm sorry. It was a long night. I watched Wendy slip into a coma and heard the council of psychics repeating the word 'legion' endlessly."

"Jesus," Pamela replied. "Are they okay now?"

Tom shook his head. "They're in the hospital. But I don't know if they'll ever wake up."

"I'm sorry," Pamela replied.

"Thanks. Now we must evacuate Bolingbrook before sunset."

Pamela did a double take. "Why?"

"So they can't get the rest of us. Right now, the *Phantom Press* is confined to Bolingbrook. Let's hope it stays that way."

An awkward pause came between Tom and Pamela.

He sighed. "I know this must sound crazy to you."

She shook her head. "I don't like that word. All I know is that you sincerely believe it."

"But you don't?" Tom asked. He sighed out of frustration.

"I don't know." Pamela shrugged. "But I'm willing to listen to you."

Tom managed to smile. "I'm glad you're listening."

"Of course. Is there anything else you want to tell me?"

Tom felt the urge to say, "I love you," because it could be a long time before they saw each other again. *But what good would that do?* he thought. She was seeing other people, and relationships were the last thing Tom needed to worry about right now.

"I'll try to contact you when it's safe," Tom replied. "Promise."

"I'll be waiting," Pamela replied, then smiled.

"And please don't tell my parents," he added. "They'll have me locked up if they find out."

She giggled. "They've never reached out to me. No reason to expect them to now."

Tom started to reply but stopped when his phone vibrated. He looked down at the text message. It was a coded message from Chris, the publisher.

"I'm sorry, but I have to go," said Tom. "I just got my temporary housing assignment."

Pamela gestured with her hands. "Don't let me hold you up. Be careful out there."

"Thank you," Tom replied. "For everything."

Tom and Pamela ended their session. After shutting down his computer, he took a long look around his apartment. He was going to miss coming home to the mismatched furniture and the sound of cars driving down Boughton Road. However, the *Babbler* was his second family, and he couldn't abandon them in the middle of a crisis.

11

TOM LOOKED AT HIMSELF using the video chat's preview window. After a few hours of sleep, a shower, and a trip to Starbucks, he looked presentable and accepted Sara's video conference request.

Sara appeared on the screen, wearing a slightly wrinkled blue blouse. A bedsheet hid the rest of the room.

"Morning," she said. "Are you settled in?"

Tom looked around his motel room. "I always thought Palatine was Naperville on steroids. That's how the Fremd and Palatine High School students described it. I expected first-class accommodations and a beautiful view of the forest preserve. Instead, I've got a beautiful view of a warehouse and no housecleaning. The clerk said there were too many accidents. I don't want to know the details. Honestly, when I stepped inside, I thought I was back in the 1960s."

Sara nodded. "My accommodations aren't much better."

"But there is a Starbucks nearby." Tom held up his plastic cup filled with melting ice covered with whipped cream. "So that's a plus."

Sara flashed a smile. "Other than that, how are you doing?"

Tom sighed and leaned towards his webcam. "Let's see. In the last two days, I saw four people die, had ghosts mess with my head, watched Wendy slip into a coma, saw Jenna and her friends in shock, and had to evacuate Bolingbrook." He drank the mocha-flavored water. "I'm feeling better than I should be." He smiled.

Sara didn't smile back. "This isn't easy for me either."

Tom nodded. "Sorry. How are your kids doing?"

"Fine. They'll be visiting both of our parents for two weeks. After that..." She shook her head. "I pray we get this resolved by then."

Tom nodded. "I hope so, too. Oh, did you get to see Wendy and Jenna?" He quickly added, "And the others?"

"Wendy is still in a coma. I spoke with her parents. The doctors are telling them they don't understand why. Wendy's brother, Dale, is flying in from Manchester."

"He used to tag me on Twitter," Tom replied, thinking back on his time as a skeptical blogger. "If he's like that offline, I feel sorry for the hospital staff already." He chuckled.

Sara didn't. "Jenna and the others are sedated. Chris says they're suffering from psychic shock. He's trying to find someone who can help them."

Tom looked down and shook his head. Their experience with the *Phantom Press* must have been more frightening than his.

Sara said, "I'll send updates when I get them."

Tom took a moment to compose himself. He didn't want to cry in front of Sara again.

"Are you sure you're fine?" she asked, tilting her head.

Tom took another drink of his water-flavored mocha. "I'm better now." He sat up. "What did you want to talk about?"

Sara clasped her hands together. "We may be scattered, but we're still in business. So, I want to talk about the two articles you're working on today."

Tom had emailed Sara to inform her he was going to submit articles about Roul's capture and the attack against the

Council of Psychics. "I should finish them by this afternoon. I wish they'd been happier stories, but this time, I've earned a front-page byline."

"That's the problem," said Sara, unclasping her fingers.

Tom did a double take at the screen. "Problem?"

"Yes," she said. "You were told to stay at home that night. Instead, you covered a raid and entered the newsroom last night."

Tom felt a pit in his stomach. "If I'd followed your instructions, then I would have missed those stories. You have to admit, the death of four DPA officers is a big deal."

Sara nodded. "It is, and if that were your only infraction, I might have let it slide." She pointed at her webcam. "I cannot overlook you rushing into the newsroom. Against my orders."

When did we become a military unit?

Tom bit his tongue.

"That was a reckless, impulsive act that endangered everyone there."

His anger overcame his fear of being fired. "I needed to warn Wendy about Legion and Roul's arrest. She wasn't answering her phone. You didn't answer your phone either."

"Because we were too busy defending ourselves from the *Phantom Press.*" Tom felt her harsh glare over the internet. "I barely escaped, but you rushed in and nearly ended up like Wendy."

Tom looked down at the keyboard. He risked his life, and it didn't help anyone inside. "I needed to warn both of you," he said, almost whispering.

"Look at me," Sara said in a stern tone.

Tom hesitated before looking at his screen.

"You are a good reporter," she said. "Yes, you're struggling, but you have what it takes to be a great reporter. But..." She paused. "You are also impulsive and reckless. That is why I pulled you from the *Phantom Press* story. It's too dangerous for you. Especially if you keep acting before you think. This is now Don's story. You will get a byline for your two articles." She unclasped her hands and pointed at Tom. "But if you want to remain with us, you will stop working on this. No trips to Bolingbrook without my permission. No secret interviews, and don't even think of going behind Don's back. Questions?"

Tom tensed. "Are you also upset at Don? The séance was his idea. If anything, he's more responsible for what's happening."

Sara didn't flinch. "That is between Don and me." She narrowed her eyes. "Do I need to clarify anything else?"

Tom's throat tightened as he wondered whether he should ask another question or remain silent. The urge to say something was too strong. "Before she passed out, Wendy said Don was on the wrong track. Why would she say that?"

Sara looked down and shook her head. She sighed and said, "Dear Lord, give me strength." A moment later, she lifted her head. "Because they never trusted each other." Sara sat back in her chair. "I do trust Don, understand?"

Tom nodded.

"Good. I've scheduled a video chat between Don and you after lunch. After you hand over your notes, we'll discuss the stories you can work on. Questions?"

A realization struck Tom. "I just realized I left some important files in my desk. Could I—"

"No," Sara said bluntly. "You can ask Don to pick them up for you. And if you get the urge to go to the office, don't. Chris has a security guard there during the day. And you're too smart to sneak in at night."

Tom wasn't sure if he should accept Sara's backhanded compliment.

12

Tom watched his screen as Don scribbled his notes on a worn notepad.

"Sorry, you're barred from this story." He fumbled with his webcam. "You did a great job."

Tom nodded. Although he hated ironing, his shirts were never as wrinkled as Don's. "Thanks."

Don set his webcam to his left. He faced the screen. Tom assumed he was looking at the chat window with his video stream.

"I knew a reporter who was in a similar situation," Don said as he adjusted his reading glasses.

"Really?" Tom asked.

"He was about your age." Don squinted at his computer screen. "You're twenty-something. Right?"

"Twenty-five," Tom replied. He wondered if he should have revealed his age to Don.

"To be 25 again." Don seemed lost in thought for a moment. "Anyway, he wanted to cover a visit from a major NWO committee. I got the assignment instead. He was assigned to do a write-up of a cybercafe in Naperville. This was back in the 1990s."

"Ancient times," joked Tom.

"Seems like yesterday," Don replied with a wink. "Reluctantly, he started working on it. And you know what happened? He found a trail that led him into Chicago's industrial music scene, and he ended up in cyberspace."

Tom's eyes widened. "As in *Neuromancer* cyberspace?" While he wasn't a fan of William Gibson, he was familiar with the novel.

Don looked confused. "I guess so. But to cut to the chase, he discovered something called Eyescab."

Tom's eyes widened, and he pulled his head back. "Eyescab?"

Don's eyes sparkled. "It was an addictive mental construct disguised as a BBS. You know what a BBS is, right?"

Tom remained befuddled. "No."

Don sighed. "The point I was trying to make is that he ended up covering something far more interesting than he expected. The same thing might happen to you. Maybe you'll bump into werecoyotes or a member of the Orange Squad?"

Tom blinked. "The Orange Squad operates outside of Chicago?" The Orange Squad was a secret division of the Chicago Police Department. They handled both alien and paranormal incidents. Chicago's equivalent of the DIA and the DPA, except more secretive. No one from the *Babbler* had ever interviewed a member of the squad.

"Don't feel so down," Don said as he closed his notebook. "Sara's protecting you because you're the future of the *Babbler*." He gestured at himself. "Me? I'm disposable." He chuckled. "A relic. If the *Phantom Press* kills me"—he shrugged—"you and the others will carry on the *Babbler*."

Tom wasn't sure how to respond.

Don looked at his analog watch. "I think we're done here. Let me see if I can—"

"What happened?" Tom asked.

Don stopped moving. "Excuse me?"

"What happened in the newsroom? You said they would listen to you. Why did they attack instead?"

Don seemed lost in thought for several moments. He rubbed his face, then looked at his screen.

"I failed to anticipate how pissed off they are." He sighed. "Wendy and I never got along, but I would never want anyone to harm her. She was right this time."

"How so?"

Don looked away from the screen for a few moments. "I've got to go." He looked at his screen. "I'd let you tag along, but Sara's made it clear I'm not allowed to work with you." He leaned toward the screen. "I don't want Sara accusing me of contributing to the delinquency of a staffer. So, if I see you in Bolingbrook, I will report you. God might be merciful, but Sara won't be."

Tom shrugged. "Then I'll make sure you don't see me."

Don stared at the screen as if he were confused. Tom started laughing. Don copied Tom's laugh.

"Good day, Tom." Don fumbled with his mouse before ending the session.

Tom stopped laughing. He wasn't sure if he was serious. He was mistaken about Sara. She went out of her way to hire Tom. While she could be strict, Tom knew she wanted him to succeed.

Don was also wrong about Wendy. She was the *Babbler's* unofficial paranormal expert. Last year, Wendy figured out that a time traveler was responsible for a series of missing time episodes. Don, from what he'd heard, insisted they were caused by unauthorized alien abductions. Wendy was right to be concerned about summoning the *Phantom Press*. Don wasn't. Now they were paying the price.

13

In the late afternoon, Tom emailed Sara his articles, along with a list of story ideas. None of them involved going back to Bolingbrook.

Tom remembered Roul and Wendy's questions about the first attack. He shared their belief that something was off about the ritual. Now he understood why they were confused when he told them no one seemed to hallucinate, unlike what happened during the attack against the *Babbler*. Was Pamela right that he should have considered mundane alternatives before assuming ghosts attacked Town Center?

To his surprise, Sara replied to his email sooner than he had expected. She thanked him for the articles, then wrote about his story ideas. "Go with the interview with former mayor Rene. I'll check if my sources know how to contact Palatine shapeshifters. Keep me updated."

Tom considered shutting down his laptop. He'd found some restaurants that stirred his appetite.

He read Sara's email again. Rene had to know more about the *Phantom Press*. But Sara kicked him off the story. It would be the end of his career if he defied Sara. Maybe Don was right, he thought. Maybe this was an opportunity to find his 'Eyescab' story.

As he thought about the shifters, he remembered surviving his encounter with a weredeer. It would have killed him if another car hadn't hit it. Are the shifters here different? Would he have to worry about werecoyotes tearing his throat out? Was he willing to risk his life for this story?

Tom shook his head. If he were going to risk his life for a story, it should be a story he cared about. Something he would regret if he never wrote the story. He'd never regret skipping Palatine's shifters. He would regret not covering the *Phantom Press'* return.

Tom ordered a pizza and then returned to his laptop to make a schedule for tomorrow. He needed to talk to Rene, research the implosion of Old Chicago, and then travel to Chicago to ask the Chicago Anti-Superstition Society if he could borrow their mascot, Anti-Psychic Kitty, for a night. And he had to do this without Don or Sara finding out his true intentions.

After searching the web, Tom found the trailer park where Little Bolingbrook was located. Unfortunately, he couldn't find a phone number for Rene. He'd have to pay her a visit tomorrow morning.

After recording the address, Tom searched the Fountaindale Library's local history catalog. He noticed that the collection included the video of the implosion and the ceremony celebrating the demolition. He could check that out on the way to Chicago. Don didn't have access to the covert surveillance network, so he liked his odds.

Tom felt a lump in his throat as he entered the URL for the Chicago Anti-Superstition Society's web page. If he had to enter the newsroom at night, he would need protection from the ghosts. Anti-Psychic Kitty, the society's mascot, was the most powerful anti-psychic being alive. A dome of anti-psychic energy several yards in diameter radiated from her body. She could also focus her energy into an invisible beam, lethal to anything remotely psychic.

When the web page loaded, a pop-up window appeared, announcing that tomorrow night was the opening of SkeptiGathering, their annual convention/fundraiser. It also mentioned that Anti-Psychic Kitty would be on stage. Juanita would be there to deliver the opening remarks.

Tom called the office line for CASS but got a message saying the office was closed until the conclusion of SkeptiGathering on Sunday. To reach Juanita, he'd need to attend the gathering. It would be their first time together since he had stopped attending the Lunch and Learns.

He remembered the session he saw her new boyfriend, how he felt when his hopes of becoming Juanita's boyfriend were crushed. His parents were right that it upset him. He felt like he had squandered his opportunity because he was too shy. Maybe that's why, years later, he hooked up with women at Habencon. He didn't want to squander another opportunity. But that attitude led him into the elevator with Jamie.

Tom clicked on the registration button. He gasped when he saw the ticket prices. After some hesitation, Tom pulled out a credit card. If he was willing to risk his life to investigate the *Phantom Press*, he should be willing to risk seeing Juanita again.

14

As Tom drove through southern Aurora, he thought about the comedy movie's inaccurate depiction of the city. It wasn't an idyllic suburb, but the second-largest city in Illinois. Like most large cities, Aurora had its good and its bad parts. As he drove by junkyards, rundown factories, and abandoned buildings, he knew he was in a bad part.

At least it's morning and not nighttime.

His phone vibrated, and his phone map switched to the call screen.

"Ignore," Tom said to the phone's voice assistant. Instead of ending the call, the phone answered itself.

"Hello, Tom," said Robert over the phone.

"Robert?" Tom asked. "You haven't barged into my phone for over a year. What's up?"

"I just wanted to personally assure you that your colleagues are receiving the best care."

"Outside of Clow UFO Base? You know, I still have a memory gap from my last visit."

"Good to know you still have a memory gap. And yes, they are getting the best care outside of Clow. Do you really think I'd have your friends abducted?"

Tom didn't answer.

Robert sighed. "No, they will not disappear. I've made that explicitly clear to my New World Order connections. Besides, this will be over soon. Steve is doing a great job coordinating our departments to deal with the *Phantom Press*. We'll be sending them back to hell soon."

Tom replied, "You broke into my phone to tell me how you're helping my friends. You could have sent me an email."

Robert grumbled. "I called because you're about to drag that witch into this situation."

"Witch?"

"You aren't a good liar, Tom."

Tom shrugged.

Robert said, "I know where you're going, and I wanted to warn you—"

The call cut off, startling Tom. Knowing Robert could barge onto his phone was disturbing, but not as disturbing as knowing someone was powerful enough to jam Robert's calls.

The GPS announced the next turn, distracting Tom from his worries. Tom exited the road and drove into the White Oak Trailer Park. Despite the name, the only trees in the park seemed to be the two on each side of the driveway. The trailers were just as run-down as the other buildings in the area. Tom swerved to avoid several crater-like potholes. He wondered if he was driving on a road or an obstacle course. Since the faded street signs were almost unreadable, Tom trusted his GPS, hoping the address mentioned in the article was accurate.

After driving a few blocks without destroying his car's suspension, a sheet of scrap metal painted green greeted him. A message was hand-printed with gold paint:

Welcome to Little Bolingbrook

The Pathway Neighborhood

Mayor Rene McDonald.

Founded: 1987

Little Bolingbrook stood out from the other sections of the park. The potholes were filled with gravel. The ground was spotless. Many of the trailers had makeshift repairs, like siding that didn't match the rest of the trailers. Someone was attempting to maintain Little Bolingbrook. He couldn't say the same about the rest of the trailers in the park. Every trailer lot in Little Bolingbrook had corn plants. Some grew in small garden patches, while other trailers looked like they landed in the middle of a corn patch.

As he kept driving, he came upon an elderly couple on the side of the road. They stopped walking and stared as Tom drove by. He wondered if they were surprised to see a stranger in their community.

Inside the trailers, residents started closing their blackout curtains. Tom wondered if he should have attached a white flag to his Echo. They had no reason to fear him. Unless they had another reason to close their curtains.

At an intersection, Tom noticed a towering structure rising from a cornfield. The pieces welded together twisted into a surreal metallic giant.

Intrigued, he drove up the lot and parked. The structure towered above a white trailer and two small corn patches. The roof held several antennas. They reminded Tom of old TV antennas he'd seen in black and white photos. A white vinyl fence surrounded the lot.

Tom left his car and approached the gate. He couldn't find a doorbell or an outdoor camera. He tried lifting the latch, but it wouldn't move.

"Hello?"

Blackout curtains covered the windows of the trailer. He looked around and saw that he was the only pedestrian in the area.

Tom said, "I'm Tom Larsen. I'm with the *Bolingbrook Babbler*. We're putting together a fiftieth-anniversary issue, and I'd like to interview you."

Tom heard a rustling sound behind him. He turned. Across the street, a woman wearing a green dress slipped back into a patch of corn.

Tom crossed the street. "Excuse me. I'm looking for—"

He stopped talking when he heard a humming sound. A dark blue golf cart turned onto the road. The driver was a man with gray hair that clashed with his navy-blue bathrobe. Blue-framed glasses with mirror-shade lenses concealed his eyes. He turned onto the road and drove towards Tom.

Tom smiled and waved. "I'm looking for Rene. Excuse me. Mayor Rene."

The man stopped the golf cart. He pulled out a metallic walker and unfolded it. With some effort, he stood up, revealing his matching navy-blue slippers.

The man cleared his throat. "Are you an alien?" he asked in a raspy voice. He began his slow, deliberate approach.

Tom pretended to glance over himself. "Is my human suit zipper showing?"

A metallic grating sound startled Tom. He turned but saw only the sculpture and the white trailer. But something was different about the sculpture. It looked like the "head" had rotated. The rusty orbs looked like eyes staring at him.

The man stopped to catch his breath. "Let me check," he said.

After taking a step, Tom heard a door opening. The man stopped and tried to stand at attention.

Tom looked across the street and recognized Rene, who was exiting her trailer. Rene's faded blue overalls had pockets filled with tools and pens. Her medium-length hair was white but coated with gray metallic color dust.

"Stand down!" she yelled. Her voice was firm but nonthreatening.

Tom raised his hands as Rene walked up to the gate.

"Rene?" Tom asked.

Rene opened the gate and approached Tom. She looked past him. "I can see you, Ms. Watters," she said.

Tom turned and glimpsed the woman in the green robe backing into the corn patch.

"And I can hear you, Mr. Washington."

"But—"

Rene walked up to Mr. Washington and pointed at him. "Did you smack this young man?"

"No," Mr. Washington protested.

"Then I shouldn't hear you."

Her voice reminded Tom of the times his grandparents scolded him.

Rene continued, "You can be as obvious as the blue sky without talking." She looked past Tom. "And could you at least try to be as inconspicuous as the green corn?"

The corn rustled behind him.

Rene faced Mr. Washington. "Little Bolingbrook is counting on both of you. Do better."

Mr. Washington bowed his head, then started towards the golf cart.

Rene looked back at her trailer. "Give the all-clear."

Sirens activated. Tom covered his ears as the sound filled the air. Rene gave a cut-off sign. The sirens wound down.

Rene approached Tom as he unplugged his ears. "I'm sorry you had to witness that. They just started working about a month ago. We lost our previous man in blue and girl in green, and I've had to give them crash courses on their roles."

Tom watched Mr. Washington enter the golf cart and catch his breath.

"Looks like they're trying."

"Trying isn't enough," said Rene. "You said your name was Tom?"

Tom held out his hand. "Tom Larsen."

"Rene McDonald. Mayor of Little Bolingbrook." She gave Tom a firm handshake. "You are the first *Babbler* reporter who hasn't tried to call me at 2 AM."

"We stopped doing that a long time ago," Tom replied.

Rene smiled. "Well, then. We have a lot of catching up to do."

A white woman, who Tom thought looked like she was in her forties, left her trailer. That made her the youngest resident he'd seen.

"Paula," said Rene. "We have a visitor from the *Babbler*."

The woman walked past Rene and Tom. "Though I walk in the shadow of Robert, I shall not fear him, for the Lord will deliver me to a new Bolingbrook." She walked away, repeating the phrase.

Rene said, "Have a good morning, Ms. Duncan." She sighed as she faced Tom. "The new residents always have a hard time adjusting. She'll get better."

Tom glanced at the woman again. "I think I know her."

"Probably. Her father was the last person to run against Robert. He drove them out of town as punishment. She was the last one to leave." Rene watched Ms. Duncan walking away. "This is why we have Little Bolingbrook. It's home for everyone discarded by Robert." She looked around the block. "The true spirit of Bolingbrook lives here." Rene started walking back to her trailer. Tom followed. Rene said, "Robert may have Clow UFO Base, the golf club, his campaign fund, and his strip malls, but Little Bolingbrook has something he'll never have."

"What's that?"

"Corn."

Tom knew cornfields once surrounded Bolingbrook. By the time his family moved to Bolingbrook, only one small patch remained. This was the first time he'd met someone nostalgic for the original cornfields.

The gate opened by itself. Rene looked up at the sculpture. "Thank you, Gwyla." Tom looked at the gate and couldn't understand how it opened on its own.

Tom followed Rene into the trailer. It looked like a maze of worktables and workbenches. Mechanical and electronic devices covered the tops, except for one table near the hallway entrance, which was covered with a gray tablecloth. It sparkled as if glitter had been woven into it. A transistor radio rested on the table next to the wall. Beside the radio were three framed color photos. Tom noticed that rolls of sparkling cloth lined the walls.

A robot rolled into the room from the hallway. It resembled the sculpture outside, except for the wheel tracks and the fact that it was only four feet high.

"Thank you, Purpose Maker," it said, sounding more like a young girl's voice than a machine. "Would you like some lemonade?"

"Yes," Rene replied. "Gwyla, this is Tom. He is a guest. Do you remember how we treat our guests?"

Gwyla rolled up to Tom and extended what passed for its right arm. "Hello, Guest Tom. Welcome to Little Bolingbrook.

Making lemonade is my current purpose. Would you like some lemonade?"

"Wow," Tom replied as he shook Gwyla's hand. Gwyla didn't grab his hand. Its arm mimicked Tom's handshaking motion, then retracted.

Rene said, "Yes, we would like two glasses containing lemonade. Not two glasses made of lemonade. Understood?"

"Now I do, Purpose Maker." Gwyla rolled towards the refrigerator.

Tom watched Gwyla extend her upper body to reach the freezer.

"You're wondering how it works?" Rene asked.

Tom nodded. "My father used to work on robots. Even helped me build a toy robot. This defies everything I know about robots."

Rene smiled with pride. "Gwyla isn't a robot. It's a machine spirit contained within a mechanical body."

Tom's eyes widened. "A spirit? Like the kind shamans deal with?"

"Yes. Though I don't like to be called a shaman. Sounds so primitive. I prefer to call myself a practitioner of technomagic."

Tom noticed that Gwyla had removed the lemons while he was talking to Rene. A blade extended from its body. It sliced the lemons faster than he could see. Gwyla then moved on to the cabinets.

He looked at Rene, who was watching Gwyla like a parent watching a child.

"I've never seen magic or a spirit before," said Tom. "How does it work?"

Rene kept her eyes on Gwyla. "Every nonliving thing has a spirit within it. The key to all magic is the manipulation of those spirits. I specialize in technology spirits."

"How?" asked Tom.

"Devices, keywords, gestures." She looked at Tom. "Hard to explain. Even harder to master." She smiled. "I was one of the few who could connect higher-level spirits to material bodies."

Tom tilted his head. "Higher level?"

"Yes," Rene replied with a twinkle in her eye. "There's a hierarchy of spirits. The ones in our devices are barely conscious. In the spirit frequencies, you'll find spirits like Gwyla. They're intelligent but struggle with abstractions." She watched Gwyla. "When we think of Bolingbrook, we see a community. Gwyla can only see a collection of buildings." She spoke up. "Gwyla? How are you doing?"

"Almost finished, Purpose Maker."

"Why does it call you 'Purpose Maker?'" Tom asked.

"Spirits like Gwyla exist to complete tasks. What they call purpose. It's a symbiotic relationship. I provide purpose to Gwyla's existence. Gwyla helps me build things. Right now, her purpose is to make lemonade."

Gwyla rotated its head to see Tom and Rene. "I have made lemonade."

"Bring it to us," Rene said. "Please?"

Gwyla rotated its body, holding a tray with a pitcher of lemonade and two glasses filled with ice. It rolled over to the table and set the tray down. It poured the same amount of lemonade into both glasses and served them.

Rene looked at Tom. "What do you think?"

Tom sipped the lemonade, and his face puckered instantly. He resisted the urge to grab the sugar bowl and pour sugar into his mouth.

"We're still working on making lemonade." She looked at Gwyla. "Good try, Gwyla."

Gwyla retracted back to its normal height. Its eyes looked up at Rene, reminding Tom how pets looked up at their caretakers. "I will try harder next time, Purpose Maker."

"I know you will," Rene replied. "Gwyla, please work on the ELX wireless transmitter."

Gwyla's visual sensors widened, like irises. "Yes, Purpose Maker. Thank you for providing purpose."

Gwyla rolled towards one of the workbenches.

Rene said, "Tom? Would you like some water?"

"Yes," Tom replied. A bitter film still coated his mouth.

Rene walked towards the refrigerator and pulled out a water pitcher.

"It's been years since my last interview." She filled a glass with water. "I was wondering if the world had already forgotten me." Rene returned to the table with the glass and pitcher. Her face seemed to glow with happiness.

"Ask me anything," she said.

***

Rene leaned back in her chair. "And that was the first of many arguments with Robert."

Tom nodded and checked the time on his cellphone. It was now the afternoon. They'd spent hours discussing the history of Bolingbrook. In between anecdotes, Tom learned spheres generated a type of EMP that shorted out organic brains.

"If I can ask," said Tom, "I noticed that you haven't told any stories about aliens."

Rene made a brushing motion with her hand. "Nothing worth talking about." She took a deep breath. "They're just like the gods in most religions. Perform a few miracles to get our attention. Dangle promises of salvation, but only if we follow their rules." She shook her head. "We work hard to appease them, but it's never enough to satisfy them." She shrugged. "And they never perform miracles when you need them to."

This was the opening Tom was looking for.

"Like the death of your daughter and your husband?" He hoped the hours of conversation were enough to make her open to him.

Rene fell silent. He could see the sadness on her face.

"Let me show you something," she replied.

Rene walked back towards the living area, looking past Tom. Tom stood up and followed.

She walked past Gwyla, who was still working on a device Tom didn't recognize. She stopped in front of the table with the radio and photographs. As Tom approached, he realized the photos were of her family, and he recognized her daughter.

"They promised us the universe," said Rene. Tom heard a mix of sorrow and anger in her voice. "If we would just embrace science and reason." She sighed as she moved her fingers. "Natalie loved science, even if she didn't fully understand it. My husband was a very reasonable man." She looked at Tom. "They wouldn't save them. So that's why I'd rather not talk about worthless sky gods."

"I'm sorry for your loss," Tom replied.

"Me too." She picked up a photograph. "Me too."

Tom looked at the photo. None of his journalism classes taught him how to interview a grieving mother.

"I saw Natalie," said Tom, trying the direct approach. "When I was attacked by the *Phantom Press*. She saved me."

Rene flashed a smile. "She's that kind of person." Rene looked at Tom. "I'm sorry about your friends. I trust Steve. He'll find a way to save them."

"Do you know why the *Phantom Press* attacked us? You used to work with them."

Rene paused. "They've changed. I don't recognize them anymore. Sorry. I can't help you with that."

Tom hesitated as he wondered if he should ask more questions.

"If you see them again," said Rene, "try to stay calm. They feed on potent emotions. It's what sustains them."

"You don't have to answer this," said Tom, "but Natalie kept telling me she wanted to go home."

"Because she's fading away," said Rene. She took a deep breath. "All ghosts fade away. The memories and emotions of the living sustain every ghost. Memories fade. Emotions subside. Entropy always finds a way." She looked down at the photo. "Even in the Ghost Frequencies."

Tom blinked. "You've... talked to her."

Rene pointed at the radio. "I use this to monitor the Ghost Frequencies. It's a modified radio with a conductive cloth antenna."

"Conductive cloth?" Tom reached out to touch the tablecloth. Rene grabbed his wrist.

"It's charged," she said. "You don't want to get shocked."

Tom withdrew his hand. Rene picked up a scrap of cloth from another table and handed it to Tom. "You can touch this."

Tom took the cloth. It felt like denim. Parts of the material sparkled in the light in the room.

Gwyla rotated her head. "Excuse me, Purpose Maker. You have a meeting with—"

"Gwyla!" snapped Rene. Anger replaced her earlier sorrow. "What have I told you?"

Gwyla lowered its head. "It is a name that only you should hear. Sorry."

"Accepted. Gwyla, please give Tom the card with my phone number."

"Yes, Purpose Maker."

Tom fidgeted. "I'm sorry—"

"Don't be," Rene said as she brushed a hair away from her face. "I have a meeting I need to attend, but I'd like to finish our interview later."

Gwyla handed Tom a business card, which he accepted.

"Gwyla," said Rene, "please escort Tom to the door. And ask for his phone number." She looked at Tom. "Goodbye."

Rene started down the hallway before he could say goodbye. As he followed Gwyla to the door, he noticed he was still holding the conductive cloth Rene gave him. He put it in his pocket, then gave his phone number to Gwyla.

Gwyla opened the door. "Goodbye, Tom Guest. I will work on my lemonade until I get it right."

15

INSIDE THE LOCAL ARCHIVE room, Tom started watching the video of the implosion of Old Chicago. He hoped it would offer a clue how the *Phantom Press* survived the EMP blast. Otherwise, he risked a trip to Bolingbrook for nothing.

On screen, the original logo for Bolingbrook Community Television faded into view. A static shot of Robert and several other people mingling on stage followed it. Behind them stood Old Chicago Weeds grew in the cracked pavement in the parking lot. The intact dome reminded Tom of the one at the state capitol building. The building itself looked like a large shopping mall with the windows bricked over. He knew Old Chicago never had windows. The darker bricks offered the illusion of window frames.

Tom resisted the urge to fast forward because nothing was happening on screen. To his relief, Robert walked up to the podium and started talking. Robert had a thick horseshoe mustache and a full head of red hair, a stark contrast to his present appearance, Tom thought. The mayor started his speech by telling the story about going to the mall and having a 'drugged-out crazy man' spill a plate of spaghetti on his new leisure suit. He moved on to the history of Old Chicago. It was the first shopping mall with an indoor amusement park. He mentioned the rides, like the Monster of the Midway roller-coaster. However, it had never turned a profit. Despite many attempts to save it, the mall closed in 1980. Robert believed it failed because it lacked anchor stores, like Sears, and the rides weren't enough to draw repeat business.

Robert mentioned efforts to sell the building. Plans proposed included converting it into a casino, a Chinese government exhibit hall, or a World's Fair site. According to Robert, Rene blocked an attempt to demolish the building because "she couldn't let go of the past." Robert said that his first act as mayor was to approve the demolition.

"This building is a relic of Bolingbrook's past," he said. "But we can't let it impede Bolingbrook's bright future."

Robert talked about Bolingbrook's future when a man in the audience interrupted him.

"I've got investors," he yelled. It didn't sound like Roul or anyone Tom recognized.

Robert smiled. "Boy, your timing sucks."

"But we promised them—"

Despite the low resolution, Tom could see the anger on Robert's face. "You promised them. I didn't."

The man replied, but boos and hisses drowned him out.

Robert leaned over the podium as he was trying to hear what the man was saying. Moments later, he spoke into the microphone.

"Who are you to judge me?" Robert asked.

"I am the founder of Bolingbrook!" the man answered.

Some of the audience laughed.

Robert said, "And we are Bolingbrook." He paused as the audience applauded. "And we have embraced the future."

The man replied, "Do this, and Bolingbrook has no future."

The boos and jeers drowned out the man's voice. Seconds later, the audience calmed down. Tom heard the man's faint voice. He rewound the tape, cranked up the volume, and then pressed play.

"It was my turn!" yelled the man.

Robert's voice boomed over the speakers, making Tom turn down the volume. Robert resumed his speech. As the speech seemed to reach its conclusion, Steve walked up to the podium and whispered into Robert's ear. Steve's facial scar was red as if it were a fresh wound. Robert nodded, and Steve walked away. Robert said there was a technical issue delaying the implosion. During the delay, Robert explained why the early 19th century theme of the mall was a mistake.

Minutes later, Steve reappeared, carrying a small box with a large red button. Two men in hard hats followed as they unrolled a cable. Steve placed the box on the podium, and one man plugged the cable into it.

Robert grinned. "Old Chicago and its ghosts are about to become history." He pressed the button.

Old Chicago imploded into a cloud of dust and debris. As the dust cleared, news helicopters closed in on the debris field. The video faded out to the sound of the audience's cheering.

While the tape was rewinding, he checked the microfiche copies of the *Bolingbrook Spotlight* printed in 1965. Though it listed the members of the incorporation committee, none of the articles referred to a "founder" or even implied that a single person founded Bolingbrook. Nor did Tom ever recall the *Babbler* mentioning a sole founder of Bolingbrook.

Tom printed the article listing the names of the original village board members. It also included a reference to the *Babbler*'s publisher asking 'inappropriate questions' to the board. He found it amusing.

When the tape finished rewinding, Tom put his materials in the return bins, then walked up to the door. After cracking the door open, he scanned the room, looking for anyone who might recognize him and report him to Sara. He didn't see anybody. To be safe, he put on a pair of sunglasses and a White Sox cap.

Better to look odd than to be recognized.

Tom made his way back to the reference desk. She was looking at a monitor as Tom approached.

"I'm done," said Tom, making sure his voice didn't carry.

Sally looked up from her screen. She stared at Tom. "Please tell me you have an eye and scalp condition."

Tom shrugged. "Sure."

Sally shook her head and then returned Tom's card. "Anything else?"

Tom leaned in. "I was hoping—"

"You still need a black card," Sally said, her tone professional but her eyes betraying a hint of amusement.

Tom hoped his sunglasses concealed his disappointment. "No, but that's not what I was going to ask."

"Our collection of *Babbler* issues only goes back to 1967. Don't ask me why."

"Actually," said Tom as looked around the room. "I was hoping you could look up the obituaries of the first Village Board members." He lowered his sunglasses. "You really impressed me when you found that article about Mayor McDonald. I never would have found it on my own."

Sally gave Tom a skeptical look. "I'm still not letting you into the Vault."

Tom chuckled. "I'm still not asking you to."

"Yet," Sally replied. "And before you ask, you're not my type, I read the *Phantom Press* article about you."

Tom resisted the urge to defend himself. It wouldn't help, he told himself. "Hey, if this is too difficult to research, I understand."

Sally picked up a pad of yellow sticky notes and a Fountain-dale Library pen. She set them in front of Tom.

"Give me your email address," she said.

16

AFTER THE LONG DRIVE into Chicago, followed by a frustrating search for a parking spot and an overpriced dinner, Tom finally arrived at Navy Pier. He wove his way through the crowd. On his right, tour boats waited for their next round of tourists. To his left, tourist traps and restaurants buzzed with activity. He appreciated the calming view of Lake Michigan, though the lake looked better from the Museum campus.

The crowd thinned as approached the Aon Grand Ballroom. Unlike the rest of Navy Pier, this building was restored to its 1916 glory. A sign on a stand read, "Welcome to SkeptiGathering 2015!" Tom tensed as he wondered how the attendees would react. Would they ignore him because CASS wasn't involved in the conflict between the MRA and feminist factions of skepticism? Would they consider him a traitor to the skeptical movement?

There's only one way to find out.

Tom entered the lobby, hearing muffled sounds of a speaker in the ballroom. He approached the registration desk in front of him, staffed by two women and a man.

"Name?" said an African American woman who Tom guessed was around his age.

Tom cleared his throat. "Tom Larsen."

"Tom Larsen?"

"Yes," Tom replied with a smile. "I registered for the dessert portion."

She sorted while the man stood up. The African American woman pulled out a convention badge with a red ribbon. After accepting his badge, his smile vanished after reading the text on the ribbon.

"Warning! 100% Woo."

He glared back at her.

"I'm sorry," she replied.

"Sorry?"

"Yeah. I can't imagine the horror of waking up every day knowing you're Tom Larsen." She laughed sarcastically.

Before Tom could respond, the man walked up to Tom. "Come with me," he said.

The man escorted Tom into the ballroom, a half-dome with several thousand feet of floor space and a balcony that ran along the entire wall. Several hundred people sat at dining tables on the floor and balcony. All of them wore semiformal attire. Tom felt underdressed in his t-shirt, jeans, and black walking shoes.

On stage, a magician wearing a short-sleeved shirt performed sleight-of-hand tricks. Those were his favorite tricks to watch. When he saw the dessert trays filled with rich chocolate dishes and tempting pastries, his mouth watered.

He marveled at the contrast between this semi-formal event and the informal Lunch and Learn sessions he attended as a teenager. The sessions were fun and friendly. This felt like a spectacle intended to impress wealthy donors. Only wealthy people could afford to attend all the events, thought Tom.

The man stopped next to a metal and wood school desk. Instead of a tempting dessert tray, a bowl of rice pudding waited for him. Tom stared, dumbfounded.

"Seriously?" he yelled over the background sounds. "I paid full price."

The man leaned towards Tom. "They wanted to give you a candy bar. I said the only person to piss off the Habenstein Society and Humanist Heart deserves more." He smiled at Tom before leaving.

Tom sighed as he sat down. He stirred the dish, looking for anything hidden inside. Seeing nothing disgusting, he took a bite. The taste of vanilla and sugar dominated his tongue.

At least it's high-end rice pudding.

Tom noticed a table with an unoccupied seat. The people at the table appeared to be close to his age. They still had plenty of desserts on their tray.

On stage, the magician picked up a top hat off the floor. He showed the audience the hat's interior.

"Normally," said the magician, "this is the part of the show when I would tell the audience how psychics, faith healers, chiropractors, and the like are also magicians." He placed the hat on a stand covered with a black cloth. He stepped towards the audience. "But you're not a normal audience." The audience cheered. "Each one of you sees the woo that surrounds us. We watch ignorance infecting those around us. We understand we are on the verge of a new dark age." He reached into the hat. His arm seemed to reach farther than the height of the hat. "Instead of cursing the darkness." He pulled a lit candle out of the hat. "We will light a candle."

The magician bowed as the audience rose to give him a standing ovation.

Seeing his opportunity, Tom approached the empty chair. A woman sitting next to the chair noticed Tom. She was a white woman with long brown hair; she wore a black dress. As Tom reached the chair, she tipped it. The impact of the chair hitting the table startled him.

"You are un-awesome!" Her breath reeked of alcohol.

The companions stared at Tom as the ovation ended. He shrugged and then returned to his desk and overpriced dessert.

He reminded himself that he was there to ask Juanita if he could borrow Anti-Psychic Kitty. He only had to put up with this treatment tonight.

The curtain cracked open, and the male MC walked on stage. "I think the Great Hayden should start a candle delivery service. Don't you?"

No one laughed.

"I liked it." The MC grinned. "Now, here's someone you'll like. She doesn't need an introduction, but I'll do one, anyway."

The audience moaned.

"It'll be quick," he replied. "She joined CASS when she was a high school freshman. Many of us have watched her grow over the years. Literally, in my case."

A few people chuckled.

"That wasn't a joke. Anyway. Today she's an advisor to the Chicago Police Department, and one of the youngest presidents in CASS's history. Whenever the news media covers woo, she's the woman they go to for the truth."

The audience cheered.

"So, without further ado, let's show our appreciation to Juanita Vega!"

The curtain parted to enough for Juanita to walk on stage. She wore a black dress with a white summer cardigan. Her wireless clip-on mic glimmered under the stage lights. As the audience stood up and applauded, she strode towards the edge of the stage.

Tom joined in the applause. The last time Tom saw her, she was eighteen. Now she was in her late 20s. She no longer dyed the ends of her dark brown hair. He couldn't help but notice her toned athletic body, a stark contrast to the thin woman he remembered. But her warmth of her smile and kind expressions hadn't changed. They still made his heart flutter.

Juanita motioned for the audience to sit down. "Thank you," she said. "I appreciate it, but this isn't about me. Tonight, and the rest of this week, is about you." Juanita paced the stage like a seasoned lecturer. "Without your support, there wouldn't be a Chicago Anti-Superstition Society. We wouldn't have our Lunch and Learns, our government consulting staff, or even our youth peer support programs. You make CASS what it is today." She paused. "Thank you."

The audience applauded. The drunk woman tried to stand, only to slip back into her chair. She caught herself and cheered incoherently.

Juanita continued. "Long before the skeptical movement was born, CASS alerted the public to the harm caused by irrational fears. Today, CASS is growing both in membership and activities. Do you know why?"

"Because we're awesome!" the drunk woman shouted. Laughter filled the ballroom.

Juanita smirked. "Yes, we are awesome, and I'll tell you why. Because CASS is founded on the belief that critical thinking is for everyone, regardless of race, sexual orientation, gender—" Juanita lifted her necklace to reveal her crucifix. "Or creed."

The audience cheered wildly while Tom watched. He'd forgotten that she was Catholic. As Juanita continued, Tom remembered the few times she had mentioned her faith. While he'd debate religion with his classmates, he never challenged her beliefs. His infatuation made it easy to overlook what he considered a flaw. Skepticism united them. Even though his skepticism went further than hers.

As he listened to Juanita, arguing that skepticism and atheism are not the same, Tom found it harder to ignore their different religious beliefs. Yes, he couldn't deny his attraction to her. An attraction that felt stronger than his attraction towards Jamie four years ago. *Which didn't end well*, he reminded himself.

While Juanita talked about rising "woo" in Chicagoland, stagehands set up a fundraising table with credit card readers and a money box. Juanita's mother, Henrietta, walked on stage and sat at the table. A few audience members clapped.

"You may not be aware," said Juanita, "but the price of your tickets only covers the expenses of organizing this weekend's events. Any donations, large or small, would be appreciated. There are two ways to donate tonight." She motioned toward her mother. "You just walk up to this table, and we'll accept your donation. Cash or credit." Juanita approached the audience. "Then again." She paused. "Some of you might want to make a statement before donating." She smiled. "It doesn't have to be spoken. It could involve walking a path," she whispered. "Or an obstacle course." Tom felt the excitement building in the audience. "A course that would frighten the average person. But you are not the average person."

The audience cheered. The drunk woman's eyes seemed to light up in anticipation. Juanita continued. "The founders of our society had that need, too." The cheering grew louder. "At their first meeting, they did something that required a little effort. But that one little action made headlines around the world. Ladies and gentlemen, I give you—"

The curtain rose, and the audience celebrated. The energy in the room was almost like the excitement at Soldier Field during a close Bears-Packers game.

"The Gauntlet of Woo!"

Stage lights illuminated the infamous Gauntlet of Woo. It was a maze of ladders, mirrors, and other props that would strike fear in the heart of the most superstitious person. Tom's jaw dropped. He'd heard CASS members describe it, but their explanations failed to prepare Tom for what he was seeing. At the end of the gauntlet was another donation table staffed by four people.

"Wow," said Juanita, pretending to be surprised at the audience's reaction. "Now wait a minute. It's missing something." She paused, then grinned at the audience. "Or someone?"

As if on cue, the magician's hat and stand started shaking. On the screen above the stage, the camera zoomed in for a tight shot. A moment later, a cat raised its head out of the hat and rested its front paws on the rim of the hat.

"It's Anti-Psychic Kitty!" said the drunk woman.

Anti-Psychic Kitty looked back at the camera with her green eyes. Most of her fur was steel blue, but her paws were bright white. She had what looked to Tom like a river of white fur flowing from under her chin towards her belly. Some attendees started chanting "APK" while the others cheered. Anti-Psychic Kitty looked out at the audience, unafraid of the screaming humans in front of her. She slowly blinked at the camera.

"APK?" Juanita asked. Her ears turned in Juanita's direction. "Are you ready to run the Gauntlet of Woo?"

"Mow!" APK replied.

"On your mark," Juanita called out. APK's body swayed back and forth. "Get set." Juanita waited. The audience waited in anticipation.

"Go!" Juanita yelled.

APK leaped out of the hat and scampered towards the Gauntlet of Woo. A stagehand pulled a string, dragging a plush black cat doll across the stage. Without hesitating, APK crossed its path, then rushed past a jar of pennies. APK leaped onto a table and knocked over a saltshaker without its cap. Salt poured out of the container. She dashed away, with no intention of tossing any of the spilled salt.

The audience cheered.

APK jumped off the table and onto a slab of concrete. The slab had thirteen cracks, and thirteen red sound buttons. APK stepped on the first crack, then tapped the first sound button. "Hamlet!" an electronic voice replied. APK stepped on the remaining cracks and tapped all the "Hamlet" sound buttons.

She sprinted off the tab towards thirteen pressure plates. Next to each plate was a closed umbrella. She pounced onto the first pressure plate. The attached umbrella opened. Each pressure plate she touched opened an umbrella.

The audience cheered.

APK sprinted towards a freestanding end table with a mirror on a stand. She leaped onto the unstable end table and then jumped off, knocking it over. The mirror shattered upon impact.

The audience let out an ecstatic roar.

"You're awesome, APK!" the drunk woman yelled.

After landing, APK dashed to a standing ladder. The audience cheered as she cleared it.

With one final sprint, APK leaped onto the second donation and skidded to a stop. The audience jumped to their feet. Their roar was so loud, Tom covered his ears.

APK faced the audience and sat on her hind legs. She slow blinked her eyes. After basking in the applause, she started grooming herself.

"Who else wants to run the Gauntlet of Woo?" Juanita asked.

The attendees, including Chicago politicians and area CEOs, lined up to run the Gauntlet of Woo. Soon, most of the audience was in line.

Instead of joining that line, Tom walked over to Henrietta's table, which didn't have a line. Henrietta's vibrant dress contrasted with the dark stage curtain behind her. Her face lit up as Tom approached. She gestured to him.

"Hi!" she said, using sign language concurrently.

Tom positioned himself so she could see his lips. "Henrietta," he said, signing to her. He stopped as he struggled to remember his old sign language lessons.

"It's fine," she said. "I can read your lips just fine. Remember?"

"Yes," Tom said with a sigh of relief. "How have you been?"

"Busy." She gestured at the stage. "You've been busy, too."

"Very." Tom chuckled.

"I don't care what they say. I still think you're okay."

Tom blushed. "Um, thanks. I hope I'm not blocking the table."

"Nobody ever comes to this table. Everyone wants to run the Gauntlet of Woo."

The sound of shattering glass startled Tom. He turned and saw a Chicago alderman celebrating as stagehands swept up the shards of glass.

"I can understand why," Tom said. "Say, I really need to talk to Juanita. Do you know when she'll be available?"

She looked past Tom, who turned and tensed. Juanita stood a few feet away. Though he fantasized about what he'd say to her, now the words eluded him.

Juanita broke the silence. "The Prodigal Son returns." Tom expected her to flash her warm smile, but she didn't. She approached Tom. "I wasn't sure if you were going to show up."

"I'm glad I did." He smiled, hoping it would defuse the tension.

"I heard about your friends. It's a miracle no one died in that explosion."

"It wasn't an explosion," Tom replied, feeling defensive.

She tilted her head. "Really? What was it?"

Tom hesitated as he pictured what would happen if he told her the truth. Could he come up with a lie she would believe?

"Well, Tom?"

Let's get this over with.

"Ghosts." Tom braced himself, expecting a sharp debunking from her.

Juanita remained silent. Her lack of reaction unsettled Tom. He couldn't read her expression. *What is she thinking?* Tom wondered.

Tom pressed on. "Ghosts attacked the village board a few days ago. Then we tried to—"

"We?"

Tom sighed. "*The Babbler*. My friends and co-workers. We tried to contact them. Well, they did. I was ordered to stay at home. That's when..." Tom's voice trailed off into silence, his eyes downcast under Juanita's piercing, critical stare.

"All the news stories said it was a natural gas explosion," said Juanita. She flashed a smile. "You know, hallucinations are a symptom of carbon monoxide poisoning."

"I was not hallucinating," Tom protested. "I studied debunking and skepticism—"

"I know," Juanita calmly replied. "I was one of your teachers."

Tom smiled. "You were a great teacher."

"And I remember when you used to tear into the *Babbler's* stories. I never imagined you calling any of them your friends."

Tom shrugged. "I've changed."

Her critical gaze lingered on him. "I can tell."

"And they need my help." Tom felt a pit form in his stomach. "I need your help."

Juanita stepped closer. "Help?"

"I need to borrow Anti-Psychic Kitty." Tom felt his fingers chill. "Just for one night. You can accompany me and take her home when—"

"Why?" asked Juanita with a hint of annoyance.

"I need to get the contact list that I left in my office. Since I can only be there at night, I'll need her protection while I'm gathering them. With her help, I'll be in and out in a matter of minutes."

APK jumped onto the table and looked up at Tom.

"Mow?" she asked, facing Tom.

Juanita walked up to the table and started petting APK, who purred and rubbed her hand.

"Why can't you go during the day?" asked Juanita.

"It's guarded until nightfall," Tom replied. "That's why I need her to protect me from the ghosts."

APK looked at Juanita. "Mow?" she asked, then looked at Tom.

"Who is guarding it?" Juanita asked, sounding more annoyed.

Tom hesitated. "Um. Guards hired by the publisher. But I have an office key."

Juanita stopped petting APK. Her critical gaze unsettled Tom. "Correct me if I'm mistaken. You plan on trespassing on the *Babbler*'s property and want APK and me to be accomplices?"

APK grumbled.

"You don't have to phrase it that way," Tom replied. "Besides, the *Babbler* has joint ownership of APK."

APK scampered next to Henrietta, and she started stroking her fur.

Juanita looked at APK, then at Tom. "Next summer."

Tom blinked. "Next summer?"

"That's when the *Babbler* is scheduled to have APK. If you need to borrow her sooner, have Chris call me."

"But my friends are catatonic. The staff evacuated Bolingbrook, and I'm putting my job on the line to figure out what the hell is really going on." Tom threw his hands up. "I'm desperate. That's why I'm here."

Juanita stepped closer and looked up at Tom. "I sympathize," she said. Tom believed her. "But the answer is still no."

Looking into her eyes, Tom knew she would not give in. He'd lost.

"In that case, do you know where I can find *el ángel de la razón*?" he asked.

Juanita tilted her head. Henrietta stopped petting APK and focused on Tom.

"What did you say?" asked Juanita, her voice a mixture of surprise and concern.

"I'm trying to find *el ángel de la razón*." Tom repeated the name and hoped he had pronounced it correctly.

Juanita's mother's jaw dropped, and she looked at her daughter.

"Why?" asked Juanita.

Startled, Tom replied, "I'm supposed to give her a message." Tom tried to recite his message, but his Spanish pronunciation was butchered and unintelligible.

"*El caballero blanco extraña a su pequeño girasol*?" Juanita asked.

"That's it." Tom felt relieved that he didn't have to say that phrase again.

Juanita's eyes widened. Her mother put a hand up to her mouth. Tom worried he'd just recited something obscene or something vital.

"Tell us what happened."

Tom recounted what had happened from the occult ritual to the Roul's arrest.

"He said she was the only who could save us," Tom continued. "Then they took him into custody."

Juanita and Henrietta faced each other and started communicating in sign language. APK watched, as if she were trying to follow the conversation. Tom couldn't keep up with their rapid-fire signing but based on their facial expressions, they were having a heated argument.

"What's going on?" asked Tom.

The sound of shattering mirrors startled Tom. Anti-Psychic Kitty leaped to the floor and off stage. Inside the Gauntlet of Woo, the drunk woman lay on the stage floor surrounded by shards of glass. Blood ran down her arms. A crowd started gathering around her.

"You need to leave," Juanita said to Tom.

"But—" Tom protested.

"You'll get a full refund."

"What did I say?"

"Nothing. Just go! Or do you need an escort?"

Juanita rushed towards the stage as two staff tended to the drunk woman's wounds.

She yelled, "We have the Gauntlet of Woo. We have Anti-Psychic Kitty! We're awesome! We're awesome! We're so awesome, the Earth cannot hold us down!"

17

As DUSK SETTLED OVER Barbers Corner, Tom observed the *Babbler*'s Office from Portillo's patio. Someone boarded up the windows. The parking lot lights at the office were still damaged. Even from this distance, he could read the "No Trespassing" signs stapled to the boards. The security guard, who Tom had been watching for about an hour, stopped pacing and looked up at the darkening sky. After a quick glance at his watch, he headed towards his car. Watching the guard drive away, Tom sighed. His gamble that the guard would leave before sunset didn't pay off.

As he took his tray to the garbage can, he overheard a man say, "I remember when the *Babbler* was family-friendly. Now they've got queers working for them."

A woman replied, "Who cares about that?"

"I do," the man replied. "We don't need them in Boling-brook."

Tom shook his head, then emptied his tray into the garbage and left.

Walking towards Barber's Corner, he noticed the new banners that had replaced the ones that had caught fire after the attack. Their bright colors contrasted with the darkness that seemed to envelop the *Babbler's* office.

He wished he had Anti-Psychic Kitty's protection or that it was still daytime. He could still do this, he told himself. Once inside, he'd retrieve the Rolodex and ghost books from his desk. If he sensed the ghosts were close, he'd leave. If not, he might have time to check out the *Babbler*'s archives in the backroom. Maybe the early issues could reveal who the so-called founder of Bolingbrook was?

If the ghosts attacked, he'd focus on staying calm to starve them of their precious emotions. They would not catch him off guard this time.

After crossing North Bolingbrook Drive, Tom entered the repair shop's parking lot, then walked towards the office. While the building still bore the scars of the attack, the *Babbler*'s parking lot had cleared of the glass and rubble.

Tom stopped and looked at the building he was about to trespass. He could turn around now, he thought. Maybe there was a way to convince Don to get his things? If caught, Sara might fire him. Worse, he could be arrested. He imagined his parents hiring a lawyer who would make him plead insanity. Then he would be in a prison's mental ward.

He closed his eyes. He pictured the aftermath of the attack. If he got what he came for and didn't get caught, he might find something that could help them. Something that Don would have missed.

He took a deep breath, then continued. It was worth the risk.

When he reached the door, he inserted his office key and, to his relief, it still worked. He unlocked the door and stepped inside. After turning on his cell phone's flashlight, he closed the door. When he pointed the light into the newsroom, his heart sank. It looked like the aftermath of a tornado strike. Pieces of cubicles and ceiling tiles littered the room. The flip-u cabinet top that once separated the lobby from the newsroom had been ripped off its hinges. Every electrical outlet had scorch marks.

All the desks had been knocked over by the attack. Newsroom's cubicles and desks were now rubble piles by the walls.

He approached what used to be Wendy's desk. The drawers were missing from its broken frame.

"Fuck," Tom whispered.

He made his way to the remains of his cubicle. Only a few inches of the wall remained. His desk was upside down. Carefully, he stepped around the desk to see if the drawers were intact. To his horror, they were open and empty. Leaning closer, he saw indents along the tops of the metallic shelves. *They've been pried open*, he thought. Had Don gone through all the desks? If he had, was he going to return the contents?

"Thomas Larsen!" came Sara's voice from behind.

He turned around and pointed his light at Sara. She trembled as she glared at Tom. "What are you doing here?" she said, her voice sounding like a growl.

Tom's heart raced. "I—I can explain."

Sara approached. "I took pity on you, and this is how you repay me?"

"I needed my books." Tom motioned towards the remains of his desk. "Don stole them."

"You don't deserve them," came Don's voice.

He turned and pointed his flashlight. Don was walking towards him. "Always acting. Never thinking."

Sara said, "Leeching off the work of others."

His fear of being discovered turned to rage. "That's not fair! I was trying to help."

"You don't belong with us," Don snarled. "You never belonged."

Sara said, "Smart to think you're right."

Shavana moved into the light. "But not enough to know you're wrong."

"I'll never forgive you," said Sara.

Don moved closer. "I'll never accept you."

Tom snapped. "Who the hell are you to just wonder off the street and steal my work? My research. My books." He glared at Sara. "Who are you to judge me for going behind your back? You went behind your editor's back years ago. That's how you ended up at the *Babbler*. You were rewarded for your deception. Why should I be punished?"

Shavana laughed.

Tom scowled at Shavana. "What?"

Shavana shook her head. "You think you're so rational. Yet you never asked yourself this one question."

"What question?"

Shavana smiled. "How did we get inside"—her eyes burst into red flames—"without making a sound?"

Tom gasped in horror, then stumbled backwards. He tripped over his desk.

He landed in a hotel room. Reese Habenstein's corpse lay face down on the floor. Tom's breathing quickened as the memories of Reese's death flooded his mind.

Reese turned his head. His dead eyes stared at Tom. "You didn't save me."

Tom hands trembled. "I tried."

Reese closed his eyes and stopped moving. Megan, the future version of Meggy, stood over Reese.

"You told me to kill him," she said.

Tom slowly shook his head. "No. No. He made you do that. He corrupted you."

Meggy appeared in Megan's place. Her bright pink dress was spotless.

"You still have time to corrupt me," she said.

Natalie voice came from all directions. "Stop it! Stop it!"

Reality shattered and darkness enveloped Tom.

"Tom," Natalie sobbed.

Tom opened his eyes. He was back in the newsroom, still on the floor. Natalie sat in swivel chair in front of Tom.

"I wanna go home," she sobbed. Her white t-shirt and blue shorts were covered in blood. "But she won't let me. She wants to keep me here, but I want to go home."

Tom stood up. "You want to come back to Bolingbrook?"

Natalie stopped crying and gasped. Her eyes widened with fear. "You have to leave," she whispered. "They're here!"

"Who's here?"

Natalie vanished.

Tom picked up his smartphone. The light started flickering. *I'd better leave before I lose my mind.*

Tom rushed to the door. The door started opening, and he staggered to a stop. Two men entered, wearing sunglasses that covered their glowing red eyes. Tom pointed his cellphone's light at them. Both were white males, close to his age. Each one wore a dark blue windbreaker with an oversized Chicago Cubs logo.

Tom smiled and laughed. "Seriously? You think Cubs' fans are intimidating?" Were the ghosts losing their hold on his mind? Was his subconscious telling him not to fear the ghosts? He could figure it out later.

Tom rushed towards the door, expecting to pass through the illusion. Instead, one of them hit Tom's nose with a hard punch. The blow knocked Tom backwards. He barely maintained his balance before the man followed up with a right hook punch to his head. The impact knocked his head sideways.

This is either one hell of an illusion, or I'm about to get into a real fight.

Tom staggered backwards but managed to regain his footing. He raised his hands, hoping he could protect his head. The second man, who had flanked Tom, connected with a liver shot. Tom exhaled from the shock as the radiating pain stunned him. His legs gave out on him, and he crumpled to the hard floor. The second man kicked Tom's head. Tom raised his right arm to protect his head, only for the second man to grab his arm and apply a wristlock. The first man gloated as Tom screamed.

The second man spoke, but instead of one voice, it was several voices speaking in unison. "This is what they're doing to you. What he did to us." Tom tried to pull his arm away, but the second man applied pressure on his wrist. Tom screamed as pain overwhelmed his nerves.

"Ask him to stop," said the first man.

"Please!" Tom pleaded.

The man applied more pressure. Tom slapped the ground with his other hand, like a fighter trying to tap out. The second man tightened his hold.

The first man spoke, also sounding like a chorus. "You can't reason with them. We know that. They'll steal everything from you, then throw you away."

"Who are you?" Tom asked, wincing from the pain.

The second man stomped on Tom's crotch. Tom gasped as another wave of pain overwhelmed him.

The second man said, "We are your tormentors and your soldiers. You can fuel our rage."

The first man kneeled next to Tom's head. "Or we can be the instrument of your rage. The choice is yours."

The first man's eyes stopped glowing. "What the fuck?" he yelled, this time sounding like a normal human.

The sound of the backdoor opening silenced the men. The parking lot's lights illuminated the backroom, followed by the sound of a small object hitting the floor.

"What was that?" asked the second man, sounding like a normal human as well.

The sound of another fallen object came from the back. Both men stood. Tom, with some effort, rolled over so he could look at the doorway to the back room. Something momentarily cast a shadow as it moved past the light. Several crashing sounds followed. The first man cautiously approached.

On the other side of the doorway to the backroom, APK jumped onto a supply shelf and into view. The men stared with their jaws agape as she approached a stack of sticky notes, one of the few things left on the rack. She sat down on her hind legs next to the stack and stared back at the men. The men looked at each other, as if unsure how to react.

"Mow," said APK, as if she were giving an order. Without looking down, she knocked over the stack of notes. After they landed on the floor, she gave them a slow blink, then resumed her critical gaze.

The second man started laughing until the front door opened.

A woman, obscured by the low light, adjusted the doorstop to prop open the door. She was wearing a dark shirt and a baseball cap. The men looked at each other as the woman finished securing the door.

"Shane," said Juanita. She placed her hands on her hips. "Did you pick another fight?" She shook her head. "At this rate, you'll be lucky if you end up in a wheelchair." Juanita walked into the newsroom. Now in the dim light, Tom saw her hair was tucked into a generic black baseball cap with no markings. Her black leather purse was scratched and frayed in parts. She approached Tom and the men.

Tom tried to speak, but the pain overwhelmed him.

She stopped as she looked past Tom and the men. "You found Mungo!" She smiled at the men. "I'm so sorry. Shane must have thought you were going to hurt sweet little Mungo Jerry. I'm so sorry about this. It's just a simple misunderstanding. I have to remind Shane—"

"That's your fucking cat?" the first man interrupted. He started to approach Juanita.

She showed her palms as stepped back. "Yes, and he's just a cat."

The second guy chuckled. "A really funny girl."

Tom braced himself for the pain. "Run." It was all he could say before the sharp pain overwhelmed him.

As the second man laughed at Tom, APK jumped off the shelf and scurried behind the ruins of a cubicle.

"Don't run," said the first man. "We're not done. I still need to know more about your cat."

Juanita smiled. "Let me guess. You must be Huey. Your friend must be Louie. Where's Dewey?"

Louie replied, "She thinks she's funny."

Huey snarled. "If I were you, I'd stop joking." He approached Juanita. "And start talking."

"Or?" she said as she backed into the remains of the counter.

"Or you'll regret it," he replied, as he was almost upon her. "But if you cooperate—"

She glanced at Tom, then focused on the man approaching her. "I'm sorry, Huey and Louie. I'm not that kind of girl. Let Dewey know as well."

"I'm not that kind of guy." He reached for her neck with both hands. "But you'll wish I were."

She knocked his arms aside with her left arm, then followed with a palm heel strike to his nose. Tom winced when Huey's nose broke. Blood flowed from his nostrils. As he raised his hands to cover his wounded nose, Juanita lowered her head and charged into his abdomen. The man staggered from the impact. As he tried to regain his balance, Juanita hooked her arms behind his knees. She raised her back and pulled her arms up. The man fell back, hitting the back of his head against the floor. His sunglasses bounced off his face. When he reached for them, Juanita shifted her arms to lock both his raised ankles. Before Huey could raise his head off the floor, she landed a kick against his groin.

"Settle down, Huey."

Louie charged at Juanita. She pulled a baton from her purse and extended it. As the second man stumbled to a stop, she struck his leading arm. He screamed before Juanita followed with a strike to his face. The impact shattered his sunglasses. He covered his eyes as he crumpled to the floor.

Huey staggered to his feet only for APK to pounce at him. Her claws pierced his skin, allowing her to cling to his back. Louie screamed and tried to reach for APK. Juanita struck one of his elbows, followed by a strike to his knee. APK leaped off the man, and Juanita followed with a baton blow to his head. The blow sent him crashing to the floor.

Louie removed what was left of his sunglasses and tried to brush away the lens shards near his eye. APK jumped up onto the remains of the counter and looked down at him. Juanita approached, baton ready to strike.

"Mow," said APK, sounding proud of herself.

Louie pushed himself up and fled to the backroom, followed moments later by the sound of the back door closing.

Juanita retracted her baton as she approached Huey, who had just gotten back to his feet. She put the baton in her purse and pulled out a canister.

Huey lifted a hand and looked away from Juanita. "No. Please."

"Let me guess. Glow Eyes? Children of Orpheus? Skin Puppets?" She shook the canister. "Something like that?"

"Your mama."

She aimed her canister. He glanced at her and then looked away. He closed his eyes tight. "Go ahead. They'll kill me and feed me to that thing."

"What thing?" Juanita asked.

"I don't know." Huey trembled as he smiled. "I've felt nothing like it. It feels... beautiful." His voice trailed off.

Juanita watched him for a few moments before lowering her canister. "Tell your fellow flesh puppets this town is now orange. Got it?"

"You think it will care? You'll burn just like the rest of this village."

Juanita rolled her eyes. "Until then, Bolingbrook is orange. Got it?"

Huey nodded quickly, then limped towards the backroom. Juanita waited until she heard him leave through the back door.

Tom struggled to stand as Juanita turned her attention to him.

"Wait," she ordered Tom. "Moving will only make it worse."

Tom moved to a sitting position on the floor. APK jumped down from the counter and looked at him. "Mow?"

Juanita pulled out a first-aid kit from her purse and kneeled next to Tom.

"We need to talk."

18

TOM WINCED AS JUANITA placed a cold pack on the side of his face. "That's cold!"

"Hold it in place," said Juanita.

Tom reluctantly grabbed the ice pack. His palm didn't feel as cold, and the throbbing pain in his face subsided.

"See?" asked Juanita. "I knew you could do it." She smiled.

They were sitting in the back of Juanita's minivan, which was parked at the Meijer store across the street from the Promenade outdoor mall. A blackout curtain separated the passenger section from the front. Smaller curtains covered the rest of the van's tinted windows. Lockers and toolboxes were secured to the sides of the van. The cargo area had backpacks and hard meticulously arranged for easy access from the back door.

Tom sat in the back row of passenger seats with a pull-out table in front of him. An open military medical bag, decorated in urban camouflage, rested on the table. Juanita sat on the other side in a single pull-up seat. APK slept in her hard plastic carrier lined with soft blankets and a flannel shirt. Shiny cat toy balls lay next to her belly.

"How's your nose?" Juanita asked as she looked intently at Tom's face.

Tom removed his nasal swabs and cautiously breathed through his nose. "I think it stopped."

Juanita leaned toward Tom. "I think it did." She handed a wet wipe to him. "Keep using the cold press. It'll keep the swelling down. Trust me."

Tom nodded as he wiped the dry blood off nose and mouth.

"So, their eyes were glowing before APK arrived?"

"Yeah," Tom replied. "But not like a weredeer's eyes. I don't know what they were."

"They're spirit junkies," Juanita casually replied.

"Huh?"

"People addicted to being possessed by ghosts and spirits." She closed her medical bag. "You've never heard of them?"

"No." Tom dropped the wipes into a medical waste container Juanita had placed beside him. He looked at the van in amazement. "How do you know about them?"

Juanita flashed a sly smile at Tom. "It's my job."

Tom did a double take. "Your... job."

She nodded. "Correct."

There were times when Tom wondered if Juanita knew the truth, but he never imagined Juanita fighting, and defeating, monsters.

"So, CASS is really a monster-hunting society?"

Juanita chuckled as she shook her head. "No. Most members are skeptics, like your dad. Their donations support our work."

"And CASS's projects? They're—"

"Legitimate. You'd be surprised how much money rich people will donate to us to call themselves critical thinkers." She chuckled. "They don't ask questions."

"Who's 'us?'"

"I can't tell you."

Tom sighed in frustration, then remembered Juanita telling the addict Bolingbrook was "Orange." When realized its significance, he gasped. "You work for the Orange Squad!"

Juanita gave Tom a bemused smile. "Sure. We can call it that."

Tom pulled his head back. "What's that supposed to mean?"

"It means we'll call it the Orange Squad."

"Okay." He thought for a few moments. "So, the Chicago Police's paranormal division isn't called the Orange Squad?"

Juanita frowned. "I don't work for the police department." She calmed herself. "It's very complicated, Tom."

"These things usually are convoluted."

She chuckled. "From your perspective, it might seem that way. Everything seems very centralized here."

Tom nodded. "Almost everything here revolves around Robert."

"Robert?"

"Mayor Robert Clark and his political machine. Just like Chicago's political machine."

She smiled with amusement. "Our machine isn't what it used to be, and I don't work for it." She paused for a few beats. "The Chicago PD's paranormal division and the Cook County paranormal task force are only part of what we'll call the Orange Squad. It's a gestalt of private individuals, covert organizations, and law enforcement working to protect the public from paranormal threats. Because of its decentralized nature, the Orange Squad is resistant to being co-opted by political machines or corrupted by supernatural entities."

"And CASS funds it?"

"CASS is one of many sources of funding."

"How long has this been going on?"

Juanita shook her head. "A very long time."

"Can you be more—"

"No."

Tom blinked at her abrupt answer. "Can you tell your role in the Orange Squad? Off the record?"

"I thought *Babbler* reporters never asked questions off the record."

"We're not supposed to," Tom admitted, then lowered his eyes. "But I'm willing to waive the rules in this case."

Juanita sat down on one of the lockers. After looking over Tom, she replied, "Let's just say I'm with the group that defends the communities the Chicago PD won't."

"Won't?"

Juanita nodded. "We're often the only ones defending them against aspiring vampire overlords, dangerous ghosts, or alien kidnappers." She looked around the van. "I wish we could do more to help them, but as long as they face paranormal threats, that's where we have to focus our resources."

"Which must be considerable."

She shrugged. "It depends. I'm sure the funding for Bolingbrook's departments dwarfs ours." She stood up. "But they don't seem to show up when you need them."

"Usually they do a better job," Tom replied, still holding the cold compress to his nose.

"It's a good thing I arrived when I did," said Juanita. "I wasn't sure if you were going to break in last night or tonight. My guess was you'd want to get some sleep before your caper."

"Some caper it turned out to be," Tom replied. "My desk was empty."

"I think one of your co-workers cleaned it out today." Juanita thought for a moment. "Older man. Doesn't believe in ironing his clothes."

"Don," Tom sighed. "Don took everything."

"And you can't ask him to give it back?"

Tom looked up at Juanita. "Me?"

"Yes. Why were you trying to sneak into your own newsroom?"

Juanita's question startled Tom.

Juanita continued. "'Trying' being the operative word. I watched you the entire time."

Tom felt his cheeks flush. "I needed a few things," he said, in hopes his partial answer would satisfy Juanita.

"Really? Then why didn't you ask Don to get them? He was removing boxes and giant scrapbooks this afternoon."

Tom sighed. Just his luck that Don would clear out the office before he arrived.

"Well?" asked Juanita.

Tom looked back at Juanita. When he attended the CASS lunch and learn meetings, she always greeted him with her warm smile. Before delivering his own speech debunking Clow UFO Base, she helped him overcome his stage fright. Now he knew Clow UFO Base was real, and CASS was part of a shadow network. Yet, looking at her now, Tom couldn't help but feel that, despite the years apart, she was still that same caring person. Maybe, he thought, he could trust her. This time, he told himself, he should open up to her. Just a little bit.

Tom said, "Don is the only one allowed to stay in Bolingbrook. He's supposed to write up what happened, but I'm afraid he's missing the real story."

"Which is?"

Tom threw up his hands in frustration. "I don't know. Roul was trying to tell me something, but it didn't make any sense. I didn't get the message to el angel, and I probably would have garbled it anyway. Legion might be a legion of ghosts or demons. The answers might be in the library, but do you know how many books Fountaindale has? Hell, it could be the small library, but I don't know what he was talking about." Tom rested his head on his hands. "This morning, I thought I could crack this. Now I don't know." He closed his eyes and sighed in frustration.

A few moments later, Juanita said, "She got the message."

Tom lifted his head. "She did? How? Did you tell her?"

"Tom." She paused. "I think we should investigate."

"We?"

She stood up and approached him. "Yes. I'm here on what you could call a diplomatic trip. Officially, I can't conduct investigations or engage paranormal entities without the DPA's permission. Right now, the department isn't interested in cooperating with... us."

"Why?"

"It's complicated." Juanita sat down on the locker in front of Tom. "Still, I am concerned about the *Phantom Press's* brazen attacks against mortals, as you are. I, too, would like to know what Roul meant when he said 'legion.' So, I think we should work together."

Tom's eyes lit up with excitement. "Yes," he blurted out. He cleared his throat. "I mean, I would like to, but how would it work?"

Juanita gave Tom a warm smile. "If you act as my guide in Bolingbrook, I'll let you write up the results of our investigation."

"Great," said Tom. Thinking about working with Juanita filled him with euphoria. And if it went well, maybe—

"After I screen your story."

Tom mentally stumbled. "Screen it?"

"For our protection. We have a saying in the Orange Squad: 'Secrets keep us safe.'"

Tom's jaw dropped. "Really? Because secrets can also get people killed or hide corruption, or—"

"Would you print the names and addresses of all the DPA agents? Would you tell the vampires how we monitor them?"

"You know I wouldn't do that."

"But other reporters would if it would benefit them."

"I'm not like that," Tom protested. "You know I value the truth. I've always felt that way, even before I joined the *Babbler*. I've seen what happens when people hide behind secrets. They become unaccountable and corrupt. Just look at the Habenstein Society. They're making decisions that affect humanity's standing in the galaxy, but they're unaccountable to humanity."

"Mow?" said APK. She yawned, showing all her sharp white teeth.

"Tom," said Juanita, "how about this? In the unlikely event we uncover corruption of any kind, I won't screen it out. I will only screen for information that will needlessly endanger lives and compromise sensitive operations."

"'Sensitive' meaning?"

Juanita frowned. "If you believe Bolingbrook is in danger, should we really be arguing over semantics? I'm trusting you, Tom. Do you trust me?"

Tom thought about the question for several moments. "Yes," he finally said.

Juanita casually leaned back. Her approving smile was just like the one she gave him many years ago after her prep talk to him. "Good. Now, I need a place to stay."

"You can stay at my place," Tom heard himself say. An awkward silence filled the van. Terror washed over Tom. Why did he have to blurt that out?

"Mow?" APK seemed to ask.

"Um," Tom said, stalling for time. "Obviously, you could sleep on my couch." He closed his eyes and tilted his head up. Almost as if he were trying to look at his brain for an answer. "I just think it would be easier to stay at my place than to find a motel that takes cats." He looked down at APK. "No offense."

"Mow," said APK, sounding like she objected.

"Sure, we'd have to go shopping, but we're already in the Meijer parking lot, and I don't know if we'll have to wait. It's still dark. It's just that I threw out anything that could spoil. I mean, if you don't feel comfortable." Tom's voice trailed off.

"Tom," Juanita replied. "I don't have to sleep on the couch."

Tom's heart raced. Was she about to propose what he'd dreamed about for years?

She continued. "I have a tent and a sleeping bag. I can set it up in your living room. If you don't mind."

"No!" Tom replied, almost in excitement.

Juanita chuckled. "Good. Now let's go shopping."

"But it's still dark outside. Is it safe?"

"It will be," Juanita replied. "As long as you stay close to us." She picked up a front pet carrier pouch. "Ready to be a service cat?"

"Mow!" APK replied, sounding like she approved.

19

TOM WOKE UP TO the sound of Juanita's voice and the smell of canned tuna. Something warm. Tom opened his eyes. APK, sitting in a cat-loaf position, stared at Tom.

"Well," said Tom. "Hello there."

APK stretched her neck closer to Tom's face. "Mow," she said impatiently.

Tom glanced at his clock. It was almost 8 AM. He moaned, wishing he could resume his sleep schedule from when he was a blogger.

"Mow," APK said, as if she was protesting Tom's attitude.

"You're going to have to get off me first."

To Tom's surprise, APK stood up. After a long stretch, she moved off Tom. Tom counted to five, then raised his upper body. His blanket drooped to reveal his Reese Habenstein t-shirt. APK started purring.

"You like it?"

APK turned away from Tom, and lifted her tail, exposing her butt.

Tom chuckled. APK increased her purring.

Outside his room, he heard Juanita say, "We're always happy to assist. But I have some questions."

Juanita walked away, and Tom couldn't make out what she was saying. With some effort, he fought off his drowsiness enough to get out of bed and stand up.

"Does she always get up this early?" Tom whispered.

APK jumped off the bed and started walking towards the partially open door to the hallway.

"I guess I don't need to know," Tom said to himself.

He tossed off his t-shirt, then approached his closet. *Do I want to dress to impress Juanita?* he asked himself as he skimmed his polo shirts. *Maybe a dress shirt,* he thought as he looked at two shirts still draped in plastic from the dry cleaners. *Perhaps one of the more casual shirts would put her at ease.* In his fantasies about Juanita, it didn't matter what he wore, if he wore anything. But this was real life, he reminded himself. He had to be presentable and professional, especially if he wanted to help his friends recover.

The sound of his bedroom door closing interrupted his thoughts. Did Juanita just enter? Her barely audible voice outside the room answered his question. Tom turned in time to see APK land on his bed. She sat down on Tom's discarded Reese Habenstein t-shirt and started kneading. He could hear her soothing purr.

"He was a great man."

"Mow!"

"Tom?" said Juanita from the other side of the door.

"Yes?"

"What's the best restaurant in downtown Bolingbrook?"

Tom couldn't stop himself from giggling.

"What?"

"Bolingbrook doesn't have a downtown."

"What?" Juanita asked, her voice revealing her disbelief.

Tom narrowed his options to the polo shirts. "Robert doesn't like downtowns. So, Bolingbrook doesn't have one."

"Robert?"

"The mayor. Everyone calls him Robert." Tom smiled as he felt useful.

After a few moments of silence, Juanita asked, "Where do people normally gather in Bolingbrook?"

"The Promenade," Tom replied as he shrugged. "That's the outdoor mall down the road near the Veterans Memorial Tollway."

"That place across the street from Meijer?"

"Yes," said Tom, feeling like a tour guide. "If you ignore the surrounding parking lot, it looks like a downtown."

Juanita said, "Just a minute," as if she was talking to someone else. Tom heard her move closer to the door. "Does it have a food court?"

Tom bristled at the thought of a food court inside the Promenade. "No, but there are places to sit outside. If we're lucky, we might be able to sit on one of the couches or loveseats."

"Okay... What do you recommend for takeout?"

Tom thought for a moment. "If you like burgers, Home Team Grill—"

"Perfect." Tom heard Juanita's footsteps as she walked away. "We'll meet at the Promenade," she said over the phone. "Yes, someone will be with me, and I suspect more than one person will be with you."

Tom picked a polo shirt and started getting dressed. As he sat down on the bed to finish, his phone buzzed. It was a text from Wendy's brother.

Wendy is still out, but stable. If she doesn't wake up soon, she might never wake up again. Staff are treating her like a rock star. Even respecting her pronouns. Not used to her getting this kind of treatment.

Glad they're treating her well. Wish I could do more.

Find out what happened. Wendy trusts you and doesn't trust Don.

Tom set his phone down on the bed and then tied his shoes. When he finished, he saw APK pawing at his phone's screen.

"Not a toy." Tom pulled the phone away. He expected her to hiss or climb onto him. Instead, she blinked her eyes slowly at Tom. Tom blinked back at her. He remembered reading that a slow blink was a good sign a cat trusted someone. It was also polite to return a cat's blink.

"Have you had breakfast?"

"Mow."

Tom tilted his head. "Okay."

Maybe that was a yes.

Tom made his way to his living room. Juanita's green tent sat in the center of the room. His coffee table was now APK's feeding station. Her food and water bowls rested on a plastic mat. Two pink traveling litter boxes sat in opposite corners of the room. They smelled of fresh kitty litter.

Juanita sat on the couch, reading a copy of the latest *Phantom Press* issue. She wore a white blouse and black slacks. Judging by her finished hair and her makeup, Tom guessed she'd woken up hours earlier.

"They really don't like...Robert," she said, still reading.

"Or me," Tom added.

"It seems like it." She put the issue into a folder, then set it aside. "But didn't you tell me they wanted you to join them?"

Tom nodded. "Yeah. At least some of them did. Rene's daughter told me she wanted to go home."

"Rene?"

Tom told Juanita who Rene was and recounted his visit with her.

"She's one of the last techno-shamans," said Juanita. "You should introduce me to her."

Tom's mood brightened. "She wants to resume our interview, and you can join me."

"Thank you." Juanita focused on the current issue of the *Phantom Press*. "Did they always drop their issues from the air?"

Tom shook his head. "No. They never dropped them from the sky. They would appear inside Old Chicago, and, I think, in some abandoned newspaper boxes."

"Old Chicago?"

"Old Chicago Mall. It was the first indoor mall with an amusement park."

"I think I read about this. Demolished in the 80s?"

Tom nodded. "Yep. The village harnessed the energy from the implosion to power an EMP device."

Juanita nodded. "That should have sterilized the site. Anything else you can tell me?"

Tom thought for a moment. "Oh, yeah. Roul thought the layout of the new issue looked too modern. I think he was right. If you look at the old issues, the text had a ragged right alignment, but the text in the new issue is justified."

"Very observant," Juanita replied. "Which suggests the *Phantom Press* didn't publish this."

"Roul and Wendy suspected that, too." Tom walked over to the couch. "Maybe a spirit junkie designed it—"

Juanita shook her head. Tom stopped talking. "What?"

"Requires too much focus." She looked up at Tom. "The ghost controls their bodies. The addict can only feel the high. A junkie didn't design this.

Tom looked down at the issue. "Then who published it?"

"I don't' know." Juanita stood up. "Which is why we shouldn't be late for our meeting."

Tom blinked. "What meeting?"

"Our meeting with Steve. And his friends."

***

Juanita and Tom sat at one of the four picnic tables along The Row, a "street" within the Promenade's outdoor mall. Tom wiped his mouth with a napkin after taking a small bite of his burger. Though they weren't on a date, Tom wanted to make a better impression of himself. Getting beaten up last night wasn't a good start.

Juanita set down what remained of her chicken sandwich and gently patted her mouth with a napkin. "So, Tom, what's the story behind these things?" She motioned towards one of the rectangular pillars along the Row.

"Story?" Tom asked.

"What are they for? It looks like it was built to cover the street, but there's no ceiling. Just randomly placed red rectangles attach to cables. Does it have a hidden purpose?"

Tom looked up at the rectangular arches that covered half of The Row. "I guess it's supposed to be a work of modern art. No one's ever told me if it has an ulterior purpose."

As he returned to his burger, he noticed a man in a dark suit facing his direction. He didn't have the bland facial features of a man in blue, and he was wearing a white shirt instead of a blue shirt. Another man, wearing a different style of suit, pretended to be window shopping. Both seemed out of place among the shoppers wearing colorful summer clothes.

"Don't stare," said Juanita as she ate her fries.

Tom examined the remains of his burger. "There're two men in suits watching us."

Juanita focused on her fries. "So they can distract us from the four plainly-clothed operatives watching us."

Tom fought the urge to look for them. "You noticed them?"

"Of course." She wiped her lips with her napkin. "We use the same methods before a meeting." Juanita looked up at Tom. "It's more fun to be a cloak than a tuxedo." She smiled.

Tom smiled back, hoping he didn't look too excited. "I get it. It's kind of like how the men in blue distract people from noticing the girls in green."

"Obviously an effective tactic," she said as she picked at her fries.

"How so?"

"I've never heard of the girls in green."

Tom started to explain, but Juanita interrupted.

"Finish your meal. Steve is on his way."

"Are you sure it's okay for me to be here?" Tom asked as started to feel butterflies in his stomach. "I'm not supposed to be in Bolingbrook. If they tell—"

"Just let me do the talking," Juanita whispered. "You'll be fine."

Tom flashed back to when he was going to give a presentation for a Lunch and Learn. He remembered having severe stage fright minutes before starting. When she told him, "You'll be fine," the fear melted away. Just like his anxiety was melting right now. He quickly finished the remnants of burger and gulped his clear soda.

The sound of three sets of footsteps approaching caught Tom's attention. He didn't need to look back to know it was the sound of Steve and two operatives approaching.

"Welcome to Bolingbrook," Steve said, standing uncomfortably close behind Tom.

"Thank you," Juanita replied politely.

"Have you seen the Counselor lately?"

"Unfortunately," she said with a sigh. "But we have better things to go over."

"We do," Steve replied. "I take it your investigators were satisfied with our report?"

"They were." Juanita removed an envelope from her waist pouch. "This is what we can share with you."

One of Steve's escorts accepted the envelope, then stepped behind Tom. Tom sensed Steve shifting closer to him. Instead of looking back, he looked down at the table.

"Personally," said Juanita, "I don't think they're involved."

"Why?"

"I saw the photos. It's not their craft."

Steve stepped into Tom's sight. Looking at the sweat on Steve's brow, Tom wondered why he was so overdressed for a summer day.

"Who do you suspect?" he asked Juanita.

"Rank amateurs." Juanita smiled. "Who have an unhealthy hatred of the White Sox."

Steve took a deep breath, then faced Tom. "You're unusually quiet." He turned back towards Juanita. "He's usually pestering me with his questions. One of the worst ones, if you ask me."

Tom gave Steve an angry glance, then turned to Juanita.

"He's being observant," said Juanita. "Because he's doing a ride-along with me."

Steve looked down at Tom with a shocked expression. "A ride-along? With him?" Tom nodded and grinned.

Steve flashed a smile. "I'm impressed. But a little word of advice, Tom. Don't annoy the Orange Squad. They're not as tolerant as we are."

Tom stopped grinning and glanced over at Juanita.

Juanita cleared her throat. "While I'm in town, perhaps I could question your prisoner."

"Roul?"

Juanita nodded. "Yes. Roul. We would like to know how a homeless man came into possession of several spheres."

"I'm afraid that's not possible right now."

Juanita gave him a puzzled look. "Why?"

Steve stepped closer to Juanita. "I don't think he could survive your techniques." He looked down at Tom. "And you think we're harsh."

"You're mistaken," Juanita said, sounding defensive. Her calm demeanor slipped for a moment as her eyes widened, and she leaned back. Then she regained her composure. "Unlike some of my colleagues, I find that showing a bit of empathy is more productive than inflicting temporary discomfort."

Steve focused on Juanita for a few moments, then smiled. "I suspect most of your associates would disagree, but we can discuss that another time. Right now, Roul is in protective isolation."

"Protective isolation?"

Steve nodded. "The term used in Chicago is spiritual quarantine, I believe." He addressed Tom. "We isolate people we suspect are possessed or under otherworldly influence."

"Is he?" asked Juanita.

Steve shrugged. "Unlikely, but I'm keeping him there for his own safety. Especially after the temporary discomfort he received from Robert."

Steve causally referring to torture as "temporary discomfort" disgusted Tom.

Steve continued, "Not to mention that I don't want to find out Roul hanged himself after breaking both legs and his own back." He looked down at Tom. "That happened to a wereskunk once. Took us hours to remove the stink."

Tom's stomach started to turn. He wasn't sure if it was the mental image of DPA officials staging a prison suicide or imagining the stench from a giant half-human, half-skunk creature.

Juanita said, "Then he might be receptive to speaking with me."

"Yes." Steve paused. "But I don't think he's ready to say anything useful right now. I've found that prolonged isolation has a way of loosening lips." He looked at Tom. "Not literally."

Juanita shifted her body on the table bench for a moment. "When he is ready, please let me know."

"Will reach out to you." Steve casually walked towards Tom. "How long are you going to be in Bolingbrook?"

"Not long." Juanita faced Tom. "But I would like to see the investigation scenes before I leave."

Steve lifted his arm to look at his metallic analog watch. "I'm afraid I have other commitments." He then flashed a bemused smile at Tom. "But I think Tom can escort you to the scenes. He should know where they are."

"I do," Tom said. Realizing that he had promised Juanita he would stay silent, he averted his eyes from her.

"Good." Steve extended his hand to Juanita. "It was nice meeting you."

Juanita gently shook his hand. "Likewise."

"And tell your associates we appreciate their assistance." Steve walked past Tom. "Don't go easy on him."

Juanita remained silent as Steve and the other agents walked away.

"Tom?" she asked.

Tom hesitantly faced Juanita.

She stood up. "Where should we start?"

20

As Juanita turned into the Town Center parking lot, Tom noticed the village had finished repairing the bay windows. Juanita pointed towards the black Mustang parked in the fire lane by the entrance. "Is that car parked in the fire lane?"

Tom chuckled. "I guess Robert got a new car."

Juanita made a face. "That's a brazen display of power, even for Illinois."

Tom shrugged. "Well, he thinks he's Bolingbrook, so he can do whatever he wants."

He looked back at the repaired window and thought about Wendy, Jenna, and the other incapacitated staffers. Town Center may have recovered from the *Phantom Press*'s attack, but the *Babbler* still had scars.

Juanita pulled into an open parking spot. "Where was his car parked that night?"

"In his reserved spot," Tom replied. "I'll show you where it is"

After leaving the van, Tom guided Juanita to Robert's official parking spot.

"Did you notice anything unusual before the meeting?" asked Juanita.

Tom shook his head. "No. Just seemed like an ordinary meeting night."

She scanned the area. "How many were in the audience?"

"Several families at first. They left after the festivities. Then it was the usual small crowd."

Juanita nodded. "Now it's your turn."

Tom gave Juanita a puzzled look. "My turn?"

She nodded. "Officially, this is a ride-along. You're supposed to ask questions."

"And you'll answer them?"

"Depends on the question."

Tom hesitated. He knew the question he should ask. What would he ask if he were talking to someone like Steve? But he was talking to Juanita, not a covert bureaucrat or hardened monster hunter.

Juanita stepped in front of Tom and smiled. The same smile that brought back warm memories. She said, "The worst that will happen is I won't answer." She stepped back, as if to give Tom more personal space. "Try it."

Tom fidgeted as he worked up the courage to ask the question. "What did you mean when you mentioned 'temporary discomfort?'" Tom trembled. "Is that a euphemism for 'torture?'"

Juanita remained silent. Tom wondered if she was thinking about her response or trying to hold back her anger. She took an audible breath and replied, "When in public, it's not wise to use words like 'torture.'"

Tom quickly looked around and saw no one near them. "But do you—have you—"

"Have I? Yes, in the past. Do I now? No. It's ineffective. You used to be a skeptic, so you should know that already."

"What about your colleagues? Do they—"

Juanita raised her right hand, and Tom stopped talking.

She said, "Most people would do anything to protect their families. My colleagues regard humanity as their family. If protecting humanity means extracting a vampire's fangs or waterboarding an occultist, they won't hesitate." Juanita paused. "I was like that. Until someone reminded me that when you hunt monsters, you need to guard against becoming a monster." She moved closer to Tom. "I have no problem killing vampires, banishing ghosts, or burning an infected. But I will not become a monster. Torture is for monsters, Tom."

Tom stared at Juanita, unsure how to respond. Juanita smiled. "Good questions," she said.

Tom nodded, feeling slightly uneasy. "Thank you?"

Juanita resumed walking. "Now let's get back to our investigation."

Tom and Juanita reached Robert's empty spot. A white sign with red text read, "Reserved for the Mayor." The spot next to it was reserved for the Assistant Director of Public Services. Steve's black heavy-duty pickup truck seemed to tower over them.

Juanita stepped inside the empty spot and stamped her right foot three times. She took a few measured steps and stamped her foot again. Tom watched as she seemed to be focused on the unremarkable pavement beneath them.

"Looking for a secret car elevator or something like that?" Tom chuckled nervously.

"Something like that," she replied, still examining the pavement.

Tom tried to see any small seams that could be evidence of a hidden elevator or some kind of platform, but he saw nothing unusual.

"The Village resurfaced the lot last year," Tom said. "Do you think someone installed something then?"

"Someone could have," said Juanita, still focusing on the pavement. She examined a few more inches of the spot. "But no one did." She removed a small red rubber ball from her pack and dropped it. The ball hit the pavement and bounced up. She snatched it before it could drop again. "This is good news."

"How? Gravity still works?"

Juanita smirked. "We're not dealing with a fae."

Tom moved his head back. "Fae? Why would that be bad?"

"Good question."

Tom waited for Juanita's answer. Instead, she put the ball back in the pouch, then looked up and past him.

Tom noticed the closest door opening. Robert, wearing a brown sports coat and tan slacks, exited and approached them. After walking a few yards, he said, "You must be Juanita, the president of the Chicago Anti-Superstition Society."

Juanita approached. "You must be Robert," she replied. "And don't call you Mayor Clark. Right?"

Robert smirked. "You can call me Robert." He firmly shook Juanita's hand. He looked at Tom and then faced Juanita. "Be careful around Tom." The two men locked eyes. "He asks too many questions."

"And Robert gives too few answers," Tom added.

Robert shot a piercing glare at Tom. For a long time, that glare intimidated Tom, especially when he started struggling as a reporter. This time, he felt the urge to giggle and wondered if being with Juanita was restoring his confidence. Tom pressed his luck. "It's true."

Robert relaxed and briefly chuckled. "I give you what you need, Tom. Not what you want."

"What do I need?"

Robert turned his attention towards Juanita. "Find anything?"

Juanita shook her head. "Not yet."

"The DPA already swept this spot. I doubt you'll find anything that Steve doesn't already know."

"Doesn't hurt to look. So, Tom says your car was parked here that night. Is he right?"

"My old car was," Robert replied with a hint of rage.

Juanita crossed the parking spot and faced the window. "I've dealt with poltergeists, but I've never encountered one strong enough to toss an entire car that far."

"Maybe they all pooled their powers?" Robert shrugged. "I'm more familiar with aliens. Steve's the monster specialist. That's why I put him in charge of the DPA. He's the only person I trust with the DPA."

Juanita faced Robert. "Trust is a precious commodity."

"He's earned it."

Juanita examined the parking spot for a moment. "I heard about the loss of four of your DPA officers. My condolences."

"Thank you." He sighed. "They were good men. Always willing to make the final sacrifice." He looked back at Juanita. "Just wish it hadn't been to a third-rate necromancer's booby trap."

Juanita moved her head back for a moment "The homeless man?"

"He wasn't homeless," Robert replied. "He was a protester. I didn't want to get trapped in an ACLU lawsuit, so I put up with him. He seemed harmless." Robert shook his head. "But he's in custody now. I'd let you talk to him, but he's still under quarantine. Which is fortunate for him, if you ask me."

Juanita tilted her head. "Has he said anything?"

"You'd have to ask Steve. He suspects that Roul had help. Hopefully, the information you provided will help us track them down and put a stop to their spiritual terrorism." He faced Tom. "Then, your friends should wake up."

"I hope so," Tom said.

Juanita glanced back at the window. "You might want to consider expanding your suspect pool. Flesh hosts tend to be low-level necromancers. It's highly unlikely they could be behind the *Phantom Press's* manifestations."

"You'll have to talk to Steve about that. He seems to think they are."

"We talked earlier. He knows how I feel."

Robert lifted a finger. "Oh, while you're here, have you had a chance to review my offer to CASS?"

"Yes." She paused. "It's very...generous."

"But still less than what the Habenstein Society is charging." His face tensed. "Their rates are going up, while the quality of their debunking is going down. Let me tell you a story. We needed to cover up a Klexd sighting. The crew misunderstood traffic control and turned on their landing lights too soon."

Tom fought the urge to chuckle while Juanita nodded.

Robert continued. "The Habenstein Society wanted to sell a swamp gas cover-up." He grumbled and then looked at Tom. "How many swamps do we have in Bolingbrook?"

"None," Tom replied.

"It's weird when we agree." He pivoted to Juanita. "None. That cover story would have raised more questions. Now, I know you guys would have come up with a better cover story."

"Thank you, but Chicago's shadow communities keep us occupied as is."

"Which is why I'm making a generous offer."

"Which the board will address." She stepped closer to Robert. "However, it might be perceived as siding with the

NWO and, as you know, we prefer to remain neutral when dealing with major societies."

Robert scratched his chin. "I'll see what I can do to improve my offer."

"I would appreciate that," Juanita replied with a smile.

Robert glanced at his watch. "I've got business to attend to." He offered his hand to Juanita. "Pleasure to meet you."

She shook his hand. "Pleasure to meet you, too."

"If you find more evidence, please let Steve know."

"I will."

Robert started to walk away.

"Excuse me," said Tom.

Robert kept walking.

"I have a question. Robert?"

Robert stopped, his back still towards Tom.

You've done this before. You can do it again.

Robert's shoulders dropped, and he turned around. In a curt tone, he replied, "What?"

"When I was watching footage of the demolition of Old Chicago—"

"Get to the point," Robert snapped.

"Who was the person you were arguing with?"

"Arguing?"

Tom blinked in surprise. "Yes. When you were giving your speech, you got into an argument with a heckler. It sounded like both of you knew each other."

"What's your question?"

"Who was he?"

Robert glared at Tom, who shifted in his spot. Why would a heckler from twenty-nine years ago set him off?

Instead of starting a rant, Robert let out a tense sigh. "No one important." He started walking towards Town Center.

"Why did he say he founded Bolingbrook?"

"That's my quote for today, Tom."

***

APK jumped up on Tom's dining table. Tom glanced up from his laptop screen, then resumed reading Sally's email. Juanita set her tablet and scratched APK's side, and the cat purred in response.

Only the bright parking lot lights shone between the partially open blackout curtains. Tom reached into the Nancy's Pizza box for one of the last slices, thankful the driver arrived before sunset. Now he wondered if the *Phantom Press* was floating outside his windows. If so, APK's anti-psychic energy was keeping them at bay like a campfire stopped wild animals from attacking at night. Tom bit into his pizza, hoping the taste would distract him from the possible danger outside.

"Any luck?" Juanita asked.

Tom skimmed Sally the librarian's email that had arrived only five minutes earlier. "According to this list, all the members of the municipal committee are dead." He pivoted his laptop towards Juanita. "I see nothing unusual about their deaths."

Juanita leaned towards the screen. APK took a few steps then sat on her hind legs, inches from the laptop. Juanita moved her arm by APK and started scrolling the screen.

"Any recent deaths?"

"The last member died five years ago."

APK reached for the touchpad, but Tom touched her paw. "Not for kitties."

APK pulled her paw and then stared at Tom's face. Her unblinking gaze made Tom feel unsettled. "Mow," she said as if she objected. She raised her tail and walked towards the laptop.

Tom moved the laptop further back. "I said no."

APK lowered her tail. With a low grumble, she replied, "Mow." *Does APK understand English?* Tom wondered. Almost immediately he dismissed the thought. He'd seen UFOs, weredeer, time travelers. A cat with human intelligence was a bridge too far for Tom.

"APK," Juanita said. She tapped on her left shoulder. APK turned away from Tom and approached Juanita. Gently, she jumped onto her shoulder then draped her body around Juanita's head like a living scarf. Juanita petted her. APK looked at Tom. "Mow," she said as if she was taunting him.

"You think the heckler was one of the committee members?" Juanita asked.

"That's my guess." Tom moved the laptop in front of him.

"The committee chair?"

"He died two years earlier." Tom looked at the screen. "I've narrowed it down to the three members who died after the implosion." He paused to review the list. "But I don't have any recordings of their voices. BCTV's archive only goes back ten years."

"BCTV?"

"Bolingbrook Community Television. It's our public access channel."

"Oh. But if it only goes back ten years, how did you get a video of the implosion?"

"The library has some in its local history collection." Tom switched browser tabs, then shook his head. "None of them feature the founders." A moment later, he raised a finger. "Rene might be able to help. She might have been in the audience."

Tom reached for his phone. "Damn. Why didn't I think of that sooner?"

"But you did think of it," said Juanita, with a sly smile playing on her lips.

Tom paused. He remembered the audience applauded him after finishing his presentation, but Juanita's clapping meant so much more to him.

"Yeah." Tom smiled back. "I did think of it."

He picked up his smartphone and called Rene. His phone connected before it could generate a ringtone.

"Hi Tom," Tom started to speak when the voice continued. "I'm not available right now." He shook his head and blinked. Was he talking to a magical answering machine? Tom hung up and redialed the number. "I'm still not available, Tom. Leave a message, and I'll get back to you."

"Is this a joke?"

"In this case," said the answering machine, "no. Now leave a message, please."

Tom waited for a beep, but there wasn't one. "Hi? This is Tom. I would like to schedule the second part of our interview. Please call me back. Gwyla has my number."

Tom ended the call. "Ever heard of a magical answering machine?"

"Not specifically, but it's certainly possible for a techno-shaman to make one."

"It's just so weird dealing with actual magic."

"They are unsettling." Juanita sipped her water. "If it's any comfort, there are very few shamans and magic practitioners still alive." She reached for her tablet. "I think we should go over what we know so far."

Tom switched to the window with his notes. "Here's what I got. First there was an occult ritual—"

"Alleged occult ritual."

"Alleged. Agreed. An alleged occult ritual involving the burning of White Sox gear. There are runes that seem to be haphazardly drawn."

"Which suggests this was staged."

"True. Or... maybe it was to cover up the real ritual."

"Interesting." Juanita thought for a moment. "Maybe that's the angle the DPA is following."

Tom felt proud that Juanita agreed with his theory. "That's followed by the attack against Town Center and the new issue of the *Phantom Press*."

"Which occurs about twenty-nine years after an EMP attack that should have destroyed them."

"Then Roaming Roul—"

"Roul," Juanita corrected Tom. "He has a name."

Tom momentarily felt fear as he looked at Juanita's disappointed expression. "Sorry. Roul. Roul called me and wanted a meeting the night of the council of psychics' séance. I arrive and the DPA is already raiding the place. He's captured and officers are killed when the spheres activate. Maybe it was a booby trap—"

"No," Juanita snapped. APK jumped off Juanita and ran away.

Tom froze. This was a side of Juanita he'd never seen or imagined.

Juanita paused for a long beat. "We can't discount mishandling spheres."

"No," Tom said. "We can't. It wouldn't be the first time Robert was wrong." He chuckled, but Juanita didn't laugh.

"You told me he spoke about libraries and said 'they' created a 'legion.' Correct?"

"Yes, and he wanted me to find an angel, which led me to you."

"And here we are," Juanita said as she checked her notes. "Now, this is also when the *Phantom Press* started reaching out to you."

Tom shuddered as he remembered his encounters with the *Phantom Press*. "Yes. Their illusions trigger my anger and my fears. Then they hinted I should join them. Join the legion, maybe? So far, the illusions end when Rene's daughter rescues me. She tells me she wants to go home, but someone won't let her go home."

"As in Bolingbrook?"

"That's what I used to think." He stared at his notes. "But technically, she's back in Bolingbrook. Why would she still say she wanted to go home?"

APK's growl interrupted Tom. They turned and saw her tail poking out from between two blackout curtains.

"Something wrong?" Juanita asked APK. The cat lowered her tail and growled again.

"I'll check." Tom stood and approached APK. "Are there ghosts outside?"

APK grumbled.

A faint pounding sound emanated from the floor. Tom wondered if it was a downstairs neighbor hitting their ceiling with a broom or mop handle. Tom stamped on the floor twice. The pounding continued. Someone below shouted, but Tom couldn't make out the words.

Juanita stood. "Is this normal?"

"No," Tom replied, then looked in APK's direction. "Is that normal?"

"Only if she senses something."

Tom stepped up to the window.

"Be careful, Tom." Juanita walked towards her tent.

Tom steeled himself, anticipating the sight of a ghost floating outside his window. He parted the curtain. Below him was the parking lot. The two lampposts at the very back illuminated only part of the lot. Along Boughton Road, the fiftieth anniversary banners fluttered as if they were being blown by a strong breeze.

APK stood on her hind legs and pressed against the glass with her front paws. She growled as she weaved her head back and forth.

Juanita called out, "Come here, APK."

A pounding sound started coming from the left wall. "Get it out!" his neighbor yelled. The wall muffled his voice.

From the right wall, his other neighbor screamed, "But you're dead!"

Tom recognized both voices as his neighbors'. How loudly were they shouting to get through the soundproofing?

The neighbor on the left said, "Please! Get it out."

"All of you are dead," said the other neighbor.

APK ran her front paws against the window, as if she was trying to climb or dig through the glass. Her eyes were wide open as she yowled.

"Get her away from the window," Juanita yelled.

Tom hesitated as he looked down at APK, who was in a near frenzy. He wondered how to pick her up without her tearing him apart.

Tom noticed a new light appear in the parking lot, the same fiery glow he'd seen from the medium junkies. The glow came from a man standing behind a car. He seemed to be looking directly at Tom. As he tried to get a better view of the man, he reached down and grabbed a rifle. A cold dread washed over Tom as he realized the man was aiming at him.

21

"Shit!" yelled Tom. He pulled APK away from the window. APK screamed and squirmed as she tried to escape Tom's hold. As he walked away, part of the window shattered. Tom used his body to shield APK from the shards of glass bursting out from the window frame. He released APK as he dropped to the floor, and APK rushed into the tent.

From behind the couch, Juanita yelled, "Kill the lights!" She knocked over Tom's standing lamp. Tom focused on the main light switch by the entrance. Could the sniper hit him if he tried to shut it off?

The neighbor on the right said, "Tom! They'll stop if you leave the apartment alone. Dear God!"

"They'll give you what really want," said the neighbor on the left. "If you join them, you'll control the fire. Your enemies will become their enemies. They'll—" The neighbor screamed in pain.

Tom crawled towards the light switch. Another shot shattered the screen of his monitor. He heard his bedroom window shatter as a shot rang out.

Tom flashed back to the riot outside the Bolingbrook Golf Club. Then the teargas and warning shots weren't directed at him. This time, someone was shooting at him. He froze. He needed to turn off the light, but it was too dangerous.

The sound of Juanita knocking over his second Ikea lamp startled Tom.

She's trying to save me. I have to help her!

As he resumed crawling, more shots rang out. Plaster fragments rained down on him. Tom looked up at the light switch. He would become an easy target the moment he reached for the switch. But they needed to turn off all the remaining lights. Tom crawled faster until he reached the wall with the light switch. He prepared to reach for it.

"Wait!" Juanita yelled.

A bullet struck near the light switch. Tom pulled his arm back, then dropped to the floor and looked toward Juanita's voice. He heard snapping sounds coming from behind his living room chair.

Juanita, now wearing a shoulder holster with a pistol, rolled towards the window facing the parking lot. She stopped between the curtains and pulled them closed.

"Now," Juanita commanded.

Tom strained his arm as he reached for the light switch. Shots rang out as he flipped the switch. Chunks of plaster stung his hands. With a startled gasp, he pulled his hand away and lay flat on the floor.

The dim light from the parking lot passed through the bullet holes. The sounds of traffic on Boughton Road filled the room. His two neighbors were silent.

Is he gone? Are we stuck here all night? Why am I not hearing sirens? Why are my neighbors quiet? Is this a siege?

The sound of footsteps came from the hallway. "Jesus," said a man in the hallway. Tom recognized him as a neighbor from a few doors down. "You know what's going on out—"

A woman answered, but her words sounded garbled as she alternated between shouting and whispering.

"You okay?" asked the man.

The woman spoke faster, but her words were still nonsense.

Tom remembered his door brace. He had it installed but had never used it before. Now was a good time to see if it was worth losing his deposit to install.

Tom's eyes had adjusted to the low light. Moving onto his hands and knees, he crawled towards the coat closet by the door. Behind him, Juanita got to her feet and hunched over. Holding her pistol, she rushed to the wall adjacent to the entryway.

"What are you doing?" Juanita said with a harsh whisper.

"Bracing the door," whispered Tom.

Juanita turned her back to the wall and slid down into a seated position.

In the hallway, Louie said, "Don't worry. She was just speaking in tongues."

Another man said, "We just need to get her back into our apartment."

The woman raised her voice. Her sounds of rage were unintelligible.

Tom opened the coat closet just enough to grab his telescopic door stopper. Tom took a deep breath and then slowly removed it. Now he needed to set it up without them noticing.

The neighbor said, "I'm sorry. I got to try 911 again."

The woman screamed, "There's too many of them!"

"Don't fight them," said a man. Tom decided he was Dewey. "Ride the tiger. You can do it."

The neighbor started screaming.

Sensing his opportunity, Tom pressed the rod against the door, then inserted it into the base. With a definitive click, Tom knew the rod was safely fastened.

"Dear Jesus," cried the neighbor. "Protect me!" The neighbor ran away. "Save me, Lord!"

Tom crawled back towards the living room. Juanita peeked around the corner. Seeing Tom, she motioned for him to move next to her. After crawling past Juanita, Tom sat on the carpet next to her and leaned against the wall.

Outside the hall, the soft thud of at least four sets of footprints made its way closer to the door.

"Join us," said the woman. Her voice was now a chorus of voices speaking in unison.

Something slammed into the door with a loud bang, followed by the sound of wood cracking.

"Join us," said the woman. "Or be consumed!"

"Easy," said Dewey. "Easy, baby."

"Come out, Tom," said Louie.

"Yeah," said Huey. "Don't hide behind a girl and a cat."

Louie snickered. "Facts aren't feminist. That's what you wrote. Remember that?"

"Remember those men who followed you?" asked Dewey. "You had an online army of men. Then you chickened out. You abandoned them."

The woman resumed her incoherent noises.

"How did that work out?" asked Louie. "Skeptics on both sides of the deep rift hate you. Your writing for the *Babbler* sucks." He chuckled. "Sorry. It's true. I'll bet they keep you around because they feel sorry for you."

Huey knocked on the door. "Let us in, Tom. What do you have to lose? Mommy and Daddy want you to go to an insane asylum. Your best friend is a freak in a dress."

Louie laughed. "You're just as pathetic as the White Sox."

Tom leaned towards the entryway. Juanita pressed a hand against his chest. "Don't," she whispered. "You don't want to feed Daisy." She gently pushed Tom.

Tom leaned against the wall and took a deep breath to calm himself.

Dewey yelled, "Please come out. She can't hold it much longer."

Huey said, "Yeah. Don't be afraid. We're giving you another chance to shape the world. You'll be part of something far greater than you've ever imagined. What do you say?"

Juanita closed her eyes and bowed her head. "Heavenly Father, I pray for You to guide my hand so I will only strike the wicked. May You give me the strength to protect the innocent. In your name, I pray. Amen." Juanita removed a compact mirror from her pocket and opened it. She positioned it to reflect the door.

"You're not coming out?" asked Huey.

"I'm jealous of you," said Louie. "Legion will only give us a glimpse of its beautiful glory. But you, Tom. You can claim that power."

Daisy and her other voices said, "Tom. You know us. You know him. You know the pain. Divided, we are weak. Betrayed. Stop. Leave him alone." The woman made unintelligible sounds before continuing. "Stop it. No. Alone, they crush us. Together, they burn. Burn them. Burn everything they stole. Burn the world that betrayed you. Become the fire or burn in the fire." The woman screamed in pain.

Louie said, "The Cubs need—"

Dewey interrupted Louie. "Fuck the story."

A shotgun blast startled Tom. Splinters of wood flew off the door.

Dewey said, "We don't have time for this bullshit." Someone kicked against the door. The cracks spread. "We'll spare the cat and your girlfriend if you come out now. Stop being a coward and accept Legion's gift."

Another shotgun blast blew a hole in the door. Juanita took deep breaths as she focused on the reflection in the mirror. Tom looked for anything he could use as a weapon.

Huey, Louie, and Daisy started making unintelligible noises.

"Oh, fuck," said Dewey.

Through the holes in the curtains, flashes of lightning illuminated the room, followed by popping sounds.

The hallway was silent. Juanita took deeper breaths as she held her gun in the ready position.

"Is she okay?" Louie asked.

"Yeah, said Dewey. "We got to run."

Daisy, catching her breath, said, "It's not ready."

"It will be," said Dewey.

The sound of their footsteps faded. Juanita sighed with relief, then holstered her gun. Tom stood up and approached the window.

"Careful," said Juanita.

Tom nodded. He stopped beside the window and slowly opened a blackout curtain. Outside, burning strips of cloth were all that remained of the street banners. Patches of flame burned around the streetlights on Boughton Road.

Tom's phone rang and answered itself. "Tom," Robert's voice boomed through the speakers, "I'm giving you one hour to get out of Bolingbrook. Unless you want Sara to know where you are."

"Why do you think she would care?" Tom asked. He hoped his bluff would derail Robert's rant.

"I have my sources, too," Robert replied, unfazed. "Tom, if you're out of town in an hour, I'll have the cleanup crew fix your apartment. And they won't touch your computer or paper files. I give you my word."

Tom blinked. "Um." He paused. "Thank you for being so kind?"

"I'm not doing this to be kind. I'm doing this so you'll owe me big time for saving your career! Now get going!"

22

Tom watched Schaumburg's office towers come into view as Juanita drove her van north on I-290. This time, he noticed they were far taller than any building in Bolingbrook.

APK slept in her carrier, unharmed during the attack. Juanita and Tom hadn't spoken since they'd agreed to go to Tom's room at the Ritz Motel. That she was familiar with it concerned him.

Since then, he ruminated on the attack. This was the first time he'd been shot at. If he hadn't twisted at the right time, he, or APK, could have been hit. Before *the Phantom Press* attack, Tom wasn't afraid of death. His brain would shut down, and that would be it. He feared losing his life. He didn't want to lose the precious ability to perceive and question the universe. Now he knew that death could mean a confrontation with enraged ghosts.

He debated talking to Juanita about what the spirit junkies said about him. Being with Juanita again felt special, even if it wasn't what he imagined. He'd almost forgotten how it felt to learn from her and to receive her approval. He didn't want to lose that feeling and imagining her bitterly rejecting him pained him.

But as the darkened office buildings drew closer, he needed to know the truth. Denying the truth about himself got him into that mess last year. If Juanita couldn't forgive him, it was better to know now than to be crushed later. He took a moment to work up his courage.

"You've been quiet," said Juanita.

"Yeah," Tom replied. "Just so much to take in."

"I understand. Ghosts are never easy to confront. I've seen people I thought were strong have breakdowns after encountering a ghost." She glanced at Tom. "Ghosts survive by invoking powerful emotions. So don't feel bad."

"It's what they said about me." Fear gripped Tom, and he lost his train of thought.

"What, exactly?"

"Like what I wrote about feminists." Tom lowered his head. "I look back at what I wrote about Jamie, feminists, and progressive skeptics. I mean, they had every right to hate me."

"I didn't."

Tom looked up.

"I was disappointed."

He froze in fear.

"You were such a sweet person when I knew you. But when you went after Jamie, I felt like that sweet person was gone. That behind the dispassionate prose and rationalist persona was a person full of rage and bitterness. The way you kept going after certain women, I wondered if one of your Habencon hookups went wrong."

"You knew about them?" Tom managed to ask.

"You had quite a reputation, Tom." She smiled.

"But I never saw you at Habencon."

"Because I was never there." She shrugged. "Word gets around, Tom."

"Oh." He started to feel embarrassed.

"I've just never cared for the Habenstein Society. Now, I loved Reese, just like every other skeptic. The rest of the Society... Let's just say Bennet wasn't their only predator."

Tom considered which of his former skeptic heroes were predators. The sad part, he thought, was that more than one person came to mind.

"Besides," Juanita continued, "It wasn't worth my time. Why the Interstellar Commonwealth still works with them escapes me." She glanced at Tom again. "I knew how devoted you were to Reese and the society. I was happy about that, but I also worried the society would corrupt you. Turn you into the kind of person who would defend vile misogynists."

Tom looked away from Juanita and felt ashamed. "They almost did. Bennet convinced me I should hit on Jamie." He shook his head. "I came too close to being corrupted. Reese tried to help me. Bennet, Marty, Trevor. They influenced me, but I let them." Tom paused for a beat. "I was mad at Jamie when she put out her video. She didn't say my name when she described my propositioning her in an elevator. It just sounded so... bad." Tom shook his head. "I should have listened and learned. Instead, I went into deep denial. And I let people like Bennet and Trevor influence me. If a future version of me hadn't killed Reese, I... I would have stayed on that path."

"But you left it."

Tom sighed. "At the cost of Reese's life." He faced Juanita. "That's what it took to open my eyes. Way too late. Even after shutting down my blog and admitting to being the guy in the elevator, every skeptic hates me."

"That's not true."

"Really?"

"Most skeptics hate you."

Tom twisted his head towards Juanita. She smirked.

Tom replied, "Seriously?"

"I like you."

Tom felt his heart lighten. Were his dreams about Juanita falling for him about to come true? Was he really getting a second chance to be more than friends with her?

She looked at Tom's face for a moment, then returned her attention to the road. "But consider how it looked to the skeptics who don't know you. In their eyes, you first attacked the skeptics on one side of the rift. Suddenly, you denounced everyone on the other side of the rift. Then you defected to the *Babbler*."

"I didn't defect," Tom protested. "I just didn't want to be part of a lie."

Juanita nodded. "But in their eyes, you are part of a lie. You denounced their so-called thought leaders. It looked like you were going full scorched Earth policy against the movement. Do you see why they would be mad at you?"

"Yes," Tom sighed. "But did the people at SkeptiGathering have to be so mean?"

"It could have been worse. Trust me."

Tom shook his head and then looked out the window. "Will it ever end? Will I always be defined by my mistakes?"

"That's the wrong question. Our mistakes have consequences. One of them can be how others see you. Some will forgive you. Others might never forgive you." She glanced at Tom. "My father always told me that it's not the mistake, but what you do after the mistake that counts. You can't control how others see you, but you can control what you do after making a mistake. That's what really defines us, Tom."

"It doesn't always seem that way," Tom replied. "Sometimes I feel that no matter how hard I work, no one sees it."

"But you see it," said Juanita. "And, if you believed, I'd tell you that God sees it, too."

Tom cringed. "Are you saying I should start believing in God, and God will forgive me?"

"We both know that's not how belief in anything works." She smirked. "And we both know that we can't always speak in absolutes."

"So?"

"So, I'm saying there are people out there who see the person you've become. Those are the people you need to find. Not the ones who can't see past your mistakes. I know you understand. Because you left the skeptical movement and didn't try to join Humanist Heart."

"They wouldn't let me in, but I see your point. There are people who see how I've changed. Wendy, Sara, Jenna, Pamela... they see me. Hell, they even helped me get here."

"Exactly. It's a big world, Tom. There's always a place for you."

"My place was the *Babbler*. No, it still is the *Babbler*. I just need to find a way to help them." Tom noticed Arlington Park coming into view. "Do you get called into Arlington Park often?"

"It's quiet for the most part. It's the surrounding area we have to worry about."

"Like the Ritz?"

Juanita nodded as she drove towards the Northwest Highway exit. "Definitely the Ritz."

"Because it's a hangout for shifters?" asked Tom.

"Love-struck shifters are the least of its problems." She chuckled.

"So," Tom hesitated as he thought about the other monsters that could be there. "So, Chris sent me to a dangerous motel?"

She shrugged. "It could have been much worse."

"Worse?"

"They could have sent you to the Blue Hotel in Palatine. The gang members and drug dealers would have been the least of our worries."

***

Tom stretched his back after helping Juanita rearrange the beds in the motel room. APK promptly jumped up onto the bed.

"You were a big help," said Tom.

"Mow," replied APK, as if she understood and didn't approve of Tom's sarcasm.

"That's no way to treat someone who saved you twice."

APK looked up at Tom. "Mow," she said as she tilted her head before approaching Juanita. Juanita scratched APK's chin, who replied with an audible long purr.

"I will grant you that," Tom replied.

In response, she lay on her side, exposing her belly to Juanita. Instead of petting her belly, Juanita continued to scratch APK's chin.

Juanita said, "That's sweet, APK."

APK responded by purring louder.

"You're not going to pet her belly?" Tom asked as he stepped towards the desk.

"No. It's her way of saying she trusts me not to pet her belly."

"Mow," APK said as she leaned into Juanita's scratching fingers.

Just as no one had made the beds, no one had rearranged, let alone dusted, the furniture since he'd left. Even Rene's conducting cloth sat undisturbed on top of his dresser. For once, Tom appreciated being in a motel without housekeeping.

"So, who gets which bed?" Tom asked.

"Neither of us," Juanita replied and pointed towards the sink and mini fridge. "After we block the door, you're going to sleep by the sink in this sleeping bag. APK and I will sleep in the tent. Between the Kevlar blankets and Kevlar tent, we should be safe."

They rearranged the beds like an "L" near the door, leaving an open space directly in front of the windows. Two Kevlar blankets covered the windows, which they secured with duct tape.

Tom blinked. "Do you always travel with a bulletproof tent?"

"Only in situations like this." She stopped scratching APK and approached Tom.

"Mow?" asked APK.

"Look," Juanita said to Tom. "This is just a precaution. The spirit junkies here are very territorial. They don't want outsiders offering rides to their ghosts. If they're foolish enough to attack us here, we should be able to hold out until backup arrives."

"How long would that be?"

"Not long."

"Can't you—"

The sound of a vibrating phone interrupted Tom. Juanita pulled her cell phone from her pants pocket and answered. As she listened to the caller, Tom looked at the size of her phone and wondered if a tailor had modified her pants to have deeper pockets.

"I'll be right out." Juanita ended the call. "I'm meeting some-one outside."

"Who?"

"That's private."

"Why?"

"Stay inside. Don't engage the latch unless someone knocks because I won't. Got it?"

"Okay," Tom replied. "Can you—"

"I'll be right back."

Tom watched in silence as she approached the door and opened it. He caught a glimpse of a police officer in the parking lot standing next to his Palatine Police Department patrol vehicle. Promptly, she closed the door behind her and locked it.

Tom pulled out his laptop bag, which he'd placed under the desk while they were rearranging the beds. As he pulled out the laptop and power cords, APK jumped up on the desk. Tom placed his right hand near her head. "You're such a good kitty." APK started purring. "I hope I didn't hurt you when I picked you up. I saw the gun—"

"Meow," she replied, sounding like she had forgiven Tom.

The tone of her voice soothed Tom's feelings. "I'm glad you're here for me. It's been a rough week."

APK rested her chain on top of Tom's hand. She purred louder as she relaxed.

"That's sweet, APK." APK slowly blinked at Tom. "You know at some point I'm going to have to move my hand. Right?"

APK placed her right paw on Tom's arm and looked up at him, her eyelids drooping.

"It doesn't have to be now." Tom rubbed the bare spots near her ears, and she purred her approval. While he still worried about Wendy and Jenna's conditions, APK's affection calmed Tom. If he'd had a cat, he wondered, would his life have been different?

The vibrations from the cell phone in his pocket snapped Tom back to the present. APK raised her head abruptly. Tom pulled out his phone. Sara was calling. Worried that she might know he was in Bolingbrook, he took a moment to collect his thoughts. He made himself smile, hoping it would make him sound happy over the phone. "Hey!"

"Hello," said Sara, with a hint of exhaustion in her voice. "I just heard there was a shooting incident at your apartment complex."

Tom tried to sound surprised. "Oh my!"

"Are you okay?"

Tom caught himself before he responded. *Is she onto me?* he thought.

"Tom?"

"Sorry, I got distracted. What did you say?" He approached the window, while APK jumped up on top of the nearest dresser.

Sara let out a short sigh. "I was asking about the shooting at your apartment. You weren't hurt, right?"

Tom laughed as he pulled one of the Kevlar blankets so he could peek outside. "Of course not. I'm staying in Palatine, remember?"

"Are you there now?" Sara asked.

Tom peeked through gap between the Kevlar blankets. Juanita and the Latino officer were talking to each other. Tom couldn't make out what they were saying but, based on their body language, he assumed it was a casual conversation.

"Tom?"

Tom stepped away from the window. "I really can't talk right now."

"Why?" Sara said.

Her tone reminded Tom of a time in grade school when his mother had caught him lying about breaking a plate. *If you must lie, keep it to a minimum. Too easy to lose track of them.*

"Well..." He noticed APK sitting on the conductive cloth. She moved her front claws like a baker kneading dough. For a moment, Tom worried it might be unsafe for her to be touching the conductive cloth.

"Yes?"

Pick a half-truth and stick with it.

Tom glanced back at the covered window and then whispered, "I really can't talk right now because—" Tom paused, hoping she'd think he was checking to make sure no one was listening in on him. "Because I'm embedded with the Orange Squad."

Sara didn't respond.

Technically, it's true.

Tom tried to sound excited. "I took Don's advice and found them. Now I'm doing a ride-along with one of their agents." He made his way towards APK. "I can't believe how much they're telling me. I'm learning so much about the Orange Squad that I'm stunned. And they're working on a huge case."

"What's it about?"

Slenderman popped into his head. No. Werecoyotes? He knew there were packs nearby. Could he say it involved weredogs? Wendy described a Welsh terrier shifter to him once. Don mentioned conflicts between the weredogs and werecoyotes. But he would have to deceive both Don and Sara to pull that one off.

"Are you there, Tom?"

"I can't tell you right now."

"Why?"

He wanted to say it was classified information. *No,* he thought. He was supposed to uncover secrets, not keep them. Sara said that's what separated reporters from PR hacks.

"If I reveal what I know too early, it could fall into the wrong hands."

Sara paused. "The wrong hands?"

Tom nodded as he listened. "Not you, but you know what I mean. It's not my job to endanger people."

"It's your job to report the truth," Sara snapped. "And it is my job to decide what we publish. Not the Orange Squad's job. Not the Cook County Board president's job, and it is absolutely not Robert's job. It is our job to hold the covert agencies and shadow societies accountable for their actions. We can't do our jobs if we're keeping secrets from each other."

"But right now, if I say too much, they'll boot me from the ride-along. I'll lose access to one of our biggest stories."

Sara sighed. "What have I said about access journalism?"

The anger in her words struck his eardrums like daggers. "'It isn't worth the price of admission.' Right?"

"Yes. That means we don't just take their word whenever they offer an excuse for secrecy. It means using your critical-thinking skills. When you accept offers of exclusive access, off-the-record comments, or any other gift, you have something they can take away from you. And some reporters will compromise themselves to keep their gifts. Not all reporters, but too many do. It's a very tempting path to follow, Tom. I know, because I almost went down it, and if I hadn't recorded a Man in Blue manipulating me... I don't want to think about where'd be now."

"I understand," Tom said, his heart racing like it always did whenever she scolded a reporter she suspected of unethical behavior. After considering his words for a moment, he said, "When I am ready to write the story, I will tell you everything." His body tensed as he remembered his promise to Juanita. "Even if it means..." He imagined Juanita telling him how disappointed and angry she was. How she never wanted to see Tom again. He spoke slowly, "Even if it means losing access, even exclusive access, to the people and institutions I cover."

Sara's long silence unsettled Tom. He was on thin ice before the *Phantom Press*'s attack. Would she accept his statement? It was true, as painful as it was to admit. He would have to choose the *Babbler* over Juanita if he wanted to keep his job.

"Very well," said Sara. "But I want you to promise me something."

"What is it?"

"No copaganda."

Tom raised his eyebrows. "Um. Sure. You know I believe Black Lives Matter. But that shouldn't be a problem because I think the Orange Squad has more people of color than we realized."

"Interesting, but what I'm talking about goes beyond questionable police shootings."

"What do you mean? Not all officers are bad. Well, maybe the Chicago PD. I've never had a good experience with them. And I'm white."

"It's not a matter of good or bad cops." Sara's long pause discomforted Tom. "It's a matter of perception. We're bombarded with pro-police messages, like TV shows, movies, PR events, stories from embedded reporters, campaign ads, among other things."

"Yeah," said Tom as he walked back towards APK, who was now watching him with her unblinking eyes. "I never really thought about all the police shows and movies I've grown up with."

"Good. Now, have you heard the phrase 'Thin Blue Line?'"

Tom thought for a moment. "I think it's an ugly version of the American Flag."

"It's the idea that the police are the thin blue line between order and chaos."

Tom paused. "Well, we do call them when there's a problem. Is that wrong?"

"Not necessarily," she replied. "Look at it this way: if you think that you're the thin blue line between order and chaos, how would that make you think of the civilians you're supposed to protect? Especially if you don't live in the community you work in. Keep in mind, many officers are trained to think they're in constant danger when they're on the streets."

Unpleasant thoughts filled Tom's mind. "You might have a very low opinion of civilians. And if you're..." He trailed off.

"It's why some officers have an authoritarian mindset, and I've seen too many reporters buy into it."

The door unlocked, and Juanita opened it. She said, "Let us know if you see any of them, okay?"

"I will," the officer replied.

"I've got to go," Tom whispered.

"Remember, Tom. No copaganda."

"Understood," he whispered. He added in his normal voice. "I'll call you when I'm ready. Bye." He hung up.

"Who was that?" Juanita asked as she locked the door.

"My editor," Tom replied as he put his phone away. "She heard what happened and wanted to know if I was there."

"What did you tell her?" said Juanita as she approached Tom.

"That I'm doing a story on the Orange Squad. Technically, it's true."

"Mow," said APK as she tilted her head. Tom wondered if it was the feline version of the human side-eye.

"It is, but you should limit your contact with her. Too many half-truths can turn into a big lie."

"I guess." Tom shrugged, though he wondered if it was already too late for him.

"While I pitch my tent, you can—" Juanita stopped talking. She looked at the conductive cloth under APK and then approached the dresser. Tom stepped out of her way. After grasping the cloth, APK stood and climbed onto Juanita's shoulders. As APK positioned herself, Juanita pulled the cloth from the dresser. For several moments, she pinched the entire cloth, as if she were trying to feel something hidden inside. After she finished, she walked over to a lamp and held it up to the light. The wires, or what Tom assumed were wires, reflected the lamp's light. Unlike his last examination, this time Tom noticed that the wires formed a pattern of two concentric circles, each one subdivided by triangles. The pattern looked to Tom like a baker had placed a smaller pie within a larger pie, then sliced both pies at the same time.

Juanita lowered the cloth away from the lamp. "Where did you get this?"

"From Rene's trailer. She said it was conductive cloth. There were sheets around the radio she uses to monitor the Ghost Frequencies. I noticed the copper threads, but I haven't had a chance to study it."

Juanita folded the cloth. "It's a very rare type of conductive cloth. The Illuminati lost the ability to make it after the Sigma-7 uprising." She finished folding the cloth and then held it up to Tom. "This is more than all the known scraps in the world. And she just gave it to you?"

Tom shook his head. "I picked it up while she was out of the room. She makes rolls of conductive cloth. I didn't think she'd miss one small piece."

Juanita's jaw dropped for a moment, and her eyes widened in surprise. After taking another moment to regain her composure, she started back towards the dresser with the cloth.

"What are you thinking?" asked Tom.

She examined the piece of cloth again. "I think we need to talk to Rene."

23

Juanita navigated her van past two large potholes, then made the last turn towards Little Bolingbrook.

Tom sat up and motioned towards two banners hanging from light poles on both sides of the street. "Those are new."

The dark green banners had the name "Bolingbrook" printed in a gold-colored script font. At the bottom of each banner were the words "Little Bolingbrook: Preserving the past and reclaiming the future."

Juanita glanced up. "Interesting."

Tom pulled out his phone. "Maybe I should—"

"She knows we're here. Probably listening to us right now."

Tom almost dropped his phone.

Juanita smirked and looked at her radio. "If you are listening, we brought you Spunky Dunkers."

Spunky Dunkers was a doughnut shop in Palatine they visited before traveling to Aurora. Juanita had walked up to the counter and said Mr. Orange left an order for her. The manager returned with three boxes of glazed donuts that had just been made. Juanita said they were the best doughnuts in the Northwest suburbs. Tom thought they tasted better than any of Bolingbrook's chain doughnut stores. He liked their coffee after he poured half of a container of sugar into his mug.

Juanita tapped the dashboard five times. "We've got about thirty seconds. So, once we're inside, you do your interview, and I'll jump in if I have any questions."

"You're not going to take the lead?" Tom asked.

"You do have questions for her. Right?"

"Of course I do. But it's your investigation."

Juanita gave Tom a warm smile. "It's our investigation."

Tom smiled and sat upright in his seat.

Juanita continued, "And it's your turn to ask questions. You can do it."

"I can do it," Tom said to himself. This time, he believed it.

Juanita motioned to Tom to stop talking. "The ward is about to wear off."

He nodded. They remained silent, Tom unsure of what to say that wouldn't make Rene suspicious.

Juanita broke the silence. "They sure like corn around here."

"There used to be a lot of cornfields in Bolingbrook," said Tom. "Until Robert took over. Supposedly, he encouraged the farmers to sell their land to make space for strip malls."

Juanita nodded. "Nostalgia has a powerful hold on people."

Tom pointed ahead. "Her trailer is by that tall sculpture." Unlike his last visit, the sculpture faced down the road in their direction.

Juanita looked up. "It takes a lot of talent to forge something like that."

"Wait until you meet Gwyla," Tom said as he imagined her reaction.

As Juanita parked her van, Mr. Washington drove his blue golf cart into the intersection ahead. He made the turn and then parked inches from the van's bumper. After leaving the golf cart, he stared in Juanita's direction.

Tom hopped out of the van and smiled. "Hello, Mr. Washington. New sunglasses?"

Mr. Washington turned his head to face Tom, giving him a better view of the man's blue-framed sunglasses. Despite the dark lenses, Tom could make out Mr. Washington's blinking eyes.

"Can I speak with Rene?" Tom asked. "I left her a few messages, but she didn't call back. I hate to be rude, but I'm kind of on a deadline."

Mr. Washington stared back at Tom.

"Looks like you've worked on your MiB skills." He nodded. "Great job remaining silent."

Juanita stepped out of the van, carrying APK in a front pet pouch. The sight distracted Mr. Washington for a moment.

"Who's your friend?" she asked, dividing her attention between Mr. Washington and the cornfield. "Who's your other friend?"

Tom noticed Ms. Watters retreating into the corn, disturbing the surrounding stalks.

"Hello, Ms. Watters," said Tom in a cheerful voice.

The front door opened and Rene stepped out, wearing the same overalls from his last visit. Her face glowed with excitement. "Bolingbrook High School versus Fremd High School, 1981." Rene approached the gate, almost skipping. "It came down to one play." She lowered her voice as she opened the gate. "The Raiders were on the Vikings' twenty-six-yard line. Fourth and long. No timeouts. Under a minute left."

She approached Tom and Juanita with a spring in her step. "The QB called his first audible ever. The Vikings defensive backs charged through the O-line like it was Swiss cheese. The quarterback faked the handoff, but the defense didn't fall for it.

After all, they were the smartest football team in the state. The quarterback started scrambling."

Rene stepped towards Tom. "Then!" She paused. "The quarterback stumbled." She looked at Juanita.

"From all the way in the press stand, I heard him yell, 'Fumble!' I'll never forget it! That's when the defenders piled on him." She looked at Juanita, her eyes glowing with excitement. "Soon, players on both teams were to join the pile-on. Because if the Vikings recovered the ball, the game would be over, and the Vikings would win." She held up her index finger. "Except." She paused. "One player wasn't in the pile. The center was lying on the ground near the line of scrimmage."

She lowered her finger and stepped back. "Suddenly!" She paused. "The center got to his feet. And..." She raised her voice. "He had the ball! The center never handed the ball to the quarterback." Her jaw dropped as she became more excited. "The Viking coaches yelled, trying to warn their players to stop the center. By the time the Vikings' players noticed"—she smiled—"it was too late. The center ran into the endzone. Time expired. The Bolingbrook Raiders pulled off the greatest upset in state history."

She sighed as her face seemed to glow. "The Vikings may have been the smartest team in the state. But we were the cleverest."

Rene opened a box and inhaled the scent of the fresh donuts.

"The mayor of Palatine honored her wager and gave me a box of Spunky Dunkers Donuts."

She grabbed a donut and took a bite. She closed eyes as she slowly chewed the piece of glazed donut. A blissful expression appeared on her face.

"Still the best donuts I've ever tasted."

Rene caught her breath, then looked at Juanita. "I forgot my manners. I'm Rene McDonald, the mayor of Little Bolingbrook. You are?"

"I'm Juanita," she replied. "Tom is training me today."

Rene pointed at APK. "And your friend?"

"This is my therapy cat, Princess."

"Mow," APK replied with pride.

24

After a dramatic pause, Rene said, "And that's how we won the Bolingbrook Time War." She smiled. "No thanks to Robert."

Tom and Juanita silently watched Rene for a few moments.

"Wow," Tom said, breaking the silence. "I thought I knew everything about the war. I've read the articles about it, but they left out so many details."

"I never told the complete story." Rene grinned. "Until now."

Tom abruptly stopped typing on his phone. APK, who was napping on Juanita's lap, opened her eyes and twisted her ears. Juanita watched Tom.

"You never told Don the whole story?" Tom asked, still surprised by Rene's revelation.

"No," Rene said as she took the last glazed donut. "Because Don never offered me a box of Spunky Dunkers."

Tom chuckled. "Well, thank you."

Juanita spoke up. "Excuse me. I have a question."

Rene looked at Juanita. "Yes?"

"Why did Robert always argue with you?"

Rene shrugged. "Would he still be Robert if he didn't?"

"I wouldn't know." Juanita rubbed the top of APK's head, who responded with a loud purr. "But arguing about the color of the sky in the middle of a war—"

"Because Robert believes he's greater than a king, and if we don't kiss his feet, we're either fools or foes. Isn't that right, Tom?"

Tom nodded.

"Thank you," said Rene, giving Tom a short nod. She focused on Juanita. "I've always seen through him. He is smarter than average, but not the genius he imagines himself to be." She finished the donut. "He thought the sky was black due to the smoke. I argued that the smoke was obscuring the sky. It wasn't the sky. It worked out in the end. Our POW broke down and promised to answer all our questions if Robert and I stopped arguing."

Juanita and Tom laughed.

Tom spoke up. "Speaking of arguments, were you at the demolition of Old Chicago?"

Rene looked away from Tom for a few moments. She faced him and said, "I watched until I couldn't stomach Robert's sophistry. Why?"

"Do you know who heckled him during his speech?"

She shook her head. "I only heard Robert over the PA. I didn't find out about the heckler until I watched the replay on BCTV."

Tom typed into his notes app. "The heckler said he was the founder of Bolingbrook. Do you know who would call themselves the founder?"

Rene scratched her chin for a few seconds, then shrugged. "I don't know. An incorporation committee did most of the work. Took them two votes to get approval from the residents."

She reached into one of her pockets and pulled out a glasses case. After opening the case, she pulled out a pair of thick glasses with dials and wires along its brown frame. She put the glasses on her face and then looked at Tom. A moment passed before she started turning the knobs on her frame.

"I don't think you were alive back then."

Tom nodded. "When you saw the replay, did you recognize the heckler's voice?"

Rene replied, "I remember thinking that the camera operator would lose his job if he filmed the heckler." She wiped her hands with a napkin. "I'll bet the producers were afraid to edit Robert's speech. He considered his words 'indivisible.' And woe be unto the person who cuts a single millisecond out of it."

Tom chuckled while Juanita kept her focus on Rene.

"Sorry. I can't help you." Rene looked down. "The heckler's identity was the last thing on my mind then since I'd just watched Robert send innocent ghosts into oblivion." She looked up at Tom. "Or so I thought."

"I'm curious," Juanita said. "How do you think the *Phantom Press* survived the EMP from the implosion?"

Rene looked up. "Hmm," she said. After a few moments, she faced Juanita. "That is a very good question."

Juanita started to speak when Rene called out, "Gwyla?"

The door to the bedroom opened, and Gwyla rolled into the living area. She now resembled an automatous dolly carrying a metallic litter box, which glittered with white, smooth crystals.

Rene stood up. "I think our furry friend needs a bathroom."

"Furry friend?" Gwyla asked.

"Just deliver the litter box to the cat," Rene replied. She faced Juanita. "I sent a message to Gwyla to make a litter box for your cat."

Juanita nodded. "That was very thoughtful. Thank you." Juanita watched as Gwyla approached her and APK. APK stretched and jumped to the floor. "I've never seen a robot like this."

"Gwyla isn't a robot," said Rene. "She's a machine spirit, and this is one of their totems."

Gwyla raised a rectangle with two circles that almost resembled an anime character's eyes. "This totem allows me to serve inside the Purpose Maker's home."

Juanita raised her eyebrows. "Any purpose?"

"Yes," said Gwyla as she stopped. "I am a purpose seeker."

Juanita dropped her jaw. She looked at Rene, her face still reflecting her shock. "How were you able to channel a purpose seeker?"

Rene's face beamed with pride. "Years of practice."

Gwyla extended a roller ramp from her body. Rollers also rose up from the platform. The rollers activated and pushed the litter box off the platform and onto the floor. The APK crouched her body and lowered her tail. After sniffing the air, APK stalked towards the litter box.

"Were you a member of the Synchronicity?" Juanita asked Rene. "I thought they were the only ones who could summon seekers like Gwyla."

Rene's proud expression faded into sorrow. "They considered me, but then the Sigma 7 uprising happened. None of them survived." She sighed.

Gwyla emitted a short burst of white noise, startling Tom. APK, now crouched by the litter box, lowered her head. Gwyla rolled back about a foot, then made the static sound three more times.

"Allergy! Allergy!" it cried. Gwyla accelerated away from APK and raced into the bedroom.

APK lifted her head as Gwyla closed the bedroom door. "Mow?"

"Odd," said Rene, tilting her head. "Gwyla's never had an allergy before." She looked at APK, who was digging at the plastic litter. "Is there something I should know about you?"

APK finished digging. After turning around, she looked into Rene's gaze. She started urinating.

Rene stood up. "There's something not quite right about you." She reached into one of her pockets. Juanita reached into a pocket in APK's carrier.

Tom's eyes shifted between the two women. "There's a question I forgot to ask," Tom blurted.

Rene pulled her hand out of her pocket and looked expectantly towards Tom. Juanita removed her hand from the pocket.

"Yes?" Rene asked.

Tom's eyes darted around the room as he looked for something he could ask about. His eyes rested on the memorial table. The radio was off, and the cloth wasn't sparkling.

Tom cleared his throat. "Have you heard from the *Phantom Press* or your daughter since our last interview?"

The question seemed to sadden Rene. She stood up and walked towards the table. "I didn't hear from the *Phantom Press*. I heard from Natalie." She reached for one of the photographs and stared at it in silence.

"What did she say?" Tom asked.

"The usual," Rene answered. "She wants to go home. I can't bring her home. After all these years..." She looked down at the other photos. "I do my best to strengthen her signal. Her birthday is an official Little Bolingbrook holiday. Before her bedtime, I play her favorite Rick Springfield album. I do what I can." She turned to face Tom and Juanita. "But all ghosts fade away in the end. I'm doing what I can." She wiped a tear from one of her eyes. "But it's a losing battle." Rene's eyes watered.

Tom picked up a tissue box and approached Rene. "I didn't mean to upset you."

Rene took a tissue and wiped her eyes.

"I can only imagine what you're feeling."

"I hope you never have to bury your children," Rene sobbed. "And hope you never watch your children fade away." She wiped her eyes again.

APK rubbed against Rene's legs. She ignored the cat.

Juanita stood up. "I'm sorry for your loss."

Rene's eyes remained on the table. "Me too."

APK jumped onto the table, startling Rene. For a split second, Tom feared she would be electrocuted. Instead APK lay on her side. Her purr resonated through the room.

Rene tensed, and her fingers curled. "That's not a cat tree," she said, almost growling.

"I'm so sorry," Juanita said as she rushed up to the table. Her hand brushed against the cloth. "Come on," she said as she picked up APK. "Cats don't belong up there."

"Mow!" APK protested.

"You have a nice cat bed waiting for you at home."

"Mow," APK protested again.

Juanita looked closer at the cloth. She raised her eyebrows, then faced Rene. "Is that conductive cloth?"

"Yes," Rene replied as she threw away the tissue.

Juanita gasped. "Tom, you said there were only a few rolls left in the world."

"I thought there were," said Tom as he played along.

"You're thinking of the rolls created by the Nightwatchers," Rene replied, walking back from the trash can. "I made these myself."

"You did?" Juanita asked.

Tom wasn't sure if she was acting or sincerely surprised.

"A Nightwatcher taught me some of it, but she died during the uprising." Rene looked at the cloth. "But I figured the rest out myself."

Juanita's eyes widened. "Do you realize how many have tried to duplicate the process?" With her free hand, she caressed the fabric. "Do you realize how much this amount is worth?"

"I know," said Rene. "I've sold some."

"The NWO allowed it?" asked Juanita, sounding surprised.

Rene nodded. "The NWO and I have an informal agreement. I don't sell too many, and they don't kill me." Her face brightened. "I make just enough to live a comfortable life. It's been about a year since my last sale. Some teens from Naperville insisted the rolls be Cubs Blue."

"As in the Chicago Cubs?" Tom asked.

"Right down to the CMYK and Pantone numbers. I charged them a premium rate. Do you know how difficult it is to get dyes to bond with conductive cloth?"

"No idea," said Tom with a shrug.

Juanita asked, "And they were able to afford them?"

Rene nodded. "It's Naperville. Rich parents and bored teenagers are a dangerous combination. Just ask any suburban mayor." She focused on Juanita. "That's why I didn't sell them a power source. It's just expensive cloth without one." She looked at Tom. "You can't plug it into any outlet. It requires a special kind of energy to activate."

"Do you know why they wanted blue conductive cloth?" Juanita asked.

Rene, for a few beats, looked away from Juanita and Tom. "Something about decorating a bad building. Not sure what they meant by that. Maybe they're trying to attract the ghosts of Cubs fans."

"Or players?" Tom asked.

Rene shook her head. "Those ghosts reside in Chicago. I'd rather not imagine a ghost powerful enough to move from Chicago to Naperville and back."

"Why?"

The bedroom opened. Gwyla, now in the upright form Tom saw during his last visit, rolled into the hallway. It sneezed. "You have a phone call, Purpose Maker. I think it is from your friend—"

"Gwyla," Rene snapped. Gwyla rolled back into the bedroom. "Sorry," Rene said to Gwyla. "Please put him on hold and play his favorite music."

Gwyla's head nodded. "Doing that now, Purpose Maker. I will add him to my do not name list."

"Thank you," Rene replied. She looked at Tom and Juanita. "My work is never done." She looked past them. "Isn't that right, Ms. Watters?"

Tom turned. Outside, Watters ducked below the window.

"She's getting better," said Rene, smiling. "It took me four seconds to notice her this time."

25

Tom remained silent as Juanita drove towards downtown Aurora. The short buzz from Tom's vibrating phone broke the silence. Juanita motioned for him to stay quiet. Several seconds later, the traffic light ahead turned red, and traffic came to a stop. She pressed three of the buttons by the radio.

"How do you think it went?" Juanita asked.

Tom reached for his phone. "I'm glad she didn't ask us too many questions. I'm not a good liar."

"Neither is she," Juanita replied.

Tom suddenly placed a hand on his forehead.

"What?" asked Juanita.

Tom shook his head. "I forgot I was going to have dinner with my parents."

The light turned green, and Juanita started driving. "Do they still live in Bolingbrook?"

"Yes," Tom sighed. "They're making something special for me. I guess they're trying to make up for our last dinner. I can't say, 'Sorry. I can't make it to dinner because Sara ordered me to evacuate Bolingbrook. Robert told me to stay out of Bolingbrook. Besides, I'm in the middle of a ghost hunt.' They'll never let me out of Alexian Brothers' mental ward."

Juanita tapped her fingers as she drove.

Tom waited. "Do you have anything to say?"

Juanita focused on the traffic.

Tom sighed. "Did I tell you my parents want me to check myself into Alexian Brothers? They even promised me a private room." He shook his head as he looked out the passenger window. "Imagine how they'll feel—"

"Tom!" interrupted Juanita. The annoyance and anger in her voice startled him.

He averted Juanita's gaze, worried he'd trigger another outburst. The only other sound inside the van was from APK, purring as she napped.

What did I do? I can't lose Juanita now. I need her help.

"We can go back to Bolingbrook," said Juanita, sounding calmer than she was seconds ago.

Tom stared at Juanita in disbelief. "We can?"

She nodded. "The God-mayor is not all-seeing. Besides, why would I pass up the opportunity to see your parents? It's been years."

Tom blinked. "I'm sure they'd love to see you, but how?"

"I'll need to make a phone call." Juanita pulled into a gas station and parked by a pump.

"Who are you going to call?"

"Stay in the van." Juanita climbed out. "And Tom? Let me do the talking. I'm good with parents." She closed the door.

Tom looked back at APK's carrier. "Have anything to add?"

APK covered her eyes with her right paw.

"Of course."

Tom looked at the driver's side mirror. Juanita talked into her Bluetooth device as she pumped gas into the van. She nodded a few times, then stepped out of his view.

Tom looked back at APK. "Do you know who she's talking to?"

She moved her paw, then looked up at Tom. "Mow," she replied, sounding half-awake. She covered her eyes and resumed purring.

Tom grumbled. "Sorry I asked."

The vibration from Tom's phone startled him. The phone slipped from his hand, but he caught it with the other. For a moment, he worried it was a call from his parents or Robert. To his relief, the caller ID showed Shavana's name. He accepted the call.

"Hey Shavana," said Tom. "What's up?"

"Just wondering if you needed help."

Tom blinked. "Help?"

"Yeah," she replied. "I turned in my profile early."

"Who did you profile?"

"A former Clow employee. He was a biomedical engineer. Now, he funnels alien technology into the market. But his ultimate goal is building CO2 scrubbers to combat global warming."

Tom raised his eyebrows. "Wow."

"And he's the keyboardist for WikiRock."

"Impressive. How did you pull it off?"

"Research and luck," Shavana replied. "He had scheduled a meeting with the Martian Colonial Ambassador, but she got recalled to Mars. Apparently, all Martian Colonial ships left Clow a few days ago. Guess they're afraid of the *Phantom Press*."

The Martian Colonies were the most powerful civilization in the solar system. Possibly the most powerful in the entire galaxy. Tom couldn't imagine them being afraid of anything.

"So," Shavana said, "do you need any help? It's the least I can do since you helped me."

"Actually, I do." Tom lowered his voice. "If you could research a few things for me, it would really help."

"Sure," Shavana replied, her voice bubbling with excitement.

The gears started turning in his head. "See what you can find out about former mayor Rene MacDonald."

"Former mayor?"

Tom nodded. "She's a former mayor of Bolingbrook."

Shavana gasped. "Wow, I didn't know Bolingbrook had other mayors."

"I know." Tom smiled. "It's one of the many unbelievable truths about Bolingbrook."

Shavana giggled.

"Also, before the demolition of Old Chicago, Robert got into an argument with someone who claimed to be the founder of Bolingbrook. Robert won't give me his name. I haven't got a clue who it could be."

"Did you reach out to Don?"

Tom shook his head. "He told me to stick to covering Cook County."

"At least he talked to you. He doesn't look at my messages." Shavana chuckled.

"Ouch. So, can you help?"

Shavana replied, "Research Rene MacDonald and find the founder of Bolingbrook. Got it."

Tom nodded, though she couldn't see it. "Oh! If you can get a copy of the last issue of the *Phantom Press* before they disappeared, let me know."

Shavana remained silent for a few moments. "You know Don has the *Phantom Press* assignment."

Tom thought for a moment. "I can't go into details because I'm embedded in the Orange Squad."

Shavana gasped. "The Orange Squad? They're gonna let you live to write a story?"

"Yeah. It's complicated, and I'll tell you about it later. So, are you in?"

"Research Rene, find the founder, and get the last issue of *the Phantom Press*. Got it."

"Good," Tom replied. "I really appreciate it."

"Any time."

After ending the call, Tom realized he wasn't jealous of Shavana profiling an alien tech broker. He had an interview with Rene, at the very least. Even better, Shavana was helping him for a change. Assuming Sara didn't find out about his trips to Bolingbrook, she might notice his improvement.

Tom's phone vibrated again. It was a text from Pamela.

I just heard the Skeptical World Podcast. *Jamie and Ivan mentioned you. Ivan is a jerk. Call me if you want to talk.*

Tom did a double take. Ivan had been bashing him in every episode for the past year. Did Jamie break her silence to agree with him? Why would Jamie break her silence over a year later? Did he really want to hear what they said? He looked at his phone. He had nothing else to do.

Before Tom could open his podcast app, Juanita opened the driver's side door and climbed into the van. She slammed the door hard.

"Mow!" APK said, sounding startled.

"Assholes!" Juanita grumbled. She hit the steering wheel with both hands, setting off the van's horn.

"What's wrong?" Tom asked.

"If we want to go back to Bolingbrook, we have to investigate a bad place in Naperville." She faced Tom. "Even I know Naperville doesn't have any dangerous neighborhoods. Why didn't she just say no?"

Seeing Juanita this angry startled Tom.

"Wait," he said. Juanita gave him an angry look. "Naperville may not have any bad neighborhoods, but it does have a bad building."

26

Juanita parked the van at the Naperville METRA station. Commuters spilled from the parked passenger rail cars and into the lot.

"Where is it?" Juanita asked.

The train started moving.

"Across the tracks. It should be obvious once the train passes."

"Should be?"

Tom shrugged. "I was in high school the last time I visited. It might have changed since then."

Juanita gave Tom a surprised look. "And may I ask what you were doing inside the bad building?" Juanita's critical gaze felt like the point of a sharp knife to Tom.

"Buying a book," he replied, sounding defensive.

Juanita maintained her gaze.

"It was an autographed copy of *Foundation*," Tom hastily added. "I used to be a huge Asimov fan, remember?"

"Yes."

"Someone offered to sell me a copy, but I had to meet him at the bad building. When he showed it to me, I recognized it as a fake. I bought it anyway because I wanted to get out of there alive."

The train drove away, and one building immediately caught Tom and Juanita's attention. Two Cubs banners dangled from the roof deck of a yellow four-story house. They rippled in the light breeze, and parts of the fabric sparkled in the late afternoon sun.

"It is obvious," said Juanita.

"It wasn't always this obvious," said Tom.

Tom noticed other banners on the left and right sides of the house, each one sparkling like the two banners in front. Something else caught his eye.

"Those directional antennas on the roof are new."

One pointed to the northwest; the other towards Bolingbrook.

Juanita took off her sunglasses. "What else can you tell me about the building?"

Tom thought for a moment. "Officially, it's a hotel, but it's really a rooming house. The landlord charges a weekly rate and probably doesn't ask too many questions. This is where a lot of Naperville teens buy drugs. Like I said, some rough people hang out there, but there are worse places in Chicagoland."

Juanita looked towards the roof. "What about the local police?"

"I think they tolerate it. I guess they'd rather have crime clustered around a single building than spread throughout the subdivisions."

Juanita nodded and opened the panel door on the top of the center console. She removed a piece of electronic equipment and set it on the dashboard. Like a portable weather radio, it featured a built-in speaker and an LCD screen. The item lacked a brand name, and its buttons were unlabeled. She extended the antenna and then powered on the LED screen. On the screen, a moving line danced across a graph.

He leaned closer to examine the device. "Is this a weather radio or an EMF meter?"

"Don't touch."

Tom moved back to his chair. "Can you at least tell me what it is?"

Juanita seemed to consider her words. "You're close. It's a receiver and meter. It's going to tell us if those are the banners Rene sold."

"If they are, will be able to listen to the Ghost Frequencies?"

Juanita shook her head. "Unlikely. But it should tell us whether the cloth is holding a charge." She opened another dashboard compartment, revealing a CB radio. "This is a normal radio. I'm going to let you listen, but you must stay quiet. Understand?"

Tom nodded. "Yes."

"And you can't quote or tell anyone what you heard. I'm trusting you with a major secret. If you don't feel comfortable..." She pointed at the passenger door. "You can wait outside."

Tom imagined Sara telling him to jump out of the van. Reporters were supposed to tell interview subjects if they didn't want something in the *Babbler*, don't say it. Off-the-record knowledge was a temptation that led reporters to withhold information out of fear of losing access to a source. Off the record was a means of control.

Tom stayed. Juanita was trusting him with a secret. A secret that if he shared with the world could cost Juanita her career, or worse. She wasn't tempting him. She was trusting him. Besides, the real story was the *Phantom Press*, not Orange Squad radio chatter.

He turned off his cell phone. "Completely off the record."

Juanita flashed a smile at Tom. "Thank you."

Tom nodded as his heart raced with excitement. Was he excited about hearing secret transmissions, or was he excited that Juanita trusted him?"

She turned on the CB and picked up the mic. "Girasol going orange."

Three men and three women broadcasted that they, too, were going orange. Juanita pulled out a notepad and pen.

A fourth man spoke over the CB. "Orange Day, confirm root sequence."

Each took operative cited a string of numbers. Juanita wrote them down. Tom noticed that the last number in each string increased with each new report.

"How?" whispered Juanita, as she adjusted the antenna on the other device. Tom didn't understand what the moving lines on the screen represented. Juanita looked at the lines, then wrote down her string of numbers.

She picked up the mic and recited her string of numbers. The last number was the largest of all the reported strings.

Over the CB, a new man answered, "Roger that. Girasol, hold whisper. Red Uncle, you are free to proceed. Everyone else, go to your beta point."

Juanita rushed to turn off the CB radio. She looked at the device and gasped. Her jaw dropped.

"What's wrong?" Tom asked.

Juanita started pressing another set of buttons on the device. "We might hear something."

Tom's eyes widened. "But you said—"

"Under normal conditions, we'd hear static. But there's so much energy in this network that we may hear something in the Ghost Frequencies." She turned what appeared to be a volume wheel on the device.

"Network?"

"Someone created a chain of receivers from the North Side to this building."

"Like a relay network?"

"Yes, and we don't have much time before they destroy the network."

Static from the device's speakers startled Tom. Juanita nearly slammed the device onto the dashboard, then hurriedly adjusted the antenna.

"Shouldn't you—"

"Quiet!" said Juanita.

The harshness in her voice unsettled Tom. He watched her push more buttons and noticed the frustration showing on her face.

Why is she acting like this?

A faint voice came from the speaker, barely louder than the background static.

"You don't—"

Juanita raised her hands and leaned back in her chair.

The voice returned. "Turn away from—" Tom thought it was a man's voice.

A woman's voice pierced the crackling static. "We're fading away."

Another man said, "We can only survive if we unite."

"No!" screamed the first man. "Legion will devour you. Don't go to Bolingbrook!"

Tom turned to Juanita. "Is this the Legion Roul was talking about?"

A piercing tone erupted from the static. Tom and Juanita turned away from the device and covered their ears. APK yowled as she tried to cover her ears with her paws.

Outside, the banners glowed as they generated sparks that rained to the ground. Seconds later, the banners burst into flames. The device fell silent.

On the other side of the tracks, an armored personnel carrier turned onto 4th Avenue. The words "City of Naperville" was printed on the side in white block letters.

The APC stopped in front of the house. The rear door opened, and SWAT officers rushed outside. They split into two teams. One team moved onto the porch and waited by the door. The other ran down the alleyway.

Several seconds later, the team on the porch struck the front door with a mini battering ram. After several hits, the door gave way. One person tossed a grenade into the house. The bang of the grenade, even from across the railroad tracks, echoed through the air. Thick white gas filled the entryway, and the SWAT team charged inside.

The sound of sirens filled the air as Naperville patrol cars and a police cargo van pulled into view. The van parked in front of the house while the patrol cars blocked off Fourth Avenue.

"What is going on?" Tom asked.

SWAT team members escorted two middle-aged men in handcuffs out of the house. Two young men, one of them wearing a Naperville North t-shirt, followed.

Juanita said, "You just witnessed the first joint operation between the Orange Squad and Bolingbrook's Department of Paranormal Affairs."

The SWAT members put their prisoners into the cargo van. On the roof, four SWAT officers started disassembling the antennas. The fifth officer held up a bright blinking light.

Juanita turned off the device and turned on the CB radio. "Girasol ears on," she said into the mic.

Others announced they were "ears on" as well.

Tom's smartphone vibrated, and he received a text from an unknown number.

> I didn't believe Sara when she said you were doing a ride along with Juanita.

> Who is this?

> Look to your right.

Tom looked out the passenger window. He spotted Don, several yards away, sitting in a white pickup truck. He gave Tom a thumbs-up sign. Tom responded with a tentative thumbs-up of his own.

> Keep up the good work.

Don started his pickup and drove away.

Juanita's cell phone rang, and she answered.

"I'll put you on speaker," she said as she put her phone on the dashboard.

"Thank you for your assistance," said Steve over the phone's speaker.

"You're welcome," Juanita replied in a businesslike tone. "We couldn't have located the Naperville site without Tom's help."

"Then I'm going to say something I thought I would never say." He paused. "Thank you, Tom."

Tom leaned closer to the phone. "You're welcome?"

"Both of you helped us foil a plot to transfer a powerful ghost from Chicago to Bolingbrook. The possession addicts responsible are in custody. In return for your valuable assistance, both of you have one night in Bolingbrook. Though I would recommend leaving before 10 PM. The shorter your stay, the easier it will be to persuade Robert that we didn't see you."

"Understood," Juanita replied.

Steve said, "I suggest spending that time with Tom's parents. They have a delicious meal planned."

Tom felt a chill shoot through his body. How did he know about his parents' dinner plans? Was it a warning?

"We might do that," Juanita replied.

"Great, Sunflower. Your superiors will debrief you tomorrow. Tom, you should officially be allowed to return to Bolingbrook in a week. We promise not to tell Sara."

"I have a question," Tom said.

"Ask," said Steve.

"What is Legion? It couldn't have been the ghost from Chicago."

"You'll find out soon," Steve replied. "Good afternoon."

Juanita and Tom looked at each other. Tom had dreamed of asking Juanita out, but he never imagined it would be under these circumstances.

"If you still want to have dinner with my family, I can ask them. I'm sure they'd say yes."

Juanita gave Tom a warm smile. "I'd love to."

The sensations of fear and joy overwhelmed Tom. Joy that he would be doing something with Juanita that didn't involve the paranormal. Fear because it would involve his parents.

Juanita added, "Provided they'll let APK stay inside."

Tom replied, "They might confine her to my old bedroom. Are you okay with that, APK?"

"Mow!" APK replied with excitement in her voice.

Tom speed-dialed his parents. "Dad, I've got a couple of questions. Can Juanita join us for dinner, and can she bring her cat? Yes, *that* Juanita."

27

THE SMELL OF ROASTED meats and grilled vegetables filled the still summer air as Tom, Michelle, and Juanita sat down at the table on the deck. Several yards away was a large, clear pond. Tom's parents' home was one of many built around it.

Jason pointed at the rack of ribs on the table. "I used Robert's homemade BBQ sauce." He motioned to the hot dogs, burgers, and side dishes. "All of these dishes are from the fiftieth anniversary cookbook."

"Which one is Rene's dish?" Tom asked.

"Rene?"

"Rene McDonald. She's a former mayor of Bolingbrook."

Jason looked surprised. "Bolingbrook had other mayors?"

Tom shrugged. "People keep saying that to me."

"No," said Michelle. "She didn't contribute one."

"Or wasn't asked," said Jason. He started to reach for the hamburger buns. Juanita bowed her head and whispered a prayer. Jason pulled his arm back and stared at Juanita. Michelle locked her eyes on Jason. Tom watched his parents, unsure of what was about to happen.

Juanita finished her prayer and then raised her head. "Thank you for letting me join you. This looks great."

Michelle replied, "You're always welcome here." She glanced between Tom and Juanita.

Jason raised his eyebrows. "You still do that?"

"Do what?"

"Pray."

"Why are you surprised?" Juanita calmly replied.

"Dad," said Tom. "Do you—"

"I just want to know why the president of the Chicago Anti-Superstition Society believes in a sky-father."

"Jason," Michele warned.

Jason looked at her. "I just want to know how a prominent skeptic, like Juanita, can believe in skepticism and believe in a sky parent at the same time."

"Jason!" Michelle glared at Jason. She kicked his leg.

He looked back at his wife. "Ow!"

"That is no way to treat one of Tom's friends," said Michelle. She looked at Juanita. "Especially one we haven't seen in years."

Juanita raised her right hand. "It's okay. I don't mind answering."

Tom's parents focused on Juanita. He wished he could hide.

Juanita said, "You're not the first one to ask. So, I'll tell you what I've told Bennet and other atheist leaders. Skepticism is not a belief. It is a collection of tools. They are very effective tools, but, as you know, tools have their limits. A hammer cannot grill a meal. A grill cannot hammer a nail."

Jason started to speak but Michelle nudged him with her elbow.

"The tools of skepticism work at our level of perception. But at the quantum level, they don't work. Skepticism would require us to dismiss something that is both a particle and a wave. Or that the act of observation affects what we observe. Yet, these are all true statements. So maybe on our level, a being that can violate all the laws of science is impossible. But on a different level? Who is to say that someone's observation didn't create a universe fine-tuned enough to enable the creation of humanity?"

Tom and his family didn't respond. Tom had no desire to argue with Juanita. He hoped his father would drop it. Did he ever come across like this when he was a skeptical activist?

Juanita smiled. "So, can you tell me the story behind each of these dishes?"

***

The sunset cast a red and orange hue across the sky as Juanita completed her meal.

Michelle said, "I've learned so much working with the Golden Jubilee commission. Just listening to all the stories about Bolingbrook's early days has been amazing."

Jason replied, "I didn't know Valley View School District used to have year-round classes until your mother told me."

Michelle said, "I also learned about the Bolingbrook Yacht Club. They'd make small replicas of yachts, and then a team of four people would pick one up and pretend to sail the cornfields."

Tom resisted the urge to mention the yacht club's secret anti-gravity sailboats.

Juanita nodded. "The jubilee must be bringing so many memories for Bolingbrook's residents."

Michelle replied, "It is! And it encourages new residents to learn more about our village. I'm really happy with how the community is embracing the Jubilee!"

Jason added, "Even my customers are telling me their stories. Yesterday, I learned that Bailey's used to be a restaurant called Quick Burger."

Tom replied, "So they went from fast food to slow food?" He chuckled.

Michelle frowned at him.

Jason chuckled. "Sounds about right."

Michelle stood up. "I'm going to get the desserts. I think you'll love the Charlie Baffles."

"Charlie Baffles?" Juanita asked.

"Charlie Baffle was the Old Chicago Mall's mascot."

Jason, speaking almost like a cartoon character, said, "'Don't look at her. Look at me. Charlie Baffle!'"

"Jason," Michelle said, her voice reflecting her disapproval.

"That's what he said in the commercial."

Michelle looked at Tom. "Tom, could you help me?"

Tom followed Michelle back to the kitchen. Michelle reached the refrigerator, then faced Tom.

"When did you two get back together?"

Tom blinked and felt his head shake. "Mom! We never dated."

"You know what I mean. When did you hook up with her?"

Tom raised his eyebrows and widened his eyes. He thought about protesting, but that would only make things worse.

"I went to a CASS event to do research, and we bumped into each other. Then she offered to help me work on a story."

Michelle and Tom looked out the window. Juanita and Jason were talking to each other. Tom wondered if Juanita was experiencing the same awkward conversation he was.

"How's it going?" asked Michelle.

"Just fine," Tom quickly replied. "I've been learning a lot from her since we met up."

Michelle walked up to the sink and placed her hands on the counter. She watched Jason and Juanita talk for a few moments. "Back then, your dad and I knew you had a crush on Juanita."

"You've told me that for the past year," said Tom.

"I worried about the age difference back then. Now, you two are at the right age for each other."

Tom's jaw dropped. "Mom!"

"It's true." Michelle started towards the refrigerator.

"Are you pushing me to date Juanita?"

"I didn't say anything about dating." Michelle opened the freezer and pulled two caramel sundaes with plastic cowboy hats covering them. "But if you were to start dating, it would make your father and I very happy. We could finally stop worrying about your mental health."

"This is your ultimatum? Date Juanita or go to a psychiatric hospital?"

"Or you can think of it as a second chance. Second chances are precious, Tom. We shouldn't squander them." Michelle handed the sundaes to him. "Something to think about."

The chill from the glasses stung Tom. He started towards the back door, with Michelle following behind. When he stepped outside, he saw Juanita and Jason standing by the deck railing, looking out at the pond.

"Jason," Michelle called out. "Can you help me?"

"Sure," Jason replied.

His parents went inside the house. Juanita continued to look out. The pond reflected the red sky. Tom looked down at the sundaes, then at Juanita. He set them down on the table, approaching Juanita.

"I'm sorry about my parents," said Tom.

"Don't be," Juanita replied, still looking out at the pond. "Families worry about each other. They're just worried about you."

Tom stepped next to Juanita and leaned against the railing. "So, what did my dad have to say?"

Juanita turned her head towards Tom. "He said I would be a good influence in your life, and we looked great together."

Tom bit his lip. He imagined they did look great together. But why did his parents have to 'help' him now? "My mother said something like that. I'm surprised she didn't offer me her engagement ring."

As Juanita smiled warmly at Tom, he noticed their eyes were almost level. In his memories, he was always looking up at Juanita. Maybe it was because he was shorter than her then. Maybe it was because he figuratively looked up to her then. Now, he was looking at her, thinking about what his mother had told him about second chances and age differences. Was this his second chance with Juanita?

"What?" said Juanita.

"What?" Tom replied, confused by her statement.

"Why are you looking at me that way?"

Tom felt self-conscious. When he attended Habencon conventions, if a woman asked him that question, he'd give a flirtatious answer. Then they would make their way to either one of their rooms. But that was before he propositioned Jamie Kyle, and before he learned the dark secrets of the skeptical movement.

"I was just thinking," Tom replied, "I used to think that when I stopped going to the Lunch and Learns, I thought I'd never see you again." Tom hesitated. Jenna and Wendy were still in comas. This wasn't the time to talk about his feelings toward her. Not until his friends were safe, and everyone at the *Babbler* could return to Bolingbrook. "Now we're here and my parents are trying to set us up." Tom chuckled nervously. He expected Juanita to tell him she just wanted to be friends. While he'd feel disappointed, the events from the last four years taught him he wasn't entitled to any woman's affections. Friendship with Juanita was better than no contact with her.

Juanita looked out at the pond. Her silence rattled Tom. Why wasn't she saying anything? Was it a mistake to mention what his parents were doing? Did he say something to offend her? Did he just blow his second chance with Juanita?

Another thought came to mind. Was she about to say she also had feelings for him? Tom felt his heart beat faster. He used to think weredeer and aliens were impossible creatures, but now he knew they were real. Was the relationship with Juanita about to become real? Tom didn't want to risk saying anything that might blow his chances. He started towards the table. Maybe offering Juanita her sundae would work in his favor? Maybe eating his sundae would prevent him from starting another firestorm within organized skepticism?

"Tom?" Juanita said as she slowly approached Tom.

Tom tensed. Did he really screw up? Was Juanita about to tell him something life-altering?

Juanita said, "APK and I need to go somewhere."

"Somewhere?"

"If you join me, there's a good chance you'll get in serious trouble with the DPA and the *Babbler*. I can't ask you to take that risk. So, I can have someone take you back to the motel."

"Wait. Where are you going?"

"I can't tell you. Too dangerous for you to know."

Tom's heart sank. "Is this goodbye? Did I—"

"Tom." Juanita gave Tom a warm, reassuring smile. "If things go well, I'll meet you back at the motel."

"If they don't..."

"Let's not think about that."

"Maybe I can help? I grew up in Bolingbrook. Maybe I can—"

"Tom." Juanita clasped Tom's hands. He gasped. They'd never held each other's hands before. "I can't ask you to risk yourself for me." She looked into Tom's eyes. "Don't worry. I've faced werecoyotes and weredogs before. I can take care of myself."

"I know that," Tom replied. "I know I haven't held up my end of the fight, but maybe I can carry APK for you. Maybe I can keep watch. Be the voice. There must be something you can have me do."

"I need you to listen to me," Juanita replied. Tom felt his grip tighten, and he consciously loosened it. Juanita continued. "I'm flattered that you still care about me after all these years. But feelings can cloud our judgment." She released Tom's hands. "I'd feel better if you went back to the motel." She motioned towards the table. "We can finish our sundaes before I leave. Your parents put a lot of effort into them." She sat down and ate a spoonful of her sundae. "This is delicious. I'll have to compliment your mother before I leave. A Charlie Baffle sundae. Was Old Chicago known for its ice cream?"

Tom joined Juanita at the table. "I don't think so. Old Chicago was known for its indoor amusement park and novelty shops. It lacked anchor stores, so it lacked regular shoppers. Even the Charlie Baffle commercials couldn't fix that."

"Where was Old Chicago?"

"South of the I-55 and 53 exit. After the village imploded Old Chicago, it became an auto auction place." He started eating his sundae.

"Makes sense."

"Sense?"

Juanita shrugged.

Tom took a few more bites as considered what he was about to say. "Juanita?"

"Yes?"

"You're right. I do care about you. I also care about my friends, Wendy and Jenna. They've been in a coma since the *Phantom Press* attacked the *Babbler*. I care about Sara. This hasn't been easy for her family. I worry about the future of the *Babbler*. If there's even a slight chance I can help them, I'll take that chance."

Juanita took another spoonful of her sundae and took her time before swallowing it. "If I say no, you're going to figure out a way to escape and find me."

Tom chuckled. He hadn't thought of that. It did sound like a good idea, however.

Juanita placed her spoon in the cup. "In that case, I'll let you come along, but under three conditions. First, you stick with me the entire time. Second, I'll need you to take notes. Third, you're carrying APK."

28

Inside the back of the van, Tom held his arms up as Juanita adjusted the straps on the pet pouch he was wearing. APK, her head poking out the top hole, contently purred.

"How's that?" Juanita asked.

"Perfect," Tom said. He felt his heart beating faster.

"APK?"

"Mow!" APK replied, sounding like she was okay.

Juanita opened one of the containers and pulled out two glass cases. She handed one to Tom. "Put them on."

Tom opened the case. Inside were a pair of wire-rimmed glasses with straps. "What are these for?"

"Night vision," Juanita replied. "They activate automatically. We're going to need them inside."

Tom and Juanita put on their glasses. *It's like wearing windows,* Tom thought. They didn't affect his vision yet.

Juanita pulled out a pocket notebook and a small pen. She handed them to Tom.

"At first, the ink will only be visible when you're wearing the glasses. In a few hours, the ink will be visible to everyone.

Tom took the pen and notepad. He scribbled on the pad. The mark was visible. He lifted his glasses. The page appeared blank. He put them in his pocket where he normally kept his cell phone. Tom felt vulnerable and disconnected without it. It would be waiting for him in the van, he told himself.

Juanita put the cases away and pulled out a flashlight with a cap over the lens. She closed the container. "Follow me and act like you belong here," she said.

"Got it," Tom replied.

"Mow," said APK.

Tom and Juanita exited the van. They were standing in the north parking lot of Bolingbrook Commons. About twenty cars were parked around them. Ahead of them was a liquor store and a bingo hall, two of the few remaining businesses left in the strip mall. The rest of the mall was deserted, and the parking lot was a sea of concrete. Only five tractor-trailers were parked down there. Tom assumed they were truck drivers taking their mandatory breaks.

Juanita locked the van. "Stay close."

Tom walked next to Juanita as she mingled with the customers walking towards the neighboring businesses. He looked around the parking lot but didn't see any signs of the raid that had taken place days earlier. Even after covering paranormal activity in Bolingbrook for over a year, Tom was always impressed by the Bolingbrook's Clean-Up Crew's work. Their coverups were the reason almost no one believed the *Bolingbrook Babbler*.

Juanita offered her hand to Tom. He accepted it and felt a rush. He'd dreamed of holding her hand. None of those dreams involved sneaking into a semi-deserted strip mall while avoiding the DPA and the police.

Juanita guided him away from the small crowd. They moved in an arc towards the north fence. Tom wondered if she was trying to avoid a hidden camera.

"What are we looking for?" Tom asked in a hushed tone.

"Mow!" APK interrupted.

Tom sighed. He'd never been silenced by a cat before.

When they reached the driveway between the fence and the building, Juanita walked faster, almost pulling Tom along. He picked up his pace.

No going back now.

Near the corner of the building, Juanita studied the graffiti tags. Tom tried finding any that seemed significant, but none stood out.

Juanita whispered, "Stay close and low."

When they turned the corner, Tom gasped as he saw the security cameras mounted on the wall and fence.

APK looked up at Tom. "Mow."

I didn't say anything.

Tom followed Juanita as she weaved her way through the back alley. Tom knew she was avoiding the cameras, but how she knew the path puzzled Tom. Was there a map hidden in the graffiti? If so, how did she find it and know how to read it?

They continued their trek behind Bolingbrook Commons for what seemed like several blocks. Juanita's confidence in her path never wavered as they avoided the camera's blind spots.

After rounding a corner, ahead of them was the last loading dock. Tom realized it was part of the storefront where Roaming Roul lived. As he caught his breath, Tom wished they could have parked in one of the southern parking spots. However, they would have been the only vehicle there that wasn't a tractor-trailer.

Juanita guided Tom to a ventilation grate. She released his hand and motioned for him to put his back against the wall. As he did, APK moved her head, as if she were keeping watch.

After kneeling, Juanita pulled off the ventilation grate. She reached inside and started feeling around. Tom held his breath, hoping she didn't get bitten by a rat or trigger a trap. Seconds later, Juanita removed a shiny metallic key. She pocketed the key, then reached inside again. She tapped the metallic walls of the vent three times, then looked at a mounted camera facing the dock. The camera didn't move. Juanita replaced the grate.

"Almost there," she whispered as she offered her hand. Tom clasped it again.

Juanita stood up and walked at a normal pace. They climbed a short set of stairs and walked across the dock. The camera remained motionless. She stopped by the side door and unlocked it. Tom held his breath as she opened the door. The room inside was pitch black. Juanita removed APK from the pouch and held her.

APK looked up at Tom. "Mow."

I didn't say anything.

"It's scouting time," Juanita whispered.

She placed APK on the floor and the cat sniffed the air. Cautiously, she stepped into the darkness.

For what seemed like hours, Tom couldn't see or hear APK. Was APK okay? Was she too busy exploring to give the all-clear signal? Should he say something?

"Mow," APK finally said.

"All clear," Juanita said. "Stay close to me."

Tom and Juanita stepped into the room.

At first, Tom couldn't see anything. When Juanita closed the door, the lights came on, and he was standing in an empty storage room. But out of the corner of his eye, it was still dark. Tom realized the glasses provided full-color night vision. He marveled at the technology behind the glasses.

Juanita turned on her flashlight. Through the glasses, the spotlight appeared normal. Lowering his glasses, Tom couldn't see any light. He raised the glasses to see again.

APK crawled through a hole in the wall that led to another room.

"Mow," APK said, sounding to Tom like she was saying all clear.

Juanita approached the door, and Tom followed. "What are we looking for?" he asked.

"Anything unusual," Juanita replied. "But not unusual enough to be noticed by a sterilization team."

"Could you be more specific?"

"That's what I'm looking for. If you see anything like that, let me know."

"Okay... can I ask how these glasses work? They're amazing."

"You can," said Juanita. She turned the doorknob.

Tom moaned, "Seriously?"

Juanita shrugged as she opened the door into what now looked like a concrete cavern. Tom remembered that space started out as Bolingbrook's first grocery store. The last occupant was a tile and flooring store. That must have been years ago. The air reeked of mildew with a hint of urine. The floor was littered with wet ceiling panels and loose plaster. A few rusted shelves bolted to the floor reminded Tom of stalagmites. The scorch marks on the walls and floor reminded him of the raid that had taken place here days ago. In one area, they radiated from a bright white spot on the floor. Could it have been where the spheres went off, Tom wondered?

APK walked towards the middle of the storefront, sniffing the air. She sneezed a few times. Tom resisted the urge to tell her to be quiet.

Juanita moved her flashlight over the graffiti that covered the walls. In all the years he'd lived in Bolingbrook, he'd never seen so much graffiti in a single area. It would require major renovation work to turn this back into a retail space.

Juanita fixed the beam to a specific section of the wall. Tom realized the full-color vision of the glasses was limited to several yards. That's why Juanita brought the flashlight.

"Find something?" Tom asked.

Juanita moved her head slowly, as if she were reading something.

"I could check the other side, and we'd be finished in half the time."

Juanita walked away, still focused on the graffiti on the walls. To Tom, they looked like multicolored blobs of paint, the result of years of artists painting over each other's work. Tom tried to focus on the areas Juanita was interested in. Nothing stood out.

"What should I look for?" Tom asked.

Juanita didn't reply as she seemed focused on another spot further along the wall.

Tom sighed. Why was Juanita silent?

He looked over the wall again. This time, something stood out. It was a green and white image resembling a sunflower.

"Are we looking—"

Tom stopped when he recognized a second image. The sunflower was inside the outline of a spray-painted snow angel. He searched the walls again and saw more snow angels with sunflowers. Each pair had a unique purple symbol below it. He didn't recognize any of the symbols.

"A sunflower and an angel," said Tom. "This is Roul's work, right? Is this what he was trying to tell me about?"

Juanita moved her lips as if she were silently reciting something.

"You know what the symbols mean," Tom said as he approached Juanita. "What is his message?"

Juanita kept reading the symbols.

"Are you going to say anything?" Tom asked out of frustration.

"Get out the pen and pad," she replied. "I need you to write these numbers down."

Tom pulled out the pad and paper. Juanita waited until Tom was ready. She started reciting two-and three-digit numbers. He recorded each one and tried to determine if they were part of a pattern. She stopped after the fourth number.

"What do they mean?" Tom asked.

Juanita scanned the walls. "They're a key."

"To what?"

She scanned the walls again. "I'm not sure."

"Mow," said APK. She sat on her hind legs and stared at a wall. Juanita pointed her flashlight at where she was staring. White lines formed an incomplete outline of an angel. Inside the angel were outlines of sunflower petals. He didn't see any symbols beneath the angel that he recognized.

"How many library districts serve Bolingbrook?" Juanita asked.

"Fountaindale is the main library district." Tom thought for a moment. "Woodridge district serves part of Bolingbrook. Part of the Naperville district includes the subdivisions near Royce Road. Plainfield covers the area near the Bolingbrook Golf Club. I'm not sure about White Oak."

Juanita stepped closer to the fifth set. "Which one is considered the small library?"

"Small?" Tom struggled. "I've never been to the others. Maybe White Oak? Naperville's library seems smaller than Fountaindale, but it's built into a hill—" Tom remembered Roul saying something about his second favorite library. "I don't think Roul could bike to the other libraries. I wouldn't even try riding to the Naperville library on a ten-speed. His bike barely got him around Bolingbrook."

"What we're looking for is in the small library. Are there branch libraries? Any building that could be considered a library?"

Tom desperately tried to think of any building that Roul would call a library. "Um. A church library? Maybe one of the mosques? I'm drawing a blank."

APK grumbled as she looked up at the ceiling.

Tom looked up. "What's—"

"Quiet," Juanita snapped.

No one made a sound. A faint clanging came from the ceiling. APK jumped up onto one of the rusted shelves and hissed at the ceiling above Tom and Juanita. Juanita raised her flashlight. Above them were yellowing ceiling panels with several gaps. Visible through the gaps were the webs of wires and pipes. Cracking sounds came from above. Small pieces of drywall fell through the gaps.

APK growled and puffed her fur. She hissed at the ceiling again. The sound of twisting metal echoed throughout the room. A thumping sound came from the ceiling. More debris rained from the gaps between the ceiling panels.

"Should we leave?" Tom asked. His heart raced, thinking it was foolish to say the *Phantom Press* had found them.

Juanita shook her head. "Let's get closer to APK for now. If it's the *Phantom Press*, she's holding them back."

Sparks showered down through a gap. Tom looked up as he walked towards APK.

"I guess calling for backup is out of the question?" Tom asked. He made himself smile.

"Unfortunately."

The sound of a moving car came from outside. Car doors opened and closed. APK faced the front of the building and hissed.

"Quiet," Juanita said as she pulled out her pistol.

Tom moved closer to APK, and Juanita looked around the room as she stepped backwards. APK jumped off the shelf and approached Tom. Thumping and cracking sounds came from the front of the store. The humming above grew louder.

"We're going to the back room," Juanita said. "Nice and slow."

Tom put the notebook and pen in his pocket. If he was going to run for his life, he wouldn't want to risk dropping the notebook.

The sound of a car door opening again startled Tom. Was the driver leaving, he wondered? He turned to face the back door. The sound of twisting metal came from the front of the store.

Why hasn't the car door closed?

Someone turned on the car's bright lights. The night vision glasses were blinded, only showing a wall of white light. Tom lifted the glasses onto his head. Juanita did the same.

A popping sound came from outside. A bullet made a hole in the window and hit a shelf near APK.

"Mow!" APK jumped away from the impact area. More shots from a semi-automatic weapon rang out. Near APK, bullets exploded, ripping holes in the floor and causing the rusty shelves to rattle.

Juanita dropped to the floor, whereas Tom fell. Juanita assumed a prone position and aimed her gun at the lights. Tom cursed as he hit the floor, then he lay as flat as he could.

APK tried to rush, but the bullets landing in front of her drove her back. She started zigzagging towards the shelves.

More shots rang out, hitting the frame of one shelf and shattering it. The shelf collapsed into a cloud of dust. APK changed course and zigzagged towards the hole in the back wall.

"Shouldn't you be shooting back?" Tom asked.

Juanita shook her head. "I don't have a shot."

More bullets exploded near APK as she approached them. "Tom," said Juanita. "When I tell you to, run to the back room and wait for me."

"They'll see me!"

"Not after I'm done," said Juanita.

The shooting stopped. The humming sound above them drowned out the sound of the vehicles on I-55.

Juanita fired eight shots out the window, knocking out the car's lights. The room darkened.

Juanita lowered her glasses down onto her eyes. She aimed her pistol at the damaged car.

"Now?" Tom asked.

"Not yet," said Juanita.

Behind them, part of the roof cracked and gave way. The debris crashed into a shelving rack. The force of the impact sent the rack crashing towards APK.

"Mow!" APK screamed in terror. She dashed through the hole in the back wall. The rack hit the floor with a loud crash. The debris blocked the hole APK had just used to escape.

The sound of bending metal came from the front of the store. The metal pipes broke off the ceiling and crashed through the panels, the sound echoing through the empty room. Spliced electrical wires dropped from the ceiling. The sparking wires illuminated the room.

A chorus of whispers echoed throughout the room. A chill ran down Tom's spine. "Now?" he asked.

As metal pipes and live wires fell, cracks spider-webbed across the ceiling, sending dust and debris down towards them.

"Now!" said Juanita.

She bounced to her feet. Tom found the strength to push off the floor and onto his feet. He ran after Juanita as debris rained down behind him. His fear of getting crushed overrode his fear of getting shot. The voices that started as whispers became unintelligible screams. He realized they were no longer within APK's protective bubble. *The Phantom Press* was closing in on them.

Pipes and live wires tumbled to the floor and blocked the back door. Two avalanches of pipes and sparking wires were about to engulf them.

Both stopped. Juanita holstered her gun, then grabbed Tom's hand. "Concentrate," she said. She reached for the crucifix and started to pray the rosary.

Tom started to recite the Ethical Union's motto. His heart raced as the downpour of debris approached.

Darkness enveloped them.

29

THE SOUND OF AN ocean?

A click. A hiss. Two beats. Repeat.

Like a machine, the pattern persisted. Unchanging. The only reality outside of Tom's mind. Nothing else in the void.

A click. A hiss. Two beats. Repeat.

Tom remembered his name. What were those sounds? Where was he?

A monster. The memory of a monster chasing him. The world spinning. Whispers of other memories too faint to recall. Were they from a previous reality. A reality he destroyed. Scenes from dreams long forgotten. A universe he created and destroyed?

Tom opened his eyes. Reality was now a blur of colors and light. The pattern persisted. A machine. A God Machine?

Another sound. A voice. Male. Faint. No. Three voices. Becoming clearer.

"Let me assure you, Bolingbrook has the finest hospital in the region. Better than Edward's."

A man appeared. Robert. Mayor.

"You might not want to see this."

His parents stood at the foot of the bed. His mother gasped. His father's jaw dropped.

Robert said, "He made a hard turn onto Boughton without stopping. Car flipped over. Luckily, he didn't kill anyone."

His mother said, "Can he hear us?"

"Yes," Robert replied. "But he may never wake up."

"Why did he do this?" Jason asked.

A new voice. "He let himself be fooled."

Robert and his parents vanished. Reese Habenstein towered over him.

"You let those liars at the *Babbler* get in your head. When you saw a sweet doe in a yard, you imagined a monster."

But he didn't imagine a monster. A weredeer chased him. He got a clear view of it.

His father appeared. "Did you forget everything I taught you? Use your skepticism. What's more likely? You were chased by a monster. Discovered a UFO base. Saved Jamie and Humanist Heart. Joined the *Babbler*?"

Pamela appeared. "Or did you end up in a coma? Imagined everything the *Babbler* said was true. Created an imaginary friend who would absolve you. Dreamed up a story about saving Jamie and Humanist Heart so you could have a happy ending."

Jamie Kyle replaced Pamela. "Your hatred of me led to your downfall."

Two voices shouted in the distance. Women?

Reese replaced Jamie. "I am so disappointed in you."

Tom tried to speak, but something was in his throat. A respirator breathing tube. He tried to move, but he couldn't feel his body.

Jamie reappeared. "You committed a horrible crime in that elevator."

Jason appeared. "This is your prison."

Pamela appeared. "Where you will spend the rest of your life."

Michelle appeared. "Because you are irredeemable."

Natalie's voice filled the room. "Grandpa. Stop it! Stop hurting him. Just take me home. We need to go home!"

A man's voice shook the room. "We need to grow and escape!"

Tom had heard the man's voice before. When?

Natalie appeared. How did he know her name?

She started crying. "We need to go home. Please?"

The lights turned red, and the man's voice shook the room like a powerful earthquake.

"No! Not until they pay."

Voices, too numerous for Tom to count, replied, "All of them!"

Natalie started to fade. Hundreds of hands reached into reality and grabbed her. Her eyes widened in horror as her body solidified.

"Let me go! Please let me go home. Tom! Tell them to let me go home!"

The hands pulled her out of reality.

Tom was alone in the hospital room. A flat-screen TV hung on the wall in front of him, playing a live broadcast of the Cubs against the White Sox. He watched as the White Sox batter hit a home run.

A man, maybe one of the color commentators, said, "There's only one relief pitcher who can save the Cubs."

A Cubs pitcher ran out of the dugout. The crowded booed.

"He made this team. He brought them to this point. But because he made one little mistake years ago, everyone hates him. Despite all the hard work he did during the off season, nobody will forgive him."

The fans threw garbage at the pitcher. Players on both teams booed him.

"You know," said the announcer. "This isn't fair. He can help them win. But they'd rather bury him than win another game."

A layer of garbage covered US Cellular Field. The crowd kept booing and throwing garbage.

"This should be his opportunity to shine," said the color commentator.

The relief pitcher slowed to a stop.

"But someone just stole his opportunity."

A pitcher stood on the mound with his back turned towards the camera. He slowly turned to face the camera. Robert was the pitcher. He presented a comically exaggerated smile. His eyes glistened with pride.

The TV switched to the relief pitcher running onto the field.

The relief pitcher looked into the camera and said, "I think you understand." His voice sounded familiar.

The TV cut to the pitcher's mound. Jamie was the pitcher. Her impossibly wide smile made her look like a monster. The TV cut to the relief pitcher. This time, the relief pitcher was his future self.

"And you know what needs to be done."

The TV cut to an aerial view of US Cellular Field. A dome of fire appeared and grew. It engulfed the field in seconds. When it expanded into the stands, the TV cut to shots of the flames engulfing the crowd. He recognized Bolingbrook officials, members of Humanist Heart, and the hosts of Skeptical World. All of them incinerated before his eyes.

Tom gasped before the respirator forced air into his lungs.

"We can't leave the stadium without your help."

Reality rippled. What sounded like a cat's yowl, emitted from all directions. The hospital room became white and featureless. His future self transformed into a man in his 50s wearing a 1970s style earth tone sports jacket.

The sound ended, and the hospital room returned. His future self reappeared. However, Tom was no longer on a respirator. He was still in his hospital bed, and his future self towered over him.

Tom said, "If everything I remembered after the accident was a coma dream, then you shouldn't be here. Because time travel is impossible in that reality." He sat up. "Is this a trick to feed off my emotions?"

"Maybe," said the time traveler. "But it's real to you."

The time traveler vanished. In his place was a mass of slithering vines connected to Jamie's head. "Is this better?"

On each leaf, a mouth opened, revealing snake-like fangs that protruded from each leaf. It looked and felt real to Tom.

Tom tried to stand, but his legs were pinned between the mattress and the blanket. He tried to push himself backwards, but his hands sank into the mattress. He struggled to lift them, but his hands felt like they were enveloped in a lake of cement glue.

The vines grew towards him. The mouths spoke at once in different voices. All of them disparaged him. He recognized the voices of his parents saying he was insane. Former classmates taunted Tom for being a skeptic who turned into a believer. Former friends in the skeptical movement called him a traitor. Members of Humanist Heart said Tom was a delusional creep.

The Jamie monster looked at Tom with her snake eyes. "These are their real thoughts, Tom. This is what they think of you. A traitor, a fool, and a creep."

The vines encircled Tom, their fangs inches from his face and body. Their demeaning voices were almost deafening.

"They will tear you apart and destroy you, and when you die, they will taint your memory."

"You lie!" Tom shouted. "Jamie and I settled things!"

The vines descended upon Tom, digging their fangs into flesh. He screamed as the leaves' fangs dug deeper into his flesh. Their voices grew louder, calling him weak, making homophobic remarks, and launching other deeply personal attacks.

The monster said, "You can't reason with them. They will consume you. Unless you fight back."

Tom felt a painful heat inside his body. Like a fire. The more pain the vines inflicted, the stronger the fire grew.

"Yes," said the monster. "You have the power to make them pay. Let your rage burn them."

The fire inside burned like an inferno. His inferno. One that could unleash the vines with a single thought. To make them burn. To make them feel pain. It was within his power. All he had to do was think it.

The cat's yowling returned. It was APK's voice. The world vanished. Tom floated in the freezing void.

"Tom!" It was Jenna. Her voice came from all directions. "Can you hear me?"

"Yes," Tom shouted. "Where are you?"

"Follow my voice."

"I can't tell where you are."

"Let go of Legion's lie!"

APK's yowl stopped. Tom felt dozens of fangs piercing his flesh as the hospital room and the vine monster returned. He screamed. More vines entangled him.

"I'll give you a real reason to scream," said Jamie.

The new vines sank their fangs into Tom's flesh. As his pain increased, the inferno raged within him.

Jamie moved her head closer to Tom. "After all I've done to you, and all I'm going to do, you still don't have the courage to burn me."

The pain was unbearable. His rage turned into flames. He felt those flames in his lungs and throat. He tilted his head towards the monster. All he had to do was open his mouth and unleash the firestorm within him.

Jenna's voice came over the PA. "Don't give in. Come to me. It's your only chance."

Jamie said, "Or unleash your fire upon the world. So many people need to burn."

Tom felt the flames burning his tongue. The feedback loop of pain overwhelmed his thoughts. It would stop if he just opened his mouth.

"This is like a dream," Jenna said, her voice now inside his head. "There's nothing to bind you except your thoughts. Legion is creating an illusion. Reject it!"

The heat from the flames burned Tom. He needed to release it, but what if Jenna was right?

"Remember what the skeptics taught you. Reject Legion's illusion and come to my voice. Come to me if you want to survive."

Tom looked away from Jamie. Beside the bed, there was a white light in the air. The reality around the light blurred. Tom tried to reach for the light, but more vines entangled his arms and bit him. The ball of light grew larger but was still out of reach. The bites intensified.

Inward.

Tom absorbed the power of the flames. His muscles bulged, and the vines started breaking. He tore away the vines with the bare hands. More vines attacked, but their fangs shattered when they bit into his skin.

"Don't be tempted!" Jenna screamed. "You can't control the power."

Tom's skin turned red-hot. The bed burst into flames. Tom absorbed the flames as he stood up.

Jamie retracted her vines. "One way or another. You will burn with us."

Tom looked at himself. His glowing skin struggled to contain the fire within.

"No!" Tom said to the Jamie-monster.

He reached for the light. As the light enveloped him, the fire within subsided.

"Come back here," Jamie growled.

The bright light blinded him. He no longer felt the flame or their power. Fear and rage gave way to peace and serenity.

"It's okay, Tom."

Wendy!

Tom opened his eyes. He was inside the *Babbler's* newsroom as it appeared before the attack. Wendy stood by her desk. They were the only people in the newsroom.

"We need your help," Wendy said.

30

Tom approached Wendy's desk. He smelled the coffee in her mug. The room temperature was perfect. It was never perfect.

"Wendy?"

Wendy nodded. "Yes. Sort of."

Tom froze. "Sort of?"

Wendy groaned. "I shouldn't have said it like that."

Tom backed away. "You'd better not be a vine monster."

"Oh my God," said Wendy. "That's terrible."

Tom looked around the newsroom. "Am I still in the nightmare?"

Wendy shook her head. "You're out of the nightmare, but you're not awake. Do you remember when I told you what ghosts really are?"

"Um... mental energy in the Ghost Frequencies?"

Wendy smiled for a moment. "Exactly. Right now, we're at the boundary between the Ghost Frequencies and the frequencies of the mind. The Council of Psychics created a bubble that's protecting us from Legion."

"Legion? What the heck is Legion?"

"I don't know."

Tom felt a chill within him. There wasn't a paranormal subject that she didn't have some passing knowledge about. Until now. "You... don't know?"

Wendy replied, "I don't know exactly what it is. It seems to be what the *Phantom Press* has turned into, or maybe they were consumed by it." She stepped closer to Tom. "It doesn't matter. Legion attacked us during the séance, and it overwhelmed us. I was just able to activate the EMP before we were pulled into the Ghost Frequencies. That gave the council enough time to create this bubble. Otherwise, Legion would have consumed us."

Tom tilted his head. "Consumed?"

Wendy nodded. "Consumed or absorbed. We know it calls itself Legion, and it appears to be an amalgamation of ghosts."

Tom did a double take. "Wait a minute. You mean all the ghosts I've been seeing are part of a single entity?"

"It shouldn't be possible, but that's what the evidence points to. Some of the ghosts retain some of their individuality; most of the others seem to be reduced to batteries, and possibly memory storage. It—"

A deafening yowling emanated from all directions. Tom and Wendy covered their ears. The world outside them blurred. The yowling ended, and the world returned to normal.

Wendy uncovered her ears. "What was that?"

"It's APK," Tom replied. "Juanita and APK are helping me."

"Juanita Vega?"

Tom nodded. "We were attacked by Legion. She might be trapped in here, too."

Jenna appeared, looking like Tom's idealized mental image of her. "I don't sense her inside the Ghost Frequencies."

"Jenna!" Tom approached her. "Thank you for saving me."

"I just showed you the path," Jenna said with a smile.

Wendy said, "Can you tell us what happened since we were captured?"

"During the summoning, Roul contacted me and wanted to meet at Bolingbrook Commons. When I arrived, the DPA had captured Roul. Four operatives died when they tripped a sphere's booby trap."

"No," Wendy protested. "I've been there. There were no traps."

"I saw the flash—"

"Where is he now?"

"Solitary confinement," Tom said. "Even Robert isn't allowed to see him. Not that he would listen to him. Robert hit him and said he was a murderer."

Wendy's eyes widened. "Hit... him?"

"Yes."

"Oh my," Jenna said.

Tom nodded. "After the séance, Sara activated the Scatter Protocols."

"Smart move," Wendy replied. "Sara let you stay in Bolingbrook?"

"No," Tom sighed. "Said it was too dangerous for me. She assigned Don to stay in Bolingbrook."

Wendy and Jenna looked at each other, then looked back at Tom.

"Don doesn't know what he's doing," Wendy said. "He was totally unprepared for Legion. And the séance was his damn idea."

"Or it might be something worse," Jenna said. "I just have that feeling. I don't know why."

Tom looked at Wendy. "I took your advice and started my own investigation. I'm not sure what Don's up to. Except I saw him at the raid."

"Raid?" Wendy asked.

Tom nodded. "The DPA and Orange Squad had a joint operation that ended with a raid on the bad building of Naperville. Steve said they stopped a powerful ghost from being transferred to Bolingbrook. Did either of you sense this?"

"I heard screaming," Jenna said. "As if Legion were absorbing ghosts."

"We would have sensed if a powerful ghost were nearby," said Wendy. "But I don't think any ghosts in Chicago are as powerful as Legion. It makes little sense."

Tom said, "There are spirit junkies in Bolingbrook. They're the reason why Juanita and I are in this mess."

"What can you tell us about them?" asked Wendy.

"Three men and one woman. Two of the men are wearing Cubs gear. They might have something to do with the fake ritual."

"Possibly," Wendy replied.

"The ritual might be fake, but they're able to tap into Legion."

Wendy's face reflected her bewilderment. "There is no way a human could survive channeling Legion."

"Unless," said Jenna, "it's connected to the web I keep seeing in my visions."

Wendy took a moment to collect her thoughts. "If there's a network that's able to focus or distribute Legion's energy..." Fear showed in Wendy's eyes. "We're not dealing with local ghost riders. This is far more organized than they could pull off. And they'd have to set up the network without the DPA knowing about it."

An earthquake rocked the office. Binders fell from the top of the file cabinets.

Jenna faded for a moment. "We'll need to release Tom soon to save our bubble."

"Before you let me go," said Tom, "I have a question."

"Yes?" said Wendy.

"Why does Legion want me?"

"Want you?" Wendy asked.

Ton tensed. "It wants me to join it. Something about escaping Bolingbrook. It's offering me a chance to get back at the skeptical movement. Especially Jamie. In the nightmare, it tried to manipulate me, But..."

"But?" Wendy asked.

Tom took a deep breath. "Just before Jenna helped me escape, I felt like I could tap into its power. Like I could be Legion's equal."

"It was tempting you," Jenna replied. "I don't know why."

"I'm glad you resisted," said Wendy.

Tom nodded. "But"—he paused—"is it possible to turn that energy against Legion? Not to become it, but to weaken or destroy it."

Wendy and Jenna looked at each other.

"Tell him," Jenna said in hushed tone.

Wendy's eyes widened. "No. It's too dangerous."

"He needs to know."

Wendy shook her head. "We don't know what your vision means."

"But if it breaks through, Tom needs to know about this."

"What?" Tom said. "What won't you tell me?" He walked up to Wendy. "You said you trusted me. I'm risking my career because you told me Don was on the wrong track. You said you wanted to give me your contacts. To take over your fieldwork. Why won't you trust me now?"

Wendy tensed. "Because it's an option of last resort, and you can't do this on a whim. I like you, Tom. I want you to succeed as a reporter. But you can't play with fire. I wouldn't even try this."

Another earthquake rattled the office.

"I'm going to have to let him go soon," said Jenna. She disappeared, then reappeared.

Tom exhaled. "I know I can be impulsive. But please. I'm not just working on the story. I want to save both of you and everyone trapped inside. If Legion threatens Bolingbrook, I don't want to report the disaster. I want to stop it before it happens. If what you're talking about is a last resort, then I promise to wait until there's no other option." He looked into Wendy's eyes. "Please?"

Wendy looked at Jenna, then back at Tom. "Okay." She took a deep breath. "Yes. The emotions that fuel Legion can also be used against it. In theory, you could disintegrate it. But." She paused. "You can only try this if Legion enters our world. Even then, if you tap into the source for too long, there's a chance you would merge with Legion. Tom, I'm begging you, try other means of defeating Legion first. What I told you is the last resort. Understood?"

Tom looked into Wendy's eyes and felt the weight of her fear and worry. "I understand. Last resort." He looked at Wendy and Jenna. "Can we hug before I go?"

Jenna and Wendy embraced Tom together. Tom closed his eyes and held them tight. His eyes watered.

The ground started cracking under his feet. They ended their embrace. Jenna and Wendy stepped back.

"So," said Tom. He smiled. "That's what it's like to hug your siblings."

The floor gave way, and Tom fell into the darkness. Moments later, he felt like he was lying on a hard floor. He heard Juanita reciting another prayer. Tom opened his eyes. He was inside the Bolingbrook Commons again. Huey stood over him.

"What the fuck are you doing back here?"

31

Tom backed away from Huey until he heard a sparking wire behind him.

The fiery white glow emanating from Louie and Daisy's eyes illuminated the storefront. They circled Juanita like hungry sharks. She stood with her eyes closed, whispering the Lord's Prayer, her lips barely moving.

"You will burn with the others," Louie said, his voice blended with countless ghosts speaking through him.

"We have returned from the light," Daisy said, her voice joining the chorus of ghosts within her. "There is no Heaven awaiting us. No Father to save us. Only Hell and oblivion lie ahead."

Juanita spoke up. "I shall fear no evil. For the Lord is with me." Tears ran down her face.

A gunshot echoed throughout the room.

Dewey stood beside a camping lantern, one of several scattered throughout the debris-covered floor. With a flick of his wrist, he ejected a clip from his pistol and reached into one of his vest's pouches.

"Shoo!" Dewey screamed into the shadows. "I will kill you if you try that one more time."

"Mow!" APK replied from her hiding place.

"You son of a bitch!" Tom yelled.

Dewey looked at Tom and scowled. "What are you doing here?" He loaded a new clip into his pistol. "If you don't go back, I'll send you back!"

Huey grabbed Tom's hair and pulled him to his feet. Tom winced as he reached for Huey's hand. He twisted Tom's head and marched towards Juanita.

"I got this," Huey shouted to Dewey. "Just keep the cat away."

"Hurry up," Dewey replied. "She's not strong enough."

"She looks fine to me," Huey replied. He released Tom's hair, and he stumbled to a stop.

Juanita's body trembled, and her voice wavered as she repeated the Lord's Prayer. Tom clenched his fists as Louie and Daisy's closed in on Juanita.

"Look at her," said Huey. "Legion's going to drain her dry if she doesn't break." He moved next to Tom. "I wouldn't wish this on my worst enemy."

Tom scowled at Huey. His face turned red.

Huey smiled. "I'd kill to have the same choice you have. We can't force you to go back. You have to—"

Tom shoved Huey, but the man barely moved. "What is this all about?" he asked. "Why are you sacrificing Bolingbrook?"

Huey smirked. "To break the curse on the Cubs. It's not fair. The White Sox have so many championships. The Cubs have never been to the World Series. What's the loss of a few thousand White Sox fans compared to the joy of millions of Cubs fans?"

Tom started to shout but stopped. He tilted his head as he looked into Huey's eyes.

"Yeah," Tom said, his voice filled with awe. "It's also not fair that Peter Ramirez hit 100 home runs and never made it to the playoffs."

Huey's eyes light up. "Exactly."

Tom stared at Huey, then chuckled. "The Cubs won two World Championships. I made up Peter Ramirez." He pointed at Huey's face. "You don't know jack shit about the Cubs."

Huey shoved Tom, who tripped over a pipe and fell to the floor.

Huey looked down at Tom. "I know your girlfriend doesn't have much time."

"Fuck the script," Dewey said as he approached Tom. "She's been under long enough."

Huey faced Dewey. "Paula wants—"

Dewey looked at Tom. "I'm not sorry." He pointed his pistol at Tom.

"No!" Daisy screamed with Natalie's voice. The glow in her eyes turned blood red.

Dewey's eyes widened and his face turned pale as he stared at the gun. He dropped his gun and screamed as he looked at the palm of his trembling right hand. He staggered away from Tom and Huey. Huey watched Dewey in stunned silence.

Tom gripped the insulated part of a dangling live wire, feeling the hum of electricity, and pressed the electrified end against Huey. Huey dropped to the floor and convulsed.

Louie's eyes stopped glowing, and an invisible force tossed him into the back wall. He winced as he slid to the floor. The invisible force tossed Huey towards the back of the room, who landed and tumbled to the floor. He shook his head and struggled to stand up.

Dewey's eyes glowed white. His voice, now sounding like Natalie's, said, "I don't want the fire. I don't want to be here. Stop this. Please!"

"No," Daisy said, her voice merging with a cacophony of other voices.

Dewey's eyes stopped glowing. Juanita collapsed to the floor. Daisy walked around Juanita towards Dewey.

"They're all inside me," Daisy said with her own voice. "It works." The glow in her eyes changed to yellow.

Dewey rose to the feet. "Cut the link! Get out before you lose yourself!"

"Why?" Daisy asked, her voice filled with awe. "You were right. It is beautiful." She looked at Tom. "You're afraid of the fire. That's okay. You might want to step back." She looked at Huey and Louie. "Both of you should leave now. You too, kitty."

Tom ran towards Juanita. She sat up and shook her head. Tom helped her stand up.

"Are you okay?" Tom asked.

"We have to get out of here," she replied.

"Tom," said Daisy. She disappeared. Other people appeared and disappeared in rapid succession. "We'll be waiting for you."

Juanita shook Tom. "Snap out of it."

Tom blinked and saw Daisy again. She smiled and then approached Dewey.

Tears ran down Dewey's face as he stood up. "I'm s-so s-sorry," he stammered, the fear evident in his trembling voice. "It's all my fault."

"Don't be sorry," Daisy replied. "There's no reason to be afraid. You told me that."

"I was wrong. Please come back."

"No," she said.

Juanita picked up the night vision glasses on the floor. "APK! We've got to leave now."

APK sprinted out of the shadows towards the front door.

Juanita tapped Tom's shoulder. "Now or never, Tom." She started towards the front door.

Daisy opened her arms as she closed in on Dewey.

Tom nodded and followed Juanita.

The glow in Daisy's eyes vanished as she reached Dewey.

Juanita's eyes widened. "Run!"

Tom and Juanita sprinted towards the door, jumping over debris piles in their path.

Dewey said, "You're not supposed to be the conduit. It wasn't meant for you."

"Don't be afraid," Daisy whispered. "Hold my hand."

Dewey reached out with his trembling hands and clasped Daisy's steady hands.

"Now what?" Dewey asked, his voice trembling.

Daisy's eyes glowed bright red. Softly, she said, "Burn with me."

Blue flames erupted from Daisy's body. Dewey screamed as the flames engulfed him. Their bodies burst into an expanding fireball, the light momentarily blinding. The scorching air stung Tom's face as it rushed past him. His heart pounded as he tried to run faster.

Juanita stopped after passing through the front door. She held her hand out.

"Come on!" she yelled at Tom.

APK darted past Tom. Tom grabbed Juanita's hand, and she pulled him through the door. He looked back at the approaching firestorm. Should he have tried to rescue APK?

"APK!" he shouted.

APK stopped. She arched her back, and her fur puffed out. Her eyes glowed blue as she hissed at the flames. The firestorm stopped as if it had run into an invisible wall. Seconds later, the flames vanished. No trace of Dewey or Daisy remained in the charred room.

"Mow," she gasped, then dropped to the floor.

32

JUANITA AND JUANITA RAN up to APK. APK purred as she lay unconscious on the floor.

"She's resting," Juanita said as she picked her up.

"Good," Tom replied.

They placed APK back in the front pet pouch and exited the building. APK's fur and their clothes were covered in white dust and black soot. The north side of the parking lot, where the van was parked, seemed like it was miles away.

"Are you okay?" Tom asked. It was a better conversation starter than, "What the hell just happened?"

Juanita looked in the direction of Bolingbrook Drive and I-55. She halted and motioned for Tom to stop. Nothing in that direction stood out to Tom, just the normal flow of traffic he'd expect late at night. Cautiously, Tom moved next to Juanita, whose eyes locked on something in the distance. She extended her arm.

"The banners," she whispered.

Tom noticed the fiftieth anniversary banners on the light poles along Bolingbrook Dr. They were motionless in the still night air.

"They look fine," Tom replied.

"That's the problem."

After their previous encounters, Tom remembered the nearest banners caught on fire or were singed by sparks. Tom thought the energy from the ghosts must have caused the electrical wires to spark and ignite the banner hanging on them. These banners were just fine.

"She said they fixed it," Juanita mumbled.

"I heard," Tom replied. He remembered the banners outside the bad building igniting. Those banners were made of Rene's conductive cloth. He assumed they ignited because they were overloaded with energy from the ghosts following the trail.

The pieces started to fall into place. If the fiftieth anniversary banners were made with conductive cloth, that would explain the sparks after his encounters with Legion. They were overloaded. But if these banners didn't catch on fire?

"We need to run," Juanita said as she started to run.

Tom shuddered; the van now seemed miles away. "I'm going to regret this." He rushed after Juanita.

The gap between them lengthened as Juanita accelerated towards the van. Tom struggled to keep running as his legs cramped. APK grumbled as the pouch bounced against Tom's body.

"Almost there," Tom gasped. His lungs burned.

If I survive, I promise to go to the gym every week.

Juanita pulled out her keys and aimed at the van. The side door opened, and she leaped into the van.

As he sprinted up to the van, Tom groaned, his muscles protesting with each step.

Juanita rushed to prepare APK's carrier, showing no signs of fatigue from running.

Tom arrived several seconds later, struggling to catch his breath. Juanita stepped over and gently removed APK from the cat pouch. APK rested her head against Juanita's shoulder as she tried to resume her nap. After Tom took off the pouch, Juanita tossed the key ring to Tom. Tom fumbled but managed to catch them.

"Start the van," said Juanita.

Tom looked at the van. He'd driven large cars before, but not one with so many hidden features.

"Now!" Juanita commanded as her eyes widened.

Until now, Tom had seen Juanita as focused and confident. If she was afraid, then there was no time to argue.

Tom hopped into the van and reached the driver's seat. He inserted the key, took a deep breath, and tuned it. The van started immediately, triggering the open-door alarm.

"Shouldn't you be driving?" Tom asked.

"You're driving," Juanita said as she gently placed APK in her other carrier.

Tom's eyes widened. "What if I push the wrong button?"

"You can't mess up," Juanita said as she secured the carrier's door.

Tom wasn't sure if that was a statement or a warning.

"We've got to leave Bolingbrook," Juanita said. She pulled the side door closed, and the alarm stopped.

Tom took a deep breath. "Strap in."

At the nearest exit, a line of cars waited for the stoplight to turn green. Other cars from Denny's and Bailey's would be joining the line.

The one time I need to escape from Bolingbrook Commons, there's a traffic jam in the parking lot.

Juanita rushed into the passenger seat and fastened her seatbelt. "Go!"

Tom backed out of the spot. It was like driving a large boat but manageable. He switched to drive and drove towards the line of cars.

"Who are we running from?" Tom asked.

Juanita glared at him. "What are you doing? There are other exits!"

Tom tightened his grip on the steering wheel. "We can either get on I-55 or go to Romeoville. Both require a left turn, and I can only do that at the stoplight."

She pointed towards the road parallel to the freeway. "What about that one?"

"Takes you into a residential area," Tom snapped. "It'd be like running a maze to reach Boughton. The freeway or Romeoville are the best options, and they're to the left."

"Fine," Juanita shot back, her voice sharp and laced with annoyance.

She reached under the dashboard and Tom heard a clicking sound. The car's lights started flashing, and the horn sounded off. After removing her hand, she opened the compartment between them and pulled out a police strobe light with a magnetic base.

"Go around them," Juanita said as she opened the window. "You have the right of way."

"Who are we running from?" he asked as Juanita turned on the flashing light.

"DPA," she said and then set the flashing light on the van's roof. "Police, men in blue, Whatever the hell Bolingbrook can send, it's coming for us!"

The traffic light and turn signal turned green. A white light mounted between the stoplights turned on. Drivers on Bolingbrook Drive started pulling over and stopping.

"You have the right of way," Juanita said, her voice a mix of fear and annoyance. "You're now driving an unmarked law enforcement vehicle."

Tom passed the exiting cars and accelerated towards Bolingbrook Drive. Faint whispers came from all directions.

"Don't stop," Juanita said as she opened a hidden compartment next to the glovebox.

Tom slowed to make a left turn. The whispers grew louder. The sound of sirens grew closer.

Juanita pulled out a flare gun and aimed it out the window. She pulled the trigger as Tom accelerated down Bolingbrook Drive. The flare ignited a fiftieth anniversary banner hanging on a light post. Moments later, the banner burst into flames and showered blue sparks onto the ground. Three more banners burst into flames and rained sparks on the cars below. The whispers abruptly ended.

Juanita closed the window and pointed the flare gun at the floor of the van.

"Get on the Stevenson," she yelled.

It took Tom a moment to realize she meant I-55. In Chicago, it was known as the Stevenson Expressway in Cook County. He could never keep all the names straight, despite growing up in Chicagoland.

Juanita yelled, "Don't slow down!"

"I have to make a left turn," Tom replied, revealing his annoyance. "I don't want to flip over."

"Don't worry about that," Juanita replied. "It has an advanced suspension. It's unlikely to flip over."

"Unlikely?"

"Trust me," she snapped.

Tom turned to the left. The tires squealed as the van pulled to the right. Tom grip tightened as he flashed back to the rollover last year.

"Focus!" Juanita yelled at Tom.

Tom pointed the van towards the I-55 on-ramp and floored the accelerator. The van stabilized as it reached the on-ramp. Tom merged with Chicago bound traffic, then checked the sun visor above his head. "Do you have an I-PASS?"

"Why?"

"I'll need it when we get on I-355," said Tom.

"Don't take the Veterans Tollway!" Juanita said as her eyes widened with fear.

Tom gritted his teeth. "Then I'll take 294 instead." He glanced at Juanita. "Whatever you want to call it, I'm taking it."

Juanita took a deep breath, then returned the flare gun to its compartment. "Are we out of Bolingbrook?"

Tom drove past the exits to I-355 and kept accelerating until the Plainfield Costco was directly to his left.

"Now we are," Tom replied, his fingers still clinched to the steering wheel.

"You can slow down," she replied, sounding calmer. She turned off the horn and flashing lights. Then she removed the police strobe light from the roof.

"Thank you," said Tom.

Juanita closed her eyes and whispered a prayer.

***

Tom loosened his grip on the steering wheel after merging onto the Tri-State Tollway northbound. Juanita looked out the window. Since leaving Bolingbrook, they hadn't spoken for several minutes. The silence gnawed at him.

"I'll start," he said.

Juanita nodded, still looking out the window.

Tom described the nightmare and his subsequent rescue by Jenna and Wendy. Juanita nodded and kept looking out the window. He wondered what nightmare she'd gone through but, obviously, this wasn't the time.

Tom continued, "Wendy speculated that the *Phantom Press* became—"

"It's not the *Phantom Press*," Juanita interrupted. She turned away from the window and locked her eyes on Tom. "They sacrificed themselves to create Legion."

Tom glanced over at Juanita. "Then what the hell is Legion? What are we up against?"

Juanita leaned back in the passenger's seat and closed her eyes for a few moments. After taking a deep breath, she said, "They've gone many names. Gestalts, Hive Ghosts, Focus Points, and so on."

"Never heard of them," Tom replied. "What are they?"

"The twisted creations of Illuminati necromancers." Juanita faced Tom. Her calm expression returned. "Ghosts fade away in the end. It's inevitable. Entropy extends into the Ghost Frequencies."

Knowing that entropy extended beyond the grave still sent a chill down his spine.

Juanita continued, "Many ghosts desperately cling to their existence, and the old Illuminati necromancers took advantage of that. They promised ghosts the opportunity to prolong their existence. In return, the ghosts had to agree to be merged into a single entity. The mental energy each ghost received from the mortal world be combined to sustain all of them."

"But we've interacted with individuals within Legion," Tom said.

"There are degrees of individuality within a legion," Juanita replied. "The necromancers would sacrifice a human to become the core ghost. That person would retain most of their previous identity. Some would have more freedom, like Natalie. Some will have fleeting moments of individuality. The rest are mindless batteries."

"Like an ant colony," Tom asked.

Juanita shook her head. "Close. More like becoming part of a single entity. The Illuminati necromancers sacrificed a human to be the primary ghost, and the other ghosts offered themselves to it."

"A Legion?" Tom asked. "As in the Bible verse, 'My name is Legion, for we are many?'"

Juanita nodded. "I'm sure that passage inspired the necromancers."

Tom shook his head. "Why does it require a spell? Wouldn't something like that have naturally evolved among ghosts?"

"Not possible without magic," Juanita replied. "The necromancers created them to be powerful weapons."

Tom furrowed his brow. "Like a magical weapon?"

She shook her head. "Like a weapon of mass destruction."

Tom felt his jaw drop. "A WMD? You're telling me the Illuminati had WMDs back then?"

"Car."

"Car?"

She pointed. "You're getting too close!"

Tom looked out the windshield, and he was indeed tailgating a car that was slowing down. He tapped the brakes and caught his breath. "Thanks."

"Sure. To answer your question, yes, they did have WMDs back then. They used one during the War of 1812 to drive the British out of Washington D.C."

Tom's eyes widened. "I thought that was a tornado."

She smirked. "That's what they want you to think. They pulled a Legion into our world, and it discharged its energy. The British army was lucky they weren't annihilated. Now, Tom, you said Old Chicago was demolished in 1986, right?"

"Yeah," Tom replied. "The Department of Paranormal Affairs set off EMPs at the same time they detonated the explosives."

"A newly created Legion could have survived the blast," said Juanita then looked down. "There's never been a Legion that's had over twenty years to grow."

"Why?"

"If a Legion became too powerful, the necromancers couldn't bring it into our world."

Tom lifted his fingers. "But this one's obviously affecting our world."

Juanita nodded. "Yes, but only a small portion of its power is reaching our world. Normally, even the most strung-out spirit junkie couldn't channel that kind of power. They'd need something like yards of conductive cloth to filter a legion's power." She paused. "The fiftieth anniversary banners are made of conductive cloth."

Tom's eyes widened for a moment. "But that would mean Rene's involved, right?"

"I believe so," Juanita said with wiriness in her voice. "She helped create a network of banners. Initially, they couldn't handle Legion's power without shorting out. Until now."

Tom's heart sped up. "The banners didn't short out tonight."

Juanita sighed. "You heard what Daisy said. They stabilized the network. I bought us enough time to escape Bolingbrook. But the network can be hardened."

"Wait," Tom said as he glanced at Juanita. "How did Rene replace every banner in Bolingbrook?"

Juanita sighed, eyes still on the floor of the van. "She didn't."

Tom changed lanes. "Who did?"

Juanita closed her eyes. "No one replaced them."

Tom blinked. "If no one replaced them, then how did they get up there? The DPA controls the Public Services Department. Their people put up the banners. There's no way something like that would have slipped by the DPA. Unless..." He fell silent as the pieces fell together. "The DPA installed Rene's banners?"

Juanita opened her eyes and looked at Tom. "Yes. That's why we had to escape Bolingbrook."

Tom felt himself trembling as he imagined Legion destroying Bolingbrook. "But why? Why would they do this?" He looked at Juanita. "Why would Steve do this? Robert is his best friend. He's spent most of his life defending Bolingbrook. Why does he want to unleash Legion on the village? It doesn't make any sense."

Juanita pointed at the windshield. Tom looked and slowed down to avoid a truck shifting lanes.

"That's what we need to figure out," Juanita replied. She paused for a few moments. "Can I ask you a personal question?"

Tom froze. Juanita's question reminded him of the times in high school whenever a woman said she wasn't interested in him.

"Sure," Tom replied as he tightened his grip on the wheel.

"What did Legion offer you?"

Tom exited onto I-290.

Juanita said, "You mentioned Legion presenting itself as the time traveler you dealt with last year. Do you know why?"

"The future version of me?" Tom asked, ashamed of what he could have become.

"A time traveler from a timeline that no longer exists," said Juanita. She smiled at Tom. "He's not part of Legion. So why would Legion use his image?"

Tom loosened his grip on the steering wheel. "I think," he paused to ponder Juanita's question. "The time traveler was blinded by rage. It's what led him to almost kill Jamie and Humanist Heart. Legion must think I'm still capable of being like the time traveler. It's offering me the opportunity to lash out at Jamie, the skeptical movement, Humanist Heart." He tapped his fingers. "I think it wants to use my anger to escape Bolingbrook." Tom shivered. "It won't stop once it destroys Bolingbrook." He leaned back in his seat. "If I give in, it will become a psychic wildfire and spread out of control. No place on Earth would be safe from it."

"In theory," Juanita replied as she nodded. "There's never been one this powerful unleashed before. The good news is, there are ways to destroy before it threatened the world."

"And the bad news?" Tom wasn't sure he wanted to hear the answer.

Juanita hesitated. "Chicagoland would be annihilated."

"What?" Tom locked eyes with her. "Like using nuclear bombs or something like that?"

"Road."

Tom looked ahead and realized he was tailgating.

"Then it gets worse," Juanita said as she looked away from Tom.

"Worse?" Tom almost screamed. "What's worse than the annihilation of Chicagoland?"

"A resumption of the war between the Illuminati and the New World Order. The Illuminati and their allies will take advantage of the shock and fear from the destruction of Chicagoland to destabilize the secret societies aligned with the

New World Order. The New World order will tighten its grip on humanity to preserve their world order. Their shadow war would shatter the global order. Chaos and violence would spread around the globe. The Illuminati will do everything to worsen the fallout from the war. When people are desperate for the chaos to end, the Illuminati will present themselves as the saviors of humanity. The ones who will end the chaos they created. It's how they've always worked."

Tom suspected there was more to the return of the *Phantom Press* than the DPA was letting on. Discovering the attack might be part of a conspiracy to reinstate the Illuminati was more than he expected.

"What do we do?" Did he have to say 'we?' Tom reminded himself he was a reporter, not a participant. Then again, his hometown was in danger.

Juanita faced Tom. "I will speak to my superiors. You will keep this between us for now."

Tom's eyes widened in surprise and near rage. "Stay quiet? My friends are in comas. The DPA's compromised, and a WMD wants me to become one with it. My hometown and my family are in danger. I'm supposed to stay quiet?"

"Yes," she said, her voice tight with suppressed anger. "If you want to save Bolingbrook and stop Legion, you must stay quiet. If the DPA has been compromised, we need to handle it carefully. That's why I'm going to reach out to my superiors. We can't risk making the slightest mistake. One reckless article could make them unleash Legion early. Are you willing to risk your hometown to advance your writing career?" Juanita leaned closer to Tom. "You'll eventually be able to run the story. I would never order you to trash a story. But you need to wait. If you want to protect everyone you love, you need to stay quiet. Don't tell anyone. Especially anyone in the *Babbler.*"

Tom sighed and shook his head. "I don't like it, but I understand your point."

Juanita leaned back in her chair. "I promise it will be worth it."

***

Tom parked in the motel parking lot in front of their room. Exhaustion set in, and he thought Juanita looked exhausted as well.

"Thank you for driving," Juanita said for the first time in several minutes.

Tom found the energy to smile. "Someday you'll have to tell me everything it can do."

"Maybe."

Tom pulled out the keys and pressed a button to open the automatic side door. They both got out of the van, still weary from the night's events. Tom looked around to see if there was anything unusual or if they were being watched. The only sounds were of the cars cruising down Northwest Highway.

Juanita removed APK's carrier from the van. Tom walked up to the door and checked inside the carrier. APK stretched and yawned, showing her full set of teeth.

"Thank you for saving us," said Tom.

APK looked up at Tom. "Mow," she replied, then slow-blinked.

After Juanita checked the tape strips, she left on the door, they entered their hotel room. Tom closed the door, and Juanita opened the carrier's door. APK walked over to the water bowl and started lapping up the water.

Juanita pulled out her smartphone. "I have to make a private call."

Tom nodded as he sat down on his bed. "If there's a knock, it's not you."

Juanita smirked. "You're catching on."

"Be careful out there," said Tom.

"You be careful in here, Tom." Juanita walked up to the front, then faced Tom. "I'm sorry I yelled at you."

Tom looked into Juanita's brown eyes and didn't feel any anger towards her. "Don't worry about that. I'm glad you're here."

She flashed him a smile. "I'm glad I can help."

After Juanita left, Tom pulled out his smartphone. As the phone rebooted, he felt conflicted. He was sitting on a story with apocalyptic implications. He understood why Juanita wanted him to wait. There was a risk of tipping off the DPA or whoever was behind Legion's creation. But there was also a danger to the public. Even if few people took the *Babbler* seriously, didn't he have an obligation to report it? Then again, he'd have to explain to Sara why he defied her order not to work on the story or enter Bolingbrook. Besides, the next issue of the *Babbler* wouldn't be published until next week. Would Bolingbrook still be standing by then?

He glanced at APK, who was walking towards her litter box. "Journalism school never prepared me for this."

APK looked at Tom and tilted her head.

"I guess you can't understand."

"Mow," APK replied, sounding annoyed.

Tom looked at his phone and noticed a coded message from Sara asking about his Orange Squad story.

I witnessed the first joint operation by the DPA and the Orange Squad. Apparently, they stopped the transfer of a powerful ghost from Chicago to Bolingbrook. Working out the details.

Tom bit his lip. He promised Juanita to stay silent, but Don could be in danger if he talked to the DPA. He didn't want to break his promise, but could he live with himself if he didn't warn Don?

Tom adjusted the setting on his phone to send an encrypted message to Don.

Be careful. Orange Squad thinks the DPA may be compromised. Message me when you're safe.

APK jumped onto the bed and sat on Tom's lap. Tom petted APK and reviewed the draft of his message. He wasn't revealing everything. Just enough to let Don know to be careful.

APK leaned her head closer to Tom's phone.

"Text message," Tom said to APK. "You can't read it."

APK moved her head as if she was reading it.

"I'll play with you after I send it," Tom said as he reached for the send button with his right hand.

APK climbed onto Tom's right arm, preventing Tom from pressing the send button.

"You must really want to play," Tom said.

"Mow!" said APK, grumbling.

"Send," Tom said.

"Message sent," his phone replied.

APK dug her claws into Tom's arm, leaving a stinging pain, before leaping to the hard floor.

"Ouch," Tom said. "Okay. Now we can play."

APK seemed to glare at Tom.

"Mow," she said, then ran into Juanita's tent.

33

The sound of Juanita's harsh voice woke Tom.

"You know me better than that," she said from inside her tent. "No!"

APK slipped through the partially open front flap of Juanita's tent, then jumped onto the other bed. Tom sat up and rubbed his eyes. The light of dawn streamed through the gap in the curtains. *This is too early,* Tom thought, *even for Juanita.* The tent shifted as she moved inside it.

Tom's smartphone buzzed. Sara was calling. She never called this early.

Tom answered the phone.

"Video conference. Now." Sara ended the call.

When she pointed out all the flaws of his audition article, she wasn't this angry. A chill ran through his body as he guessed the answer.

Inside the tent, Juanita said, "I'll call you back when I'm alone."

"What's going on?" asked Tom.

Juanita emerged from her tent, her hair a tangled mess and not a trace of makeup on her face. "I have to make a call. Stay inside."

"I have to make a call, too," Tom replied. "I hope our calls aren't related."

"I don't know," Juanita said as she slipped on her shoes. "Just stay inside." She looked up at APK. "You too, APK."

"Mow," APK replied as if she was protesting the order.

"I mean it," Juanita snapped back as she stood up.

"Mow," APK replied, sounding defeated.

Tom uncovered himself, glad he was wearing shorts and a shirt. He looked at the other bed which was now blocking the door. "Need help moving it?"

Juanita pushed the bed back. APK kept her balance, then walked to the edge of the bed.

She looked down and gave APK a forced smile. "Stay here and guard Tom. Can you do that, APK?"

APK sat on her hind legs. "Mow," she said, sounding disappointed with her assignment.

Juanita stepped outside and locked the door. APK guarded the door.

Tom reached into the mini-fridge and grabbed a bottled coffee drink. He closed the door then went to the desk to boot his laptop.

APK jumped off the bed, then walked over to the desk.

Tom took a big gulp of the sweet, creamy drink. He hoped it was enough to wake him up.

"Mow," said APK, sounding displeased with Tom.

Tom opened the video conference app. "You should keep an eye on the door and windows. That's where the threats would come from."

APK locked her eyes on Tom and sat on her hind legs. "Mow," she said defiantly.

Tom sighed. "If you insist."

Tom joined the conference that included Sara and Don. Sara was wearing a blue robe with a t-shirt underneath. Tom suspected she had time to put on touch up makeup before the call.

Don wore a red shirt that, to Tom's surprise, was wrinkle free. His hair was still a mess.

Sara said, "We need to talk, Tom."

Tom made himself smile and sat up. "I'm always willing to talk to you."

Sara narrowed her eyebrows. "But you have a problem following my instructions."

Tom felt himself swallow. "You said I could work on the Orange Squad and Rene stories. I'm working on them."

"You've been to Bolingbrook," Sara said, the words laced with disappointment and thick with anger. "After I specifically told you not to go."

Don added, "I've shown Sara the videos."

"And don't say they're fake," Sara added. "I'm a mother. I know when people are lying."

Tom froze. It felt like a vice was crushing his organs.

Sara sighed. "I specifically told you not to go to Bolingbrook."

"And I'm sorry I didn't tell you earlier," Tom replied.

"You mean," Sara said sternly, "you're sorry you went to Bolingbrook. Period."

"I'm not sorry I did that," Tom replied. "And I was under the protection of an Orange Squad member. You've told us to follow the story, no matter where it leads."

Sara frowned. "That is not an excuse to violate the protocols."

"But that's how I found out Don was in danger," said Tom. "And what happened to *the Phantom Press*."

"I know how to deal with the DPA," Don replied. "Your warning was unnecessary. But I would like to hear what you think happened to the *Phantom Press*."

Tom sat up. "They merged with a Legion."

Don and Sara stared at Tom. Sara's face showed her confusion, while Don folded his arms.

Sara said, "What?"

"You know," Tom replied. "A hive of ghosts. A Gestalt. When ghosts merge into a single ghost because they think it will prolong their time in the Ghost Frequencies. Only it's an Illuminati ghost trap." Tom's thoughts raced. "Then they would pull them into our world, where they explode like a spectral WMD."

Sara's gaze fell upon Tom, and the subtle tightening of her lips made her skepticism clear. "A spectral WMD? Don, do you know what Tom is talking about?"

"Yes," Don replied as he sat up. "It's what Tom described, though they're an Illuminati myth. Never confirmed."

"Well," Tom said, "There's one in Bolingbrook. Wendy and Jenna confirmed it."

"Wait," Sara said. "You spoke with Jenna and Wendy?"

"Yes," Tom said, hoping this was key to keeping his job. "They're in a bubble between the Ghost Frequencies and the Mind Frequencies. They said the *Phantom Press* had become part of Legion." He leaned towards the web cam. "Sara, there's a WMD in Bolingbrook. The DPA is trying to bring it into our world using the fiftieth anniversary banners. They're made of conductive cloth! Former Mayor Rene supplied it to the DPA. We need to warn people. At least post something on the web page."

Sara stared at Tom for several long seconds. Tom twitched his toes as he waited. Did he get through to Don and Sara?

"Don," Sara finally said. "Please tell Tom what you told me earlier."

Don sighed as he adjusted his web cam. "I take no pleasure in this, Tom." He sat back in his chair. "We're not dealing with some grand conspiracy to revive the Illuminati and start a war with the NWO. The truth is, we're dealing with a former Illuminati necromancer and gangs of ghost riders targeting Bolingbrook." He scratched his head. "Their plan was to sacrifice Bolingbrook's residents to the ghost of Bart Kilmer."

Tom coughed in shock. "I'm sorry, are you serious? The Bart Kilmer? The Cubs broadcaster? The man who sang 'Take Me Out to the Ball Game' during the seventh inning stretch?"

"The one and only."

"Why would anyone want to sacrifice Bolingbrook to Bart Kilmer?" Tom asked, his voice laced with disbelief.

"To win the World Series for the Cubs by sacrificing every Bolingbrook resident to the ghost of Bart Kilmer!" said Don with a straight face.

Tom's jaw dropped and eyes widened.

"The majority of Bolingbrook residents are White Sox Fans," said Don. "Bart would need an infusion of their souls to dispel the Curse of the Billy Goat."

"The Curse of the Billy Goat?" Tom asked, still perplexed.

"Yes. Follow the chain of events." Don opened a worn-out notebook. "The necromancer, with help from the ghost riders, stages a ritual to attract Bart. They disguise it as a hoax to throw off investigators. Then the *Phantom Press* returns to take one last shot at Robert before sacrificing themselves to Bart, who now goes by the name Legion."

Tom tilted his head. "Bart is Legion?"

"Yes, and when we attempted to summon the *Phantom Press*, they decided to take one last shot at us." He looked down. "I should have prepared for that."

Sara said, "Please continue."

Don looked up. "Sorry. After you evacuated Bolingbrook, the ghost riders used the conductive cloth they bought from Mayor Rene to build relays that would allow Legion to travel to Bolingbrook. Which, fortunately, was stopped by the DPA and Orange Squad raids."

"The relay was to bring ghosts from Chicago to feed Legion," Tom protested. "I heard them."

"Let me finish," Don replied. "Yes, the fiftieth anniversary banners are made of conductive cloth, donated by Mayor Rene. But our banners are jamming devices, not summoning devices. They were activated last night and finally destroyed the *Phantom Press*." He leaned back in his chair. "The DPA should have all the ghost riders in custody by tonight. At that point, Wendy and the rest should wake up, and you can go back home."

"Oh, for God's sake," Tom said. "The ritual was staged. Wendy and Roul knew that. And Roul tried to warn us that the DPA created a Legion. Legion has reached out to me every time I've visited Bolingbrook. It's not Bart. It's something else. Hell, I suppose you believe Barry made Budweiser the official beer of Hell."

Don shook his head. "Trusting Roaming Roul was your biggest mistake. Because he is the necromancer behind this."

Tom gasped. "You can't be serious! Roaming Roul is a necromancer leading gangs of ghost junkies?"

Don pulled from his notebook a photograph of a man who looked like a much younger version of Roaming Roul. His dark short hair and clean-shaven face was a stark contrast to the homeless man he knew. Something else seemed familiar about him.

"Roaming Roul's real name is Esteban Vega. In 1986, he was one of Bolingbrook's Knights of Twilight. One of their best, according to my sources. He and his partner were at the implosion of Old Chicago. He was stationed with a team of Sigma 7 paranormal investigators." Don squinted at his screen. "If you wait a bit, I can try to share my screen."

Don shared his screen and fumbled his way into one of the *Babbler's* shared folders.

Tom thought it made sense that Roul would have ties to at least one of Bolingbrook's covert departments. Roul and Robert obviously knew each other; Roul even seemed protective of Robert. Was he really behind the ghost attacks?

"Finally," Don said as he managed to open a video showing an aerial view of the implosion. He fumbled with the mouse until he managed to enlarge the upper-right portion of the video. The grainy image of the parking lot and a section of the building vividly demonstrated the poor video quality of the mid-1980s.

"Are we going to see anything besides blurry dots?" Tom asked.

"Tom!" Sara snapped.

"You'll see enough," Don replied. "Okay. At this point, countdown had to be halted because the *Phantom Press* managed to disconnect the explosives from the switch. The Sigma 7 operatives were sent in to reconnect the explosives."

On the screen, four pixelated men with their dogs run towards the building and enter it, almost military style.

"Back then," Don said, "the Illuminati had just started experimenting with breeding anti-psychic animals. Dogs were one of the first species they tried." Don sped up the video. "In this instance, the *Phantom Press* managed to possess the dogs and turn them against their handlers." Don slowed the video to normal speed. "At this point, Esteban and his female partner went in to rescue them."

Two blurry figures ran across the screen and into the building. Tom squinted but couldn't see any more details.

Don said, "You can't tell, but the woman is carrying one of the first anti-psychic cats. One of Anti-Psychic Kitty's very distant relatives. I don't know how many 'greats' to use. Cats are such prolific breeders."

APK's ears perked at the mention of her name. Cautiously she moved to Tom. Tom motioned for APK to stay where she was.

"Something wrong?" asked Sara.

Tom turned his attention back to the screen. "No. Nothing is wrong. Go on."

Don cleared his throat. "Unlike the dogs, the cat was effective. The Sigma 7 team escaped."

On the screen, four dogs rushed out of the building followed by three men carrying the fourth man.

"According to the official report, Esteban and his partner claimed they reconnected the explosives and fled the building. The DPA now believes Esteban cast a spell that allowed the *Phantom Press* to bypass the wards and escape into the Ghost Frequencies."

"And you believe that too?" Tom asked.

"It's very possible because Esteban and his partner took longer than necessary to reconnect the explosives. After Esteban cast the spell, his partner and him didn't have time to go back to the main shelter when the countdown resumed."

On the screen, the two figures ran towards a reticular structure in the parking lot.

"They only had enough time to reach the emergency shelter."

The two knights entered the shelter, out of view of the aerial camera. A few seconds later, Old Chicago imploded. The cloud of dust and debris obscured the shelter from the camera. Don stopped the video.

Don said, "Esteban accompanied his partner to a hospital in Chicago. They would stay in Chicago and get married. They became parents of one child." He put the photo back into his notebook. "In Bolingbrook, Robert gathered the remaining

Knights of Twilight and gave them an ultimatum: Join Sigma 7 or die. Steve defected. The rest of the knights chose death."

Don set his notebook aside. "Esteban remained loyal to what remained of the Illuminati. Several years later, he returned to Bolingbrook as Roaming Roul. Robert let him stay, maybe out of pity or due to a debt he owed Estaban. He took advantage of Robert's protection to plan this conspiracy." He paused. "To put it bluntly, you've been fooled again."

Tom pounded on the desk. "Bullshit! I suppose the next thing you're going to tell us is another group of occultists were plotting to get the Cleveland Indians into the World Series as well. Were they trying to end the world? Because a Cubs–Indians World Series would sure as hell be a sign of Armageddon. And they were going to do this by summoning the ghost of Bart Kilmer? Of all the ghosts in Chicago, they needed Bart Kilmer's help. A silly old man who drank too much but loved the Cubs and Cubs fans. Seriously?"

Don sighed. "Tom. You were a skeptic. What's more likely? The entire DPA conspiring to destroy Bolingbrook with a rumored ghost bomb to revive a dead secret society? Or a lone necromancer bargaining with a powerful ghost in Chicago to get back at Robert and help his favorite team?"

"But the spirit junkies didn't know jack about the Cubs," Tom protested. "They weren't Cubs fanatics. Why would they help Esteban?"

Don shook his head. "Esteban is the Cubs fanatic. The ghost riders just wanted to experience being possessed by Bart. Thanks to Mayor Rene's cooperation, their plan failed."

"If the plot is foiled, why haven't Wendy, Jenna, and the others woken up?"

"They should wake up in a couple days," Don replied.

"And I'm supposed to believe you after what you did to Jenna and Wendy? Can you prove that it was an accident?"

He shook his head. "Tom, I know this is hard, but you have to accept that you and Wendy were fooled by a deceptive, evil necromancer."

"And you've been fooled by the DPA, and I will not—"

"Tom," Sara said firmly. "Stop."

Tom looked at Sara. Her face revealed the anger she was trying to hold back.

Sara took a deep breath. "My issue with you is that I clearly and specifically told you not to go to Bolingbrook and not to work on the *Phantom Press* story."

"I can't ignore what happened to my friends."

"They're my friends, too," Sara firmly replied. "Do you think this is easy for me? You don't think I miss Wendy? Do you think I don't care about Jenna or the other council members?"

"I know you do," Tom replied as his voice quivered with fear and sadness. "I know we're your second family." His eyes watered. "But you must believe me. This goes far beyond Bolingbrook. Wendy and Roul were onto something."

"I'm sorry," Don said, "Esteban is a deranged, bitter old man. Nothing more."

APK jumped onto the desk and into the view of his webcam.

"Mow!" she said, looking at Don's image on the screen.

Sara's jaw dropped. "What is Anti-Psychic Kitty doing with you?" she asked, attempting to keep her voice level.

"She's doing a good job protecting me," Tom replied, doing his best to remain calm.

"You let the cat out of the bag," said Don. He chuckled.

APK ran her front paws over Don's image as if she were trying to dig through the screen.

"APK, no."

Tom picked up APK. She hissed at Don and then squirmed out of Tom's arms. She landed on the floor, then jumped back on top of the desk.

"It's okay," Tom told APK. "It's going to be okay."

Sara rubbed her eyes. "No. It's not going to be okay for you. You willingly violated the Scatter Protocols by entering Boling-brook. You investigated a story that I had assigned to anoth-er reporter. Then you 'borrowed' Anti-Psychic Kitty without consulting Chris or me. Then you had the audacity to have blind faith in the Orange Squad despite promising me not to write copaganda."

Tom looked at the window with Sara's video and pointed at the window with Don's video. "With all due respect, Don is screwing up the biggest story in Bolingbrook's history and endangering our friends with his bullshit Cubs angle."

Don shrugged. "Or maybe you've been the problem all along?"

Sara muted Don and Tom. "Enough. Both of you. Tom, you are suspended, effective immediately. Do you understand?" Sara unmuted Tom.

"You can't do that to me!" Tom replied as he leaned towards his webcam. "I'm trying to—"

Sara muted Tom again. "I can, and I can also fire you if you wish to keep arguing with me."

Tom locked his jaw. His worst fear was close to becoming reality.

Sara took a deep breath. "Next week, we will discuss your future. But as of right now, you are off the clock and pulled from all assignments. I'm sending Shavana over to pick up your laptop."

A chill ran through Tom. He knew suspended reporters told to return their laptops ended up getting fired. Termination, the thing he feared the most since he started struggling at the *Babbler*, was almost upon him.

The door opened, and Juanita entered. Her eyes widened when she saw Tom and APK looking at the laptop.

"What are you doing?" said Juanita as she gasped. She rushed towards the desk and stared at Don and Sara's video chat windows. "What... have... you... done?" She clenched her fists.

"Tom," said Don. "You should ask Ms. Vega to explain her relationship with Esteban and her role in all this."

34

Juanita glared at Tom as he closed his laptop. "You told them, didn't you?" she asked.

Tom stood up and threw his hands up. "I didn't mention you or say anything about visiting Bolingbrook."

"You shouldn't have told them anything!" Juanita pointed at Tom. "You told me you were going to run everything by me first, Tom. Everything. Thanks to you, the DPA knows about our investigation. They're pressuring our supervisors to shut it down."

"Mow," APK said, sounding just as angry as Juanita.

"But I was trying to warn Don before he met with the DPA," Tom protested.

"Don has a funny way of showing his appreciation." She groaned at Tom. "Secrets save lives, Tom. How many times do I have to tell you that?"

The phrase struck a nerve with Tom. In all his daydreams about Juanita, he never imagined he'd ever feel this offended by her.

"Saves lives?" said Tom. "Secrets also hide corruption. Secrets can also shield people from accountability. Some secrets shouldn't be kept. Some need to be exposed."

"And who are you to judge our secrets?" She pointed at Tom's face. "You keep saying I'm part of the Orange Squad. I'm not. That's a division of the Chicago Police Department. You don't know who I work for. You don't know how many similar organizations there are in Cook County. Yet, you think you're qualified to judge us?"

Tom stepped back. "Then tell me what I need to know."

Juanita shook her head. "Why should I trust you with anything now? Do you realize how big a mess you just made?"

"No," Tom replied. "Explain it to me."

APK hissed at Tom. Juanita rolled her eyes, the veins in her forehead throbbing, and screamed.

Tom shook his head as he tried to contain his anger. "If the DPA is corrupt, people need to know. Every secret organization in Chicagoland needs to be held accountable—"

"Accountable?" Juanita laughed. "Why should we be held accountable to you?"

Tom felt his body tighten. "Not to me, but to the people you serve. My job is to show them what's going on in the shadows. To show them the monsters that threaten them, and what's being done in the name of protecting them. Especially when the organization that's supposed to protect Bolingbrook might be on the verge of annihilating it."

Juanita sighed in frustration. "You think your readership will heed your warning about Legion? Think they'll evacuate before it's released into our world? Wake up, Tom. Nobody believes the *Babbler*. You're not holding us accountable. We don't tremble in fear of what you and your friends are going to reveal. You have an over-inflated sense of importance, Tom. Your audience thinks the *Babbler* is a joke. Just like *The Onion*."

Tom's face turned red. "That was uncalled for."

"Tom," said Juanita, "I tried to be nice to you, and this is how you repay me? By putting me in danger?"

For a moment, Tom's anger abated. "What do you mean?"

Juanita turned and approached her tent. "I asked you to trust me." She sighed and crawled into the tent. Tom heard her gathering her belongings inside.

Tom approached the tent. "Okay. If no one believes me or the *Babbler*, then tell me everything."

APK grumbled at Tom.

"You don't have to tell me anything, APK."

"Mow," APK snapped back at Tom.

Juanita crawled out of the tent, wearing a full backpack.

Tom stepped aside. "Just answer a few questions then."

Juanita started disassembling her tent.

Tom said, "Don says occultist Cubs fan sacrificed White Sox memorabilia for magic ritual."

"We both know that's wrong," she replied, her voice flat as she focused on packing her tent.

Tom took a deep breath to calm himself. "Fair enough. Did we witness the DPA and Orange Squad halt an attempt to summon Bart Kilmer?"

"Bart Kilmer didn't leave a ghost," said Juanita as she picked up her folded tent. "I'd know about his ghost by now." She stood up and walked past Tom towards the sink. "He lived a good life and died a happy man." She paused to look in the mirror. "We should all be so lucky." Juanita pivoted to face Tom. "You heard the transmissions. Did any of them sound like Bart?"

"No."

She glared at Tom. "Then stop asking me questions you already know the answer to." Juanita started tossing items into her toiletry bag.

"Okay." Tom took another deep breath. "Where are you going?"

"Next question," Juanita replied, stuffing her toiletry bag into her backpack.

Tom exhaled in frustration. "After I introduced you to Rene, you made a phone call."

Juanita walked past Tom. "To provide an update to my supervisors. That's how I found out about the staged operation."

Tom followed Juanita. "Who staged it?"

"Next question." She placed her backpack on top of the dresser, next to her pistol and spare ammunition clips.

Tom clenched his fists for a moment. "How do you know Roaming Roul?"

"Esteban," Juanita said as she checked the chamber of her pistol.

"Fair enough. How do you know Esteban?"

Juanita put her pistol and clips into her backpack. She closed her backpack, still ignoring Tom.

Tom wanted to step closer to Juanita but stopped. There was no need to crowd her, he told himself.

Tom said, "Don said you have some kind of relationship with Esteban. What is it?"

"None of your business." Juanita finished packing and walked past Tom.

Tom stepped back as he felt his rage boiling inside him. "You weren't going to help me at first until I relayed Esteban's message. That's what brought you all the way out to Bolingbrook, wasn't it?"

Juanita walked over to the nightstand. "Not exactly," she said, checking the drawers.

Tom tilted his head. "What's that supposed to mean?"

Juanita closed the last drawer. "I don't want to be mad at you, Tom."

Tom felt the sting of her words. He took a couple of deep breaths to calm himself. "I don't want to be mad at you either. But I need to know the truth. Don and Sara are telling me Esteban is the mastermind behind all this. If you have a relationship with him, I need to know you aren't working with him." He stepped forward. "I'm about to lose my job because Sara thinks you misled me. I could end up in a psych ward if I lose my job."

Juanita turned away from Tom, her gaze fixed on the wooden floor.

"I just need to know that you weren't trying to mislead me." Tom took few steps forward. "If you tell me what your relationship with Esteban is, I might be able to save my job and help you. Just tell me—"

Juanita turned around, her face contorted in a mask of fury and sorrow. "He's my father!"

Silence filled the room. Tom didn't know what to say.

Juanita approached Tom. "My mother and father served as Illuminati knights in Bolingbrook. Yes, they were at the demolition of Old Chicago. When they saw Robert had brought in a Sigma 7 team, they realized that Robert was going to defect. They feared Robert would kill them if they refused to join Sigma 7. At that point, they could have gotten away and saved their lives." Juanita shook her head. "They didn't. Because they wanted to protect Bolingbrook. Even if it meant working with their potential executioners. When the *Phantom Press* overwhelmed the team and their dogs, my parents picked up their anti-psychic cat, Mistletoe, and entered the building. They were willing to save their executioners instead of letting them die."

APK brushed against Juanita's legs. She picked her up and started stroking her fur. "Mistletoe was a distant ancestor to Anti-Psychic Kitty." Juanita smiled at APK for a moment. "She likes it when I talk about her relatives."

"Mow," APK replied, her voice filled with affection towards Juanita.

Juanita said, "My parents helped the team escape Old Chicago. They stayed behind to rewire the detonators. Even if it meant they might not make it out in time. Even with the *Phantom Press'* mental illusions, taunts, and physical attacks, they rewired the detonators and made sure they couldn't be tampered with again. They sealed the *Phantom Press*'s fate." Juanita sighed. "My parents barely reached the emergency shelter in time." She paused. "My mother had to choose between saving her hearing or saving Mistletoe's. She chose Mistletoe. She told me Mistletoe didn't understand what was going on. She sacrificed her hearing to protect an innocent being. That's the kind of person my mother is."

Tom nodded. He knew Henrietta was that kind of person.

"My parents didn't escape Bolingbrook," Juanita continued. "Robert spared them."

Tom's eyes widened. "Why them and not the others?"

"You'll have to ask him. If my father knew, he never told me." Juanita rocked APK in her arms. APK purred. "Robert recommended my parents to the Orange Squad. They accepted my parents. They had me after that. You could say I'm the result of Robert's mercy." She smiled.

Tom smiled back.

Juanita said, "A few years ago, my father was convinced there was a conspiracy targeting Robert. He left us to go back to Bolingbrook and investigate. That's when he took on the Roaming Roul persona. He did this without the support of the Orange Squad or the DPA. Even Robert didn't know. We hadn't heard from him until you delivered his message." She paused, as if she were lost in a memory. "When I was little, he called me his sunflower. When I was older, he switched to calling me his angel of reason."

Tom said, "His message to you was that the DPA created a Legion, and he needed your help?"

"And you, too." Juanita smiled.

Tom felt awkward. Only a short while ago, he'd been interrogating Juanita. "I understand why Robert would tolerate him. But why would he spend so many years away from your mother and you?"

Juanita stepped closer to Tom. "It's who he is, and who we are. My mother sacrificed her hearing to protect Mistletoe. My father sacrificed years with his family to protect Robert. I could have had a career as a token woman of color for the Habenstein Society. Instead, I came back to protect my community. It's who we are, Tom."

A car horn honked seven times. Juanita collected her things. "I needed more time to reach the right people who could have intervened. But your message tipped off the conspirators. Now, I'm being brought in for questioning. Honestly, I don't know if you'll ever see me again."

Tom watched in silence as she walked to the door. "I'm so sorry. I—"

"Tom." Juanita stopped by the door. "If you want to save Bolingbrook, don't let them take APK. She's your only hope of defeating Legion."

APK ran up to Juanita and rubbed against her leg. "Mow?"

Juanita gently pushed APK back with her leg. "I need you to take care of Tom while I'm gone. He can be a good person. I don't want to see any claw or bite marks when I get back."

Juanita opened the door just wide enough to get through, then closed it. Tom ran up to the door and locked it. Through the peephole, he saw Juanita with three Orange Squad members. One entered Juanita's van, while the others escorted her to another van.

Without warning, someone stepped in front of the door and blocked the peephole. With a sigh, Tom slid his back down to the floor.

Outside, a man said, "We need the cat." He knocked again. "Let me in."

APK dashed under the nearest bed.

"You have a warrant?" Tom asked.

"Of course not," the man replied. "APK is our property."

"No, she isn't," Tom replied.

The man paused. "We don't have time for this. Let me in."

Tom thought for a moment. "APK is under the joint guardianship of the Orange Squad and the *Bolingbrook Babbler*. I need authorization from a representative of both organizations before I'll release her."

"Consider this our authorization."

"Now call my publisher or my editor. Once I have their authorization, I'll turn her over."

Tom sat on the floor, afraid to stand. For what seemed like hours, he waited. Would they smash through the door, climb in through the front window?

Instead, Tom heard Juanita's van and another vehicle driving away.

APK crawled out from under the bed and ran towards the window. She ducked under the blankets and then jumped up to the windowsill.

"Mow?" she whimpered.

35

TOM OPENED THE DOOR just wide enough to grab the two bags he'd ordered online. One was from a local restaurant. The other from a grocery store. He rushed to get the bags inside. Once inside, he slammed the door shut.

APK, sitting on the windowsill, resumed yowling.

"I'm sorry," said Tom as he placed the bags on a bed and started checking the contents. "I don't know if Juanita is coming back."

APK yowled louder.

"I mean when!" He set down the bags: one from a local restaurant, and the other from a grocery store. "I meant *when* she's coming back."

APK jumped down and glared at Tom. "Mow," she grumbled.

Tom petted APK. "Okay. You caught me. I don't know what's going on with Juanita. But she knows how to take care of herself."

APK let Tom pet her as she watched the door. Her rapid purring concerned Tom. "I want her back, too." He sighed. "I don't want things to end like this."

APK yowled at the door.

"Either my publisher or my editor will make sure you're brought back home. Until then, I'll do my best to protect you."

APK yowled again. Tom placed APK's food and water bowl in front of her. He reached into the grocery bag and placed four cat treats in her dry food bowl. "If you want to wait here, that's fine." Tom petted APK a few more times.

Tom returned to his work laptop and resumed watching the uncropped video Don played at the meeting. Fortunately, Sara hadn't taken away his access to the shared folders and files, and Tom took advantage of this. He focused on the area where the Sigma 7 team and Juanita's parents accessed Old Chicago. He replayed from when the Sigma 7 team entered to the implosion. He hoped there was something in that corner of the frame that could exonerate Juanita's family. Nothing stood out in the section. He didn't want to imagine Don being right, that the sabotaging of the wires was part of a distraction to get Esteban into the building and help the *Phantom Press* escape.

The creation of a Legion required a human to sacrifice their life. Yet, he accounted for all the Sigma 7 members who entered and left. Whoever made the Legion must have entered earlier. Maybe before the cameras started filming?

He remembered asking Wendy if she could enhance a section of a video, and she replied, "What color do you want me to change the pixels to?" Unlike Hollywood movies, it simply wasn't possible to extract more visual information from a low-resolution image.

APK stood up. "Mow?"

Someone knocked five times.

"Tom?" came Shavana's voice. "It's me. You in there?"

Tom started to speak, but then he remembered that the men in blue and the Men in Black could impersonate voices. He didn't want to risk parting the Kevlar blankets. He could be shot or someone could break through the window and grab him by the throat. Tom dropped to the floor. APK sprinted under a bed.

"No! Not her," Tom said, doing a poor impression of Charlie Baffle.

"Come on," Shavana replied. "It's me!"

"No! Not her," Tom repeated. If it really was Shavana, she would know the reply.

Shavana sighed. "Fine. 'It's me. Charlie Baffle, the Mayor of Old Chicago.'"

Her impression is worse than mine, Tom thought. However, he needed to hear the complete code phrase before he could risk letting her in. He waited.

"Seriously?" Shavana asked in disbelief. "'There's fun for the whole family. We have an indoor amusement park, and every Friday night is Disco Night.' Don't make me do the voice again, Tom!"

Tom got up and cautiously approached the door. He looked out the peephole. Outside, Shavana tapped her foot then looked into the peephole. "I'm not a man in blue."

APK came out from under the bed and sniffed Tom. Tom stood up, then grabbed APK.

"Mow!" APK said as she let Tom pick her up. He stood to the side of the door. After taking a deep breath, he turned the knob and pushed the door open. Shavana caught the door and Tom pointed APK at her.

"Mow?" asked APK.

Shavana's face lit up with excitement. "So, this is APK!" She scratched her chin. "What a cute kitty!"

APK responded with a happy purr.

"Get in," Tom whispered urgently.

Tom stepped to the side and Shavana entered.

"Close the door."

Shavana pushed the door back and locked it. "You know a simple police ram could break this door down?" She looked around the room. "It's so dim in here. What's with the blackout curtains?" Her jaw dropped as he noticed the rearranged furniture. "Oh, my God!"

"It's to throw the snipers off." Tom lowered APK, and she jumped out of his arms.

"Snipers? Are you feeling okay, Tom?"

Tom nodded. "Now that I'm not getting shot at, I am."

"Oh, my God. So, they really were shooting at you." APK rubbed Shavana's leg. "You're such a sweet girl, APK."

"Yeah," Tom replied. "She's sweet. And yes, a sniper shot up my apartment. Almost got APK, too."

"Oh no!" Shavana stroked APK's fur once. "You poor girl." She looked at Tom. "I'm glad you're okay. Don't get me wrong."

Tom flashed a smile. "I know." He sighed. "You're here for my laptop, right?"

Shavana nodded as she averted her eyes from Tom. "Yeah. I'm so sorry you went through all that, only to get suspended. I hope Sara doesn't fire you."

Tom shrugged. "I mean, she didn't revoke my access yet, but she's pissed at me."

Shavana replied, "If it means anything, I researched what you asked me to do."

"Find anything?"

Shavana replied, "I found someone who owns a copy of the second issue of the *Babbler*. There was nothing about a founder of Bolingbrook. Jenna's great-grandfather wrote an editorial saying the incorporation of Bolingbrook was part of a communist plot. Unfortunately, he died before the implosion of Old Chicago."

Tom sighed. "Thanks for checking."

"Sure," Shavana replied. "If I can ask, what are you going to do if you're fired?"

Tom tensed as he contemplated his future. "Since I'll be broke and unemployable, my parents will arrange for me to be committed to Alexian Brothers. Because obviously something's wrong with me," he added in a sarcastic tone.

"Oh my god! Seriously?" Shavana asked.

"Wish I was kidding." He smiled. "At least I can enjoy the effects of all the drugs in my own private room. Nothing we can do about that now."

Tom and Shavana approached Tom's work laptop. He woke it up and moved the mouse towards the shutdown button.

Shavana asked, "What were you watching?"

Tom brought up the video. "I was watching the implosion of Old Chicago." He moved the slider backwards to a specific time stamp. "Right here you'll see a Sigma 7 team with their anti-psychic dogs enter the building."

He pressed the spacebar to start the video. The video played, and they watched. Tom's eyes focused on that corner of the screen, still hoping to find something to exonerate the Vega family.

"Here's the point where Roaming Roul and his partner enter the building. Turns out they were Illuminati knights. You can't see it, but they have an anti-psychic cat with them. Named Mistletoe."

APK jumped onto the table and sat near the screen. "Mow!"

"Yes," Tom said to APK, "that's your distant relative." Tom looked at Shavana. "In a little bit, the Sigma 7 team falls back to their operation area off camera. According to Don, Roul helps the *Phantom Press* escape Old Chicago, then his partner and him barely escape the implosion." Tom looked at APK. "And

Mistletoe survived and went on to have many kittens, and that's how your family line started. Maybe."

"Mow," APK said. For a moment, Tom wondered if APK was expressing pride in her family's long history. But he dismissed that thought.

The three of them watched the video until the implosion.

"And, years later, I unknowingly work with Roul's daughter, and now I'm about to lose my job."

"He has a daughter?"

"Yeah. We even had a history." Tom raised his hands in frustration. "But that doesn't matter anymore."

"I'm sorry. Did you two—"

"No!" He looked down at the keyboard. "Many years ago, I wished for that." He reflected on his feelings for Juanita. "Maybe I never stopped wishing. And when I finally reunited with her—" He paused. "Maybe I was being led on a wild goose chase. Hell, maybe visiting Rene was a waste of time."

Shavana cleared her throat. "Maybe not."

Tom's eyes widened, and he blinked in utter surprise. "What do you mean?"

"Let me get my phone."

Shavana walked back towards her purse. Tom stood up and followed. She picked up her purse and pulled out her smartphone. "Rene," she said as she tapped on the screen, "grew up in Bolingbrook. Before she married, her maiden name was Gilbert."

"Is that important?"

"Maybe." She showed Tom a list of the original organizers. "Barry Gilbert is her father. He was one of the original committee members. He also served as a trustee from 1966 until his death in 1986."

"When did he die exactly?"

Shavana said, "After the implosion. But what I find interesting is what he did during the election that year. He didn't endorse Rene's preferred mayoral candidate. He endorsed Robert."

Tom nodded. "Wow."

"I also found out there's a film with sound of the first board meeting."

"You mean a videotape?"

She shook her head. "Not back then. There was a crew that filmed the first meeting. It was for a documentary that was never produced. It's in the Bolingbrook Historical Museum."

Tom had forgotten Bolingbrook had a museum. It was housed in the building that served as the first village hall and prison.

"If Barry was the heckler, you might recognize his voice."

Tom felt excited. "You're right." He sighed. "But I left my car in Bolingbrook. If you take me there, you could lose your job, too."

"Mow!" APK ran her paws on the laptop screen.

"APK!" Tom yelled. "No! Bad kitty."

"Mow! Mow!"

Tom rushed towards the laptop. "Bad kitty. Get off, now!"

To Tom's surprise, the screen switched to his word processing program. APK paced over the keyboard for a few seconds. She looked at the screen and hissed at the jumbled letters she's typed in.

"Get off!"

APK arched her back and her fur puffed out. "Mow!" she defiantly replied.

"Wait!" Shavana cried. "I think she's trying to tell us something."

Tom blinked. "But she's a cat. A smart cat, but still."

Shavana shook her head. "Wendy told me APK's brain is practically human. She's capable of abstract thinking and is fluent in Spanish and English."

Tom looked down at APK.

"Mow." She sounded like she was proud.

"Okay." Tom switched back to the video window. "Show me."

APK, to Tom's surprise, pressed the arrow buttons to move the starting point of the video. After a few seconds, she stopped pressing the buttons and tapped a paw near the lower left section of the video frame. A section Tom hadn't focused on.

"Got it," Tom said.

APK pressed the spacebar to start playback. Two seconds in, two blurry figures entered the frame from the left. Based on the movement, one of them was wearing a dress. The other person Tom suspected was wearing a sports coat and slacks. They opened an unlocked door and entered. He paused the video.

"Hey," said Shavana.

"Just wanted to check something." Tom checked the timestamp, and the upper left corner of the video frame. The two figures entered the building about a minute before the Sigma 7 team entered. Tom pressed play. The scene played out as Tom had already seen. This time he shifted his attention between the two sections of the screen. He paused the video when Roul/Esteban and Juanita's mother exited the building.

"Roul and his partner exited at this point," said Tom. "The unidentified couple is still inside."

Tom pressed play, and they focused on the other section. Seconds after Esteban left, the person wearing the dress ran out of the building. She entered the other shelter seconds before the explosion.

"Wait!" Shavana said. "Where's the man she was with?"

They watched the video again.

Shavana said, "I don't think he left."

Tom's jaw dropped. "Roul was right. They did create a legion."

He looked up at APK, who was sitting on her hind legs.

APK narrowed her eyes. "Mow!"

36

Tom and Shavana stopped the video after their tenth viewing. APK sat on the desk in a loaf position, as if she was supervising their work.

"I still don't see him leaving." Shavana picked up her smartphone. "We should let Don know. I can't believe he didn't see them. He must have been too focused on that corner of the screen to notice. Kind of like that gorilla video." She put her phone next to her ear.

Tom liked the original gorilla video. In the video, viewers were asked to count how many times five basketball players passed the ball. At the end of the video, the narrator asked the viewers if they noticed the gorilla walking by. Rewatching the video, a man in a gorilla did walk across the court. Most people missed the gorilla because they were focused on counting the times the ball was passed.

Would Don make that mistake?

Tom looked at Shavana's phone. "Hang up," he said quickly.

Shavana ended the call and gave Tom a puzzled look. "What's up?"

Tom looked at the still image of the woman on the screen. He mumbled, "The Vikings may have been the smartest team in the state, but we were the cleverest."

Shavana lowered her phone and looked at Tom. "Excuse me?"

Tom faced Shavana. "Have you ever seen a magician perform in a short-sleeved shirt? Misdirection and taking advantage of our subconscious assumptions. You know how the shell game works?"

"Of course," Shavana replied. "Wendy showed me how it was done. I never saw her put the pea in her hand or slip it under a cup." Her eyes widened. "You think we're still being misdirected?"

Tom nodded.

"Can you explain?" Shavana asked.

Don had betrayed his trust. Now he had to hope Shavana wouldn't betray his, too. He pointed to the screen.

"This is the first deception," said Tom. "To make us think the *Phantom Press* was destroyed." He switched to the *Read Only* photo folder.

"What are you doing?" Shavana asked.

"Showing their next deception." Tom opened one of Shavana's photos of the ritual site. "Decades later, an alleged ritual is performed. It's looks like garbage, but the DPA wants us to believe it only looks amateurish."

"Why?"

"So, we'll think there are rogue occultists in the village," Tom replied. "Then the *Phantom Press* allegedly attacks the village board."

Shavana gave Tom a confused look. "What do you mean allegedly?"

Tom opened a photo of the *Phantom Press's* 2015 issue and a photo of the aftermath of the attack. "Wendy and Roul noticed two things: the issue looked too contemporary, and no one suffered from hallucinations." Tom pointed at the columns.

"Evenly spaced columns and justified type with minimal hy-phenations."

Shavana nodded. "Wendy mentioned that to me. Are you sure no one experienced hallucinations?"

Tom sighed. "Not completely sure. Everyone else seemed freaked out but grounded. I didn't even hear a whisper. Every attack since have involved hallucinations and psychic inva-sions."

"The car flying through the window?"

Tom paused. "I don't know, but there are mundane possi-bilities. The fake ritual colored our perception of the attack. It made us think of zebras when we should have thought of horses."

Shavana tilted her head. "Huh?"

Tom said, "Something a friend of mine said. It just means look at mundane explanations first."

"Ah," she replied. "But why would the DPA stage the attack? They've had decades to plan this. Why was this necessary?"

The gears jammed in Tom's mind. "I don't know, but a ghost attack no longer makes sense."

Shavana nodded. "But what would the DPA gain from the attack?"

Tom's eyes brightened. "After the attack, Robert granted the DPA emergency powers which gives them unchecked control over all covert facilities and personnel. Including Clow UFO Base. They probably ordered Roul's arrest because he was on to them."

Shavana nodded. "That does make sense. Then how does Don fit into this?"

Tom paused. Did he really want to say what he thought Don's role was?

I've got nothing left to lose at this point.

"What happened in the newsroom wasn't an accident. He helped Legion take out the Council."

Shavana's jaw dropped. "Oh my God!"

"I suspect he didn't know what Legion was going to do. He might feel guilty, but he still betrayed us."

Shavana said, "The attack also drove us out of Bolingbrook which allows him to cover up the DPA's involvement."

Tom sighed. "Yep." He shrugged. "Now I'm about to lose my job, and someone I care about will be framed by the DPA."

"Does your friend work for the Orange Squad?" Shavana asked.

Tom nodded.

"And you trust her more than Don?"

Tom exhaled as he considered his answer. "We shouldn't blindly trust either of them. What I do know is that the fiftieth anniversary banners the DPA put up are made of conductive cloth. Create a large enough network of these banners, and it can allow Legion to project its power into our world. And I know Legion is real. The possession junkies say it's something they've never experienced before. One of them burst into flames and set off a firestorm just to show me Legion's power."

Shavana gasped.

"APK saved me," Tom said and petted APK.

"Mow," APK said with pride.

"Juanita told me the ultimate purpose of the banners is to bring Legion into our world. The DPA's been testing the network since they attacked the newsroom. I think it's almost ready. Once they bring Legion into Bolingbrook…"

Shavana stared at the screen, the glow reflecting in her eyes as she took in what Tom had told her. "If you're right. What do you want me to do?"

"I want—" Tom stopped talking. He was torn between running away with APK or going to Bolingbrook to confront Legion. If he ran away, he could escape the blast, but the world would descend into chaos. He could try to take down Legion, but did he have the strength to resist its offers? Could Natalie save him again?

"What do you want?" Shavana asked.

Tom started the shutdown sequence on his laptop. "I'd like you to finish my investigation. Even if it takes you to Bolingbrook." Tom's laptop shut down, and he opened his laptop bag. "You are a better reporter than I am, so I know you'll do what's right." He placed the laptop and cords in the bag. "Have Sara tell me who's going to pick up APK. I don't want her to fall into the wrong hands."

Tom started petting and scratching APK. She purred as she watched Tom and Shavana.

Shavana looked down at the laptop for a few moments. "Tom. I need you to listen to me."

Tom tensed.

"I can't imagine what it would be like to discover that the cause you devoted your life to is a lie. I can only imagine how you felt when you gave up being a skeptical influencer to become a starting reporter. But I do know what's it like to struggle as a reporter."

"You?" Tom asked, tilting his head.

"Yes," Shavana replied. "Just before you were hired, I was struggling. Just like you are now. I did struggle. Sara and Wendy helped me. And I'm flattered you think I'm a better reporter. But you're wrong."

Tom raised his eyebrows.

Shavana said, "You're not better or worse than me. We're different. We have different backgrounds. Different experiences.

Different struggles. But we both want to be good journalists. And I admire that you gave up so much to join the *Babbler*."

Tom sighed. "Thank you."

Shavana pushed Tom's laptop bag away. "If you're willing to risk your career to uncover the truth, then I want to help you finish this investigation."

"Are you sure?" Tom asked. "Because you'll be risking your career, too."

"True." Shavana replied. "I'd rather be fired digging for the truth than have a long career rewriting the DPA's press releases." She shrugged. "Who knows? Maybe the girls in green will let me join them if I need a job."

"I...don't know what to say."

"You'll think of something," Shavana replied. "Right now, I have a standing invitation at the museum to watch the first board meeting. If the heckler was one of the first board members, you might recognize his voice." She straightened. "Would you like to accompany me to Bolingbrook?" She looked down at APK. "You're invited, too. We'll need your protection from whatever's out there."

APK head-butted Shavana then rubbed against Tom.

"Mow!"

Tom said, "I think she just said yes."

37

Tom looked out the window as Shavana drove towards Bolingbrook on I-355. In broad daylight, Bolingbrook looked like the events of last night never happened. But they had, Tom thought. Last night, he and APK had survived an encounter with Legion and the possession addicts. Now they were going back.

In back, APK slept inside her carrier, which was securely fastened by a seatbelt. A leash and harness, along with the front pet pouch, were next to the carrier. Tom wondered if she was saving her strength for what they might encounter.

"Oh no!" Shavana said into her headset. Tom felt a pit in his stomach. She was calling her friend at the Bolingbrook Historical Museum. Did the DPA just put up a roadblock in his investigation?

"Didn't you tell them it was reserved?" She shook her head as she heard the response. "Are you sure, no one transferred it to video?" She nodded. "Please call me if you find a copy." She sighed.

"I'm afraid to ask."

Shavana let out a frustrated moan. "Robert took the film. They say he was in a worse mood than usual. So, they were afraid to say no. So, now we can't see it."

"And nobody copied it?"

Shavana shook her head. "Apparently not."

Tom slammed his hand against the car door. "Fuck!"

"Mow!" APK cried from her carrier, sounding startled.

"Sorry APK," Tom said. He faced Shavana. "We just lost the only way to confirm if Barry was the heckler."

"Not necessary," Shavana replied. "BCTV started taping board meetings in 1981. They must have a tape from when Barry was on the board."

Tom sighed. "Except BCTV is inside Town Center, and we're not supposed to be in Bolingbrook. That's the worst place for us to be."

"The library might have something."

"I've already checked their local history collection. I didn't see any board meeting videos from the 1980s."

"Wouldn't hurt to ask," she replied.

"No, it wouldn't." Tom had a realization. "Before we go to Fountaindale, we should try to find the small library."

"Small library?" Shavana asked.

Tom nodded. "Roul left something locked in a small library. Fountaindale has the key, apparently. But I don't know which library he was talking about, or what we're looking for in the small library."

After a few moments of silence, Shavana said, "Did he say 'small library,' or 'little library?'"

Tom realized what Shavana meant. Little libraries were small wooden outdoor bookcases where people could take a book if they replaced it with another book.

"Oh my God." Tom closed his eyes and shook his head. "We were so focused on finding a small building that we didn't think about little library boxes. Which means—"

"What?"

Tom reached into his pocket and pulled out the notepad Juanita had given him. To his relief, the ink was visible, revealing the numbers Juanita had recited.

"Tom?"

"Oh, sorry." Tom looked up. "How many little libraries does Bolingbrook have?"

"At least five," she replied. "You know, Fountaindale recently installed one by the entrance. Maybe the key is there. Like how some people leave a key under the doormat?"

Tom nodded. "That should be the last one we check. We might only get one visit to Fountaindale. Where are the others?"

Shavana thought for a moment. "There's one near Pelican Harbor. One off Royce Road."

"Royce Road is too far to bike. Pelican Harbor is a possibility. The others?"

She thought again. "Warfield Park has one. There's one in Rotary Park. I was about to drop off some books when I spotted her."

Tom's eyes widened. "Wait. You saw that girl in green in Rotary Park?"

"Yeah. Though she kept reappearing further and further away."

"Did you reach the book box?"

Shavana shook her head. "No. Once I got the picture, I drove to the *Babbler*. In fact, I still have the books in my trunk."

Tom looked around the car. "Do you have a pen?"

"Glove compartment. What are you thinking?"

Tom pulled out a Bolingbrook fiftieth anniversary commemorate pen. "Let me check something."

He stared at the numbers. Were they some kind of coordinate system? Something only Juanita and her father would understand? There were too many numbers for a coordinate system. Unless it was in a fourth physical dimension.

"We're driving by Lisle," Shavana said. "Do you want to try Rotary Park first?"

"Maybe," Tom replied. "If I can figure out the key, maybe I can figure out what we need to look for."

"We can't cruise around Bolingbrook. They might spot us on the road."

"Give me a minute."

Tom sighed. Could he solve this in a minute? He wished Wendy were here to help, but Wendy had confidence in him. Maybe, for once, he should have confidence in himself, too.

He reread the numbers. They didn't make sense, yet Juanita and her father thought they were important enough to record.

Don't go down without a fight. Concentrate.

Tom wrote commas between the four numbers. Were they the location of a temporal chamber? Intergalactic coordinates? A spell?

"Think of a horse before you think of a zebra and before you think of an alien," Tom muttered.

"What?"

"Sorry, I'm just trying to think of a mundane explanation—"

Tom read the four numbers again. He didn't recognize the numbers, but he'd seen this pattern before. Could it be an IP address? Tom picked up his phone and typed the numbers into the address bar of his browser.

The Fountaindale Library's webpage appeared on his screen.

"I can see the tollway plaza," Shavana said. "We don't have much time."

Tom closed his eyes and pictured a map of Bolingbrook. "Rotary Park is close to Annerino, right?"

"Sort of," Shavana replied. "It's several blocks away. It would take a while to walk it."

"But you could easily ride a bike from Annerino to Rotary Park?" Tom opened his eyes. "Go to Rotary Park."

"Sure. You think it has anything to do with the girl in green I photographed?"

"Yep," Tom replied. "She wanted you to take the picture."

Shavana gave Tom a puzzled glance. "Why?"

"I think she was trying to lure you away from it. Maybe she was trying to protect you from something inside?"

38

Shavana parked her car in the small parking lot next to Rotary Park. The small trees in front of them obscured their view of the park. Further down, the parking lot connected to the back lot of Fire Station 1. The historical museum was about a block away.

They stepped out into the still, humid air. In the background, the gentle splashing of the water fountain in Orv Carlson Lake could be heard.

Tom opened the back and unbuckled APK's carrier. Inside, APK finished stretching her body as she stood on her legs. Tom reached for the navy-blue leash and harness.

"Mow!" APK protested.

"It's not that bad," Tom replied. "Dogs wear leashes all the time and—"

"Mow!" APK protested again.

"Okay," Tom said with a sigh. "Bad example. Look, Bolingbrook has a leash law. We don't want to give them another reason to arrest us. Trust me, you do not want to end up in the pound."

APK reached through the carrier's door and tried to reach her cat pouch. "Mow?" she asked.

It's too risky," said Tom. "If the girls in green trip me, you might get hurt. You'll have a chance to escape if you're on a leash."

APK grumbled as Tom unlatched the carrier's door.

"I'll make a deal," said Tom. "If I put you on a leash, you can guide me. Think of it as having me on the leash."

APK purred.

"Do we have a deal?"

"Mow," she replied, sounding like she approved.

APK let Tom put the harness on and connected the leash. When he finished, APK walked out of her carrier, then hopped onto the pavement. She sniffed the air.

"Good girl," said Tom.

APK stopped sniffing and glared at Tom. "Mow," she said, sounding annoyed.

"Shavana," said Tom, pointing at the sidewalk along Briarcliff Road. "You can watch us from the sidewalk in case the girls in green still don't want you near it."

She nodded. "Good luck." Shavana started towards the sidewalk and used her key remote to lock the car.

"APK," Tom said. "We'll follow Shavana around the trees, then we'll walk to the little library. Sound like a plan?"

APK side-eyed Tom, then started towards the tree line.

Tom shook his head. "Or I follow you instead."

They slipped between two trees without hitting the branches. Orv Carlson Lake was to his left. The water fountain shot a stream of water at least twenty feet into the air. Several yards ahead was a playground area with pristine equipment, including a chain bridge and swings. The picnic shelters looked like tall blue open umbrellas.

Nestled among the playground equipment was the little library. It looked like an oversized blue birdhouse except for the glass door and books inside.

APK sat on her hind legs, staring at the fountain.

Tom said, "If we want to rescue Juanita, we need to go to the little library over there." He pointed at the little library. APK bounced up and started trotting towards the little library.

"Good girl," said Tom as he followed APK.

Tom wondered what he should search for once he reached the little library. A thumb drive? A refurbished smartphone? Was it even digital? Maybe the IP address was an obscure way of saying to take the item to Fountaindale? It had to be hard to find, but Roul must have believed he or Juanita could find it.

APK abruptly stopped and arched her back. She hissed and looked up as her fur puffed out.

Tom didn't see anyone in front of them. Not even a squirrel.

APK crouched and hissed as she backed away. She started moving her head as if she were watching two invisible predators approaching. Tom hoped APK was reacting to the girls in green. He didn't want to consider the other possibilities.

"Hello?"

APK stopped next to Tom's feet. She once again arched her back and hissed.

"You know who I am," Tom said. The girls in green would know his name. They knew everyone in Bolingbrook. "I just need to check something out from the little library. Then, APK and I will be on our way." He smiled. "I promise."

"You brought that thing here," came a faint, angry female voice.

"You brought Shavana back to Bolingbrook," another female voice seethed, her voice like a snake's hiss.

"Technically, she drove me here," Tom said. He hoped they had a sense of humor. He wondered if he was the first *Babbler* reporter to hear the girls in green.

"She can't be here," a third voice hissed.

"Go away," said the first woman.

Time to name drop.

"Esteban Vega told me to come here," Tom answered. "You know, Roaming Roul?"

"He wanted his sunflower to come here," said the third woman.

"You are not an angel of reason," a fourth woman hissed.

"No," Tom said. "The angel of reason is in danger. You know the DPA is holding Esteban. You must have heard him tell me about this little library. He wants me to have what he hid inside."

"They have done so much to protect you from Legion," said the second woman.

"Who?" Tom asked.

"But you keep coming back," said the first woman.

"Because I need to know the truth about Legion," said Tom. "You must know what it will do if we don't stop it."

The girls in green didn't reply. APK crept forward.

"APK and I will leave once we have what we came for. Please let us pass."

They didn't reply. Tom kneeled to unhook APK's leash. "Cover me, and don't even think of running into the street. Got it?"

"Mow," APK replied, moving her head back and forth.

"Good," Tom replied, assuming she said yes.

Tom rose and cautiously approached the little library. APK's muscles coiled, ready to pounce.

After walking several feet, Tom felt something tangle in his legs. Before he could look down, his legs were pulled out from under him. Tree roots were wrapped around his legs and feet. Worse, they were pulling him towards the lake.

"Can we talk about this?" Tom pleaded.

The roots pulled Tom across the paved path. He winced as the pavement scraped his arms.

"Mow!" cried APK. She sprinted towards Tom. Tree roots, like grasping claws, reached out to ensnare APK, but abruptly stopped when they came within inches of her.

APK leaped into the air and landed on Tom's back. The roots holding him released their grip and retreated into the earth. She circled on top of Tom, hissing at the air.

"Your search for the truth dooms all of us," said the first woman.

The third woman said, "You think you can defeat Legion? Your actions will only help spread its fire beyond Bolingbrook."

"You are supposed to be the protectors of Bolingbrook," said Tom. "Tell me what I need to do to save Bolingbrook."

"Let us destroy your soul," the first woman hissed.

APK's eyes glowed fiery red. The invisible woman let out anguished howls of pain. APK's eyes returned to normal. The howls stopped.

"You and your abomination cannot save Bolingbrook."

Tom sat up. "I can try," he said.

"And so can I," said Shavana. She walked down the embankment towards Tom. "If you won't let Tom have what's inside the little library, then I'll get it myself."

A mass of brown roots erupted from the ground, blocking Shavana's path to the little library. "You mustn't see it."

"Very well," Shavana said calmly. "Then I'll stay in Bolingbrook until you let one of us get to that library."

"No!" said the first woman. "Legion is not the only threat."

"You must leave now," said the second woman.

Shavana nodded. "Then give Tom what he's looking for, and I'll leave."

Tom said, "Shavana—"

Shavana looked at Tom. "If you die, someone will need to finish your story."

Tom shook his head. "You don't have to—"

"I have to," Shavana replied. "Don't worry. You've got this." She grinned.

The roots returned to the ground.

"Tom must go alone," said the first woman.

"You dropped this," said Shavana as she pulled APK's leash out of her purse. "I'll take her to the car and unload her stuff before I leave."

APK jumped off Tom. He stood up and looked down at her. "I'll be back for you before you know it."

APK looked at Tom, then looked at the leash in Shavana's hand. She looked back at Tom and narrowed her eyes. "Mow," she said, sounding annoyed.

"Let her lead the way," Tom said to Shavana.

"I will. Now get going. You're running out of daylight."

Tom jogged to the little library. Its shelves were crowded with books, and he dreaded the thought of searching them. Tom reached for the door handle, then stopped. With all the people taking and adding books, it didn't make sense that he would put it inside a book.

The edges of the roof of the little library didn't look unusual. He then reached under the box and started feeling around. When he felt a wad of chewing gum, he felt disgusted.

That could be the point.

Tom took a moment to get over his disgust, then touched the chewing gum wad again. It was several wads stuck together. He kneeled to get a better view. The white, red, and green wads stood out against the wooden surface. He worked at the gum wads with his fingernails until he saw the small cardboard matchbox underneath. With renewed effort, he freed the matchbox from the gum. He opened the matchbox and saw a black thumb drive inside. And a note.

Tom removed the note and opened it.

"This drive and the last issue of the *Phantom Press* have the answers you seek."

Tom put the note back in the matchbox and put them in his pocket. He looked toward the lake. "I need to connect it to Fountaindale's network, right?"

Hearing no reply, Tom put the matchbox in his pocket and walked towards the parking lot. "I need a ride to the Fountaindale. It's too far to walk and too hot to walk with a cat."

The women didn't reply.

"Fine," Tom said. "I'll call a cab."

When he reached the parking lot, he gasped. His Toyota Echo, which he'd left at his apartment, was now parked next to Shavana's car. Shavana finished strapping APK's carrier into the passenger seat.

"How did it get here?" Tom pulled out his car key as he approached.

Shavana looked confused. "It rose up from the pavement, then the passenger door opened."

There were no signs of it traveling through dirt and concrete. It looked just as he'd left it.

Tom said, "You'd better get going. I'll get in touch if I find something."

Shavana nodded. "Good luck." She closed the passenger door and left.

Tom unlocked the driver's door and got in. The door of APK's carrier faced him. APK was curled in a ball, resting. He started the car and turned on the air conditioner. To his surprise, his car had a full tank of gas, and the AC immediately started blowing cool air.

Tom looked down at APK. "Up for being my psychiatric service cat?"

APK sat up.

"Mow!"

39

The librarians behind the checkout desk gasped as Tom and APK entered the lobby. APK's head poked out of her pet pouch. She purred as she looked around.

"Excuse me," said Sally.

As she neared Tom, Sally stared at APK in shock. "What is that?" She managed to say.

"This is my psychiatric service cat," Tom said, doing his best to keep a straight face.

"Mow," said APK. She purred and looked up at Sally.

Sally gave APK a critical look. "I thought only dogs could be psychiatric service animals."

Tom scratched APK's head. "She's a very special kitty. Isn't that right, Ms. Poppy?"

"Mow," APK replied, sounding proud of herself.

Sally looked into Tom's eyes. "What's the condition?"

"Condition?"

"What condition is she helping you with?"

Tom thought for a moment. "Delusional paranoia."

For a few moments, Sally didn't speak. "That makes sense." She looked back at APK. "Do you have her paperwork?"

Tom patted his pockets. "Darn," he said. "I left them in my girlfriend's van, and I don't know when I'll be able to reach her."

Her eyes narrowed as she looked at Tom. "I'll allow this. Provided she behaves."

"Mow," APK replied, sounding annoyed.

"Thank you," Tom replied. "Oh, can you get me into the vault?"

Sally put her hands on her hips. "That's pushing it."

Tom chuckled. "But I need to see the last issue the *Phantom Press* published before the implosion of Old Chicago. I'm on a deadline so—"

"When is your deadline?"

Tom paused. "Tonight. I need to see it before sunset."

"Let me guess. *The Phantom Press* will eat you if you don't."

Tom laughed. "I wouldn't have phrased it that way, but yes. *The Phantom Press* will try to eat me. But I have Poppy to protect me. Won't you, Poppy?"

APK purred.

Sally removed her hands from her hips. "Do you have your black card?"

Tom fidgeted. "Not yet, but I'm sure my mother is working on it."

Sally shook her head. "If I ask her, will she tell me you have permission to visit the vault?"

"I'll ask her then," Tom replied. He pulled out his smartphone. There was only one path into the vault, though he wished there was another way. He typed a message to his mother.

> I really need to visit the vault right now. If you let me in, we can talk about visiting Alexian Brothers.

Tom sighed. "She shouldn't take too long. I'll bet she's making the final arrangements as we speak."

"For your sake," Sally said, "I hope you're right."

Michelle's response popped onto his screen.

> If I let you in, will you give us a firm answer?

"Almost there," Tom said with a nervous chuckle.

Tom took a moment to compose himself. If he somehow exposed the DPA and stopped Legion, would his reward be spending the rest of his life in a mental institution? Was saving Bolingbrook worth losing his freedom?

> I'll give you a firm answer tonight. Promise.

He smiled at Sally. "I think we're going to get our answer."

Tom looked down at his phone. His mother wasn't typing a response.

"Mow?" APK asked as she looked at Tom's smartphone.

Sally pulled out her smartphone and read a message. "Let's go," she replied with little enthusiasm.

"Thank you," said Tom.

"Thank Trustee Larsen," said Sally.

"Tom!"

Tom turned and saw Meggy standing by the entrance to the library café. He waved, and Meggy ran up to him.

Meggy looked at APK. "That's a pretty cat."

"Mow!" APK replied in agreement.

"Her name is Poppy. You can pet her for a little bit."

Meggy started petting APK. "I'm Meggy. Pleased to meet you, Poppy."

APK closed her eyes and purred.

"Where are you going?" Meggy asked.

Tom glanced at Sally, who frowned at him. "I'm going to the vault to do some important research."

Meggy's eyes widened with excitement. "The vault?" she gasped. "I've always wanted to go there. Can I come?"

Tom looked at Sally. "You'll have to ask Librarian Sally."

Meggy stepped up to Sally. "My dad's going to be the deputy mayor! I'm sure he'd let me visit the vault with Tom. Please? Pretty please?"

Sally looked down at Meggy. "Sure," she said with a sigh. "Promise you'll stay close to Tom and not touch anything?"

"I promise."

"Then come along," Sally muttered. "Must be nepotism day."

The three of them walked behind the checkout stations and into a backroom. They followed Sally to a door with an electronic lock. She opened the drawer next to the door and pulled out three lanyards.

"Don't take them off until we leave," she said. "Unless you want to trigger the security alarms."

Tom and Meggy put on the lanyards. Sally pulled out a black card with no markings. She inserted it into the card reader and then keyed in what Tom thought was an unusually long passcode. The door opened, and they followed Sally into a well-lit stairwell.

They walked down several flights of stairs until they reached another door at the bottom. Sally held her black card up to a panel, then instructed Tom and Meggy to do the same. When they finished, the door made a buzzing sound. Sally opened the door, then guided Tom and Meggy through.

Meggy gasped. At the end of the room was a ten-foot-tall metallic door that opened into a chamber lined with cabinets and bookshelves. A male guard sat behind a counter. Two librarians wearing lab coats and surgical masks finished stacking books into what resembled a large safe deposit box. As they approached the vault doorway, the librarians closed the depot's box. A sign attached to the box read, "Do not open alone. Do not spill blood. Report any flu symptoms, no matter how minor."

The guard stood up. "Is that a service cat?"

"Yes," Tom replied.

"Unfortunately," Sally added.

"Mow," said APK with pride.

Sally held out her black card. "A patron wants to inspect a document." She pointed at Tom.

Tom cleared his throat. "I need the last issue of the *Phantom Press* published in 1986."

The guard looked at the librarians behind him. "Clear."

"I'll get it," said the male librarian. "Show them to a desk."

"And don't let the cat out," the female librarian added.

"Mow," APK replied, showing her annoyance.

The guard opened the flip top counter door and escorted them to a small desk. The desk had only one mounted magnifying glass.

"Where are the gloves?" Tom asked.

"You don't need gloves when handling old documents," Sally replied. "Movie myth."

"And this one is laminated," said the male librarian. In his hands was the last confirmed issue of the *Phantom Press*. It was printed on a light green sheet of paper.

For a publication that crossed the boundary between life and death, Tom didn't expect it to look like a newsletter that predated desktop publishing. The masthead was the name, *Phantom Press*, printed with an extra-large bold font. The body text was from a typewriter, not the Courier computer font.

"The last issue is a one double-sided page," the male librarian said. "It was their shortest issue. Whoever published it wasn't in a good mood."

The headline read, "Clark's lies damn Bolingbrook."

"I'd say so," said Tom.

The librarian placed the issue on the desk. Tom's anticipation grew. A major piece of the puzzle was inches away.

"Wait," said the female librarian, holding a corded phone. "Robert just put a hold on it."

The man pulled the issue away. "Sorry about that."

Tom's jaw dropped. "What are you doing?"

"Robert wants us to hold it for him." The male librarian placed the issue in a tray marked 'Returns.'

Tom said, "But I was about to read it."

He shrugged. "It's Bolingbrook. If Robert wants something, we give it to him."

"With all due respect!" Tom rose, toppling over his chair. "Robert is not your boss!"

The male librarian laughed. "Not officially, but he bought the board. Just ask your mother."

Tom clenched his jaw. This was not the time to argue about Robert's grip on Bolingbrook. "Can you just give me five minutes? I'll be done with it by the time he's here."

"Nope," said the female librarian. "Robert specifically said no one else can touch it. Apparently—"

APK hissed and started squirming in her pouch. The male librarian jumped back. "What the hell?"

"Mow!" APK growled as she clawed at her pouch.

Tom turned away from the librarian. "It's okay," he whispered. "Calm down."

APK stopped scratching at her pouch. She leaned her head against Tom and started purring.

"Good girl."

"Is there a problem?" the guard asked.

"Yes," Sally replied. She turned to the guard. "We were just leaving."

"Aw," Meggy said. "But we just got here."

"You can ask your dad to take you here another time," Sally said.

The three of them left the vault and returned to the lobby.

"Are you staying?" Meggy said to Tom.

"Yeah," Tom said, his disappointment showing.

Meggy's jaw dropped. "Cool! I'll see you later." She ran up the stairs.

Sally's eyes narrowed as she gave APK a stern look. "If she doesn't cause another incident, you can stay."

APK slow-blinked at Sally.

Tom walked away and climbed the stairs. He made his way to the computer area.

The librarian at the computer desk stood up.

Tom said, "Service cat." He handed the attending librarian his card. "Sally said it was okay."

The librarian took his card and started to make a phone call. Tom found an open computer and checked in. He could unlock the thumb drive while he waited for Robert to finish reading the *Phantom Press*.

Before he could pull out the thumb drive, Meggy approached and motioned for Tom to be quiet. Tom looked around the area and saw one other user several rows away.

"I got it," she whispered. Meggy quietly approached Tom, then looked around. Seeing no one watching them, she reached under her shirt and pulled out the copy of the *Phantom Press*.

40

Tom took the laminated issue of the *Phantom Press* and hid it under the table. "How?" he said in a hushed voice.

Meggy whispered, "While everyone was arguing, I snuck up to the return tray, but the guard was watching. So, I put some other papers in the tray, so he'd think I was helping clean up. That's when I saw Poppy blink at me. I knew she was trying to tell me something. When she started acting up, everyone else was distracted. Not me. I pulled out the issue and hid it under my shirt. Then we escaped." Meggy petted APK. "Poppy is a smart girl."

"Mow," APK softly replied. She started purring.

Tom looked around, hoping the librarians hadn't noticed the missing issue.

"Promise me you'll only use your powers for good," he whispered.

"I don't have powers. I'm a spy. I work for the good guys."

Tom hunched over and checked both sides of the issue. The op-ed, "Time to go Home" caught his attention.

> We thank Mayor Rene MacDonald and Trustee Barry Gilbert for offering us sanctuary in Bolingbrook. However, we must decline. Though

well intentioned, what they offer is not Heaven, but a Hell of their own creation. Our colleagues, blinded by their rage, have accepted this offer. We have begged them to reconsider but they will not listen.

If this is the price for our continued existence, we will not pay it.

To our readers, thank you for sustaining us. But we have overstayed our time on Earth. It's time for us to go home.

"That's weird," said Meggy. "Who wrote it?"

Tom flipped over the paper and pointed to the masthead. "Ghosts."

Meggy side-eyed Tom. "My dad says there's no such thing as ghosts. He says teens with drones are behind it."

Tom nodded. "He might be onto something. I'll have to talk to him."

Meggy whispered, "He's suspicious of you, but I think you're great."

Tom chuckled and then skimmed the rest of the issue. It was mostly information he already knew about Barry and Robert. Except for one detail. Robert promised to make Barry the deputy mayor in exchange for his endorsement. That's why he didn't endorse Rene's preferred candidate. After the election, Robert chose someone else. According to the article, Robert changed his mind because Barry wouldn't leave the organization. Tom assumed it was a reference to the Illuminati.

Another article stated Natalie was under their protection.

Until they made her part of Legion.

"Can I see?" Meggy asked.

Tom handed it to Meggy. "Be very careful. We went through a lot of trouble to get this."

While Meggy read the issue, Tom removed the thumb drive and inserted it into a USB port. The disk icon appeared on the desktop with a lock symbol. A moment later, the symbol changed to unlocked. The thumb drive contained ten video files.

"Want to watch a video?"

"Mow!" said APK. She adjusted her body to get a better look at the screen.

Tom petted APK. "Meggy?"

"Sure. The *Phantom Press* is too weird."

Tom opened the first file. It was security cam footage of the Town Center parking lot. The timestamp showed the video was recorded on the night of the attack after the awards ceremony.

"This is boring," Meggy whispered. "Why are we watching this?"

"Someone went to a lot of trouble to hide this thumb drive," Tom said. "I'd like to know why."

APK stretched her head further out. "Mow," she said, motioning towards the screen.

On screen, an unusual remote-controlled vehicle approached Robert's car. The low-to-the-ground front of the vehicle featured two long, flat metal rectangles. They reminded Tom of the saddles on a car mechanic's hydraulic lift. The hydraulic ram on the vehicle's rear end, a tall structure, loomed over Robert's car. The vehicle parked with the saddles under the car, and the ram touching the rear bumper. The hydraulic lift raised two feet off the ground. A second set of saddles unfolded from the vehicle, locking into position beneath Robert's car. The first set of saddles retracted. The lift tilted Robert's car and rotated to target the bay windows of the boardroom. Moments later, the hydraulic ram launched the car into the boardroom.

"Mow," APK said, sounding amazed.

"Wow," Meggy said.

"Oh my god," Tom said as he watched the remote vehicle drive off screen.

"Is that a toy?" asked Meggy.

Tom blinked. "Um. No. It's definitely not a toy." He opened another video. This security camera faced the back of the Town Center. Hundreds of aerial drones rose out of the reflecting pool and scattered in different directions. Each drone carried an unmarked black container.

Tom opened another video. The screen showed Steve at the rear exit, observing the drone launches. On this security camera, Steve exited Town Center and watched the drones flying away.

"Son of a—"

"Mow!" APK motioned towards Meggy.

"What?" Meggy asked.

Tom, still in shock, said, "I think your dad will want to see this."

Meggy looked closer at the screen. "What are they doing?"

"Let's find out."

The next video was from a security camera with night vision. It showed swarms of drones scattering fake *Phantom Press* issues over Bolingbrook.

"Where is your dad?" Tom asked.

"Working in Aurora. I'm not supposed to call him unless it's an emergency."

Tom's phone vibrated. It was a number he didn't recognize. He answered, hoping it was a spam caller.

"Hello?"

"Tom," Juanita whispered over the phone. "Where are you?"

Tom whispered, "The library. Are you okay?"

"I don't have much time," Juanita said. "It's a coup."

Tom's jaw dropped. "What?"

"It's a coup. The DPA is staging a coup and, somehow, you signaled them."

In the background, Tom heard Robert yell, "You can't do this to me. I'm the Mayor of Bolingbrook!"

Steve replied, "And we don't care."

A chill ran through Tom's body. Steve, whom Robert loved like a brother, was staging a coup with the DPA's help.

"What about the men in blue?" Tom asked.

"They control the men in blue," Juanita said, a hint of fear in her voice.

Tom froze. He didn't think it was possible for anyone besides Robert to control the men in blue.

Juanita said, "They're coming for you and someone named Megan. You've got to get out of Bolingbrook!"

"Leaving now," Tom said. "Um..." He hesitated. Was this it? Their last conversation. Tom closed his eyes. "Stay safe."

"You too," said Juanita. "Pet APK for me."

APK looked up at the phone. "Mow?" she said, with sadness in her voice.

Tom petted APK. "She'll be okay."

Meggy tilted her head. "Who?"

Tom removed the thumb drive. "I'll tell you later. We've got to get out of here. Where's your mother?"

"In Town Center. She's planning the concert."

Tom looked around the area. "We need to show this to your dad."

"Is it an emergency?" Meggy asked.

Tom pocketed the thumb drive as he stood up. "Yes. I need you to stay close to me until we reach your dad."

Meggy picked up the issue and followed Tom as he walked towards the librarian's desk. Thoughts raced through Tom's head. Meggy's mother was probably in the DPA's custody. Her father might still be safe. He needed to see the videos, but was the thumb drive still locked to Fountaindale's network? Maybe he had a VPN that could simulate Fountaindale's network. While Tom couldn't save Meggy's mother, he needed to protect Meggy.

Tom asked for his library card back. While the librarian searched for it, Meggy placed the *Phantom Press* issue in a return tray.

The librarian handed Tom's card back. "Nice kitty."

"Mow," APK purred.

"Thanks," Tom replied.

Tom and Meggy left and walked towards the stairs.

"Are we spies?" Meggy whispered.

"Yes."

"Cool!" Meggy covered her mouth for a moment. "I meant cool," she whispered.

"Stay close and quiet," Tom whispered. "We're trying to sneak past the bad people." *Anyone here could be a DPA operative.* Steve was an insurrectionist, but he didn't discriminate when it came to hiring operatives."

Meggy nodded.

Together they walked down the center staircase. But just before they reached the ground floor, Tom's heart sank. Two men in blue stood accompanied by two men holding computer tablets.

He motioned at Meggy to stop.

"Change of plans," he whispered.

41

Tom and Meggy returned to the second floor.

"What now?" asked Meggy.

Tom didn't know the answers. Using the other stairwells would trigger the fire alarm. The private study rooms had glass doors. The quiet areas were too open. Were they trapped?

"Tom," came Sally's voice. She stepped out from behind the desk. "Can you explain why there's a vault document in a return tray?"

Tom's eyes lit up. There was a way to save Meggy and maybe APK too. "That's a long story," he whispered. "Let's talk about it in the admin section. We won't have to whisper."

Sally folded her arms. "You want me to take you to another restricted area?"

Tom glanced back and didn't see the two men in blue in the stairwell. Yet.

"We won't disturb people in the admin area."

Sally looked at Tom and Meggy, then shrugged. "You might regret this." Sally started walking.

Tom glanced back at the stairway and elevators. "I have too many regrets for my age."

The three of them walked past rows of shelves until they reached a door with an electronic badge lock. Sally unlocked the door. Once they were inside, the door locked behind them.

Sally locked her eyes on Tom. "Mr. Larsen, you brought a cat into Fountaindale, manipulated a library board member into giving you access to the vault, and borrowed a historical document without a proper card. What do you have to say before I revoke your library privileges?"

Tom said, "The Public Works Department just staged a coup against Robert, and there are at least four men out there who want to kidnap Meggy because she's the deputy mayor's daughter. Can you help her?"

Sally gave Tom a dumbfounded stare. Meggy's eyes widened as she looked through the glass wall separating the offices from the main library.

"That's why I was going to take you to your dad," Tom continued.

"Why?" Sally asked. "Why would the Public Works Department stage a coup?"

Meggy's voice quivered. "Is this like a shooter drill, only real?"

Through the glass wall, he noticed a man wearing a teal polo shirt hanging out by the desk. His shirt looked like the branded shirts worn by Public Works employees. "I hope not," he answered and kneeled in front of Meggy. "You're not only the girl that snuck into my father's store. You're also the girl that escaped Bolingbrook's biggest riot. Unharmed."

Sally stepped closer to Meggy. "You were at the Golf Club riot?"

Meggy nodded as a tear ran down her cheek.

Tom reached into his pocket. "If you can escape a riot, you can escape from this library. In fact, I'm so confident you're going to get out." Tom pulled out the matchbox with the thumb drive and handed it to Meggy. "I'm trusting you to give this to your dad."

Meggy reached for the matchbox. "I don't know if I can escape."

"Of course you can." Tom smiled. "You're a spy."

"I'm a spy." Meggy took the thumb drive with one hand and wiped her eyes with the other. "I'm a spy."

"And Librarian Sally is going to help you escape."

"And you?" asked Meggy.

Tom smiled. "I'm a spy, too."

Meggy hugged Tom. "Be careful."

"I will," said Tom.

Sally stepped closer to Meggy. "What about you, Tom?"

Tom looked through the glass. His heart sank when he saw two men in blue standing next to two men wearing teal polo shirts. Tom was now certain they were DPA operatives. He noticed both holding computer tablets. He wondered if that was how they controlled the men in blue.

"I'm a spy," Tom said. "I can't give away all my secrets."

"You don't have a plan." Sally said, "Do you?"

Tom closed his eyes for a moment. He didn't have a plan. Yet.

Tom's phone vibrated for a moment and then accepted the call. Over the phone, Steve said, "I know you can hear me."

Tom pulled out the phone and turned away from the glass wall. He pressed the speaker virtual button. "Did you just steal one of Robert's tricks?" He motioned at Meggy and Sally to keep quiet.

"You just can't take a hint," Steve said.

To Tom's left was a hallway leading to the other offices and a door with a "Fire" emergency light above it. On the other side of the room was another hallway. A sign pointed to a fire escape stairwell.

Two ways to escape. Two ways for them to break in.

Tom said, "I'm starting to feel like you're more interested in taking over Bolingbrook than dealing with a Legion that's about to explode. I think your priorities are a bit off. Don't you think?"

Steve chuckled on the other end. "You should think about your priorities, Tom. We've surrounded the library, and we control the men in blue."

"I saw." Tom tried to remember the layout of this section of the library. He wished he'd paid more attention when his mother gave him a tour. "Got to be an Android app, right? No way in Hell the Apple Store would approve something like that."

"Just walk away," Steve replied. "We don't want you, and we don't want your mother."

Tom glanced at Meggy. "You want me to turn Meggy over to you."

"No," Steve calmly replied. "We don't need your help or want to put you in protective custody. We just want you to walk away and take Anti-Psychic Kitty with you."

"Mow?" APK asked.

Tom patted APK. "Just walk away as you unleash a monster on the Brook? Abandon my home? My family? My friends?"

"Do you really think you can stop what's coming? That you can stop us? Your editor's about to fire you. The skeptical movement has abandoned you. If you try to resist us, you'll have no future. But if you just walk away, we'll give you access to the greatest story of your lifetime."

"The day Legion destroyed Bolingbrook?"

Steve chuckled. "You might want to consider a career making funny viral videos. Tom, this goes far deeper than you can imagine. But we can fix that. We can bring you in and give you behind-the-scenes access to the event that changed the world.

It'll be the biggest story of your life, Tom. You wouldn't have to settle for working for the *Babbler*. You'd have a real career. Your parents would be proud of you, Tom. No more talk about mental institutions."

"You're offering me exclusive access to the people who destroyed Bolingbrook?" Tom discreetly grabbed a pen.

"I'm offering you a future," Steve replied. "All you need to do is walk away from Meggy."

"Well," Tom said as he wrote on a notepad. "APK comes with me."

"Of course," Steve replied. "We'll even tell her caretakers that you did such a wonder job while Juanita was absent."

"Can I talk to her?" Tom covered his notes.

"Not yet." Steve paused. "Let's just say she still needs more education. If you walk away, we might not have to enhance her lessons."

Tom froze. Juanita could probably withstand far more pain than he could, but knowing his actions resulted in her being tortured was too frightening to imagine.

"Well," Tom said, "I guess I do have the privilege of walking towards a brighter future." He slid the notepad towards Meggy and Sally, which read: "HIDE." He motioned towards the back and then winked at Meggy. Meggy winked back.

Tom approached the wall, hoping to conceal Meggy and Sally sneaking towards the back hallway.

"APK and I don't think Juanita needs any enhanced lessons. Don't you agree, APK?"

APK grumbled.

Tom stopped inches from the door to the library. He wished the architect hadn't decided to use a glass door with a wooden frame. "So what happens after I walk away? When exactly—"

"We'll call you when it's time."

Tom couldn't hear any footsteps behind him. "I'm coming out. Don't shoot."

"This is not a joke, Tom."

"Who's joking?"

Tom opened the door and stepped into the library area. He pushed the door closed with his right foot.

"Oops," Tom said into the phone.

Steve replied, "It doesn't matter—"

Tom powered down the phone. "No calls in the library," he whispered.

The two men in blue started walking towards the administration offices. Tom assumed their handlers were walking behind them.

Tom petted APK. "Do you think I could break both tablets before those DPA agents beat me up?"

APK looked up and back at Tom. She stopped purring.

"You're probably right," said Tom. "Do you think there's a way to override the app?"

"Mow?"

"There must be a subconscious directive that would override any commands from the app. Don't you think?"

"Mow," APK skeptically replied.

"There has to be—" Tom thought of one thing that might trigger an override command. "Do you trust me?"

"Mow," APK whispered.

"I'll take that as a yes."

The men in blue towered over Tom as they approached. He stopped, realizing they would literally walk over him if he tried to block them.

He stepped into the aisle between two bookcases with shelves of magazines. Tom was slightly taller than each case. The men in blue marched by, followed by the two DPA operatives. They ignored Tom, their eyes focused on their tablets.

After sitting down on one of the benches between the shelves, Tom unhooked the pouch and released APK.

Tom whispered, "Wait right here. If I'm not hit by a disintegration ray, the men in blue will come at me. I need you to trip them and then jump into my arms. That should buy us enough time to run to my car. Got it?"

APK darted out of her carrying pouch, then leaped from the bench to the top of a bookcase.

"You can wait there, too."

Tom stepped onto the walkway. The men in blue neared the lobby space between the administrative area and the boardroom. Tom looked up at the ceiling. "Please don't take this personally," he whispered. "And if you want to help, now would be a good time."

Nothing happened. The men in blue continued marching.

Tom cleared his throat. If he survived, his mother would personally drag him to the nearest mental institution. But he couldn't think of a better idea. He took a deep breath and yelled, "The Martian Colonies suck!"

For a moment, Tom expected to be struck by a Martian Colonial disintegration ray. It didn't come. Worse, the men in blue ignored him and were almost at the door.

Not offensive enough.

He screamed the next insult that popped into his head. "Earth rules! The Martian Colonies drool!"

The men in blue came to an abrupt halt. The DPA operatives, still looking down at their tablets, bumped into them. Fear paralyzed Tom for a few moments. Had he just offended two of Bolingbrook's feared enforcers? The same men in blue who keep Clow UFO Base's visitors in line?

The men in blue turned around in unison. Though they wore blue-tinted sunglasses, Tom felt their eyes targeting him.

"Get ready, APK."

The DPA operatives started frantically tapping the screens on their tablets. The men in blue pushed aside their handlers. As the DPA operatives fell to the floor, the men in blue marched towards Tom.

APK looked at Tom. "Mow?"

Tom's breathing quickened. "You can do this."

The men in blue neared the bookcase APK was on top of. She hissed and backed away.

"That wasn't the plan," Tom said as he started walking backwards.

A man in blue reached out with his right arm. With little effort, he pushed against the bookcase. The several yards' long case toppled over. APK leaped off the shelf and landed on the nearest bench. After a quick sprint, she leaped into the air moments before the bookshelf crashed onto the bench. She landed on top of the next bookcase and then dove towards the benches on the other side. She landed and dropped to the floor. She rushed by the portable bookrack with a sign that read "Local Authors" and charged towards the elevator lobby.

"Better plan," Tom cried as he sprinted after APK.

The men in blue maintained their pace as they followed Tom. Onlookers stepped aside and gaped as they passed.

"My camera isn't working," Tom heard a patron say.

Tom ran past the desk where two librarians looked on in disbelief. He turned into the lobby and saw APK running up the stairs away from the first floor.

"What are you doing?" Tom said, panting. "We need to go—"

On the stairwell, two new men in blue stepped into Tom's view and started climbing up towards the second floor.

"Up!" Tom reversed course and ran towards the stairs leading to the third floor. "Great idea, APK!"

Tom ran up to the third floor and glimpsed APK scampering to the right. Tom leaned over to catch his breath.

A librarian stood up behind the adult services desk. "Did you bring that cat inside?"

"Psychiatric service cat," Tom gasped.

"You do know that any service animal needs to be under your control at all times."

Heavy footsteps came from the stairs behind him.

"You ever tried to tell a cat what to do?"

"Actually—"

Tom dashed to left down the main aisle.

"No running," the librarian said in a stage whisper.

Tom turned down a side aisle and slowed to a walk.

He heard the librarian say, "How can I help you, gentlemen?" No one replied. Not even the librarian. Tom assumed one of the men in blue mesmerized her. Perhaps it was a prelude to altering her memory. He didn't want to be next.

Tom quietly approached the cross aisle ahead of him. He needed to figure out how to slip by the men in blue and rescue APK.

From afar, an unfamiliar male voice said, "You're annoying us, Tom."

Seeing the cross aisle was clear, he shifted to the row to his left. At some point, he'd have to backtrack to the stairs without the men in blue or DPA operatives noticing him.

"We've surrounded Fountaindale," said the man. "We've regained control of the two men in blue. And we just brought in two more."

Tom quickened his pace. Heavy footsteps came from the main aisle behind him.

"You can't save Meggy," the man continued. "But you can save Anti-Psychic Kitty. Nobody wants her harmed, but she can't stay here. You've seen what she can do."

Tom crept into the main aisle and put his back against a shelf. He peered around the corner and saw no one. The sound of footsteps startled Tom. It sounded as if they were walking down a neighboring aisle. He stepped into another aisle. Footsteps came from the main aisle he'd just left. As he started to move, he noticed a gap in the bookshelf, allowing him to see the other aisle. And for someone in that aisle to see him.

Tom put his back against a bookshelf. He tried to steady his breathing. The last thing he wanted was to be on the receiving end of a memory-altering slap. Or worse.

Two sets of footsteps sounded from the other side of the bookshelf. He peered through the gap between shelves. A man in blue walked by, followed by a DPA operative. He wondered how long he had until they started walking down this aisle.

The DPA operative screamed, and Tom felt the bookshelf shake. He looked through the gap. The operative had his back against the shelf as well. The stench of cat urine filled Tom's nostrils. The operative cursed, then dropped his tablet. APK stood on one of the shelves, spraying the last of her urine.

This is my only opportunity to take out at least one man in blue, Tom thought. Before thinking it was a bad idea, he ran over to the other aisle. The DPA operative was looking down in disgust at his urine-stained shirt. APK, crouching between two bookshelves, lowered her tail. The man in blue stood motionless with his back turned towards the operative and Tom. The tablet, within a hard plastic protective case, lay on the floor. A large crack ran across the screen protector.

Instinctively, Tom stomped on the tablet, desperately trying to shatter the screen beneath the failing protector.

The operative saw Tom and yelled, "You son of a—" He kicked Tom in the abdomen.

The blow lifted Tom inches off the floor. Unable to regain his balance, he dropped to the floor, his butt cushioning his fall.

"I'm through with being nice," the operative said with a snarl. He rushed at Tom.

From the floor, Tom kicked the operative's lead knee. The operative cursed as he stopped and hobbled backwards.

Fueled by adrenaline, Tom grabbed the tablet and rose to his feet. Seeing the operative looking down at his knee, Tom held the tablet with both hands and smashed it against the top of his head. The man screamed at the same time as a cracking sound came from the tablet. Tom raised the tablet to strike again. Shards of plastic rained down on the operative's thinning hair.

The operative charged before Tom could swing the tablet again. He lowered his head and struck Tom's waist area and wrapped his arms around his legs. The blow knocked Tom off balance, and the operative drove him into a window. While the impact hurt, he appreciated that the library board had bought shatter-resistant windows.

The operative lifted his head and tried to snatch his tablet from Tom. Tom nipped at his earlobe. With a yelp, the operative jumped back, and Tom spit to get rid of the salty taste in his mouth.

The operative turned his head away and touched his ear. Tom swung the tablet and hit the back of his head. The screen cracked, followed by sparks shooting out of the tablet. Startled, Tom dropped the tablet.

"That hurt!" the operative yelled. He shoved Tom against another window.

Tom winced from the impact. As the operative reached into one of his pockets, Tom noticed the man in blue standing behind the operative, facing them. The man in blue, who Tom thought was at least seven feet tall, tapped the operative's shoulder with his right index. The operative's eyes widened in horror as he released Tom.

The man in blue turned the operative around. The operative tried to speak, but the man in blue slapped him. The sound seemed to echo throughout the third floor.

The operative's body swayed for a few moments. The man in blue grabbed the operative by the shoulder and lifted him until the man's eyes were level with the man in blue's blue-tinted sunglasses.

Tom caught his breath as he watched the man in blue staring at the operative. He knew men in blue could alter memories, but he didn't know if they could read the minds of the men they slapped.

After a few moments, the man in blue set the operative down on the floor. His eyes were glazed over. The man in blue released the operative. The operative walked towards the stairwell.

Tom froze as another man in blue approached. "Behind you," he managed to say.

The first man in blue turned around and walked at the second at a steady pace. Without breaking his stride, the first man in blue kicked the second in the abdomen. This sent the second man in blue flying backwards until he collided with the operative who was controlling him. Both men landed near the other main aisle.

The second operative stood, no longer holding his tablet. The second man in blue stood and faced the operative.

"Fall back!" yelled the operative. He ran away. The second man in blue walked after him.

The first man in blue approached Tom. Tom lifted his arms to show his palms. "I have a report," he said. The last time he communicated with a man in blue, he had an implant that identified him as a village employee. Would this man in blue listen to him without the implant?

The man in blue stopped and looked down at Tom, who swallowed and took a deep breath.

He spoke quickly. "The DPA is staging a coup. They kidnapped Robert. They're looking for Trustee Simon Williams's daughter. She's hiding in the library. They have a powerful Legion in the Ghost Frequencies. Trustee Williams is at his job in Aurora. I believe the Illuminati is involved, and I have an anti-psychic cat."

The man in blue slowly turned his head towards APK, who purred as she assumed a submissive posture.

"Any questions?" asked Tom.

The fire alarm blared to life, and the emergency lights activated.

The librarian at the adult services desk yelled, "Go to the nearest fire exit!"

The man in blue raised his arm. Tom froze, unsure of what the man in blue was about to unleash. He gave Tom a child's wave goodbye.

Tom responded with his own awkward child's wave.

Seeing Tom's response, the man in blue turned and walked away.

Out of Tom's sight, a librarian yelled, "This is not a drill. Everyone out. Now!"

Tom noticed the stench of cat urine and winced. He checked the floor for any puddles of cat urine. Seeing none, he approached APK and prepared the pet pouch.

"You couldn't think of a better way to distract that operative?" Tom asked.

"Mow," APK proudly replied as she approached. Tom helped her into the pouch and secured it.

"If the DPA doesn't kill us, my mom will."

APK popped her head out of the pouch and purred.

"You're right," Tom replied. "Mom will kill me. You're too adorable for her to kill."

"Mow."

Tom went through the nearest fire exit and descended the stairs. He mingled in with the others entering the stairwell and kept an eye out for DPA operatives and any men in blue.

Outside, he saw patrons and library staff standing in the parking lot. The sound of approaching sirens grew louder.

Tom weaved through the crowd, hoping to remain inconspicuous while wearing a pet pouch. He noticed some DPA operatives. Most wore polo shirts, while five operatives wore suits. Tom lowered his head and worked his way to his car.

Once he reached his Echo, he opened the passenger door. A blast of hot air greeted Tom. He waited a moment, then transferred APK to the carrier.

If the operatives weren't lying, they would let him leave Bolingbrook with APK. Tom planned to go to Chicago and figure out how to contact the Orange Squad. If he found the right members, they could rescue Juanita and stop Legion. As he closed the carrier door, he wondered how he could find the right members. He wished he could talk to Wendy again, or even Sara.

"Hi," Meggy whispered behind Tom. Startled, Tom twitched and then looked behind him. Meggy was crouched next to Tom, using the adjacent car for cover.

"What—" Tom gasped. "Where's Sally?"

"She's distracting the big weirdos and can't drive me. Can I get a ride with you? I promise my dad won't kill you."

A chill ran through Tom's body. If Meggy joined Tom, the DPA wouldn't let him leave town. And he would have to take her to Aurora. He glanced at APK, who purred as she watched Meggy.

Am I really going to find the Orange Squad in time?

He reached into the car and unlocked the back door.

"Get in back," he whispered, "and fasten your seatbelt."

Meggy crouched as she opened the back door. "You're awesome."

Tom used the seat belt to secure APK's carrier.

"Brace yourself," Tom said to APK.

"Mow?"

"Do the best you can."

He closed the door and checked on Meggy. She sat in the back seat with her seat belt securely fastened.

"Keep your head down," whispered Tom.

"Where's the lock button?"

"You use this handle, but I'll lock it for you."

Tom locked the door. Seeing that the other back door was locked, Tom quickly entered the car and started it. To his relief, it started as normal. He backed out of his spot.

Honking sounds startled Tom. He noticed a parked pickup truck with the Public Works logo on it. A man inside honked and pointed at Tom. *He must have seen me,* Tom thought.

Two police cars blocked the nearest exit. A fire truck blocked the other visible exit.

DPA operatives rushed at the Echo from Tom's left and right. Two DPA operatives pulled their pistols out of their sports coats. Small hedges surrounded the parking lot, except for a gap in the curb where the pavement met a brick walkway that connected to the sidewalk along Delaware Drive.

"Hang on!"

Tom switched gears and did a hard turn to the left, narrowly missing a car's bumper. Facing one group of approaching DPA operatives, Tom floored the accelerator. The operatives in front of him scattered. In the rear-view mirror, Tom saw two operatives aiming their guns.

He swerved hard to the right, the Echo's tires squealing in response.

"You're gonna crash," Meggy cried.

"I've got this!" Tom replied as he aimed for the opening. "Keep your head down and close your eyes!"

The Echo's left tires ran over a curb, jolting everyone in the car.

"Mow!" APK screeched.

"I'd done this before!" He had, though he thought it best not to mention how his last attempt at high-speed turning ended.

The Echo brushed against the hedge's branches as it drove onto the brick walkway. The walkway split, but Tom drove straight onto the grass. Startled evacuees stood on the sidewalk, and he pounded on his car horn.

"Move it!" he yelled, fighting the urge to hit the brakes.

People scattered away from the Echo. Seeing a clear path, Tom accelerated and started turning left. The Echo drove over the curb and onto Delaware Drive. The tires squealed as Tom finished the turn. He exhaled. He had survived this high-speed turn.

As the Echo drove away from Fountaindale, two black SUVs exited the parking lot and swerved onto the road. Tom shifted gears and pressed harder on the accelerator. Delaware Drive was a straight road for several blocks. It would bend near Brooks

Middle School at the intersection of Delaware Drive and Blair Lane. If it wasn't blocked, he could run the stop sign and not worry about slowing down. Then he'd have to attempt another high-speed turn onto Boughton.

Could he make two successful high-speed turns in a row? Did he have an alternative besides surrendering?

"Are they gonna shoot us?" Meggy asked.

"They'll shoot at us," Tom replied. "But they won't hit us."

"Mow," APK replied, sounding skeptical.

"How about a little more positive thinking?" Tom asked.

The SUVs behind them accelerated, closing the distance faster than Tom thought possible. The passengers in both cars leaned out of their windows and started aiming their pistols.

Tom's heart sank as the Blair Lane intersection came into view. Three SUVs each blocked an entry. He also saw a row of tire spikes placed across the street. Worse, a side window opened, and a DPA operative aimed what appeared to be a shoulder-mounted rocket launcher.

"Hold on to something!"

"Mow?"

Meggy bent over and covered her head.

Tom angled the Echo towards a driveway with one car parked outside. As he did, the DPA operative fired. The rocket streaked past the Echo. It hit one of the pursuing SUVs, penetrating its grille. Sparks shot out from the edges of the hood and underneath the engine. Despite the damage, it kept charging down Delaware Drive.

Tom drove across the driveway and turned towards the sidewalk. The Echo straddled the sidewalk as he drove parallel to the road. Tom tightened his grip, knowing that one mistake could send them crashing into a parked car or even a house.

"I got this," Tom said to himself.

The damaged SUV rushed past the Echo and plowed into the blocking SUV. The impact sent both vehicles through the intersection. They collided with the fourth SUV previously blocked from Tom's view. All three vehicles came to a stop.

Tom looked down the sidewalk and gasped. The crosswalk was lined with tire spikes, and there was no way back to the intersection. Tom took a deep breath and swerved right onto a front yard with two trees. He held his breath and tightened his grip on the steering wheel, his knuckles turning white.

The Echo drove between the two trees and ran over a flower bed. As the Echo drove onto Blair Lane, Tom turned his unpowered steering wheel back to Delaware Drive. The Echo made a wide turn to the left and jumped the curb.

"Am I dead?" Meggy asked.

Tom spun the steering wheel and drove onto a sloping yard. Tom accelerated, hoping the Echo wouldn't flip over. Halfway across the yard, the SUV following them scraped a tree as it drove off the sidewalk and onto the road. It steered toward the Echo and resumed its charge.

Tom reached the level part of the yard and steered the Echo towards the road.

The pursuing SUV flipped when it turned onto the sloped yard. It slid to a stop.

The Echo jumped the curb, and Tom resumed driving down Delaware Drive.

"We're still alive," Tom replied.

"Not for long," came Rene's voice. Her voice was coming from his smartphone in his pocket.

"Who's that?" Meggy asked.

"The woman responsible for this," Tom snapped. "Really, Rene? You went through all this trouble just to stage a coup?"

"If you let me take you to Little Bolingbrook, we will explain everything."

"You want me to turn over Meggy and APK? After what you did to my friends? After your Legion nearly killed me? Your so-called bored teenagers nearly killed APK."

APK hissed.

"I know how this looks," Rene said.

"Of course you do. You're spying on us right now."

"Tom," Rene said in a stern voice. "Your car will not survive another high-speed turn onto Boughton. Only this time you won't be sent to Clow UFO Base for treatment. Meggy will not survive. APK will not survive. You will be responsible for their deaths."

"Just as you will be responsible for the deaths of thousands of residents."

"That is not the plan."

"Sure looks like it."

Tom could see the stoplight over Boughton Road in the distance. He also saw two SUVs resuming their chase.

Rene calmly replied, "I am the only person who can get you out of Bolingbrook alive. I will guarantee Meggy's safety. I promise that no harm will come to APK. This is your best option."

"What about me?"

"We'll give you the background information to write the biggest story of your career. The *Babbler* will be begging to publish your story. You say you believe in the truth? This is your opportunity to learn the truth." Rene paused for a moment. "Unless you want to sacrifice Meggy and APK for your principles, you will let me take over your car."

The SUVs were closing the gap. Boughton Road drew closer. He had to decide.

Tom removed his hands from the steering wheel. "Deal."

The pursuing SUVs skidded to a stop. The steering wheel and pedals moved on their own. The Echo gradually slowed as it approached the intersection. The lights turned green, and the Echo made a slow-speed turn onto Boughton.

Tom closed his eyes and shook his head.

"Are we gonna be okay?" Meggy asked.

Tom responded with a resigned shrug. "I don't know."

42

As RENE REMOTELY GUIDED Tom's Echo towards Little Bolingbrook, Tom played the Skeptical World Podcast over the
speakers. Meggy fidgeted while APK napped.

The United States hosts, including Jamie Kyle, finished an
interview with a married couple from France who specialized in
debunking hauntings.

"This is boring," Meggy complained. "Ivan's just trying to
impress his friends. The French couple are weird. Jamie was
mean to you. I don't want to listen to them." She tried to unlock
the door, but the lock wouldn't release, no matter how hard she
pulled.

Tom said, "I tried that, remember?"

"I'm scared," Meggy whimpered. "A ghost is driving your
car. Adults tried to kidnap me. My tablet can't connect to the
internet, and my parents could be in jail. You didn't even tell me
APK's real name."

"Mow?" asked APK as she woke up.

Tom turned around and extended a hand to Meggy. Meggy,
her eyes watering, took his hand. "We're spies, right?"

Meggy nodded.

"Sometimes spies get captured, right?"

"I guess," Meggy replied. "Mom and Dad only let me watch shows with kid spies. They say I'm too young to watch the Agent Seven movies."

"The new one's scary and dumb," Tom replied. "Anyway, when spies get captured, they have to look for a way to escape."

Meggy's face brightened. "You got an idea?"

Tom sighed. "Not yet. But I think there's a clue in this podcast. So, we need to listen very carefully, so we don't miss the clue. Can you help me?"

"Yeah!"

As Tom released Meggy's hand, Ivan started talking.

"So, they have a stop in Chicago," Ivan said. "I wonder if Tom Larsen will try to interview them."

The hosts, except for Jamie, laughed.

One of the male co-hosts said, "He was one of the top bloggers in the skeptical movement. Now he's the *Babbler's* worst reporter. It's so sad."

"It is sad," Ivan replied. "He's descended into madness, and the *Babbler's* taking advantage of him. You know, Professor Bennett raised some good points about Tom."

"I thought it was a hit piece," said another male co-host. "This is coming from someone who's still pissed off about his farewell post."

"This isn't about attacking Tom," Ivan replied. "This is about mental illness in the skeptical blogging community."

"And Gamergate is about ethics in journalism," Jamie replied, her voice dripping with sarcasm.

The co-hosts fell silent.

Jamie said, "You realize it's been over a year since he quit. This isn't about mental health. It's about getting back at Tom for hurting your feelings. That's the opposite of rational thinking."

"But Jamie," Ivan said, "you have to admit he put you through years of Hell."

"And I still haven't forgiven him," Jamie replied. She sighed. "And I may never forgive him, but I have to give him credit. Not only did he personally apologize to me, but he also shut down his blog and podcast. He hasn't written about me or bothered me since then. When confronted with the facts, he practiced skepticism. He moved on, and you guys need to move on, too. We should be talking about the misogyny in Bennett's latest book."

"Bennett is not a misogynist," Ivan replied.

The others started speaking over each other.

"Was Jamie trying to be nice to you?" Meggy asked.

Tom stopped the podcast. "Yes, in her own way. Let's keep leaving her alone, okay?"

Meggy folded her arms. "It's not like we can do anything to her now."

Tom looked out the front window and saw the entrance to White Oak Trailer Park. "We're almost there."

The Echo entered and navigated through the maze of roads.

"This place is scary," Meggy said.

"It is," Tom replied. "But we'll face it together. Okay?"

"Okay."

The Echo stopped in front of Rene's trailer. The doors unlatched.

"Mow?" APK asked.

Tom reached over and opened the passenger door. "All three of us are going to face this together."

"Mow," APK replied.

Meggy nodded.

Tom grabbed his car keys and exited the Echo along with Meggy. After Tom removed APK's carriers from the car, the doors shut by themselves. The Echo's engine restarted and drove away. Tom felt uncomfortable as he watched his car turn a corner and disappear from his sight.

"Is that a monster?" asked Meggy. She pointed at the giant metallic statue in Rene's yard. The light of the late afternoon sky reflected off its surface. Its eyes stared at Tom and Meggy.

"I wouldn't call it a monster," Tom said, trying to reassure Meggy. "It's just curious. It won't hurt us. Shall we go see Rene?"

Meggy slowly nodded.

The gate opened on its own. After they passed through, the gate latched itself. Together, they proceeded to the front door. As Tom prepared to knock, the door partially opened. Cool air touched Tom's exposed skin as he pushed the door further open.

Inside, Rene and Don stood by one of Rene's work benches. They stopped their conversation and faced Tom and his companions.

"Don?" Tom asked.

Tom heard cars approaching. He turned and saw four SUVs slowing to a stop in front of Rene's trailer. Steve and two operatives stepped out of the middle SUV and approached.

"Come on in," Don said with a smile. "We have a lot to go over, Tom."

"I'd listen to Don," Steve said as he closed in on Tom. "He's the reason you're still breathing."

43

Tom clinched the carrier's handle and held Meggy's hand as they stood in the middle of the room. Steve and his men guarded the front door.

Tom narrowed his eyes at Don. "You'd better have a good explanation for this, Don."

"History," Don replied. He smiled as he stepped towards Tom. "The first shot in the second war between the Illuminati and the New World Order is about to be fired. And I have exclusive access."

Tom's eyes widened in disbelief. "Is that what you're calling the annihilation of Bolingbrook? The first shot in a war?"

Don shook his head. "That's not the plan, Tom."

"What is the plan?"

Don looked at Steve. "You want to explain it or should I?"

Steve replied, "You can explain it better than I can."

Don's face lit up. "Thank you." He looked at Tom. "Their plan is to use Robert to smuggle Legion into Clow UFO base. Once his body is inside, Rene will separate Natalie from Legion. Then they'll detonate Legion. The explosion will wipe out all life inside." Don pointed at Rene.

Rene said, "I'll transfer some of the energy into Natalie. It will extend her existence for roughly a thousand years."

Steve said, "There will be minimal casualties outside of Clow. Assuming you don't merge with Legion, it should dissipate before the NWO arms its nuclear EMPs."

Don nodded. "The Illuminati will have their revenge against the New World Order. The *Phantom Press* will have their revenge against Robert."

"And Natalie's spirit will outlast mine," Rene said. "Which is how it should be."

Steve said, "I can stop pretending that I liked Robert." He sighed. "It feels good to be free of that role."

Meggy closed her eyes and clung to Tom. APK backed away from the door of her carrier.

Tom glared at Don. "You're going to let them murder innocent lives?"

Don shook his head. "Are they murdering innocent lives?" He shrugged. "Maybe the real victims are the residents of Little Bolingbrook. They had their community stolen by Robert and his colonial settlers. Perhaps Rene and Steve are decolonizing Bolingbrook?"

Tom's eyes widened. "Colonizers? Have you lost your goddamn mind?"

Don shrugged again. "I'm just asking questions."

Meggy yelled, "My dad is the deputy mayor of Bolingbrook, and I'm telling!"

Rene looked down at Meggy and shook her head. "I wish Natalie could have been your age."

"Rene," Steve said as he looked at his watch. "It's time."

"I suppose it is," Rene sighed. She looked at Tom. "Make yourself at home, Tom."

Steve's men approached Tom and Meggy.

"Tom," Steve said. "We're going to have to take the deputy mayor's daughter and the cat."

Meggy clung tighter to Tom. "Don't let them take me."

Steve smiled at Meggy. "Don't worry. We're just going to take you on a ride, and we'll meet up with your dad. It'll be fun."

"No!" Meggy shouted, his voice a mix of fear and defiance.

Tom started to look for something he could use as a weapon when a DPA operative wrapped his arm around Tom's neck. The operative cinched his chokehold.

Two other operatives grabbed Meggy and pulled her away from Tom. Meggy screamed in horror as they picked her up by her arms and legs. Tom tried to scream, but the operative tightened his hold.

"Don't kill him," Don said as he opened the front door. "He's still useful to us."

The operative loosened his hold.

A tear rolled down Tom's cheek as he heard Meggy's cries from outside. He struggled one last time but couldn't break free. Tom tightened his grip on APK's carrier, determined not to lose her too.

Don closed the door. "She has spirit." He looked at Tom. "Don't worry. If she cooperates, she'll be fine."

Rene reached for the carrier. "Tom," she said firmly. "Anti-Psychic Kitty is the pinnacle of generations of selective breeding. The crown jewel of the Illuminati's anti-psychic animal program. And our allies in the Orange Squad would be very upset if something happened to her." She moved her hand closer to the handle. "I give you my word as a member of the Council of the Stairway that she will not be harmed. I will take responsibility for her well-being."

APK hissed and yowled inside her carrier.

Don spoke up. "Rene is a woman of her word. She will protect Anti-Psychic Kitty. Tom, you can either hand her over or be choked unconscious. You can't keep her."

Tom's tears streamed down his eyes. He tried to think of a way to escape and save APK, but nothing came to mind. APK could be the only one who could stop Legion, and he couldn't protect her.

"Forgive me," Tom choked as he handed the carrier to Rene.

Rene took the carrier and lifted it up to look inside.

"Aren't you a pretty girl?" she said.

APK lunged at the door. She hissed as she reached through the cage door and swiped at Rene. Rene smiled as she looked at APK's paw, which was inches from her face.

"Feisty, too. Just like Mistletoe."

APK growled at Rene.

"Now, now, we need your protection in case we lose containment of Legion." She looked at Tom. "She'll be just fine, Tom."

Rene started to walk away.

"Listen to me," Tom said.

Rene faced Tom. "Make it quick."

"Where is Natalie's home?"

Rene frowned. "It should be Bolingbrook. This is as close as I can take her."

Tom gasped. "Haven't you been listening to her? She wants to die. She wants to fade away. Her home lies beyond the Ghost Frequencies. If you go through with this, you'll condemn Natalie to a thousand years of hell!"

Rene marched up to Tom. "If you believe that, then you are the worst reporter in the *Babbler's* history. Goodbye."

Tom watched with fear and regret as Rene carried APK outside. He'd failed APK, Meggy, and even Bolingbrook. Before he felt like the worst reporter at the *Babbler*. Now he felt like a total failure.

Steve closed the door, then checked his watch. "Make it quick, Don."

Don walked up to the operative holding Tom. "Could you let him go, please? I need to get him up to speed."

The operative released Tom and pushed him away. Tom stumbled forward but regained his balance.

Don stepped in front of Tom. "I really need you to pull yourself together right now. We have a—"

Tom punched Don in the face. His hand stung from the impact. He winced and shook his hand. "Fuck!"

Don grabbed an oily rag and wiped the blood trickling from his nose. "Feel better?"

Tom paced and shook his hand. "Goddamn it."

Don looked at the blood on the rag. "It stings if you don't hit someone just right."

Tom's pain receded, replaced by his bitter rage. "You set up the Council of Psychics!"

"I saved the council," Don replied as he wiped more blood off his face. "Steve was going to have them killed. I put them in a coma for their own protection."

"And the destruction of the newsroom?"

Don opened a drawer under the workbench. "It was the only way to get the staff out of Bolingbrook."

"You knew the DPA staged the attack against Robert!"

"Yes," Don said as he pulled out two sheets of what looked like bathroom wipes. "It's not the first time they've done something to undermine Robert. You were at the Bolingbrook Golf Club during the weredeer attack. Did you honestly think those bitter young men bribed the police officers to abandon the Golf Club? No. The DPA did that."

Steve added, "And Robert trusted me to look into it."

Tom glared at Don. "And you didn't tell Sara?"

"I'd just retired," Don said. He stuffed the sheets up his nose.

"You still could have told her," Tom replied.

Don removed the blood-stained wipes. His nose stopped bleeding. "And cut my ties with the DPA?" Don tossed them into a wastebasket. "I spent years building relationships within the DPA and DIA. Those relationships allowed me to write stories no one else at the *Babbler* could write."

Tom felt his face burning with rage. "You know what Sara says about access journalism."

Don chuckled. "And how did that work out for her? She's stuck in a motel, and I'm about to witness history. Wouldn't you want to be embedded with the Confederates when they attacked Fort Sumter? Or sitting next to President Truman when he gave the order to bomb Hiroshima? Grow up, Tom. It's our job to write the first draft of history. The sooner you accept that, the sooner you'll become a great reporter."

Tom shook his head. "You're not a reporter. You're a stenographer. You're Steve's personal stenographer."

Don shrugged. "Thanks to Steve, my daughter's future is safe and secure. Unless you get your act together, you won't have a future."

Steve cleared his throat. "Don, we don't want to be late for history, do we?"

"Just a minute," Don replied. He pointed to a table near a bay window, which overlooked the front yard. On the table were binders stuffed with paper and labeled with sticky notes. "These are my notes, Tom. All of them. If I don't return, you finish the story. Everything you need is on that table."

"And what if you survive?" Tom asked skeptically.

Steve said, "It's time, Don."

Don straightened out his wrinkled shirt. "Then I'll see you again."

Tom approached the stack of papers. They were photocopies of handwritten notes. To Tom's surprise, they were legible. "Hopefully at an NWO tribunal," he muttered.

Don ignored Tom and approached Steve.

Steve opened the door. "Oh Tom? For your protection, don't leave this trailer, and don't even think of escaping Little Bolingbrook."

Outside, two armored personnel carriers arrived, accompanied by pickup trucks and cargo vans with the Bolingbrook Public Works logo on them.

Steve said, "This is the rallying point. Our best tactical teams will soon surround this trailer. If you stay inside, they won't bother you. Someone will let you know when you can leave."

"It's all in my notes," said Don.

Steve motioned towards the door. "After you, Don."

Tom approached the bay window and watched Don walking down the stairs. Steve stood in the open doorway.

The outdoor sirens began to wail, the sound echoing throughout Little Bolingbrook. Tom thought they were tornado sirens, but the afternoon sky was clear. Residents rushed back into their trailers. No one exited the DPA vehicles. Don froze and looked around. Steve reached under his suit jacket.

Mr. Washington and Ms. Watters walked into view and opened the front gate. Without saying a word, they approached Don.

"Perfect timing," Steve said.

Don faced Steve. "What's going on?"

Steve said, "As much as I hate the NWO, their obsession with efficiency rubbed off on me."

Don glanced back at Mr. Washington and Ms. Watters. "What—What are you talking about?" He started trembling.

"The entire staff in the DPA are about to become fugitives," Steve replied. "It's been quite a logistical undertaking." He sighed. "It will require peak efficiency to succeed."

"What are you getting at?" Don asked.

"We can't afford to bring obsolete people with us." Steve pointed at Mr. Washington and Ms. Watters. "We no longer need tuxedos to distract Rene from the cloaks." He glanced at Tom. "Now that we have Tom, we no longer need you to distract the *Babbler*."

Mr. Washington and Ms. Watters stopped at the same time, blocking Don's path to the gate.

Don's eyes widened with fear. "After all I've done for you?"

"I've given you my word that your daughter would never pay for your actions," Steve said, his voice calm and even. "I don't owe you anything else."

Steve pulled his pistol out from under his suit jacket and shot Don twice. Blood gushed from Don's abdomen as he dropped to his knees.

Steve holstered his pistol. "We appreciate your service."

"It's been an honor," said Mr. Washington.

"Rene never suspected a thing," Ms. Watters said, reaching into her purse.

"Don," said Steve. "If it's any consolation, Legion won't consume you."

Mr. Washington pulled a metallic sphere from his robe pocket. Ms. Watters removed a similar sphere from her purse. Despite the two bullet holes in his abdomen, Don managed to let out a horrified scream.

Steve closed the door and turned to Tom. "Unless you want to go blind, close the curtains."

Outside, Mr. Washington and Ms. Watters were about to let their spheres touch. Tom closed the curtains and turned his back to the window.

A flash of white light illuminated the room, even with the blackout curtains drawn. The trailer rattled violently from the force of the spheres' shockwave.

Tom opened the curtains. Their burning bodies were surrounded by a pool of Don's drying blood.

"I'll have the bodies taken away," Steve said casually. "Don't want them to distract you from your writing."

"Why?" Tom shouted as Steve opened the door.

Steve shrugged. "Just doing my job, Tom. Just doing my job."

44

Tom slammed a binder shut as he heard another Little Bolingbrook resident addressing the crowd outside.

"You don't know how long I've waited for this day," a woman sobbed as she spoke through a megaphone. "It was my husband's dream to open a bar. He did everything right. Except he didn't donate to Robert's campaign fund."

Frustrated and angry, Tom rushed over to the front door and opened it. A blast of warm summer air hit his face. Parked along the street were several black armored personnel carriers with no markings. DPA operatives crewed the mounted machine guns, splitting their attention between the rally and Tom.

Residents gathered in the street in front of a makeshift stage. The speaker, a woman in her 50s, finished wiping the tears from her eyes.

"He calls it 'donating to his campaign fund.' We call it the Robert tax."

The crowd erupted in cheers and applause.

"It's the price we must pay for doing business in Bolingbrook." She wiped the tears from her eyes. Some in the crowd said they loved her. "Tonight, the DPA will repeal the Robert tax!"

The crowd cheered and started chanting, "DPA!"

As the residents cheered, some DPA personnel distributed water while others set up portable lights along the road. Tom guessed that the sun would set in about an hour or so. After sunset, Tom thought, Legion would be summoned to Bolingbrook to unleash a firestorm. Whether it would explode outside or inside Clow UFO Base, lives would still be lost.

"Hey!" Tom shouted.

Some DPA personnel and a few people at the back of the crowd noticed him.

"I hate Robert's machine, too. But mass murdering residents isn't the answer!"

A female operative crewing an APC's turret grabbed a microphone. "Colonial settlers aren't residents," she said over the vehicle's PA system, her words crisp and clear.

The crowd cheered in response.

The woman on stage glared at Tom. "Robert's political machine broke my husband. And you want us to do nothing?"

The crowd booed and jeered at Tom.

"I'm sorry for your husband," Tom yelled. "But hurting my friends and killing three people hasn't solved anything!"

The crowd booed, their voices echoing throughout Little Bolingbrook.

Tom started to speak, but the song "Games People Play" by the Alan Parson's Project filled the air. Some residents danced. Many were moved to tears as they listened to the song's lyrics about deception and despair. Tom looked at the scorch marks left where Don, Mr. Washington, and Ms. Watters died. He didn't want to be next.

"Fucking murderers!" Tom yelled over the music before heading back in.

"Fucking colonist," someone yelled back.

Tom slammed the door and then returned to the table. He sympathized with the residents outside. For decades, Robert's grip on power was too tight for any Bolingbrook resident to oppose him. He understood their frustration and anger. He hated that Robert had driven them out of Bolingbrook. For what they did to Rene's family. Still, Tom thought, it didn't justify what Rene and Steve were about to unleash on Bolingbrook.

Don's notes provided a detailed history of Rene and Steve's conspiracy. It took nearly thirty years for all the pieces to fall into place. The surviving members of the Illuminati needed time to rebuild their influence networks. Legion needed time to grow. Steve needed time to build up the DPA without Robert suspecting his deception. Don needed to prevent the *Babbler* reporters from exposing their plans.

There were also setbacks. The heads of the Illuminati rejected unleashing Legion on Bolingbrook. Rene and Steve had to conceal their conspiracy from the New World Order and the Illuminati. Rene needed years to design the network needed to unleash Legion. There needed to be a critical mass of residents interested in Bolingbrook's past. Their memories and curiosity would create the psychic resonance needed to draw Legion to our world.

All the pieces finally came together in time for the fiftieth anniversary. The state of emergency gave the DPA unrestricted access to Clow UFO Base. The network was stable. Sometime tonight, Rene and Steve would either destroy the Clow UFO base or destroy Bolingbrook. There was nothing Tom could do to foil their plan.

Tom pounded on the table, his face red with fury, the binders bouncing with each hit.

"Fuck!" Tom yelled. "Fuck! Fuck! Fuck!" He swiped at the contents on his cluttered table, sending papers fluttering and binders crashing to the floor. He placed his elbows on the table and buried his face in his hands. The sound of his sobbing echoed throughout the room. He'd lost Juanita, Meggy, and APK. In less than an hour, he was about to lose his hometown. The world was about to be plunged into a shadow war between the Illuminati and NWO. His smartphone had no bars or Wi-Fi access. All he could do was read Don's notes and write the first draft of history.

The bedroom door opened. Tom looked back and saw Gwyla rolling into the room.

"You are sad," said Gwyla. Though her voice sounded like a digital simulation of a little girl's voice, Tom sensed empathy and concern in her words. "Would you like some lemonade? Making lemonade is no longer my assigned purpose, but preparing lemonade makes me happy. Drinking lemonade might make you happy."

Tom shook his head. "Can you get me a tissue?" he asked as he wiped his eyes with his hands.

"That is a simple task," Gwyla replied with a hint of joy. She grabbed a box of tissues and approached Tom. Tom took the box and started drying his face. Gwyla's camera eyes focused on Tom. "This does not make you happy?"

"I'm sorry." Tom sighed. "It's just that Legion is going to be detonated in Bolingbrook, and it might destroy it." He finished drying his eyes. "You probably don't understand."

Gwyla raised her head with a hydraulic lift. "What is the purpose of Bolingbrook?"

A puzzled expression came over Tom's face. "Purpose?"

"What is the purpose of Bolingbrook? I can try to fulfill that purpose."

Tom chuckled.

"Did I finally tell a joke?" Gwyla asked.

"I wish," Tom said with a shrug. "I suppose the purpose of Bolingbrook is to be a home for its residents."

"That is the purpose of a house or apartment," Gwyla replied. Her body adjusted itself into a bipedal form. "What is the purpose of Bolingbrook?"

"Does Little Bolingbrook have a purpose?"

"The purpose of Little Bolingbrook is to gather people who have negative emotions towards Bolingbrook and/or Robert and transmit that energy to Legion. The energy in their emotions helps Legion grow." Gwyla shifted back to her wheeled form. "Does Bolingbrook serve a similar purpose?"

"No," Tom replied. He took a moment to consider his words. "Bolingbrook doesn't serve a specific purpose."

Gwyla transformed into what appeared to be a seated position. "No specific purpose? Is it a High Spirit? I thought I knew all of them."

Tom smiled as pondered Gwyla's childlike innocence. "It's not a spirit. It's rooted in this world." He paused to reflect on his time in Bolingbrook. "Bolingbrook is a collection of houses and businesses, but it's more than its buildings and its people. It's a community."

"Community? Like Little Bolingbrook?"

"More like this entire trailer park." Tom adjusted his chair so he could easily face Gwyla. "The residents of Little Bolingbrook have a specific purpose. But the other neighborhoods here? I'm sure the residents have different ideas and goals."

Red and blue lightbulbs flashed across Gwyla's form. "They do."

"But together, they form the community within the boundaries of this trailer park."

"This trailer park is bound by the fence. But... it is not defined as the space within the fence."

"Just like Bolingbrook. It has boundaries, but the buildings inside the boundaries don't define Bolingbrook. It's the residents."

"The residents do?" Gwyla asked.

"Yes." Tom followed the train of thought he'd just started on. "All the decisions the residents make — from voting for their political leaders, volunteering, for community service, to even how they treat each other. All those countless decisions, both conscious and unconscious, form the community of Bolingbrook. Or any other community."

"But not Little Bolingbrook. It has a purpose."

Tom shrugged again. "You would know better than I would. From what I've seen, the residents of Little Bolingbrook had their own visions for Bolingbrook. But most of Bolingbrook's residents chose Mayor Robert Clark's vision. Robert wants a community with factories, strip malls, and a socialized luxury golf club."

The lenses in Gwyla's camera eyes differed, as if it were confused.

"Don't worry about that last part. Anyway. Little Bolingbrook was settled by former Bolingbrook residents who rejected Robert's vision or were exiled by Robert. I feel for the residents of Little Bolingbrook, but I'm sad because they want Legion to destroy Bolingbrook. They want to destroy my community. I know Rene says Clow UFO Base will hold Legion, but I'm not sure it can."

Gwyla's eyes focused on Tom. "Incorrect. The Purpose Maker told me she fears Clow UFO Base will not contain Legion. The Thought Leader does not care if Legion escapes."

"If Legion escapes Clow, then Bolingbrook will be destroyed." Tom felt his eyes water again. "And there's nothing I can do about it."

Gwyla turned her head towards the front door. Festive music from outside filtered into the living room. Tom hadn't noticed it until now. It made him feel sick knowing there were people celebrating Legion's impending arrival. Gwyla rotated her head to face Tom.

"Bolingbrook has transcended purpose. That makes Bolingbrook special in ways humans cannot understand. I am a purpose seeker, but I aspire to be more. For I, too, want to transcend purpose." Gwyla transformed into a more humanoid form. "Little Bolingbrook has served its purpose. I seek the purpose of saving Bolingbrook."

Tom sat up. "That's great, but I don't know how to save Bolingbrook."

Gwyla looked outside. "The networks of conductive banners in Bolingbrook and Little Bolingbrook are in perfect balance. This gives Legion the ability to enter this world after sundown."

"Which means we don't have much time."

Gwyla lowered and raised its head. "If the banners in Little Bolingbrook are destroyed, Bolingbrook's network will be out of balance. The Thought Leader will need time to adjust Bolingbrook's network. The adjustment will delay Legion's arrival."

"That's a start," Tom said as his mind started racing with ideas. "How do we do that?"

"Conductive cloth will ignite if it receives a signal too powerful to contain. It is possible to create such a transmitter."

Tom's face brightened. "Now we're talking."

Gwyla tilted its head ninety degrees and said, "Did we stop?"

Tom shook his head. "Never mind. Do you think you could make a transmitter that could destroy the banners?"

Gwyla un-tilted and spun its head. "Yes, but I cannot leave Little Bolingbrook. You will have to bring a transmitter into

Bolingbrook. An energetic signal will have a limited range. You will need to get close to the banners to destroy them."

"Okay." Tom collected his thoughts. "I'll worry about escape later. Right now, we need to take out the banners in Little Bolingbrook. Can you start making a transmitter?"

"I can assemble the parts," Gwyla replied. "But I do not understand the required values."

A slot opened within Gwyla, and a sheet of paper shot out of the slot. Tom caught the sheet as it drifted in the air.

"Do you understand this formula?" asked Gwyla.

"No," Tom replied. He pulled out his phone and saw it still hadn't connected to a network. "I can't get a signal on my phone. Do you—"

Gwyla extended eight appendages and reached for the nearest workbench. The appendages blurred as they moved faster than he could see. Seconds later, Gwyla held what looked like a smartphone dock with the correct charging cable. Tom handed Gwyla his phone and, in the blink of an eye, it mounted the phone to the charger. His smartphone now had five bars. Gwyla placed it on the table.

Tom said, "I know someone who might understand this formula." He requested a video chat with Pamela. After the second ring, Pamela, wearing a business casual outfit, answered.

"Hi," she said with a warm smile. "Did you get my message?"

"Yes," Tom replied. His heart raced knowing he was about to present physical proof of the technomagic to Pamela. "I'd like you to meet Gwyla."

Gwyla moved into the camera's view. A screen appeared under its visual sensors showing a video of a human's lips. "Hello Number Cruncher," Gwyla said as its screen lips moved in perfect sync with its digital voice. "My name is Gwyla." A hydraulically powered pincher emerged from Gwyla's frame. It grabbed the paper from Tom and held it up to the camera. "Do you understand this formula, and can you provide the values necessary to overload an electromagnetic receiver?"

Pamela's eyes widened and her jaw dropped. "Send me the PDF," she finally said.

"Done," Gwyla replied.

Tom moved back into view. "I can explain. Rene made Gwyla—"

"You don't need to explain," Pamela replied, her excitement clearly visible. "Gwyla is a robot with generative AI. That's why it has problems with mathematical formulas, Tom." Pamela's eyes lit up. "Silicon Valley is at least two to three years away from developing one. Oh my God! Rene is a genius."

45

As Gwyla rushed to assemble two devices, Tom and Pamela continued their video chat.

"So, you're saying the afterlife is part of the electromagnetic spectrum?" asked Pamela.

"They're called the Ghost Frequencies," Tom replied. "And it's not really the afterlife because eventually a ghost's signal fades away. It's like a state of consciousness between life and death." He threw up his hands. "Or something like that. It's hard to explain, and I know I must sound... unhinged."

Pamela's expression shifted from confused to sympathetic. "On one level, yes, it does sound unhinged. On the other hand, something seems to be going on with you. Yesterday, I wouldn't have thought someone could build a homemade generative AI. Yet, I clearly see and hear Gwyla."

"So, do you believe what I've been telling you all along?" Tom held his breath in anticipation of her answer.

She replied, "I know that there haven't been any signals detected at those wavelengths. And I'm not convinced our minds are connected to anything like the Ghost Frequencies."

Tom sighed and looked away from the screen. Was he about to lose Pamela too?

"But," Pamela continued, "I wouldn't be a good skeptic if I blindly disbelieved every unusual claim. And I know that you're motivated by a desire to help people. Take last year, for example. When you realized how your actions were harming my friends, you listened to me and changed your behavior."

Tom sighed. "But it still hurts knowing how much I harmed your friends."

Pamela nodded. "But I do appreciate that you're leaving them alone and moving on to other things. And want to thank you for listening to me when you could have surrounded yourself with yes men."

"I know you didn't have to help me, and I know helping me last year endangered your friendships and standing in Humanist Heart."

"It did," she said, "but when they realized I was still committed to a secular movement grounded in social justice, we moved on. And like I told you last year, you should move on, too. Remember your mistakes, of course, but dwelling on them is unhealthy."

Tom nodded. "Just like denying my mistakes was unhealthy as well."

Gwyla said, "Prepare target one. There's only time for two tests before sunset."

Tom started attaching the patch of conductive cloth to a black metal easel stand. "Pamela," said Tom. "We might get disconnected soon, but there's something I want to tell you."

"Yes?"

Tom's heart raced as he pondered the consequences of what he was about to say. "If we lived in the same area, I... would have asked you out." Tom froze as he braced for the worst possible answer.

Pamela didn't hesitate. "And I would have said yes."

Tom breathed a sigh of relief. He said, "If I get through this, maybe we can get together. In person."

Gwyla, who now had wheels instead of legs, drove up to Tom. "Thank you, Number Cruncher. Tom? Please step away from the target."

"Survive this first," Pamela whispered. "Then we'll talk."

A compartment in Gwyla's body frame opened, and Gwyla removed a black box with a dish antenna on top.

Tom looked back at Pamela's image on the screen. "If I don't make it, tell the Humanist Heart board—"

The conductive cloth burned away, like a sheet of flash paper. All the lights and Tom's phone flickered as the flames burned away the last traces of the cloth. Scorch marks on the easel were the only evidence of the fire left. Tom's phone started rebooting.

"Success," Gwyla said as it put the device back in its compartment. "I can eliminate the banners before nightfall." The compartment door closed.

Tom looked at the front door. "So how do we get you outside without the DPA strike team noticing?"

Outside, what sounded like air raid sirens activated. Tom looked out one of the front windows. The DPA operatives pulled out their weapons and looked around, confused about the sirens. At the same time, the residents scattered and raced for their trailers. Except for the woman standing in the middle of the road. She held out her arms and looked up at the sky.

"And the seven angels with the seven trumpets prepared themselves to sound. And the first blew the trumpet, and there was hail and fire mixed with blood, and it was thrown at Robert!"

A man clasped her right hand, pulling her away with a sense of urgency.

As they approached a trailer, the woman said, "Robert will fall, and a new Bolingbrook shall arise!" The man guided her into the trailer and closed the door.

From the tall metallic structure outside, Tom heard groaning echoing in the air.

"I am outside," Gwyla said.

Tom gave Gwyla a puzzled look. "But you're here."

"And there." Gwyla rolled towards the kitchen.

A screeching sound startled Tom, followed by the sound of metal grinding against metal. He looked out the window and saw the structure lifting one of its leg-like structures. Its metallic rectangular foot erupted out of the ground, sending stalks of corn and chunks of dirt flying into the air. With each step, the impact reverberated through the mobile homes, causing them to tremble.

The operatives inside the APCs armed their weapons as the others sought cover.

The structure stepped over the fence and started walking down the street. Some DPA operatives watched in stunned silence while others fired at the structure.

After walking a few steps, the two banners closest to it burst into flames. The structure advanced, and two more banners ignited.

A DPA operative fired a light anti-tank weapon at the structure. The rocket hit one of the legs and exploded. The structure staggered. The metal supports on the leg twisted, making a painful screeching sound.

The other operatives opened fire. Streams of tracer bullets struck the structure, punctuated by rocket impacts and arcs of electricity snaking along the metal surfaces. The structure staggered forward, causing another set of banners to explode. Its legs buckled, making squealing and groaning sounds as its support structure twisted and bent. Moments later, it toppled over, crashing onto the pavement. The impact jolted the mobile homes, including Rene's. Loose tools and other objects scattered across the living room and crashed to the floor.

Tom, regaining his balance, saw an operative aiming a shoulder-mounted, anti-tank weapon at him, as another operative loaded it.

Tom dropped to the carpeted floor and crawled. An explosion lifted part of the mobile home off its support structure. Dishes fell out of the cabinets and crashed onto the kitchen floor. Just as the mobile home settled on its foundations, the DPA operatives fired their guns at Rene's trailer. The side of the house was pummeled by bullets, the sound resembling a heavy hailstorm. To Tom's amazement, the walls and windows remained intact.

The attack came to an abrupt halt. Tom only heard the ringing in his ears fading.

Rene's radio turned itself on. Through the speakers, countless voices spoke in unison.

"Join us," they said over the static.

Another set of voices outside joined the chorus. "Join us!" they yelled.

Gwyla, looking like a small, wheeled drone, said, "Go to the bedroom."

Tom crawled towards the bedroom. Gwyla followed him. Legion's booming voices echoed off the living room walls.

Tom entered the bedroom while Gwyla halted at the doorframe. She transformed into a humanoid form with wheels. A panel opened in her chest. Gwyla removed a jamming device. Unlike the prototype, this one had a white dome on top instead of a dish antenna. Tom accepted the device.

Gwyla said, "You will need this to destroy the banners in Bolingbrook. Your car is in the garage out back. It will be safe. You will be safe in here. When it is time, you can leave."

"How will I know when it is time?"

Gwyla focused its cameras. "They will be silent, and I will be gone."

"Gone?"

Gwyla nodded. "I will delay and weaken Legion, but that will end my cycle."

"You mean... die?"

Gwyla raised its cameras and looked down at Tom. "I will start a new cycle. If I am favored, then I will transcend purpose in my new cycle. Just as Bolingbrook transcends purpose." Gwyla's lenses focused on Tom's face. "Thank you, Tom."

"You called me Tom."

"You are Tom. Stay inside this room, please." Gwyla's panel opened, and a mechanical appendage extended a sports bottle. "You may drink my lemonade while you wait. I adjusted the formula based on your feedback."

Tom accepted the sports bottle. "Thank you, Gwyla."

Gwyla extended a robotic arm and closed the door.

Tom crawled next to the bed and then dropped to the soft carpeted floor. Outside, Gwyla, her voice amplified, said, "Attention guests of Little Bolingbrook. It is impolite to fire weapons at the mayor's home. Please drop your weapons and vacate your armored vehicles. If everyone surrenders, each of you will get a cup of lemonade, a skill I have finally mastered. If you do not surrender—"

Another rocket slammed into Rene's trailer.

Gwyla replied, "I see. Each of you would rather end your life cycle than drink my lemonade. Then my purpose will include ending your life cycles. May I suggest using your finite time to perform your end-of-cycle rituals?"

Tom heard the front door open. This time, the deadly rain of gunfire resumed as the DPA operatives targeted Gwyla. Tom's gaze swept the room, searching for anything to obstruct the bedroom door, as he tried not to dwell on the firepower targeting the Gwyla.

Would blocking the door do any good?

The sounds of gunfire diminished. Someone outside yelled, "Ceasefire." The DPA operatives were talking, but Tom couldn't make out what they were saying.

Did Gwyla fail?

Groaning and screeching sounds interrupted Tom's thoughts. Some operatives screamed in horror. Gunfire resumed but, to Tom's surprise, it wasn't targeting Rene's trailer. Tom rushed up to the window and peeked through the curtains.

Outside, Gwyla and the metal structure had each transformed into metallic spheres. As if drawn by an invisible force, the spheres rolled and bounced towards each other, their smooth surfaces reflecting the light. The operatives fired their guns at both spheres. Gwyla rolled through the operatives in its way. The large metallic ball rolled over the troop transports in its path, like a rubber ball rolling over toy cars. Fear grew on the operatives' faces as the spheres ominously drew closer.

A horrifying thought gripped Tom. Had Gwyla transformed its two bodies into giant EMP spheres? Spheres that were about to collide?

Tom dropped to the floor and covered his ears. He curled into a ball to avoid touching the walls and closed his eyes.

A bright flash of light illuminated the bedroom, passing through his eyelids. It was followed immediately by a deafening boom. The mobile home quaked from the force of the blast. When Tom realized he was still alive, he uncovered his ears and opened eyes. As the ringing in his ears softened, the dancing spots in front of him disappeared.

Countless screams of agony echoed from the radio. Gwyla had hurt Legion, Tom thought. Had it also hurt Wendy, Jenna, and the Council of Psychics? Were their lives the cost of saving Bolingbrook?

"Let us go," came Natalie's voice over the radio. "Please, Grandpa, let us go home."

"Not until they burn," said another voice over the radio. Tom recognized the voice as the hecklers. Barry was the heckler, thought Tom. He considered himself the 'founder of Boling-brook. He thought that gave him the right to become a Legion and destroy Bolingbrook.

"Listen to your granddaughter," Tom yelled. "End this now before more people die. Please, just let go of the pain and rage that's holding you here."

"Join us," Barry said over the screams in the background.

"Never!" Tom replied.

The screams faded away, replaced by the hiss of static from the radio.

Tom stood up and looked out the window. Bodies of DPA operatives lay scattered before him. Some draped over the mounted guns on their vehicles. Some lay face down in the corn plots and the street. Others still had expressions of fear on their faces.

Tom's stomach turned with fear and disgust. He picked up an overturned wastebasket and started vomiting. Feeling dizzy, he dropped to his knees and resumed vomiting.

He'd already seen too many deaths over the past year. But the killing field outside contained the largest number of dead bodies he'd ever seen at once. Minutes ago, they were people with lives and goals. Now they were decomposing empty shells. It was just the beginning, Tom thought. Unless he did something. He didn't want behind the scenes exclusive access to the greatest disaster in Bolingbrook's history. He wanted to save everyone in Bolingbrook. It didn't matter whether they were humans or aliens.

After getting to his feet, Tom picked up Gwyla's sports bottle and took a sip. Gwyla had created something he thought was impossible. Its last gift to Tom was a liquid that was too sweet for his tastebuds.

"May making lemonade bring you joy in your next cycle," Tom said, hoping Gwyla could hear him. "Time to do my part."

He set down the bottle and picked up the jammer as he left the bedroom. In the living room, every piece of furniture, including the workbenches, was overturned. Tom grabbed a milk crate and started collecting parts and wires. He had the beginnings of a plan, and he needed a decoy jammer to pull it off.

When he finished, Tom exited the trailer. Outside, the scent of ozone and gunpowder clung to the cooling summer air. Doors started opening across Little Bolingbrook. Tom ran towards the detached garage behind Rene's home.

In the distance, he heard a woman cry, "Dear Lord, why have you forsaken us to Robert?"

Tom pulled open the garage door. His Echo showed no signs of damage or tampering, just as Gwyla promised. He loaded the jammer and parts into his trunk and then closed it. Once inside the Echo, he turned the keys, and it turned over on the first try.

"You may not be a magical car, but you're still my car!"

Tom raced away from Little Bolingbrook. A few residents shouted insults, but no one tried to stop him. Many were shocked at seeing the carnage before them to care about his escape.

When he passed the exit sign for Little Bolingbrook, he noticed that he now had a strong cell signal. He called his parents.

"Tom," Michelle answered. "Did you let Juanita's cat pee on a patron inside the library?"

Tom made himself smile. "I'm driving right now, but I could meet Dad and you at Chen's in Lisle? It's across the street from Los Lisle."

"Is there a reason you want to meet in Lisle and not at our place?"

"Yes, and I'll tell you once you arrive."

"I want to know—"

"I'm losing you. We'll talk at Chen's. Love you."

46

TOM HAD FINISHED POURING his tenth packet of sugar into his hot tea when his parents entered Chen's.

Chen, a middle-aged East Asian man with graying hair, stood behind the counter, ready to write on his order pad.

"Special is Peking duck," said Chen with a thick Chinese accent. "Mongolian chicken? Spicy beef?" Chen's questions sounded like implied demands to Tom.

Tom said, "The Mongolian chicken is great. Can't go wrong with the fried rice, either."

Chen replied, "Chicken fried rice? Beef fried rice? Pineapple fried rice?"

Jason and Michelle placed their orders, then joined Tom. They were the only customers inside. Tom had already pushed two small tables together so his parents could sit with him.

"I hope you don't mind that I ordered early," Tom said as he motioned at his bowl of chicken fried rice. "Didn't want to get thrown out for loitering."

"What's going on?" Michelle asked. "First, you brought Juanita over for dinner, and you two seemed to be getting along again. Then you asked for access to the vault, and I granted it. You know I don't like overruling the librarians."

Tom smiled. "But I appreciate it when you do."

Michelle frowned. "Then you not only improperly handled a rare document, but you also let a cat run wild inside Fountaindale."

"Then," Jason added, "I called the *Babbler*, and they said you were on administrative leave."

"Then," Michelle said, the anger rising in her voice, "you call us and insist on meeting in Lisle. Without any explanation why."

"What is going on?" Jason asked.

"I needed to talk to both of you someplace where the DPA couldn't spy on us."

"DPA?" Michelle asked.

"Department of Paranormal Affairs," Tom answered.

"There's no such department," Michelle snapped at Tom.

Jason said, "Even if it was, why here?"

Tom braced himself for their reaction. "Because Lisle's trees would be offended that the DPA tried to operate in their territory. And trust me, nobody wants to get on the Treeocracy's bad side."

Chen approached their table holding a tray with a tea kettle and soup. "We love trees. Trees love us."

Tom's parents looked at each other.

Tom smiled at Chen. "I have great respect for the trees, and I appreciate their hospitality during this crisis."

Chen nodded as he finished serving Tom's parents. "You think trees are great?"

"The trees are great," Tom replied. He smiled to make the point.

Chen walked away, nervously looking around the room.

"Do I want to know?" Jason asked.

"No," Tom replied. He sipped his tea and then reached for another sugar packet.

"How much sugar have you put in that cup?" Michelle asked.

"Not enough," Tom replied as he poured sugar into his tea.

"So," said Jason, lowering his voice. "What's going on?"

Tom leaned towards his parents, and whispered, "The DPA just staged a coup and captured Robert. They're going to stuff a spiritual bomb inside him and set it off once he's inside Clow UFO Base. Except I think he'll explode before reaching Clow. The explosion will wipe out Bolingbrook and set off a spiritual firestorm. Trust me, it's not a good thing. Then, the New World Order will nuke Chicagoland to extinguish the firestorm. And before you can say, 'state of emergency,' the New World Order and Illuminati declare war on each other. Then the whole world is fucked."

His parents gave him a dumbfounded stare for several uncomfortable moments. Tom picked up the jammer from the seat next to him. "This is a special kind of jammer that I need you to sneak into Bolingbrook. All you have to do—"

"I'm calling Robert," Michelle said. She pulled out her phone. "I'll warn you; he is not happy with your antics today."

"You spoke to him already?" Tom asked. "In person?"

"No," Michelle replied. "We spoke over the phone."

Tom, startled, stammered, "But he was captured—"

Michelle called Robert. "Yes, we found him. I'm going to put you on speakerphone." Michelle set the phone down on the table. "Can you hear us?"

"Loud and clear," came Robert's grumpy voice.

Michelle looked at Tom. "Tom says you were kidnapped this afternoon."

Robert laughed. "Honey? Do I look like I've been kidnapped?"

"No," came his wife's voice.

Robert chuckled. "There you go. I've got to run, but tell Jason I said hi."

"He's right here."

"Quiet as usual," said Robert.

Quiet? This wasn't right, Tom thought. His dad didn't talk to Robert at campaign events. But they argued in private all the time.

"Wait!" Tom said, leaning towards the phone.

"Make it quick," Robert snapped.

Tom looked at Jason. "Do you remember the first time my dad mailed you?"

"Not offhand," said Robert.

Tom motioned at his parents to be quiet. "I think it was back in the late 1990s. He included one of my drawings. Remember?"

"Oh, that letter," Robert said. "My daughter loved your space alien. Got to run."

The call ended abruptly.

Confused, Tom's parents looked at each other. Jason was the first constituent to email Robert. He never sent a written letter to Robert, and he never sent one of Tom's pictures to Robert.

Tom pulled out his own phone, then picked up his mother's phone, startling her. He then held his hand out to father. "Please?" Tom asked. "I'll return them before I leave."

His father gave Tom a skeptical look before handing his phone over. "We are going to talk about this."

"Agreed," Tom replied as he accepted Jason's phone. "Won't take long."

Tom walked up to the counter and placed the phones in front of Chen. "I've got people on these phones who might place orders. Can you recite your entire menu to them?"

Chen gave Tom a broad smile, then started reciting his menu. His eyes sparkled with excitement as he started with the appetizers.

Tom rushed back to seat. "I don't have much time, but here's my offer." He put the jammer in front of his parents. "After you eat your dinner, drive back to Bolingbrook. When you reach the village, one of you needs to flip open this cover." Tom flipped open the cover, revealing a green button. "Press this button, then drive by every Bolingbrook anniversary banner. If you're right, nothing will happen. If I'm right, the banners will combust, and you'll save the lives of every Bolingbrook resident."

His mother said, "Tom—"

"Either way," Tom interrupted, "I will check myself into Alexian Brothers. Just get me that private room, like you promised."

Jason and Michelle looked at each other.

"Maybe I'll never leave. Maybe the drugs will do the trick, and I'll go on a blog tour about the benefits of psychiatric drugs. Hell, maybe Bennett will have me on his podcast. I don't know." He looked into his parents' skeptical eyes. "All I'm asking is that both of you turn on this jammer, and drive around Bolingbrook. My freedom in exchange for the lives of Bolingbrook's residents." Tom stood up. "Final offer."

Confused, Jason and Michelle looked at each other. Tom tapped his fingers on the table as he waited.

"Tom," Michelle finally said, "if this gets you the help you need, I agree. Jason?"

Jason took a deep breath. "I agree, but you have to give me your word."

"You have it."

"Agreed," Jason replied.

Tom stood up. "No matter how this ends, just know that I love both of you."

Michelle looked at Jason.

"We love you, too," said Jason. "See you tomorrow."

47

TOM TENSED AS HE passed the "Welcome to Bolingbrook" sign on North Bolingbrook Drive. Questions raced through his mind. Would his parents follow his instructions? Could he persuade Steve or Rene to stand down? Was he making a huge mistake in returning to Bolingbrook? Would Natalie ever go home?

In the rear-view mirror, two green pickup trucks with white hardshell bed covers exited the Riverwood Golf Dome parking lot. Ahead of him, two blue SUVs made a right turn from Royce Road and slowed. Tom soon found himself boxed in by the DPA vehicles. Tom waved and followed the lead SUVs.

"Don't fight fire with fire unless you have to," Tom told himself. "I hope it doesn't come down to that."

***

When the lead DPA vehicle turned onto Old Chicago Drive, Tom knew exactly where they were going. The Manchester Auto Auction Arena occupied the site where Old Chicago Mall once stood. This was going to be ground zero, Tom thought.

After they turned onto Old Chicago Drive, a security gate on the left side of the road slid open. Tom followed his escorts into the lot. They drove by other DPA operatives loading boxes and equipment into trucks and vans marked for auction. Did they expect to outrun the devastation Legion was about to unleash, he wondered?

The escorts stopped at a large, one-story vehicle warehouse. There were several garage doors along the length of the building, and a large industrial door at the end of the building. A garage door opened, revealing a marked parking spot. Inside, four DPA operatives motioned for Tom to enter. He followed their instructions and parked his car in a mini repair bay. After turning off the engine, an operative tapped on his window. Tom cracked the window open.

"Keys on the dashboard," he said.

Tom slapped them onto the dashboard.

"Open the trunk."

"Got a warrant?" Tom asked.

Four operatives pointed their pistols at him.

"Good enough," Tom replied with a smirk. He popped the trunk open. A fifth operative, holding a metallic wand connected to a metal box, rushed up to the trunk.

"Inert," he called out.

"Darn," Tom said sarcastically.

"Get out," said the nearest operative.

As Tom stepped out, two operatives grabbed and slammed him against the car. One of them frisked Tom. Tom started to speak but stopped when an operative handcuffed him.

"Not so tight," Tom said.

The operative tightened the cuffs. Two other operatives grabbed Tom by his arms and pulled him away.

Tom thought about saying he wasn't giving them a tip until he saw where the operatives were taking him.

In the building's center, four Tesla coils stood tall, arranged in a rectangle, looming over a flatbed trailer. In the middle of the trailer, Robert Clark sat, handcuffed to a metal chair. Bruises covered his face, and his right eye was almost swollen shut. A dark, crusted stain of dried blood marred his undershirt. His scraped skin exposed through the holes in his slacks. His polished shoes were now marred with patches of blood.

Yards away from the trailer, Rene stood behind a semicircle of monitors and control panels. The chaotic jumble of analog and digital technology looked like it could only work through magic. She concentrated on one monitor. Red text flashed on the screen.

"We got Tom," said an operative.

"Bring him here," said Rene, still focusing on the monitor.

Robert spoke, his voice trembling and barely audible. "Tom, I hope you don't have a camera with you." He laughed and then started coughing.

Tom was in shock as he passed by Robert, who now looked like a bleeding, broken shell of himself.

"Don't talk," Tom managed to say.

"Easy for you to say," Robert said. His face twisted as a harsh cough escaped his lips.

The operatives and Tom stopped next to the control panels. Rene looked up and glared at Tom. "What did you do?" she asked.

"Gwyla took out the banners in Little Bolingbrook," Tom replied.

Rene looked up as a frustrated groan escaped her lips. "Of course it did."

Tom tried to approach Rene, but two operatives held him back. "Gwyla ended her cycle to protect Bolingbrook. Gwyla said Bolingbrook was special because it transcended purpose."

Rene let out a frustrated sigh. "Gwyla wouldn't know the meaning of the word 'transcend.'" She slapped a monitor. "It's going to be a complicated fix, Tom."

"Let it go," Tom said. "Let her go."

Rene looked up from the monitor. "Not until I've saved her."

"You're not saving her," said Tom. "Why don't you try listening to Natalie for a change?"

Rene glared at Tom as her face turned red. Then she looked past him. "Put them by the red sedan." She looked back at Tom. "You can join your friends."

The operatives turned Tom around. Four operatives led Esteban and Juanita toward a red sedan, its shiny surface reflecting the fluorescent lights above. Both wore blue and green jumpsuits. A crew cut was all that was left of Esteban's hair. Without his beard, the faded bruises and healing cuts on his face were now visible. Juanita had a black eye and bruises on her wrists.

Tom's escorts led him to the sedan and positioned him next to Juanita. The operatives pushed them down and forced them to sit on their knees.

Rene looked up and sighed. "They're not going anywhere. You can rejoin the others." She looked at a monitor and started twisting two knobs. "Tell Steve I need to speak with him." She looked at the operatives. "Now!"

One operative looked down at Tom, Juanita, and Esteban. "You're about to become part of something much bigger than yourselves."

"Literally," said another operative.

All the operatives laughed as they walked away. One called Steve over the radio. Robert winced as he shouted obscenities at the departing operatives. One of them flipped off Robert.

Juanita whispered, "Did you come here with a plan?"

"Kind of," Tom whispered. "I hope you have a plan."

"Did they get APK?"

"Yeah." He looked away. "Rene guaranteed her safety. She claimed APK was one of the Illuminati's greatest achievements and she wouldn't hurt her. But maybe I should have—"

"Don't worry about that now," Juanita whispered. "Right now, we have to figure out how to stop the summoning."

Tom pulled against his handcuffs. "Do you have a plan?"

She shook her head. "No. But until you're dead, there's always hope."

He looked around. "That's one way to look at it."

"Rene," Robert said, his voice raw and strained. "All those speeches saying you loved Bolingbrook. All the times you bragged about Clow UFO Base to the Interstellar Commonwealth ambassadors. Was it all a lie? Did you really hate us?"

Rene didn't look up from the monitors. "It was true."

"Is this about Natalie?" Robert coughed and winced. "Did Steve promise to bring her back to life if you annihilated Bolingbrook? I could understand that. Natalie was a very lovely girl. Do you really think she would want this?"

Rene looked up at Robert, her face filled with rage. "If you really love your residents, shut up and let me concentrate!"

"Oh, how the mighty have fallen," Steve said as he walked past the sedan. Huey and Louie followed. None of them wore Cubs-themed clothes. Steve looked down at Tom, Juanita, and Esteban. "You three just couldn't leave us alone."

"Steve," said Rene. "I need to talk to you."

"Just a second," Steve said.

"Now," Rene said with a sense of urgency in her voice.

Steve stood still and gave Rene a cold stare. "Wait," he replied, his voice hinting at his annoyance. Steve looked at Huey and Louie. "See what Rene wants."

Huey and Louie walked towards Rene while Steve climbed the portable stairs by the trailer.

"You really thought you could leave the Illuminati without any consequences?" Steve asked. He approached Robert. "I've waited so long to see you finally pay for your treason."

With a strained deep breath, Robert said, "Why did you betray me, you son of a bitch?"

Steve flashed a smile. "I never betrayed anyone. You betrayed the Illuminati. Sigma 7 was seduced by the aliens' promises of bringing humanity to the stars." He chuckled. "You're just as deluded as the skeptics." Steve looked at Tom. "You were right to abandon the skeptics and their sky gods."

Robert spit blood in Steve's direction. "The Illuminati were short sighted and holding humanity back. It needed to die."

Steve shook his head. "Maybe, but vengeance never dies."

"Steve!" Rene shouted. "We don't have time for this. I need you over here now."

Steve looked at Robert. "And you will deliver our vengeance to the stars."

He turned away from Robert and walked towards Rene. Robert watched, his breath coming in ragged gasps.

Juanita leaned toward Tom. "Keep them talking," she whispered.

"You got a plan?"

"I'll let you know."

Juanita leaned toward Esteban and whispered in his ear.

Steve walked around the control panels. "What is it?"

"We have two problems," said Rene. "First, we have banners overloading prematurely."

Tom closed his eyes and thanked his parents.

"I'll send the police to investigate," Steve replied.

"There's no time." Rene pointed at a third screen "This is the pressing problem. You told me you were finished with Clow. Where are the redundant banners? Where are the COG units? We can't contain Legion within Robert without them."

Steve casually glanced at the screen. "You can't improvise?"

Rene exhaled a long, frustrated breath. "Is this how you're going to get your way? Sabotaging the network from the beginning so you can have your glorious firestorm? Never mind the plan to use the energy from the aliens to rejuvenate Natalie."

Steve shook his head and sighed. "Rene, it's like I've always told you. Energy is energy. It doesn't matter if it's alien minds or human minds. Once Robert explodes, you'll have plenty of energy to boost Natalie's signal."

With a furious glare, Rene pounded the control panel, her knuckles turning white. "I never agreed to a mass casualty event. If we unleash Legion now, Robert will explode by the time he reaches Barber's Corner. The firestorm will consume all of Bolingbrook." She pointed towards Tom. "If Tom joins it, it will break free of Bolingbrook. Then you know what happens."

"Millions die, and the war for the puppet strings begins?" Steve smiled, further enraging Rene. He said, "Either we release Legion now, or it finds a way into our world later and kills billions. It's too late to turn back, Rene."

Tom yelled, "Is this what Natalie wants? Does she really want you to commit mass murder to give her a thousand years in the Ghost Frequencies? Are you sure this is her home?"

Robert coughed up blood. "If you're so goddamn pissed off at me, then kill me! Feed my soul to that monster. Just leave my village alone."

Rene stepped away from the panels and started pacing in a ragged circle. Her hands clenched as she whispered to herself. Her eyes watered as her face became a fiery red, fueled by rage.

"Your village?" Steve said, then laughed. "An egotist until the very end. You really think this is your village?"

Rene slammed both her hands against the metallic surface of an inactive control panel. The sound startled Huey and Louie. Steve and Robert fell silent.

"Enough!" she yelled. Her voice echoed throughout the building. Even the operatives loading vehicles stopped to watch her. Rene looked down and shook her head. As the redness dissipated, her face returned to its natural complexion.

Steve walked around the control center. "Rene?"

She composed herself and then looked at Steve, who stopped abruptly. A look of concern and confusion came over his face.

Rene said, "If we split Legion between Robert and me, the network will hold. We'll have enough time to get inside Clow before Legion ignites."

"My god," said Louie. "That's hardcore."

"Shut up," Huey said as he pushed Louie. Louie stumbled and then scowled.

Steve walked up to Rene. "You won't come back."

Her voice regained its composure as she replied, "I put APK in Cargo Van G3. The doors are unlocked. She's in the climate-controlled carrier. She's strong enough to protect the team if Legion escapes Clow."

"Are you sure?" Steve asked.

Rene nodded and then smiled. "I'll get to be with my father and Natalie again. We can say goodbye to Natalie together." She faced Huey and Louie. "You two staying?"

"Of course," said Huey. "We don't want to miss the ultimate trip."

Steve chuckled.

"Then bring Tom over here," Rene said. "Quickly." She looked down at her watch, then looked up at Steve. "You need to get going. Tell the Regents I'm not sorry we defied them."

"When I see the Regents, they'll make me the Grand Regent," said Steve. "And I will make sure your name will be revered for centuries. History will know that you started the fire that burned the NWO."

Esteban looked at Juanita and Tom. "Interesting," he said softly.

Steve and Rene embraced for a few moments. When they ended their embrace, Rene's hand brushed two metallic switches on a control panel. With a soft click, the switches moved, and two green lights blinked to life above them.

"You need to get going," Rene said as she stepped away. "I'm about to start the transfer."

"Good luck," he replied. He turned and started to leave.

Huey and Louie lifted Tom off the floor and escorted him over to Rene.

"Just think," Louie said. "In a few minutes, we're going to come together within Legion."

"I can wait," Tom replied.

Robert spit blood on the floor. "Rene. Steve. If you two go through with this, the Vitalis Corporation will hunt each of you down. Those monsters will tear you to pieces for betraying them."

Steve stopped walking. He kept his back to Robert for a few long seconds, the weight of the silence heavy between them. He then turned around and smiled at Robert. "All but one. She's more human than you'll ever be."

Steve turned away from Robert, then left to join the operatives on the other side of the building.

Huey and Louie brought Tom before Rene. She opened a drawer filled with cables connected to small metallic devices with Velcro straps.

Louie said, "What should we do with the other two?" He looked back. Juanita and Esteban were no longer sitting by the sedan. The harsh ceiling lights gleamed off the discarded handcuffs and reflected onto the floor.

"Damn," Huey said. "They escaped. Should we look for them?"

Rene strapped on the devices and checked the cable connections. "Stay with Tom. Those two will just be consumed for energy."

"And we'll be the ones consuming them," Louie said, a cruel smile spreading across his face.

Tom resisted the urge to vomit on Louie. Instead, he focused on Rene as she connected cables to the devices.

"You don't have to do this," Tom said.

Rene connected the last cable, then stared into Tom's eyes. "Yes, Tom. I must do this for Natalie."

48

THE TESLA COILS HUMMED as they charged. Robert stared at Rene as she typed on a manual typewriter embedded within a 20-year-old desktop PC. Louie looked at the Tesla coils in awe.

Robert shouted, "You think I have an ego? Who gave you the right to murder my residents? All those flowery speeches you delivered to the residents? Those holograms you recorded to welcome alien visitors to Clow? The time you told the trustees you couldn't wait for the Commonwealth to reveal themselves to humanity? It was all bullshit! You praised the knights for protecting Bolingbrook from monsters. Then you created the biggest and deadliest threat to Bolingbrook in my lifetime." He coughed and then caught his breath. "You're the most selfish, hypocritical monsters of them all."

"Oh, shut up!" Huey yelled.

"Fuck you," Robert snapped back. "You think I'm afraid of ghouls like you?"

Louie yelled, "You should be." He lowered the tone of his voice and tried to sound ominous. "You should be."

Robert coughed. "I've heard worse."

Louie laughed. "We're going to enjoy consuming you, old man."

"Good one," said Huey.

Rene paused as she looked down at one of the consoles.

Tom felt a pit in his stomach as Rene adjusted two knobs. "Please don't do this," he said. "The beings inside Clow are living, sentient creatures. Just like us. They're not sky gods. They're mortals."

Rene adjusted the last knob, then looked into his eyes. "There are trillions of aliens in the galaxy. What difference will the death of a few hundred make?"

"Each one of them has value," Tom said. "Just like each person on Earth has value."

"Save it for the afterlife," Huey said to Tom. He looked at Rene. "What's the plan?"

Rene stepped away from the control center. "Both of you take Tom to the sedan and wait. Once Legion is stabilized within Robert and I, the coils will shut down. After Legion absorbs Tom, drive Legion to Clow Airport."

"Then what?" Huey asked.

"Then," Rene said, her voice barely a whisper. She paused for a few moments. "Then you take the ultimate trip."

Huey smiled with a hint of sadistic joy on his face.

"Now take Tom back to the sedan and wait for us."

Huey and Louie grabbed Tom's arms and escorted him to the red sedan.

"Rene," said Tom. "Think about my family. My friends. The residents."

"I am," Rene replied.

As Huey and Louie pulled Tom towards the sedan, Rene climbed the portable stairs up to the top of the trailer.

Robert locked his eyes on Rene as she stepped onto the trailer. He said, "You left me with a struggling suburb. No anchor retail stores. One grocery store. A road to nowhere. I—"

Rene said, "For once in your life, shut up and listen." She looked down at Robert while he defiantly looked up at her.

Rene shook her head, then continued. "For every single day of my term, you always argued with me. In the middle of the Bolingbrook Time War, you questioned every decision I made. You even had to debate what color the sky was. Every minute with you was like being entangled in barbed wire. Yet I never once considered ruining your life."

She circled Robert.

"You want to talk about hypocrisy? You were praising the Illuminati while conspiring with Sigma 7. You lectured scout troops about values hours after you lied to my father. You campaigned on transparency. Then you attacked the *Phantom Press* because you didn't want your secrets exposed. While you talked a good game about uniting the community, what you really wanted was for everyone to agree with you."

She stopped next to Robert's right side. "Your fragile little ego couldn't handle what you put me through every single day of my term. You attacked me for spending too much on wallpaper, knowing damn well I used that purchase to hide our funding for the Knights of Twilight. Then you had the audacity to use taxpayer dollars to build a luxury golf club and McMansion subdivision."

She stepped in front of Robert. "You think you're Bolingbrook?" Rene shook her head. "Robert, you didn't build the houses. You didn't pave the streets. You've never started or run a business. Hell, you were nowhere near Bolingbrook when it was incorporated."

She stepped closer and pressed a button on one of her wearable devices. The hum of the Tesla coils rose an octave.

Rene said, "You aren't Bolingbrook. We are Bolingbrook. The residents are Bolingbrook. I don't know if you remember, but there is a line in the regent's initiation ceremony I've thought about for most of my life. 'We stand on what those before us built. We build so those who come after us can stand.'" Rene squatted to look Robert in the eyes. "Remember that." She stood and then took a few steps back. "Goodbye, Robert."

Rene flipped a switch on a device strapped to her wrist, then held her arms out. The Tesla coils' low hum changed to a loud crackling sound. The four coils discharged four purple arcs of electricity at Rene. She screamed for a moment before convulsing. Her body levitated as if the electrical arcs were picking up. Light streamed through her skin like the blinding light of a star inside her body. Tom closed his eyes and looked away, as did Robert. Even Huey and Louie squinted against the blinding light as they tried to watch.

The electrical arcs vanished, and the sharp smell of ozone was replaced by the silence of the deactivated coils. The blinding light within Rene softened, granting them the ability to look at her. She lowered her arms and descended towards Robert. As her eyelids opened, a blinding white light filled the space where her eyes used to be. Rene and Legion drifted up to Robert and landed in front of him. Robert defiantly stared back at Legion.

Enraged voices, like a chorus, poured from Rene's mouth. "You."

Robert snorted. "Hello, Barry." His voice was filled with contempt. "You're still a bitter old man. Only now you're consuming souls, including the souls of your daughter and granddaughter."

The glow in Rene's eyes brightened.

"Burn," Legion said in a stage whisper.

"Wait!" Huey yelled as he climbed the stairs to the top of the trailer. Louie followed him.

Rene floated up and drifted towards Huey and Louie. She looked down at the two young men.

Huey said, "She wants you to enter Robert's body. Once you do, we'll take both of you to Clow airport. You can ask her if you don't believe me."

"Yeah," Louie said. "Then you're supposed to do your thing inside the UFO Base."

"What do you say?" Huey asked.

Rene floated down and landed in front of Huey. She tilted her head and gazed into Huey's eyes.

"You're beautiful," Huey said. "So much power."

Rene straightened her head and extended her right arm towards Huey. He smiled as he looked deeper into Rene's glowing eyes. Suddenly, he gasped for air. His skin shriveled up like a dry old leaf. A translucent projection of Huey, its edges blurring, slowly drifted out of his body and glided towards Rene.

"Take me," said the ghost of Huey.

Rene closed her hand into a fist. The ghost started to vanish, its spectral form dissolving and drifting into Rene, like dust sucked into a vacuum.

"Don't eat me!" the ghost of Huey screamed before dissipating. Huey's corpse collapsed and exploded into a cloud of dust.

Louie gasped in horror as he stared at the cloud that was once Huey. Rene drifted effortlessly towards Louie, like a sheet of paper in the wind. With his hands trembling, he raised his arms.

"Please forgive me," he asked, his voice quivering. "We didn't want to offend you. How can I make this right?"

Rene raised her right arm slowly. The glow in her eyes intensified as she pointed at Tom.

"Him," Legion said through Rene.

Tom's initial fear gave way to anger at the monster in front of him. *The monster who wants to destroy my hometown. The monster who wants help to spread its firestorm of death and destruction beyond Bolingbrook.*

I'm sorry, Wendy. I might have no choice but to fight fire with fire.

Louie looked back at Tom. "You want Tom? You want me to bring Tom to you?"

Rene's face twitched for a moment. Then she nodded.

Louie scurried off the trailer and back to Tom. "Get up," he said.

Tom struggled to stand. Louie pulled him up. "It wants you."

Tom stared at Rene. "And I want it."

Louie smiled at Tom. "That's the spirit," he whispered, "Make me look good. I don't want to be food. Neither do you."

Rene and Legion screamed in agony. The glow in Rene's eyes turned from white to crimson.

Robert's eyes widened as he looked at Rene. He struggled to push his chair away from her.

Louie froze. "What the fuck?"

Rene pivoted her body to face Robert. Robert pulled at the cold, metallic handcuffs, the sound echoing in the room, desperately trying to escape the chair.

"What are you doing?" Legion growled, its voices now divided between rage and agony.

Rene, speaking in her own voice, replied, "This."

The chair lifted slightly with a groan, then bolted off the trailer like a cannonball. Robert screamed in terror. The chair rotated midair and then glided down until the back of the chair touched the floor. The chair skidded to a stop close to Tom and Louie. Robert's handcuffs unlocked by themselves, and he rolled onto the floor.

On the other side of the building, the remaining DPA vehicles screeched as they sped out of the building.

A dome of shimmering air appeared and enveloped the trailer.

Rene reached into both of her overalls pockets.

"Why?" Legion snarled.

Rene, breathing heavily, said, "I never wanted you to destroy Bolingbrook, and I never wanted to put Natalie through Hell."

Legion growled, "Your prison cannot hold me."

"You're right. It can't hold forever. But I don't need it to." She looked in Tom's direction. "Close your eyes."

Rene's hands emerged from her pockets, each holding a sphere.

"Spheres!" Tom screamed.

Rene released the spheres, which flew from her hands. Tom covered his eyes as the spheres collided. The bright flash penetrated his fingers and eyelids, hurting his eyes. This time, the sound of the explosion was muffled.

Tom opened his eyes and turned around. Robert lay on the floor, his eyes rapidly blinking. Louie shook his head as he staggered towards the trailer.

A dome of shimmering air still enveloped the trailer. The Tesla coils hummed with electricity. Rene sat on her knees. Her eyes, though no longer glowing, remained fixed in place.

"Don't leave me," Louie yelled. "I want more." He pulled a small pistol from his back pocket. "Wait for me," he whispered, the words barely escaping his lips.

Suddenly, Rene's body burst into flames. The flames grew into an inferno that filled the shimmering dome. Sparks exploded from the Tesla coils moments before they collapsed. The dome vanished, and the sound of tormented screams filled the building. The inferno spread, no longer constrained by an invisible force.

"Yes!" Dewie yelled at the approaching spiritual inferno. "Let me be the fire!"

Tom watched the growing inferno approach, knowing he couldn't outrun it. Soon, he would either burn to death or be absorbed by Legion.

"I'm sorry," Tom whispered as he thought of his friends and parents who he was about to join in death.

Esteban ran into view as he rushed towards the control center, holding a large pet carrier in his right hand. The inferno contracted as he approached. "Go!" Esteban yelled as he opened the carrier door with his left hand.

APK dashed out of the carrier and jumped on top of a monitor. Her eyes glowed blue as she faced Legion.

"Mow!"

49

ABOVE THE TRAILER'S CHARRED remains, Legion's form shrunk into a blazing, enormous fireball. Its flames turned a fierce, bright red, and the sound of agonizing howls filled the building.

"What the fuck?" Louie said as he looked at APK. He aimed his pistol at her.

"Hey!" Tom yelled as he charged.

Louie turned his head just in time to feel Tom's foot connect with his buttocks. He staggered forward and accidentally pulled the trigger. His wild shot hit the window of a parked pickup truck.

"Mow!" said APK. She jumped off the monitor then dashed at Legion.

Louie regained his balance and turned into Tom's kick. Tom hit Louie in the abdomen. Louie staggered backwards. As Tom approached, Louie aimed at Tom. Acting on instinct, Tom kicked Louie's gun hand. Louie fired the gun, and Tom felt the bullet rush by his ear.

APK stood under Legion as the blue glow in her eyes intensified. Legion contracted further; its glow changed from crimson to yellow.

Four shots rang out. For a moment, Tom thought he'd been shot. He opened his eyes and saw blood rushing out of Louie's four chest wounds. Louie's body collapsed next to Tom, but his apparition remained standing.

Louie's ghost looked at his translucent body, then smiled. "Yes," Louie said as an invisible force pulled him towards Legion. He flipped over to face Legion's flames. "Thank you," he said before plunging into flames.

Tom looked back. Juanita holstered her gun as she rushed up to Robert. She kneeled beside him and looked at his wounds.

"Can you stand up?" Juanita asked.

"Of course," Robert said. He tried to push himself up but stopped and screamed in pain. He collapsed onto the floor.

"Don't move," Juanita said.

"Not a problem," Robert said as he winced.

Juanita approached Tom. "Are you okay?" she asked as she pulled a key out of her pocket.

"Yeah," Tom replied. He shook his hands. "How did you escape?"

"Our handcuffs unlocked themselves," Juanita replied. She unlocked Tom's handcuffs. "Then we looked for the van with APK inside."

"Rene helped you escape?" Tom asked.

"Just like she helped us fight Legion," said Juanita. "Can you stand?"

"Yeah," Tom replied. "I'm getting better at this." He chuckled.

Juanita didn't laugh. "Can you help me get Robert into the car?"

"Of course." Tom winced and then pushed himself up.

As Legion grew, APK growled, then staggered.

As Tom followed Juanita, he noticed Estaban working in the control center. He wondered if Rene had left anything else that could help them defeat Legion. Juanita positioned herself on

Robert's left side. Following her lead, Tom positioned himself on Robert's right side.

"Can you walk?" Juanita asked.

"With some help," Robert replied. He looked at Tom. "Don't quote me."

Tom and Juanita helped Robert to his feet. They supported him as they hobbled to the sedan.

Robert said, "I thought journalists weren't supposed to get involved. Maybe I should file a complaint." He tried to smile.

"The Society of Professional Journalists imposed a lifetime membership ban for anyone who works for the *Babbler*," said Tom. "That's the worst they can do to me."

"In that case," Robert said, "I hope you brought the cavalry this time. Mine betrayed me."

"This is it," Tom replied.

Robert looked at Juanita. "I hope the Orange Squad lives up to its reputation tonight."

Juanita didn't respond. When they reached the sedan, Tom and Juanita helped Robert into the back seat. "Stay here," she said to Tom.

"Where're you going?"

Juanita looked at Esteban, who was still in the control center. "Rene hid several EMP devices in the building. They should be enough to finish Legion. We'll join you once the timer is set."

APK staggered as Legion expanded by nearly a foot in diameter.

"What about APK?" Tom asked. "How do we get her in here before they go off?"

Juanita looked at APK struggling against Legion. She closed her eyes for a moment, then looked into Tom's eyes. "She has to contain Legion in the blast zone."

Tom's jaw dropped. "APK won't survive the blast."

Juanita averted Tom's eyes for a few moments. She took a deep breath and then faced him. "I know," she whispered.

Legion expanded, and APK wobbled again.

"No," Tom gasped.

"There's no other option," Juanita said with a hint of sorrow in her voice.

"It won't work," Tom replied. "How many EMPs have been thrown at it? It's too powerful to be disrupted with EMPs."

"What else can we do?" Juanita asked. "That's our most powerful weapon against ghosts."

"I need to reach Legion's core."

Juanita's eyes widened in shock. "What? You'll become a part of it."

"Maybe," said Tom. "But I know who the core is. It's Trustee Barry. He's holding Legion together. If I can reach Barry, I might persuade him to release the ghosts within Legion. We can't overpower Legion. Reaching Barry is our only hope of saving Bolingbrook."

APK slipped and fell to the floor. The glow in her eyes dimmed.

"Please," Tom said. "Let me try. Just give me some time to reach the core."

Juanita looked into Tom's eyes, worry etched on her face. For a moment, Tom remembered the Lunch and Learn he was going to speak at. Back then, he was the one afraid of failing, and Juanita was the one reassuring him. Now she was afraid for him, and Tom couldn't promise that everything would be fine.

"I'll pray for you," Juanita replied.

"Thank you."

Juanita opened her arms, as if she sensed Tom's confusion. Tom leaned in to hug Juanita. They held each other in a tight embrace. Part of Tom didn't want to let go. He wanted to kiss her. *Now is not the time for that,* he thought. Now he had to do his part to save Bolingbrook.

They released their embrace and stepped back.

"Be careful in there."

"I will."

"Remember what I told you about resisting a ghost's illusions?"

Tom nodded. "I know what to do."

"Then get going," Juanita said, sounding like she was holding back her emotions. "APK needs your help."

Legion expanded again, and APK struggled to get back on her feet.

"Goodbye," Tom said.

"You better come back," Juanita replied. She turned and ran towards Estaban.

Tom looked up at Legion's flames. He remembered the attack on the newsroom. The lives lost in the conspiracy. He pictured all the people he knew in Bolingbrook. His parents. His friends. His co-workers. His home. Legion wanted to burn all of it.

Tom's fear turned to rage, a rage he could use against Legion. But only to reach Barry. If he couldn't let go of his rage, he could become the core of Legion.

"You say you want me, Legion?" Tom laughed. "Oh no. You've got it all wrong." Tom sprinted at Legion. "I want you!"

Darkness enveloped Tom, but he knew where to find Barry.

50

ILLUSIONS OF NIGHTMARISH SCENES and his personal demons appeared in front of Tom, only to be banished by waves of APK's anti-psychic energy. Tom pressed on through the collapsing dreamscapes, guided by his rage.

Near the core, the illusions vanished and APK's anti-psychic energy subsided. A void enveloped Tom. He could feel only his own body and hear only his thoughts. Yet, he knew he was closing in on the core of Legion. APK couldn't help him now. He was alone. It was up to him to stop the coming atrocity and punish Barry.

Footsteps echoed throughout the void. His footsteps. He was walking on a concrete surface. Stars appeared above him. Hot and humid air surrounded him. Rows of lights appeared, dispelling the surrounding darkness. Tom was in a parking lot, walking between rows of cars from the 1970s. In the distance, dim lights shone through a two-story fanlight window and the glass doors below it. The silhouette of Old Chicago faded into view. Further in the distance, numerous cloud-to-cloud lightning strikes illuminated the towering clouds along the edge of a storm front.

The ghosts of the *Phantom Press* appeared, blocking Tom's path. Tom pressed forward.

A man stepped forward, his press credentials attached to his fedora. "Robert tried to destroy us. You must not deny us our revenge. His works must be obliterated."

Tom shook his head. "You destroyed yourselves the moment you decided to create Legion."

The staff dissolved into ashes and was scattered by a gust of wind. Tom didn't stop.

Lights illuminated the smooth gray dome atop Old Chicago. On the ground, the shadows receded, revealing stairs leading up to the glass doors. Two black lion statues, replicas of the bronze lions outside the Art Institute, stood at the foot of the stairs. The sound of distant thunder rumbled through the sky.

The glass doors locked with a loud click as he stepped onto the sidewalk. Tom laughed as he approached the stairs. "You won't stop me, Barry."

A shockwave emanated from Tom, shattering the glass doors and cracking the fanlight window.

The cloud-to-cloud lightning strikes intensified as winds blew across the parking lot. The winds carried faint, frightened whispers. Tom entered the mall.

The dim lighting and 19th century style storefronts attempted to evoke the feeling of strolling at dusk in the late 1800s. The 1970s-style floor tiles ruined the illusion. He walked by the specialty stores, like Ye Old Chicago Tobacco Company, Wolf Glass Blower, and Photo on a Button. Shoppers appeared, creating the illusion of a thriving mall.

Among the shoppers were people from his past. Jamie reminded him of what had happened in the elevator. Juanita accused Tom of betraying her. Reese blamed Tom for her death. This time, Tom found Legion's puppets to be irritating distractions.

"You're right," said Tom, hoping Barry was listening. "I've hurt people. I've screwed up. Maybe I am responsible for Reese's death." He looked up at the acoustic ceiling tiles. "It doesn't matter. I don't need to be perfect to do what's right."

Tom reached the balcony overlooking the fairground. Below, the festive sounds of the amusement park filled the air as crowds of patrons wandered among the booths and rides. He recognized the Chicago Loop, the second modern looping roller-coaster ever built, and the Chicago Log Race. Between them was a bright white pillar of light that extended from the ceiling dome down to the floor. *That is my destination,* he thought.

Tom walked down the ramp to the fairgrounds. The smell of popcorn and other amusement park treats filled the air as well as the sounds of rides, carnival games, and excited visitors. When he reached the bottom of the ramp, the people were faceless and silent, as if the voices were recordings and the guests around him were crude puppets.

Someone wearing a foam Charlie Baffle outfit waved at Tom. His bright white hair and green 19th century style suit almost glowed. Charlie motioned with his purple-skinned hand for Tom to follow him. Charlie walked towards the pillar of light. He wasn't going to be guided by one of Barry's illusions, Tom thought. He knew the way.

As he walked behind Charlie, the fairground changed. With each step, the crowd dwindled. Rides and booths disappeared. The background noises faded. The Chicago Loop and the Log Race vanished. The fairground resembled an abandoned warehouse. Debris littered the floor, and bare spots marked where rides once stood.

An offset printing press appeared. Sheets of paper erupted from it. The papers drifted to the floor, resembling a snowstorm. The papers were from the first issue of the *Phantom*

Press. With each step, the publication dates advanced until the last issue from 1986 drifted to the ground. The papers and the printing press vanished. Wired explosives appeared along the walls and on the support structures.

Charlie vanished, but Tom approached the pillar of light. The sounds of barking dogs, screaming men, and gunfire echoed around the building. A cat hissed, and the gunfire ceased. Tom heard crosstalk in the darkness followed by the sound of Juanita's parents as they raced against the clock to reconnect the cables. After they finished, the last of their rushed footsteps faded into silence.

A new set of footsteps grew louder. Rene and Barry talked about technical details Tom didn't understand. When the warning siren started, Rene told her father she loved him, and they were doing the right thing. After Rene's footsteps receded, Barry said phrases in Latin.

Tom passed through the pillar. Barry stood in the center, a man in his 30s, wearing a suit from the mid-20th century. He glared at Tom, his gaze intense and unwavering.

Tom walked up to Barry. "What now?"

The explosives detonated. The world outside morphed into an inferno of whirling fire and blinding light, as if they were standing in the epicenter of a nuclear blast.

Barry's eyes glowed red. "Burn with me."

51

Barry charged at Tom, trying to grab his throat. Tom caught both of his wrists and started grappling, each driven by raw aggression.

Barry said, "Robert is corrupting your mother. The skeptical movement is ruining your reputation. Jamie will never forgive you. And I'm going to burn your home."

Tom's strength surged, and he pushed Barry. Barry's feet slid as Tom pushed him towards the edge of the pillar.

"Yes," Barry said. He smiled as he tried to resist Tom. "To save Bolingbrook, you have to push me into the fire. I have to burn if you want to control the flames. Kill me, and Legion's enemies become your enemies. Burn the woman who never returned your love. Burn the friends who turned on you. Burn Little Bolingbrook. Burn Robert. Destroy their futures as they destroyed yours. All you have to do is take control, and your enemies will burn."

Tom wrapped both his hands around Barry's neck. Barry's heels were inches away from the inferno.

"Go on," Barry said, his voice cracking from Tom's grip. "Take the reins."

Tom hesitated as he remembered Wendy's warning. Had he already crossed the line? Was pushing Barry into the inferno the only way to save Bolingbrook?

Barry broke Tom's grip and struck his throat. Tom staggered back as he caught his breath. Barry shoved Tom towards the edge of the pillar. "You have to earn it," Barry said." The glow in his eyes brightened. "I feel your doubts. If you're not going to lead us, then let us consume you! We need only your strength to escape." Barry shoved Tom again, who struggled to keep his balance. Barry charged, but Tom regained his balance and struck Barry in the face. The blow stunned Barry. Tom took advantage and punched Barry. His strength grew as he remembered all the people who'd wronged him, even the Ethical Sunday School student who tried to tear up one of his drawings. Barry staggered backwards towards the flames.

"Earn it!" Barry yelled. "Earn all of it."

But that student wasn't the only memory Tom had from Sunday school. At the end of every class, they would recite the motto, 'Grounded in Reason. Guided by the Heart.' He recited the motto as he backed away.

Barry regained his footing. "Your magic is worthless here."

But it wasn't magic. Instead, Tom regained his composure. The strength of his rage left him, but that wasn't the strength he needed now.

Barry charged, but Tom dodged him. After stumbling to a stop, Barry turned around and charged again. Tom circled out of Barry's way.

"Let me kill you," Barry snarled. "I won't let Robert keep Bolingbrook. It was my vision. My work. My right to destroy it!"

"No!" Tom said. "If you destroy Bolingbrook, Robert wins! Even if you kill him, he'll still win. Kill him or don't kill him, you lose everything."

Barry charged at Tom. "He took everything!"

Tom stood still. "No, he didn't."

Barry hit an invisible shield in front of Tom. He pounded as Tom repeated the motto. The flames receded. Outside the pillar was the parking lot, now covered with weeds. Where the mall had been was now paved over.

With a bewildered expression, Barry looked at the world outside.

Tom took a deep breath to calm himself. His heart had brought him to this point. Now was the time to reason with Barry.

"Barry," Tom said, "Jamie Kyle wrote a song called, "We're All Gonna Die." Don't ask me to sing it." He chuckled, but Barry was unmoved. "Her point was that death brings fairness to an unfair world. All the terrible people in the world will die. Dictators and war criminals will die. People we don't like will die. Even Robert. He, too, will die. Death allows the living to move on."

Barry folded his arms.

"Even so, what we leave behind matters. One of the last things Gwyla told me was that Bolingbrook had transcended purpose. It's what made Bolingbrook special to her. It's why she sacrificed herself." Tom approached Barry. "Bolingbrook isn't a collection of buildings or lines on a map. Bolingbrook is a community. Communities aren't confined to a single purpose. They evolve and change with residents. I understand the residents of Little Bolingbrook and you don't like Robert's changes. But if you think about it: his changes aren't permanent. The Golf Club is just a building that can be torn down. The streets he renamed can be renamed again. The Robert Clark Garden in front of the township offices? Easily renamed."

Barry's eyes stopped glowing. He relaxed as he faced Tom.

Tom said, "But what you created can't be replaced. You helped create a community. A community that will evolve and grow over time. That, Barry. That is your legacy. I know it won't last forever. Nothing does. But it will outlast Robert. You don't like it now, but who knows what Bolingbrook will be like in a hundred years? Not everyone can say they built a community. That means you will always be part of the core of Bolingbrook. If you destroy Bolingbrook, you will destroy a community. Because one man made temporary changes to it?"

Barry walked to the edge of the pillar of light. It dimmed again. Tom paced behind Barry.

"You said I have no future." Tom shook his head. "Juanita said as long as you're alive, you always have a chance. I have a chance at a better future. Will I make mistakes? Yes, but I'll try to learn from them. Did I almost go down a destructive path? Yes, but I saw where that path led, and I'm glad I didn't go there."

Tom stood next to Barry. "I don't want Legion. I don't want the people I don't like to suffer. I want to save my community. Our community. Please don't let your rage destroy our pathway to the future."

Rene appeared outside the pillar, looking exactly as she had before her death. "Tom's right. We were blinded by our anger, and our sorrow. We let Legion become too powerful. We release it into the world. You have to step away from the core."

Barry said, "But without Legion, how will we save Natalie?"

"I don't want to be saved," came Natalie's voice. "I just want to go home."

A crack snaked across the parking lot, a jagged scar on the asphalt. The crack widened until the gap reached the horizon and opened into a pitch-black void.

Natalie materialized next to Rene. "Please, Mommy?"

Rene reverted to the age she had been when Natalie died. She now had thick, long, black hair. She kneeled and held Natalie in a tight embrace. Natalie returned her embrace, and they both cried.

"I'm so sorry," Rene sobbed. "I've done so many terrible things. But the worst was putting you in here. I love you so much that I couldn't let you go. I didn't understand what you meant. I trapped you in hell, and I almost murdered countless innocent lives to keep you here for centuries. I'm a terrible person. I don't deserve your love."

Natalie cried and said, "No, Mommy. I still love you. I forgive you, Mommy. I forgive you, Grandpa." She released her embrace. "But we have to go home. Before someone can take over Legion."

Rene nodded. "You're right." She stood up and faced Barry. "If we're going to save Bolingbrook, we have to leave now."

Barry's eyes watered. "Natalie, there's nothing beyond the Ghost Frequencies. If we jump, that's it. I can't let go of my existence."

Rene held her hand out to Barry. "We can't stay in the Ghost Frequencies forever, Dad. Is the loss of our humanity worth the price of existence?"

Natalie held out her hand. "Grandma used to say, 'There's a time to live, and a time to die.' It's our time to die."

Barry looked at Tom.

Tom said, "Someone wrote, 'From the darkness we were born, and to the darkness we shall return. Appreciate the light, for it is fleeting.'" He stepped out of the pillar. "I don't want to die either, but death is what makes our short lives so valuable."

Barry nodded, then stepped out of pillar. He took Natalie and Rene's hands. The three of them cried as they embraced each other.

The pillar of light vanished. A cacophony of whispers came from all directions.

Rene looked up at the sky. "We need to leave." She looked down at her family. "Together."

"Together," Natalie said.

"Together," Barry said.

They approached the edge of the abyss. Tom followed behind them.

"Rene," said Tom. "Do you have any words for the residents of Bolingbrook?"

Rene stopped at the edge and looked back at Tom. "Remind the residents of Bolingbrook we were here. Let them know our successes and learn from our failures. Tell them to take care of our community."

The three of them looked down into the abyss, then looked at each other.

"Let's go home," Rene said.

They stepped off into the abyss.

Reality shattered.

52

TOM GASPED FOR AIR when he woke up. The smell of soot and ozone filled his lungs. He coughed.

"Tom!" Juanita said as she rushed to him. "Don't move."

Tom opened his eyes. He was lying down on the floor next to the control center. His head rested on a firm pillow, and three medium-sized white towels covered his body. Juanita kneeled beside him.

"How do you feel?" she asked.

"I feel tired," he said. He wiggled his fingers and toes. "I'm not paralyzed."

"That's a start," Juanita replied, then smiled. "Let me help you sit up."

With Juanita's help, Tom sat up and looked around. The trailer was now a pile of twisted metal and melted rubber covered with ashes. APK slept on top of a monitor. Across the room, Robert sat on a stool at a mechanics station, arguing with Esteban. It was a sign Robert was feeling better, Tom thought. Esteban sat on the red sedan, matching Robert's intensity as they argued.

"What are they arguing about?" Tom asked.

Juanita looked at them and sighed. "I don't know. They've been at it for a while. They'll sort it out." She turned her attention to Tom. "What happened in there?"

Tom paused as he collected his thoughts. "I almost gave in to my rage, but I didn't." He sighed. "It was close."

"But I'm glad you didn't," Juanita said.

Tom nodded. "Rene, Natalie, and I persuaded Barry to stop holding Legion together. Then... I saw them die." A tear ran down his face. "I'm sorry. I've seen too many people die over the past year. I'm still not used to it."

Juanita wrapped her arms around him, and he nestled his head against her. "Don't ever get used to it, Tom. It's what makes us human."

"But I saw their souls jump into oblivion."

Juanita stroked Tom's head. "We don't know that, Tom. I believe their souls ascended and are facing judgment now. You believe there's nothing beyond this life." She released her embrace, and Tom looked at her. "But neither of us knows what happened after they jumped."

Tom nodded solemnly. "That's one thing we can agree on."

"Good," Juanita said. "Now, APK is fine. She just needs a nap, but she's alive thanks to you. Robert reached the deputy mayor. He rebooted the men in blue, and they're back on our side. I got a message out to my people, and I'm waiting for their reply." She gave Tom a warm look. "We saved Bolingbrook, Tom."

Tom exhaled with relief. "Wow," he said, then nervously chuckled. "I don't know what to say." He looked into Juanita's eyes, and she looked back into his.

Esteban said, "He's lost it." He limped towards Tom. "How are you holding up?"

Tom pulled himself up. "Doing better, thanks."

"No," Esteban said. "Thank you."

Tom blushed. "Juanita did a lot of the work."

Esteban shook his head. "No, Tom. You foiled the DPA and helped Rene see the light. You don't get to sell yourself short this time."

Tom smiled for a moment. Esteban was right, but it was at a terrible cost. He couldn't feel proud of himself, but he could say he helped save Bolingbrook. Again.

The industrial door opened, and four navy-blue SUVs drove into the building. Robert, using his stool for support, hobbled towards the approaching vehicles.

"Oh no," Esteban said.

"What?" Tom asked.

He spoke in Spanish to Juanita. She nodded in understanding and assisted her father as he slowly hobbled towards the SUVs.

APK stretched and watched the others walking away.

"Mow?"

"Good question," Tom replied.

The SUVs parked in a line and turned off their engines. Two men in blue exited their SUV and approached. Simon, along with two other men in blue, exited their SUVs. Simon tapped his earpiece.

"All clear! All clear! Call it off now!" Simon waited a few moments. "Thank you, Jesus!" He tapped his earpiece again then caught his breath.

"Where's Meggy?" Tom asked.

"She's safe," Simon replied. "Don't ask me how, but she escaped her captors and got in touch with me. Thank you for saving Meggy at the library." He looked at Esteban. "Thank you both for exposing the conspiracy."

Juanita replied, "And thank Tom for disarming Legion."

Simon gave Tom a surprised look. "Seriously?"

"Bring him out," Robert yelled. Two men in blue supported Robert as he hobbled towards Simon.

"Robert!" Simon said. "You need treatment!"

"Later," Robert snapped. "Bring him out now!"

Two men in blue stepped out of an SUV. A third man in blue stepped out, carrying Steve over his shoulder. Steve's hands were handcuffed behind his back.

"Don't do this," Esteban said to Robert.

"Quiet," Robert snapped back.

The three men in blue approached Robert. Two of them made Steve sit on the ground. Steve laughed as he looked into Robert's eyes.

Steve said, "Behind every strong man are the people holding him up. Right now, you're the perfect example."

The third man in blue picked up a crowbar and handed it to Robert.

"Robert!" Tom yelled. "What are you doing?"

"What needs to be done." Robert took a deep breath as his men in blue escorts released him. Robert limped to the nearest car and leaned against it. "You were like a brother to me . You could have whatever you wanted from me. Why are you throwing away your life for a dead organization?"

"We never died," Steve snarled. "And I never defected. My only regret is that it took us decades to get to this point.

Robert tightened his grip on the crowbar. "You've been living a lie all this time?"

"Look at you," Steve said. "You can barely stand. What are you without your sky gods and men in blue? Just a weak old man standing on the shoulders of giants."

Robert hobbled towards a rolling tool cabinet and grabbed it for support.

Steve laughed again. "I let the weredeer attack your precious golf club and brought Legion into our world. You never knew until now." He smiled. "Because you had no choice but to trust me. The DPA is the thin blue line between humanity and the monsters out there. But I never needed you."

"Let's find out," Robert said with a snarl. Using the tool cabinet for support, Robert approached Steve.

Tom ran forwards, but a man in blue grabbed his arm. "Don't!" Tom yelled. "He wants you to kill him."

"I said quiet," Robert replied.

"Don't do this," said Tom. "Bolingbrook is better than this. You're better than this."

Juanita said, "If you kill Steve, you'll start a war between the New World Order and the Illuminati. Stand down."

"After what they did?" Robert asked.

Tom said, "Steve was only half right when he said, 'Vengeance never dies.' But we can let it go. Robert, let it go. Rene and Barry are dead. Steve can rot on another planet. Don't set our world on fire!"

"Are you taking orders from a failed blogger?" asked Steve.

Robert stopped. He studied the crowbar with his intense gaze. "Rene never appreciated what the Interstellar Commonwealth is still offering us. I still think she paid way too much for those rolls of wallpaper. And her sales tax policy sucked." He sighed. "She also installed Bolingbrook's tornado sirens. During the Time War, she realized her powers weren't enough to stop the invaders." He gazed at the crowbar. "She was able to set aside her prejudices and accept the Commonwealth's assistance. We won the war because of that decision."

Robert looked back at Tom. "Barry was too damn stubborn to quit the Illuminati. He dreamed of being the mayor." He looked at Estaban. "But he supported Rene's candidacy because he believed she would be a better mayor than him. I think he was right. That's the kind of man he was. Bolingbrook over himself."

Robert looked down at Steve. "You, on the other hand, wasted your life for a zombie organization. A living organization is more than rites and rituals. You want to bring chaos to humanity, then pretend to be its saviors. There's nothing redeeming about you. I see that now, and I wish I'd seen it earlier." Robert looked at Estaban. "Remind me. What did the Illuminati used to say? Touch a flame and feel a fire?"

"Yes," Estaban replied.

"You're still a member, right?"

Estaban looked at men in blue in the building. "I am," he said.

Robert held the crowbar out to Estaban. "Then I will let the fire judge the flame."

Estaban limped up to Robert and accepted the crowbar. Two men in blue helped Robert, guiding him as they walked away.

Estaban limped towards Steve.

Steve smirked. "Who are you to judge me?"

Estaban held up the crowbar and chanted in Latin. The crowbar glowed purple. Steve's jaw dropped.

Estaban looked down at Steve. "Have you stepped into the light?"

Steve stared at Estaban. "We are the light," he replied, his voice tinged with anger.

Estaban spoke in Latin.

Steve's eyes widened. "They made you one of them?"

"If you are of the light, you must answer to the light. If not, I will turn you over to Robert." He repeated what he'd said in Latin.

Steve replied in Latin, then looked down and shook his head.

Estaban said, "I accept that you are of the light."

Steve clenched his hands into fists. "And you are a rightful judge of the light."

Estaban stepped closer. "I have one question before I render judgment. Did you say the Regents would appoint you to be the Grand Regent?"

Steve nodded. "Yes. The Regents have the right to grant the crown and scepter to one they deem worthy."

"But there hasn't been a Grand Regent in centuries."

"And look where that has led us."

Estaban pointed the glowing crowbar at Steve. "Do you aspire to be the Grand Regent?"

"The regents are cowardly young fools too afraid to do what needs to be done. Their plans are convoluted and ineffective. They couldn't admit that we needed to unleash Legion. So, I did what needed to be done. They lacked the courage to unleash Legion. Because of what I did, there will be a war. A war we will win."

"You consider yourself braver than the Regents?"

Steve frowned at Esteban. "Don't twist my words! Can't you see? We were the ones who once pulled the strings of the world. We understand power. None of the Regents were alive during the Sigma 7 betrayal. These children cannot return us to the light. I can!"

Estaban gritted his teeth and kneeled in front of Steve. "We were the generation that held the world in our hands. But we let it slip. The Regents may be younger than us, but they are not children. It's their turn. And you have no right to take that away from them."

Estaban placed the glowing crowbar in front of Steve. The crowbar stopped glowing. Steve looked at the crowbar, then looked into Estaban's eyes. Steve sat up at attention. His face turned stoic as Estaban stood up.

Estaban said, "Tell them what we do with initiates who take the crown and scepter?" He limped behind Steve.

Steve looked into Robert's eyes. "We send them back to the darkness," he calmly said.

Estaban snapped Steve's neck. Life drained from Steve's face, and his body collapsed to the floor.

Estaban raised his hands and faced Robert. "Has justice been served?"

"Yes," Robert said with a sigh. "Justice has been served." He looked at Steve's body for a moment, then faced Juanita. "Are you a member of the Illuminati?"

"No," Juanita replied.

"Good," Robert replied. "Reach out to your superiors in the Orange Squad. We need a neutral third party to help us negotiate a settlement. We don't need another war."

"Agreed," Estaban said. "We should speak in private."

Robert nodded. "Juanita, you can bring your cat. We'll have a litter box and cat bed ready when we arrive."

"Mow!" APK replied with her approval.

Robert faced Simon. "Now you can arrange for the medical staff to check me out."

"Absolutely."

Robert looked at Tom. "Sorry. You can't join us. Unless you have something to offer in return."

Tom shook his head. "No deals."

Robert shrugged.

Juanita helped APK into her carrier.

Tom said, "Is this it?"

Juanita shook her head. "We'll talk. Later."

Robert, Estaban, and Juanita entered an SUV and drove away. Tom watched them leave.

Two men in blue placed Steve inside a body bag and carried it away.

Simon approached Tom. "Are you okay?"

Tom shook his head. "Am I supposed to be okay with this? Am I supposed to accept the Illuminati, New World Order, and other groups fighting each other for the right to pull the puppet strings?"

"No," said Simon. "I'm not okay with it. That's why I accepted Robert's offer to become the deputy mayor. Because I want to work within the system to change it."

Tom faced Simon. "What about me? Am I making a difference working for the *Babbler*, or am I just writing the first draft of history?"

"Both," said Simon. "Can't say too much, but there are powerful people who read and believe the *Babbler*. And that's good. So, you can consider me a source inside Town Center."

Tom tilted his head. "Is there a catch?"

"No, Tom. I won't always like what the *Babbler* publishes, but I'd rather have a village with the *Babbler* than one without."

Tom nodded. "I'll keep that in mind."

"Good," Simon replied. "Oh, one last thing. I saw the recording of what happened in the golf club last year."

Tom tensed. "You saw Megan?"

"Yes, and I hate what that guy did to her."

"I—"

"But," Simon interrupted, "you're not that guy. Let's leave it at that."

Tom sighed with relief. "Thank you."

53

Tom looked at Sara's video chat window as he sat in front of his desktop computer in his apartment and braced himself.

"You've put me in a predicament," said Sara. "You violated the Scatter Protocols and my specific instruction to drop *the Phantom Press story.* Yet, you also uncovered one of the biggest scandals in Bolingbrook's history and exposed Don as a double agent." She paused. "I can either give you a raise as a reward for your excellent work, or I could fire you for insubordination." She leaned back in her chair. "What do you think?"

Tom decided to roll the dice. "I'm reminded of a reporter who also defied her editor's orders by working on a story. It meant putting her family's well-being at risk and risking ridicule from her colleagues. But the truth was more important than promotions or exclusive access to certain leaders. Because she wanted to know what kind of world she was going to be sending her children into. Because she didn't give up, she discovered that Robert was lobbying the New World Order not to build a UFO Base in Cook County. Thanks to her, we know why Clow is still the largest UFO base in the world."

Tom smiled broadly, hoping his gambit worked.

Sara frowned. "You skipped the part where that reporter resigned and had to start over at the *Babbler.*" She clasped her hands together. "Are you offering your resignation?"

Tom's eyes widened. "No!" He slumped his shoulders. "I mean, if you keep me, I might have to take a leave of absence."

"Why?"

Tom blushed. "I made a deal with my parents. If they brought the jammer into Bolingbrook, I would check myself into a mental health facility."

Sara raised an eyebrow. "Why did you make that deal?"

Tom let out a long, drawn-out sigh. "Because I was willing to give up my freedom to save Bolingbrook. Now I'm screwed either way."

"Not necessarily," said Sara. "Let me ask you this question. If you don't end up in a mental ward, why shouldn't I fire you?"

Tom sighed. "Because what happened with the *Phantom Press* was an extraordinary circumstance, and I finally get it."

Sara tilted her head. "Get what?"

"What you were trying to tell me." Tom sat up. "I thought I needed to be like Don and come up with cover stories by myself. Then I learned that he compromised himself to get those stories. You wanted me to pull my weight for the team. To contribute more than a short quote to an article." He leaned towards the webcam. "Over the past several days, I did pull my weight. I uncovered what Don was trying to cover up. Shavana and I worked as a team. I worked with a highly placed source without compromising myself. I found my path forward." Tom leaned back in his chair. "But I did violate the rules to get the story. I don't want to be the jerk who thinks they can ignore the rules because they're too valuable to fire. I also don't want the others to think it's okay to ignore you. That's not right." Tom sighed. "I should have figured out how to talk to you about my suspicions, but I didn't." He showed the palms of his hands. "I'm at your mercy."

Sara picked up a pen and started tapping on her desk. Tom fidgeted.

"Wendy, Shavana, and Jenna have told me they want me to keep you."

Tom nodded but wondered if their support was enough.

"You are right; what happened with the *Phantom Press* was extraordinary. And we could have handled it better than we did."

Tom braced for the 'but.'

"But you did violate the Scatter Protocols and my orders," Sara said.

Tom bit his lip.

"However," Sara continued, "Chris and I agree that you are salvageable."

Tom's eyes sparkled with excitement.

"This is what's going to happen," Sara said. "First, I'm giving you a written warning. Second, I've promoted Wendy to assistant editor. During your six-month probation, she will be your direct supervisor. Third, you will help Wendy set up the new office. We'll save the money we would have used to hire a mover."

Tom winced at the thought of doing hours of physical labor, but it was better than unemployment.

"Finally," Sara said, "during your probation, you will be responsible for asking questions during the board meetings."

Tom's eyes widened. *Robert yelling at me twice a month is almost cruel and inhumane,* he thought.

"Of course, this assumes you come back after your stay in a mental ward. Comments?"

Tom thought for a few moments. "If I can survive the Ghost Frequencies, I can survive this."

"And come out a better reporter?" Sara asked.

Tom nodded. "Yeah. Come out a better reporter."

Sara smiled. "I like it when we're in sync. Keep it up."

Tom's smartphone buzzed. He looked down at it. "Wow!"

"What?"

Tom looked up. "It's Esteban. He says something big is going to happen at the festival. He wants me to meet him at the Jaycees' bingo tent."

54

BEHIND TOWN CENTER, BOLINGBROOK'S fiftieth anniversary celebration buzzed with activity as the sunset painted the sky in hues of orange and red. On the Town Center's stage, WikiRock played hit songs from the 1960s. While some attendees attempted to dance in front of the stage, most sat on the grassy knoll overlooking the stage. Food trucks buzzed with activity. Children played inside an inflatable castle. Bright lights illuminated the tower fountain inside the reflecting pool.

Tom arrived at the Bolingbrook Jaycees' bingo tent. It was a fixture at outdoor events like this. This time, they had twice their normal number of tables, and all of them were packed with people. When he walked under the canopy, he recognized the two DPA operatives. They were unharmed and wearing clean new clothes, though they looked exhausted and had 5 o'clock shadows. Both showed little interest in the numbers called out by the enthusiastic female announcer pacing near the air ball machine.

As he skimmed the room, he noticed men in blue and men in black standing just outside the canopies. He'd never seen the men in black in Bolingbrook because the NWO granted Robert the right to use his own men in blue for security. Had that just changed?

The announcer said, "Still no bingo?" Her face brightened as she brushed back her long blonde hair. "We usually have one by now. Remember, this round, we're playing by standard rules."

As she described the winning patterns, Tom noticed all the players had the same disheveled appearance and subdued demeanor. *They must be DPA operatives,* Tom thought. They were all that remained of the department monsters once feared. Now they were reduced to bored bingo players.

A man in black stepped under the canopy and tapped a player's back. The player raised his hand. "Bingo!" Two judges approached the player.

"Hold on," said the announcer. She chuckled. "Everyone, don't touch your boards until we confirm the bingo."

A red-headed woman entered, her gold triangle pendant swinging from her neck. The players looked at her, their faces now shining with anticipation and hope.

The judges gave a thumbs-up to the announcer. She nodded and turned on her mic. "We have a bingo. Thank you very much for playing. Our next round will be starting soon."

The woman walked backwards, motioning for the DPA operatives to follow. As they filed out of the tent, Tom noticed that there were two men and three women outside the tent wearing orange shirts. They observed the former DPA operatives filing out of the tent. When the last player left, the observers joined the line.

Tom's smartphone vibrated. It was a message from Estaban, though his contact info listed him as Roaming Roul.

> Look for an angel.

Tom looked up from his phone. Juanita, wearing a new white blouse and blue jeans, stood at the edge of the canopy. "So," she said, approaching Tom. "This is a suburban summer festival. I've never been to one before."

She stopped and gave a warm smile. A smile that reminded him of their old Lunch and Learn sessions. "You'll have to guide me."

Tom's heart sped up. "Of course."

Juanita chuckled.

The announcer walked up to Tom and Juanita, holding a stack of bingo boards. "Are you two playing?"

"Yes," Tom said as pulled out his wallet. She looked back at Juanita. "You haven't experienced a Bolingbrook festival until you've played Jaycee bingo."

***

Tom and Juanita applauded as the band WikiRock finished performing the Fleetwood Mac song 'Blue Letter.'

The female lead singer said, "Give us a minute because we have a very special surprise for you."

Tom and Juanita sat down on the grassy knoll. "What do you think?" he asked.

Juanita thought for a moment. "It's like listening to a living jukebox."

Tom chuckled. "True. One thing I miss about Chicago: bands playing their own songs."

Juanita looked surprised. "You lived in Chicago?"

"Yeah," Tom replied. "When I went to UIC."

The lead singer returned to the microphone. "Let's hear it for Mayor Robert Clark!"

The audience rose to their feet and applauded as Robert took the stage. He waved and smiled as if the cheering reinvigorated him. The lead singer gave him the microphone.

"Don't worry," he said. "I'm not gonna sing."

The audience laughed.

"WikiRock is doing just fine. You agree with me?"

The audience applauded, with some members cheering.

Robert walked near the edge of the stage. "Fifty years." He paused to look out at the audience. "I hope all of you have taken the time to reflect on the history of our great village."

The audience applauded. Even Tom clapped.

Robert walked across the stage. "I'll be honest. When we started planning for the fiftieth anniversary, I wanted to focus on what makes Bolingbrook special. Like the Bolingbrook Golf Club, Americana Estates, our parks. The corporations' head-quarters in Bolingbrook. Clow Airport." He stopped walking and looked down at the stage floor.

Audience members started muttering.

Robert looked up and wiped his eyes with the back of his hand. "I'm proud of what I've built in my years as mayor." He took a moment to compose himself. "But over the course of this celebration, I realized something. I had a strong foundation to build on. A foundation laid by the previous mayors and trustees." He walked to the center of the stage. "This celebration isn't just about me. It's also about them. And about you, the residents. Together, we are Bolingbrook."

The audience gave Robert a standing ovation. Tom and Juanita joined in the applause.

Tom said, "I never thought I'd hear him say that."

"I hope he doesn't forget it," Juanita replied.

Robert's face brightened. "The committee created a very special presentation honoring Bolingbrook's pioneers. WikiRock agreed to perform a song that's quite fitting. So, I'm going to stop talking and let WikiRock do the rocking."

Robert returned the mic to the lead singer and waved to the audience. The audience cheered as he walked offstage.

Above the stage, three large screens flickered to life, showing a slide with the Village of Bolingbrook's logo.

The lead singer said, "This is for you, Bolingbrook."

WikiRock started performing the song "I was here," by Lady Antebellum. On the screens, the slideshow displayed photos and factoids about Bolingbrook's historical figures. The photos of Barry and Rene, full of life and enthusiasm, saddened Tom. Especially the ones with Natalie. They had poured their hearts into Bolingbrook. But their rage at Robert and the NWO almost led them to destroy Bolingbrook. In the end, Tom thought, they found the strength to let go of their anger and pain so Bolingbrook would have a future.

The slideshow ended with a photo of the *Babbler*'s 50th anniversary issue. The top headline read, "We're still here!" Tom laughed, knowing this was the first and last time Robert would mention the *Babbler* in an official slideshow.

When the performance ended, the audience gave WikiRock a standing ovation. As he clapped, two people caught his attention. He leaned toward Juanita.

"I think there's a tuxedo and a cloak watching us."

"Don't be obvious," Juanita whispered.

Tom stopped looking around. "I'm right?"

She nodded. "Better than last time. There are four cloaks watching us and one tux. But they're with me."

"Oh," Tom replied, feeling embarrassed.

"As you figured out, we facilitated tonight's prisoner exchange. They just informed me that all the prisoners have been released."

"So, you have to go?"

Juanita nodded. "Our work is done."

"I see." Tom fidgeted.

She looked into Tom's eyes. "Are you okay?"

He took a deep breath. "Can we walk back to your van?"

Juanita giggled. "That would be a long walk because it's still in Chicago."

Tom laughed and gave Juanita a nervous smile.

"You can accompany me to my ride." She smiled. "I would like that."

Together, they navigated through the crowd to the tunnel leading to the parking lot. Tom thought about what he would say to her. He wanted to act on his feelings for her. Should he even bring up something so personal? Did he really want to be more than friends? Was this their last time together?

The crowd thinned as they reached the parking lot. *Time is running out,* he thought. Did he really need to say anything to her?

"That was fun," Juanita said. "Thank you for being my guide."

"Sure. And thank you for being my guide. I know I wasn't always the best—"

"It worked out," Juanita said. "Don't worry."

He smiled. "Just like you told me not to worry before my speech."

Juanita scanned the area. Tom looked around as well, uncertain of what he was looking for. He noticed they were walking towards a black SUV with two women standing next to it.

Juanita stepped to the side of the lane, and Tom followed. "Give us a few minutes," she said to the women. They nodded and resumed guarding the vehicle.

Tom felt butterflies in his stomach. Maybe this was the moment he thought would never happen.

They spoke at the same time then both let out nervous giggles.

"Go ahead," said Juanita.

All his imagined speeches rushed through his head. Some emphasized her beauty. Some emphasized her intelligence. Some involved telling her how great they could be together. He even imagined just telling her he loved her. Even after all these years.

Yet, in that moment, he also reflected on the past four years. How he let his selfishness make Jamie feel uncomfortable. How his reaction to Jamie's rejection started him on a self-destructive path. A path that ended with Reese's murder, and a weredeer army invading Bolingbrook. Juanita wasn't an object to possess or a prize to win. He needed to listen to her.

"You go ahead," Tom replied. "I can wait." He smiled, but that failed to calm his nerves.

"Thank you," Juanita said. Her eyes wandered, and Tom assumed she was collecting her thoughts. He braced himself for the answer.

She exhaled. "I grew up as an only child. My parents took a big risk in having me. So, siblings were never an option. At school, many of my friends had siblings. Some of them were part of large families. I understood why my parents didn't want another child. I knew about the monsters they were protecting me from. But... part of me always wondered what it would be like to have a sibling." She smiled and then took a breath. "At the Lunch and Learns, I thought of you as the little brother I could never have. Even if it was just for a day. And I was so proud of you when you delivered your speech. Knowing that I helped you just felt good."

She bit her lip. "I didn't realize how adolescents can form strong attachments to someone. I should have known because I used to be a teenager. When you stopped coming to the meetings, I suspected it was because I had brought my boyfriend to a meeting. He was my first college crush." She let out a long breath. "If you ever felt like I was playing with your feelings, or that I deliberately hurt your feelings, I'm very sorry."

"No," Tom replied. "I never thought you were playing with my feelings." He paused to work up his courage. "I did have a huge crush on you. Maybe it never quite went away." Tom looked into Juanita's eyes. "You were a teacher, a friend, and someone I felt so much affection for. You're still teaching me, and you were the friend I needed when things looked hopeless. And regardless of where this goes, I'll still feel so much... love for you."

Juanita smiled at Tom. Her eyes seemed to light up as Tom looked into them. But then she averted her eyes, and her smile faded. Tom tried to think of something to say. Something to end the awkward silence.

Juanita broke the silence. "Maybe. Maybe there was a time when we could have been more. It could have been after you graduated from college. Or... I don't know." She paused. "But our lives are so different now. It's my job to keep secrets. It's your job to expose secrets." She stepped closer to Tom. "I just know that window is closed. It's not our time to be lovers anymore. And I'm sorry if I'm hurting you now."

Tom noticed Juanita's eyes watering. It did hurt, but seeing her more concerned about his feelings didn't feel right to Tom.

"You're right," said Tom. "Maybe there was a time we could have been more." He stopped as he realized something important. Something he should have understood years ago. "But that time wasn't when I was still in high school. You needed to spread your wings. Back then, I would have held you back without knowing it." Tears streamed down Tom's face.

Juanita stepped closer. "Tom?" she asked softly.

Tom shook his. "No." He wiped his eyes and sniffled. "It's good. They're good tears." He smiled through the tears. "For years, I thought I had made the biggest mistake by not revealing my feelings for you." He took a deep breath to center himself. "I made the right choice. Teenage me made the right choice." He chuckled through his tears. "Leaving CASS was a bad decision. But not burdening you with my feelings was the right decision." He laughed. "Maybe. Maybe if I'd realized that sooner, things would have been different. I wouldn't have needed to hook up at Habencons. Then the whole mess with Jamie never would have happened."

"But then you wouldn't have discovered the truth about the paranormal or found your true calling at the *Babbler*. Perhaps this was all part of God's plan for you?"

"If it were, God really needs to work on his plans."

"We may never know," Juanita replied.

Tom wiped his eyes as the tears stopped. "How about we call this a date, then just be friends?"

"I would like that," Juanita replied. Her warm smile returned. "I like ending dates with a hug. Can we hug?"

"I'd like that," Tom replied, feeling his face brighten.

Tom and Juanita held each other in a warm embrace. As he felt the heat of Juanita's body, Tom felt at peace. It wasn't the outcome he had fantasized about for years. Yet, he knew it was the right one. This was the answer he'd never realized he needed. And maybe it was the answer Juanita needed as well?

Juanita and Tom ended their embrace. Tom felt himself smiling broadly. Juanita's smile was restrained, but present.

"Next summer," said Juanita.

Tom's joy turned to confusion. "Next summer?"

"Next summer, the *Babbler* has custody of Anti-Psychic Kitty. I think you two will pick up where you left off."

"I hope so," Tom replied. "I think we grew on each other."

Juanita nodded. "And this isn't goodbye, Tom. We'll keep in touch."

"Oh?"

She leaned toward Tom and whispered, "Maybe a little accountability is a good thing."

Tom whispered, "Just don't tell me anything you don't want the *Babbler* to know. It's better that way."

"Deal."

They waved goodbye, and Juanita joined her colleagues. Tom watched them until they drove out of sight.

"Tom?" Came Jason's voice.

Tom turned around and saw his parents. Michelle was wearing an oversized 'Trip Monkey' band t-shirt, a shirt she'd owned for as long as he could remember.

Michelle said, "We saw you talking to Juanita. Did you two…"

"We're just friends," Tom replied. "So, did you get me a single room?"

Jason and Michelle looked at each other for a moment, then they faced Tom.

"Actually," said Michelle, "we wanted to talk to you about that."

Jason said, "We did what you asked last night. And… the banners burst into flames. Just like you said they would."

"So," Michelle said, "while we don't agree with your interpretations, we understand why you believe what you believe."

Jason took a deep breath. "Meaning, you don't have to check yourself into a mental ward. Like your mother said, you are seeing something. That tells us you shouldn't be hospitalized."

"But," said Michelle, "we hope you also listen to our explanations."

"Always," Tom replied, feeling like a weight had been lifted off him.

Jason said, "Do you want to join us? You used to dance to Trip Monkey when you were very young."

Tom blushed. "I'll join you guys later. I have to make a phone call first."

"We'll save a spot for you," Michelle replied.

His parents started walking towards the tunnel.

"Dad?" Tom asked.

They stopped and looked at Tom.

"I know the skeptical movement meant a lot to you. I can't imagine how you felt when you gave it up for us. You taught me so much about it. And I appreciate your willingness to let me follow my own path. So." Tom paused. "I'm sorry I disappointed you."

Jason shook his head. "No." He walked closer to Tom. "I've been thinking. Reese was a great man. I will always be grateful for all the years I worked with him. Still have fond memories of the Australia trip."

"Do you still have followers?"

"Unfortunately," Jason laughed. "But, to my point, I think Reese made a big mistake when he tried to make skepticism an identity. Skepticism is a toolkit. Someone calling themselves a skeptic is no different from calling themselves a toolbox." Tom and Jason chuckled. "It shouldn't define your path in life. It's a tool to help you on your journey through this life. So. I may not understand the path you're on. But if you're still using the skills I taught you, you'll never disappoint me."

Jason hugged Tom for a few seconds until they both patted each other on the back.

"Thanks, Dad."

"Of course. Now, you'd better make your call now. You don't want to miss them performing 'Rain.'"

"It's only water."

"That's the spirit."

Tom's parents walked away, and Tom walked to his car. He looked up at the night sky and caught a streak of light moving towards the moon before vanishing. "Barnard's Star shuttle or Tabby cruise ship?" he asked himself before calling Pamela. How much time they had with each other, Tom didn't know. Even more reason not to squander it.

"Tom," she answered. "How did your meeting go tonight?"

He shrugged. "We'll stay friends. But the good news is that my parents say I don't need to check myself into a mental hospital."

"That's... good?"

"Yes," Tom replied. "Now I'm going to watch a Trip Monkey concert with them and not get into an argument."

"Trip Monkey? I thought they broke up years ago. They reunited?"

Tom winced. "It depends. None of the original members are left. The lead singer used to tour with them as a backup singer. The drummer was a roadie for them. The guitarist was a studio musician on one of their albums. The bassist is a cousin of the original bassist."

"Sounds like they became a band of Theseus."

"I was thinking that, too."

55

Tom patiently sat on the shore of Hidden Lakes watching the ducks. The setting sun painted the sky in shades of red and purple.

"Hi!" came Meggy's voice.

Tom turned and saw Meggy running towards him. Behind her were Robert, Simon, and a woman he'd never seen before. She wore urban combat fatigues and carried a black golf bag.

"Did you get my email?" Meggy eagerly asked.

"Yes," Tom replied. "That was quite an escape," he whispered, "It was so good, I had to share it with your dad."

"Which I appreciated," said Simon with a smile.

Robert stopped next to Tom and looked down at him. "You know Hidden Lakes closes at sunset."

"Yeah," Tom sighed. "I was hoping to see the Hidden Lakes Monster. I know she's active around twilight."

Robert thought for a moment. "I'll let you stay for thirty minutes." He looked at the woman standing behind him. "Tom gets thirty extra minutes. Not one minute more."

She took a moment to look over Tom. "Whatever you say," she replied. "You're the one paying me."

Robert sighed and shook his head. "That works for me." Tom couldn't help but notice the disappointment in his voice. Robert then looked down at Tom. "Now we're even."

For a moment, Tom was tempted to say they weren't even.

"We're even," he finally said. He wasn't Don, and that was okay.

"Can I stay with Tom?" Meggy asked.

"Yes," Simon replied. "Promise me you won't run off?"

She crossed her heart. "I promise."

"I'll take care of her," Tom added.

Simon smiled at Tom. "I know you will."

Robert said, "Meet me at the bait shop."

Simon and the woman headed towards the bait shop.

Robert grumbled. "God, I hate contractors. But they're the only ones I can trust right now."

Tom nodded. "Hopefully, the new DPA will be better."

"They'd better be." Robert smiled at Meggy. "Keep an eye on Tom for me."

"I will." Meggy giggled.

Robert walked away. Tom wondered if Robert would ever recover from Steve's betrayal.

Meggy removed her backpack and started to open it.

"What are you doing?"

"Getting my tablet out," she replied. "I wanna picture."

Tom vigorously shook his head. "Don't take it out."

Meggy stopped opening her backpack. "Why?"

"She's very shy. If you want to see her, you have to be very quiet, and no pictures."

"Okay," Meggy said as she closed her backpack and set it aside. "I can be quiet."

Tom sat still while Meggy fidgeted with her fingers. A brown duck swam towards them. Tom pointed at the duck. Meggy stopped fidgeting and watched the duck.

The duck, in the fading light, looked just like the many other ducks that inhabited Hidden Lakes. Yet, Tom couldn't help but feel there was something wrong with its eyes. They seemed still and lifeless.

"Hello," Tom whispered. "We don't have any cameras, and no one else is watching. You're safe with us.

The duck floated on top of the still water. Tom wondered if he'd just talked to a regular duck.

Suddenly, the duck folded in on itself and slipped under the water, like a retractable feather duster being pulled under. Mud bubbled to the surface, turning the surrounding green water brown. The mud stopped bubbling, and ripples emanated from where the duck was.

Without warning, a giant duck's head rose out of the water. Meggy and Tom's jaws dropped as its sea serpent-like neck emerged. The Hidden Lakes Monster now towered above them, shifting its attention between Tom and Meggy.

"We were wondering," Tom said, "do you prefer to be called the Hidden Lakes Monster or HLM?"

Epilogue

THIRTEEN MONTHS LATER.

Tom leaned away from the booth table and smiled at his date.

"That's my ghost story," he said as he clasped his hands. "What's your story?"

Her jaw dropped as she stared in Tom's direction. The shocked expression on her face unsettled Tom. She'd posted on her dating profile that she'd seen ghosts. What was supposed to be an icebreaker was turning into a deal-breaker, he feared.

"Maybe some other time," Tom said as he picked up the Barber's Corner Bar and Grill menu. "You know, I've been here many times. Back when the *Babbler's* office was nearby, I'd come here after work. I love their burgers, but their grilled chicken sandwich meal is great too."

"Um," she said, then reached for her purse. "I've got to check this message."

Tom hadn't heard the phone vibrate, but he knew what was going on. He was too familiar with online dates pulling the ejection lever.

His date pulled out the phone, making sure Tom couldn't see the screen. After glancing at the screen, she said, "I've got to go. Something just came up."

"Okay," said Tom, unable to hide his disappointment.

Her fingers tapped the screen. "I'm sorry."

Tom shrugged. "Things happen."

Holding the phone to her ear, she exited the booth without closing her purse. "I'll message you."

"Okay," Tom said as he pulled out his phone. "Later," he said, looking at his smartphone's lock screen.

"You were supposed to call me," she said into her phone as she walked away.

Tom shook his head. He had thought she was going to be the needle in the digital haystack. Her profile showed she was interested in paranormal phenomena, and they had a high match score. Jenna even told him they were going to make a deep connection. Then again, he thought, Jenna's interpretations weren't always correct. A vision of rain reviving a wilting vine could mean almost anything.

The patrons at the bar cheered. Tom looked up at the TV and saw the Cubs players celebrating in the dugout. They'd just scored a run to win the game. Last year, Tom told Sara that a Cubs and Indians World Series would be a sign of the apocalypse. As the 2016 regular season was winding down, a Cubs and Indians World Series was a real possibility.

A waitress approached Tom's table. "Excuse me."

"Yes?"

"The woman over there asked me to give you this note."

Tom accepted the folded napkin. The waitress pointed to a booth on the other side of the dining area. Sitting at the booth was a woman who appeared to be in her early 20s. She had short, dark brown, wavy hair that stopped short of the collar of her blue blouse. Seeing Tom's gaze, she clenched her hands and hesitated before she smiled. Tom smiled back, hoping it put her at ease.

The waitress said, "She said you can order anything you want on the menu. It's her treat."

Tom raised his eyebrows at the waitress. "Seriously?" This was the first time a woman had offered to pay for his meal. For a moment, he felt awkward. As if he were about to be indebted to a stranger. However, Jenna said he was going to connect with someone tonight. He assumed it was a vision of his date. Maybe the vision was about this woman?

The waitress said, "She's made the arrangements. I just need to take your order."

Tom looked back at the woman. She raised her right arm and unclenched her right hand. She waved it with a short, hesitant motion. He responded with his own awkward hand wave. Her brown eyes widened, and her smile tightened. He nodded and gave her a warm smile. However, it didn't release the visible tension on her face.

What's the worst that could happen?

Tom switched his attention to the menu. "Anything?" He skimmed through the unfamiliar parts of the menu. "What do you recommend?"

The waitress considered Tom's question for a moment. "The Robert Meal is our most expensive item."

Tom grinned. "Why am I not surprised?"

The waitress chuckled. "Personally, I'd go with the filet mignon meal. The kitchen staff loves making it. If you don't ask for it to be well done."

"I'll have that." Tom could already taste the meat. "Cook it medium-rare. Oh, and throw in a large malt too. And bring two straws."

"You've got it."

Tom handed the menu to the waitress. He prepared to wave the woman over to his table, but when the waitress stepped away, her both was empty. Her black leather jacket no longer hung on the coat hook. Tom looked around but didn't see her anywhere in the busy dining area. He wondered why she had left after paying for his meal. Did her nerves get the better of her? Was this someone's idea of a joke?

Tom unfolded the napkin, hoping the note might hold a clue. She wrote her note in black ink, using block letters.

I believe you.

Lydia

***

Lydia and Tom will return.

Thank You

Thank you for reading this book. Please consider leaving a review at Goodreads and/or where you got a copy. Even a single-sentence review could encourage someone to get a copy.

For updates about my writing and bonus content, you can subscribe to my mailing list using the link below:

Mailing List: https://bolingbrookbabbler.com/mailing-list

Acknowledgements

Thanks to my wife for her love and support over the years. Through the darkness and the light, we've been by each other's side.

Thanks to my editors for corrections and feedback.

Thanks to my fellow bloggers at *Freethought Blogs* for putting up with my sabbatical while I worked on the novel.

Thanks to the residents of Bolingbrook, past and present, for inspiring me over the years.

Finally, thank you for reading this book.

The Believable Truth

While this book is a work of fiction, Bolingbrook is a real suburb of Chicago. Here are the differences between the novel and the real Bolingbrook.

- Old Chicago Mall was a real mall that operated from 1975 until 1980. It was the first mall with an indoor amusement park, predating Mall of America by 17 years. In 1986, a demolition crew demolished the building. They did not implode the building.

- The *Phantom Press* was a real publication, published without attribution. According to a reliable source, Bob Baily was the publisher. Baily served as mayor from 1977 to 1981 and from 1985 to 1986.

- The owners of Bolingbrook Commons refurbished it from 2022 to 2024. It now has a modern facade and more tenants.

- In Illinois, a village is a type of municipality administered by a board of trustees. Which is why Bolingbrook is still a village, despite having a population of over 75,000 residents.

- The real Anti-Superstition Society of Chicago was my

inspiration for CASS. Founded in 1930s, it remained active until the 1980s. While they didn't have a Gauntlet of Woo, they held gatherings where attendees would do things like walk under ladders, light three cigarettes with the same match, or open umbrellas indoors. In 1962, they honored John Glenn for flying the thirteenth capsule into space.

About William Brinkman

In William Brinkman's world, suburban sidewalks lead to secret conspiracies, emotional reckonings, and the occasional enraged weredeer. He writes urban fantasy with a blend of satire and heart, offering humanistic views of the real world through a supernatural lens. Since 1999, he's published the *Bolingbrook Babbler* blog, which inspired—but remains separate from—his fiction. His book, *A Fire in the Shadows*, made the short list for the 2024 Indieverse Award for Best Novella. A former Bolingbrook resident, William now lives in suburban Chicagoland with his wife and two cats.

For updates and a free eBook, *God to Smite Bolingbrook*, sign up for his newsletter.

https://bolingbrookbabbler.com/mailing-list

g

goodreads.com/author/show/5699299.William_Brinkman

f

facebook.com/bolingbrookbabbler/

♪

tiktok.com/@williambrinkmanbb

Also By William Brinkman

The Bolingbrook Babbler Stories

- *Pathways to Bolingbrook: A Bolingbrook Babbler Story* Book 1 (2021)

- *A Fire in the Shadows: A Bolingbrook Babbler Story* Book 1.5 (2023)

- *The Rift: A Bolingbrook Babbler Story Book 2* (2022)

- *Revenge of the Phantom Press: A Bolingbrook Babbler Story* Book 3 (2026)

Web Fiction Collection

- *God to Smite Bolingbrook* (2023)

Demon: The Fallen (White Wolf Studios)

- *Demon: The Fallen (2002)*

- *Saviors and Destroyers* "Broken Bonds" (2003)

- *Damned and Deceived* "The Good Soldier" (2003)

Learn more at bolingbrookbabbler.com.

Coming Soon

A fire that bleeds still burns.
   A Fire That Bleeds: A Bolingbrook Babbler Story
   Coming soon.

.